AFTER I DREAM

Harold McVeq

AFTER I DREAM

RACHEL LEE

BEELER LARGE PRINT
Hampton Falls, New Hampshire, 2000

Library of Congress Cataloging-in-Publication Data

Lee, Rachel
    After I dream / Rachel Lee.
    p   cm
    ISBN 1-57490-278-4 (alk. paper)
        1. Private investigators—Florida—Florida Keys—
Fiction. 2. Brothers and sisters—Fiction. 3. Women
psychologists—Fiction. 4. Florida Keys (Fla.)—Fiction. 5.
Large type books. I. Title

    PS3562.E3596 A69 2000
    813'.54—dc21   00-036017

Published in Large Print by arrangement with
Warner Books, Inc.

BEELER LARGE PRINT
is published by
Thomas T. Beeler, *Publisher*
Post Office Box 659
Hampton Falls, New Hampshire 03844

Typeset in 16 point Times New Roman type.
Sewn and bound by
Sheridan Books in Chelsea, Michigan

For my darling, who packed up the van and headed south on a moment's notice to make the setting for this book possible.

PROLOGUE

THE DAY WAS WRONG.

Tom Akers stood on the deck of the hundred-foot-long ship *Lady Hope*, enjoying a pipe as he waited for the divers to finish their work. As captain of a salvage vessel he took his moments of peace where he could find them. Most salvage operations he and his crew performed were risky bits of business conducted in bad conditions and under immutable time constraints if they were to save a troubled vessel and its occupants. By comparison, waiting for divers to finish exploring a sunken yacht was a cakewalk, and Tom was perfectly willing to enjoy the calm.

Except that it was too calm.

Tom had spent the majority of his forty years at sea, and the sea spoke to him in a language he understood as well as his native tongue. He needed no radio weather advisories to warn him something was wrong.

Unease crawled along the cradle of his scalp, and it bothered him that he couldn't pin it down. The morning had started out almost painfully clear, with sun glinting off the waves of the Florida Straits in splinters of light that hurt the eyes. But gradually, since the divers had gone below, the day had changed.

Becalmed. The word floated up out of his subconscious, some genetic memory from ancestors who had gone to sea in wind-driven vessels. A sailor in these days of powerful engines had no need to fear the absence of wind.

But Tom found himself fearing it anyway. The Atlantic was never this quiet and still, not even here at

1

the edge of the continental shelf. Stretching away from the *Hope*, the sea was as smooth as glass. Too smooth. And the sky had grown hazy, an unsettling green-tinged haze unlike anything he could remember seeing this far from land. The sun was still up there somewhere, but the light had become so flat that he had no sense of direction. The *Hope* might have been cast adrift in some alien world where sea and sky were one.

He didn't like it.

Standing there he reminded himself of his engines, his radio, and his global positioning system, advantages his ancestors hadn't enjoyed. As long as they didn't swamp, he could get his ship home.

But modern technology and rationalization weren't quite enough to soothe the soul of a sailor. Like most of his kind, he had a superstitious streak, and right now he was trying to remember if they were in the Bermuda Triangle. If asked, he would have said he didn't believe in such tripe, but deep inside he couldn't quite shake a gut feeling no logic could touch.

His pipe was out, and he tapped it on the railing to shake the dottle into the sea below. The sound echoed in the strange silence, too loud, as if they were caught in a fog bank. But this was no fog, at least no ordinary fog.

The sea had a life of her own, and Tom respected it. He knew her moods as well or better than he had known the moods of his late wife. In his heart of hearts he felt that the sea tolerated his ship on her surface, and in some part of him he always wondered when that tolerance would end.

Today? Perhaps it would be today. It was as if she were reaching up over their heads, surrounding them in this grayish green cocoon, and at any moment she would take them down into her eternal embrace.

"Jesus, Mary, and Joseph," he muttered, appalled by the turn of his own thoughts. He shook himself and decided this was not a good day to stand alone at the bow, thinking thoughts that were as mad as any dream he'd ever had.

A shout caught his attention. Forgetting his strange meanderings, he headed swiftly toward the two men who were monitoring the divers from amidships. The *Hope* was a large vessel, crewed by ten, and it took him a minute or so to get back there.

"What's wrong?" he demanded as he reached them. Other crew members gathered, too.

"One of the divers is in trouble," said the man who was monitoring the sound-powered phones the divers were using to talk to the ship. He and his companion were employed by the insurance company that had hired Tom and his ship.

"What happened?"

"I don't know." The man looked at him, but then his eyes slid away, as if he were somehow a strange part of this strange day.

Tom felt his unease blossom into vines of ice that wrapped around his spine. "What makes you say something is wrong?" he asked again, slowly.

"He says there are monsters in the water."

The icy vines clamped Tom's spine. "Monsters?"

"Hallucinations," said the man tending the safety lines. "He must be having hallucinations. It can happen on a deep dive."

But not usually to experienced deep divers, Tom thought.

He'd known Chase for years, but the other diver wasn't as familiar to him. Just some guy the insurance company had hired.

3

"The other diver can't see anything," the phone man agreed. "It's got to be nitrogen narcosis."

Tom objected. This was something he knew a little about. "But their tanks don't have Nitrox. They've got a helium and oxygen mix."

The phone man shrugged. "He had some nitrogen in him from breathing regular air when he went over the side."

Enough for this? Tom wondered. Fearing trouble, he asked one of his sailors to get the medic they'd brought with them, a man experienced in treating diving emergencies.

Then out of the speaker came the tinny voice of one of the divers. Unidentifiable, because some of his voice was being converted to electrical power for the phone, squawky from the helium in his air mix. Let it be Chase, Tom prayed.

"I can't . . . get near him," the voice said, sounding like a cartoon character. "God . . . knife . . . out!"

"Stay back, stay back," said the first dive master into his microphone. "We're going to bring him up."

"He's . . ." The diver's words were broken, many of them distorted past Tom's ability to recognize. "Christ, he . . . thinks . . . sees something . . ."

The winch was already turning, bringing the troubled diver up a few safe feet. How long? Tom wondered. How deep were they? He hadn't really paid any attention to the details of the dive. It was out of his bailiwick. All he was supposed to do was keep his tender here until the work was done. He had no idea how long it would take to bring the man to the top safely.

"I'm . . . alongside him," the diver said. "Bring me up . . . Oh, Jesus! He's trying . . . helmet off! Get him up!

4

Get him up! *Get him up!*"

The two dive masters exchanged glances, then looked at Tom. "The bends . . ." said the man operating the winches that controlled the safety lines.

Tom might know little about diving, but he knew about the bends. When a diver descended, the increasing pressure condensed the gas bubbles in his blood, making them smaller, small enough to get into places they wouldn't usually go, into tissues and nerves. If the diver ascended too quickly, those bubbles would expand before they could work their way out of the tissues, causing serious damage and even death.

"We've got the decompression chamber," Tom said. "Preventing the bends won't matter a raindrop in a hurricane if he pulls his helmet off down there!" He was surprised he even needed to say it.

"Get him up!" yelled the diver. "Get him up, he's . . . mask, for the love of God get him up!"

The dive master slammed one of the winches to top speed. For Tom, a lifetime seemed to pass before the diver finally surfaced alongside the vessel. He was still flailing, making it difficult to winch him over the side. At least he'd lost his knife in his rapid ascent, so they only had to deal with his struggles as they hastened to unhook him from the safety line.

Helping hands were plentiful. As soon as they had the diver unhooked, they carried him as quickly as they could to the hyperbaric chamber that the insurance company had ordered bolted onto the *Hope*'s deck specifically for this deep dive. As if someone had known . . .

The thought crossed Tom's mind, then washed away on the tide of horror as he helped put the diver on the cot in the chamber.

Oh, God, he thought as he glanced at the face inside the mask. Oh, God, it was Chase.

Chase, his friend of many years. Chase, a drinking buddy since their navy days. Oh, dear Mary, Mother of God . . .

He stood outside the chamber, watching through the small, thick window, as the compressor labored to raise the pressure to sixty feet below sea level. He wanted to steam full ahead for the shore, but they couldn't budge until they safely brought up the other diver. He watched as the bends gripped his friend and twisted his body into impossible shapes. He listened to the muffled screams.

"Skipper? Bill's aboard."

Only then, with a heart as heavy as lead, did Tom order the *Lady Hope* to make full speed for port. Only then did the wind and waves return, carrying away the eerie haze.

The sea had exacted her toll.

CHAPTER 1

NIGHT BLANKETED LOWER SUGARLOAF KEY, surrounding the cottage and threatening to bury it.

Chase Mattingly looked at the 9mm Beretta sitting on the table in front of him. He took it out from time to time to clean it, then sat staring at it with a mixture of loathing and need. Sometimes he came perilously close to putting the barrel to his head, but so far it had been enough just to know it was there.

Tonight was one of those nights when he was coming close. Every light in the cottage was burning brightly to hold the night outside at bay. He couldn't stand the darkness anymore. Out of the dark came the twisting, evil things to torment him. Out of the dark came monsters that had been spawned by a nightmare that had nearly killed him.

As long as the lights were on, he could cling to the edges of reality. As long as the lights were on, he could stare at the Beretta and know that relief was only one short act away.

He scorned himself for it. He scorned his weakness in needing that gun and needing the lights that drove the demons back. He scorned himself for not being strong enough to put a bullet in his brain.

Hell, he more than scorned himself. He hated himself.

So he sat staring at the pistol while the night whispered around the walls of the cottage, and he tried not to think about the pain that gnawed at him with hungry jaws.

There was a bottle of painkillers in his medicine chest. Two tablets would dull the pain and send him over the edge into sleep.

But he didn't dare sleep while night ruled the world. In dreams, he found himself clamped in the icy black grip of the merciless sea. While he slept, not even the lights and the locked doors could keep the night outside. It crept in, clawing at his sleeping mind with icy fingers, pressing the breath right out of his body until he woke screaming and gasping for air.

The monsters had followed him back from the depths of the sea. Now they inhabited the depths of night. They had almost killed him once, and he couldn't escape the feeling that they would never quit until they succeeded.

The doctors told him he was being irrational, and he knew they were right. They told him he had suffered some weird kind of stroke or embolism that had caused hallucinations while he was diving, and he believed them. His *mind* believed them. But in the depths of night, his gut ruled, and he knew with absolute certainty that demons had tried to kill him, and were only awaiting a chance to finish the job.

The gun wouldn't work on them, but it would work on him. So he sat with it for company, drinking coffee until his nerves buzzed, waiting for the night to find some crack by which it could creep in and attack him.

He clung to his pain because it kept him awake, and he needed to stay awake.

He listened to the clatter of palm fronds in the sea breeze, and heard taunting laughter. He listened to the wind rattle the windows and shutters, and heard the night trying to break in. The darkness had shape and form and evil intent.

And he didn't believe it, but he couldn't stop believing it. He was mad, and despised himself for it. Before, he had always believed that the insane didn't know they were insane. Now he knew otherwise. There was no such mercy in madness.

Alone with his insanity and his gun, he struggled to hold on to reality. He forced himself to hear the sounds of the night and put natural interpretations on them. He forced himself to pay attention to the pain throbbing in his hip and his back, a pain that was almost as solid as the chair on which he sat.

And with every cell he strained for the sounds that would herald his release from terror for another day.

At last he heard a boat engine turn over, then chug in the restless air of the inlet. Without looking, he knew that the first pink streamers of dawn were driving the night back from the eastern rim of the world. Pushing back from the table, ignoring the grinding pain in his hip, and the stabbing pain in his back, he limped to the

8

door and threw it open.

Night was recoiling, vanquished as always by the approach of day. In the dim light, the taunting shadows were beginning to resolve into normalcy. He could see the Carlson boy across the inlet, jumping from the dock onto the battered thirty-foot fishing boat he shared with a friend. The two of them dreamed grand dreams of making enough to buy a good deep-sea fishing boat one day, something they could charter to tourists. He'd heard them spinning their dreams not too long ago as they'd worked on their old wood-hulled boat, fighting age and the elements to keep it seaworthy.

Once, he'd been like them. He'd had dreams . . . dreams that weren't filled with terror and pain.

Looking up, he saw the red streaks of dawn stretching across the sky like bloody gashes. Idiots, he thought, watching the boys' boat as it chugged out of the inlet toward the Intracoastal Waterway and the Atlantic Ocean. Jerks. A sky like that in the morning shouldn't be ignored.

Then he turned and went back inside. The sun had driven the night back into the depths of the sea.

Now he could sleep.

Calypso Carlson opened her eyes with the certain sense that something was wrong. Another person might have called it foreboding, but she had spent many years rooting out that kind of mystical garbage from her thinking. She was a psychologist, and she knew too much about the mind's workings to fall prey to such intuitions.

What was wrong—the *only* thing that was wrong— was that she and her brother Jeff had been up half the night fighting. She simply dreaded opening another

9

round with him this morning.

With a groan, Callie rolled over and tried to talk herself into going back to sleep. This was the first day of her month-long vacation, and there was no reason to drag herself out of bed. What was she going to do? Argue with Jeff again about how he should go to college and save his dreams of owning a charter service until after he had a degree?

She snorted into her pillow and wondered why she even bothered. Jeff had hit the nail on the head when he'd accused her of being afraid of the sea ever since their father had been lost out there. As far as he was concerned, that made her reasoning about college suspect.

And maybe it was, in part. God knew, the sea had taken enough from her.

But she couldn't stay in bed any longer. The morning sun was hammering on the walls of her bedroom, making it hot and stuffy, but not yet warming the rest of the house enough to make the air-conditioning turn on. But it wasn't the stuffiness that drove her to get up, though she told herself it was. It was the lingering, troubling sense of doom.

Groaning again, feeling far older than twenty-eight, she climbed out of bed and pulled on a pair of white shorts and a blue T-shirt. Coffee. Maybe Jeff had a pot going. For that she would forgive him anything.

A cloud scudded across the sun, darkening her room. She felt an inexplicable shiver of apprehension and forced it aside. Lack of sleep was making her ditzy, that was all.

In the kitchen she found coffee, but Jeff had pulled the plug, leaving it to grow cold. Impatient, she poured some into a mug and put it in the microwave to heat.

She didn't remember whether he was supposed to go to work at the hardware store this morning, so she wandered over to the refrigerator to check the schedule he kept posted there, held in place by two magnets, one shaped like a whale, the other like a dolphin.

No, he wasn't supposed to go in until three this afternoon. The microwave *pinged* but she didn't hear it. Her uneasiness overwhelmed her.

Hurrying through the house, she ran out onto the front porch and looked toward the dock.

The *Lily*, named for their mother, wasn't there. And worse, storm clouds were building on the horizon.

The sea had called to her brother, and he had gone.

She forced herself to cook breakfast, grits and cheese, and made a fresh pot of coffee. It occurred to her that she was trying to distract herself by keeping busy because she wasn't at all hungry. She ate anyway, forcing the sticky grits down with orange juice, ignoring the way the food sat like lead in her stomach.

Jeff, what are you doing?

She'd asked her brother that question many times over the years she had raised him, and she wanted to ask it again right now. Maybe he only meant to do a little fishing before it was time for work, but with those storm clouds out over the water, the waves and wind would be strengthening. It was not a good day to put out to sea.

She turned on the weather radio and listened to marine advisories that warned small craft of approaching squalls. Finally, she used the marine radio to try and raise the *Lily*, but in answer to her calls she heard only the crackle of static.

She felt a surge of anger and frustration. It would be just like Jeff to ignore her calls so she couldn't yell at him. When he got back later, she was going to have this

11

out with him once and for all. If he wanted to ignore her pleas to come home, that was one thing, but at the very least he ought to respond to her radio calls so she could know he was alive!

She walked out to the mouth of the inlet, marching along the path that wound through the mangroves, along her neighbor's seawall, and sometimes emerged onto sandy shore. Standing on the high ridge of limestone and caprock that reached out into the water, she used binoculars to peer out over the sea and try to pick out any small speck that might be the *Lily*.

The waves were high, she noticed, and the Intracoastal Waterway, calm on sunny days, was beginning to look dark and angry. The storms out at sea were causing the waves to chew up the bottom and toss all kinds of debris onto the shore. The distant thunderclouds were closer now, and with senses finely honed from years of living on the water, she could feel the changing barometer, could smell the approaching squalls.

Damn it, Jeff! Come home!

Thirteen years ago she had stood on this point, a girl of fourteen, awaiting her father's return from sea in the days after her mother's death. For the better part of three days she had stood here, paralyzed by grief, needing her father as desperately as she had ever needed anyone or anything. She needed desperately for him to be there so she wouldn't be alone with her grief. Jeff, only six at the time, had not really grasped that their mother was dead, and he had played at her feet while she watched and waited as the women of seagoing families had watched and waited since the dawn of time.

Ten years later she had stood on this same point, watching her father's boat return from a six-week shrimping trip, impatient to tell him that Jeff had dropped out of school. But their father had never come home. He had been washed overboard at sea and his crew had returned the boat to her with sorrowful faces.

Her mother, her father, and now she was waiting for her brother. When she looked at the ocean now, she felt something akin to revulsion and hatred. It was far more emotion than an inanimate body of water deserved, she told herself. The sea had done nothing to her. It couldn't *do* anything. It didn't think, or breathe, or feel. It was just a force of nature.

But she hated it anyway, and never looked out over it without remembering her losses.

Two more times in the next several hours she walked out to the headland to look at the increasingly restless water and the threatening shapes of dark gray clouds. It was two o'clock now, and there had been no sign of the *Lily*, not even through the binoculars that hung heavy around her neck.

As she walked back to her house, she had to pass the cottage that faced her house across the inlet. This time a rough voice startled her.

"You're worrying about the boy."

Looking up from the path along the seawall, she saw the man who had recently moved into the A-frame cottage some snowbird had built years before. It looked out of place amidst palms planted by previous owners and the tropical foliage of the Florida Keys, as if it had been plucked from some alpine valley and accidentally dropped here.

He was sitting on his redwood deck, one leg propped out before him on a small wicker table. Now that she was only a few feet away, she could see that his face had been gouged by life, leaving deep cuts around his eyes and mouth. He had the permanently bronzed look of someone who lived with the elements, but beneath that burnt-in color, he looked pale. Dark, shaggy hair reached his collar, and his eyes were the color of a stormy sea. A diamond twinkled in his left earlobe, even though he sat in the shade of his porch.

He looked, thought Callie, like a pirate.

"I saw him sail out this morning," the man said. "The sky looked bad. I'm surprised he went."

Without warning, it all burst out of Callie. "When he gets back, I'm going to kill him. He has less than an hour to get to work."

A laugh issued from the man, and he nodded as if he understood her feeling. "He's young."

"He's foolish! The marine advisories have been worsening all day. If he stays out there much longer—" She broke off, unwilling to give voice to the possibilities. All her efforts to pluck superstition out of her life had apparently failed. She didn't want the sea to hear her speak her worst fears.

He nodded toward the radio antenna rising beside her house. "Have you tried to raise him?"

"He's not answering." The anger went out of her as she tacitly admitted her worst fear of all.

"He's probably ignoring you," the man said almost kindly. "He knows what you're going to say."

"Probably." She turned from him and looked back toward the mouth of the inlet. The tide was rising, and the waves were stiffening, becoming whitecapped even in this protected cove. The storm was still far out, but she had no idea how far out Jeff himself and his friend Eric might have gone.

"We fought last night." The memory filled her with guilt now, because it might be the reason her headstrong

14

brother had sailed out that morning. Lead settled in her stomach.

"About what?" the man asked.

"I want him to go to college. I think he should get his degree and see what else is available out there before he throws his life away on fishing boats."

"Mmm." He was silent a while. "When the sea gets into a man's blood there's not much you can do about it."

She turned to look at him. "He's only twenty. He's been like this ever since I can remember. Just before our father died he dropped out of high school to fish. It's been a major battle just to get him to complete his G.E.D."

"But he did?"

She nodded, her gaze straying back to the water. Why was she telling him all this? He couldn't possibly care.

"So he's your brother?"

"Yes." The rules of common courtesy dragged her gaze from the water back to him. "Sorry. I'm Callie Carlson. My brother is Jeff."

"Nice to make your acquaintance. I'm Chase Mattingly."

His name struck a chord deep inside her, as if she recognized it from somewhere, but other worries concerned her more. "I guess I'd better get back to the house and try to radio him again. I can't believe he hasn't been listening to the advisories."

"I can't believe he hasn't noticed the weather conditions," Chase said. "He may be only twenty, but he's a sailor."

She nodded, fear rearing its ugly head even higher.

"I'll come with you," he offered unexpectedly. "Maybe if I call him, he'll answer."

15

It was worth a try. She nodded her thanks.

He lowered his leg to the floor and rose from the redwood chair like a man much older than his apparent years. Even in her current preoccupied state, Callie recognized the repressed flickers of pain that passed over his face. "Are you all right?" she asked impulsively, before she could reconsider.

"As right as I'll ever be." With a movement of his hand, he dismissed the subject. But he limped as he came down the steps to the sand, and limped as they made their way around the inlet to her house.

"It's a nice old house," he volunteered, with a nod toward her home.

"My granddad built it with his own two hands out of cypress and tropical hardwood. My dad put the siding on it when I was little to make it prettier for my mom. It needs paint."

"Everything by the water needs paint."

She nodded. "I'm planning to do it during my vacation."

"If you need help, holler. It'd do me some good to work."

She wondered about that, wondered why he wasn't working, if he'd been in some kind of accident and was recuperating. But she didn't ask. He would tell her what he chose to. "Thanks," she said. Once again she looked back at the mouth of the inlet, hoping to see the *Lily*. The boat wouldn't be there, but she hoped anyway.

A gust of wind blew, ruffling the surface of the inlet and making the palms clatter noisily. A heron flew in and settled in the shallows a few feet out from shore, then stood as motionless as a statue.

When they reached her veranda, Chase climbed the steps carefully, as if each movement hurt. Inside, the

16

house was cool and silent except for the tireless murmur of the air-conditioning. Callie showed him to the radio. Then, since he seemed to know what he was doing with it, she went to the kitchen to get them each a glass of lemonade. Three walks to the point in the summer heat had left her feeling as parched as Death Valley.

When she returned with the drinks, she heard her brother's voice come out of the radio. Relief washed over her so strongly that her hands started to shake. Moving quickly, she set the glasses down on the table near the radio.

"Your sister's worried half to death about you," Chase said amiably into the microphone. "Have you looked at the sky lately? Over."

"It's getting a little rough out here," Jeff replied. "Tell her we'll be back in a couple of hours. Over."

"Hours?" Callie said, fear grabbing her again. "Hours?"

"You hear that?" Chase said into the microphone. "You're giving her a heart attack."

Jeff's laugh sounded tinny but genuine. "Hey, sis, lighten up. We found a boat!"

"A boat?"

Chase looked at her and shrugged a shoulder. Leaning toward the mike, he said, "What boat? What's going on out there, *Lily*? Over."

"It's really cool!" Jeff said enthusiastically. "We found an abandoned deep-sea fishing boat. We're putting the pumps over right now to salvage her. Man, she's a beauty! Just exactly what I wanted Santa to bring."

Callie listened with dawning horror. Her baby brother was out on rough seas attempting to salvage a sinking boat? He was risking his neck for a *boat*?

She grabbed the microphone and pressed the transmit button. "Jeff, are you crazy? That boat's sinking, isn't it? You're not going to board it!"

"We already have, sis. Eric and I are setting up the pumps right now. She's not sinking any more anyway. Can you believe it? Somebody scuttled her!"

The hair on the back of Callie's neck prickled, and she found herself looking at Chase. His dark gray gaze, exactly the color of thunderheads, seemed to reflect her own concern.

"Jeff, salvage is risky even under good conditions! You're in dangerous seas!"

"Not that dangerous. Not yet, Callie. It's a little rough out here, but we're a long way from being in trouble. Besides, it's a boat! It's in almost-new condition, and she's exactly what Eric and I want for our business! I can't just leave her here!"

"Jeff . . . the boat was scuttled. Maybe there's a *reason* for that."

She was answered with a crackling silence, then, "I've gotta go help Eric, Callie. I'm going to sign off now."

Chase reached for the mike. "Jeff? Call in from time to time so your sister doesn't get any more gray hairs, okay?"

Silence, then, "Okay. Half an hour. I'll radio in half an hour. Out."

And once again the crackling of dead air filled the room.

Chase put the microphone back on the table. Callie stared off into space, fighting the fear that wanted to strangle her.

Not Jeff, too, she found herself praying. Haven't you taken enough from me? But she wasn't praying to God,

18

she realized. She was praying to the sea. Talking to that monstrous beast out there as if it were alive and could hear. As if it could be bargained with.

With a start, she realized the day outside had darkened. The dimness inside was no longer solely caused by the wide veranda that circled three sides of the house. Turning, without speaking a word to Chase Mattingly, she hurried to the front of the house and out onto the porch.

The clouds had swallowed the blue sky at last. The mangroves and the trees on the hammock behind the house tossed wildly, and strong gusts of wind lifted the spray right off the inlet and slapped her in the face with it.

"It's bad," she said, almost to herself.

Chase had followed her, and answered. "Maybe it's not as bad where he is. You know the water's so shallow around here that it doesn't take much to whip it up. From what he said, I'd guess he's farther out, in deeper water."

She was suddenly aware of his eyes on her, and she turned to look at him. In those dark depths she saw the flickers of things that frightened her, but she also saw compassion. Time seemed to fade away, and a strange stillness came to the afternoon.

But then the spray slapped her again, jerking her back to reality.

"I'll stay with you until he gets back in," Chase said.

It was the neighborly thing to do, the kind of thing people in isolated locations had always done for each other, so it didn't seem out of place to her. She nodded her thanks. "We might as well wait inside. If he radios, I don't want to miss it."

The house was a cool cocoon against the weather

building outside. The air-conditioning had been her own addition two years ago, an expensive job of running ducts through the attic in a house that had never had central heat or air. She and Jeff had done most of the ductwork themselves, laboring in the suffocating temperatures of the attic, finally deciding to add a better attic fan, too.

But now she could seal herself away from everything behind closed windows and doors. Everything except fear.

The speakers on the marine radio still crackled emptily. The weather radio was blaring another alert tone, and Callie hit the button, listening with trepidation as the U.S. Weather Service gave another small-craft advisory. Ten-foot waves were being predicted, and while the *Lily* could ride out such seas, it was another matter entirely if her brother was tied up alongside another boat, trying to salvage it.

She glanced toward Chase, and saw the awareness in his gaze. "Maybe I should call the Coast Guard," she said.

"I didn't ask his position."

"Oh. I should have thought of that!"

"Me, too." He glanced at the digital clock on the table beside the radio. "He should be calling again in about fifteen minutes."

Waiting. "You know," she said, "the thing I hate most about the sea is the way it makes you wait. I have stood for days on that headland waiting for someone to come home . . ." Her voice trailed off and she looked away, feeling she was exposing too much to a stranger.

"It's not as bad as it used to be," he said. "Radio, radiophone . . . it's a lot better."

She shook her head. "It's never any better. You never

20

know. . ."

She had the feeling he thought she was being
extreme, but he didn't say anything, and she didn't
bother to defend her feelings. They were *her* feelings,
however irrational.

"No," he said finally. "You never know what the sea
might do."

That was it exactly, she thought. She couldn't trust
the sea the same way she could trust a ribbon of
highway. If somebody took a long road trip, she just
assumed they'd arrive safely. With the sea . . . with the
sea Callie was always afraid.

She spoke. "You talk like you spend a lot of time at
sea."

"I do. I *did*. Probably not anymore."

"Why not?"

"I had an . . . accident."

Another one. Another person whose life had been
blighted by the sea. She turned away, wrapping her
arms around herself and looking out the window. The
day had turned dark, almost bottle green. Come home,
Jeff! "What happened?"

"I . . . don't like to talk about it."

"Okay." Fair enough. They *were* strangers after all.

"What do you do?" he asked, changing the subject.

"I'm a psychologist. I work in a program for abuse
and rape survivors."

"That's gotta be tough."

She nodded, still not looking at him, and changed the
subject again, wanting to stay away from memories of
her job. That was the point of a vacation, after all, to get
away from the mountains of horrible human tragedy she
dealt with on a regular basis. "I started my vacation
today."

21

"So you're planning to buy paintbrushes?"

She looked at him then, wondering what he meant. Then she remembered their earlier conversation. "I'm thinking about it. If I don't paint the house now, it'll have to wait another year, until my next vacation."

He nodded and opened his mouth to reply, but just as he started speaking, a long, low roll of thunder shook the house.

"Damn it, Jeff!" Callie said out loud. She looked at the digital clock and saw that the power must have fluctuated, because it was blinking steadily. She suddenly realized the room had become almost as gloomy as night.

"Five minutes," Chase said, looking at his watch.

"If the power doesn't go out." Something new to worry about. God, she hated this! Crossing the room, she turned on the lamp beside the radio.

She hated that radio, she realized. It sat there, ugly and gray, in a corner of the living room, a constant reminder that the Carlsons went to sea. Her dad had bought it after their mother's death. When he died, she'd come close to throwing it in the trash, but then Jeff had started going out, and she couldn't bear the thought of not being able to get in touch with him.

So it sat there, a lifeline that she hated.

She probably should have sunk the boat, she thought now. When they had sold their father's vessel after his death, to get money to live on, Jeff had insisted they take some of it and get a smaller boat. "For pleasure," he'd said. "We can go fishing, or just cruise on nice days . . ."

She'd allowed herself to be persuaded, thinking that if Jeff could take the boat out for fun, he wouldn't feel as strong a need to go out as a commercial fisherman. How

22

wrong she'd been. She'd never imagined that he would use that boat to follow the very lifestyle she wanted him to leave behind.

The radio crackled to life, Jeff's voice giving the call letters. "It's getting rough out here," he said. "We've got eight-foot waves . . ."

Chase picked up the microphone. "Are you still tied to the abandoned vessel?"

"We're almost done here . . ." His voice faded away in a burst of static.

Callie came to stand beside the table, gripping the edge of it until her knuckles turned white. Chase looked up at her, his eyes opaque.

". . . most of the water out of the boat and . . ."

Another burst of static. Callie closed her eyes, praying.

". . . engine started. Over."

Chase spoke into the microphone. "Give me your position, over."

Another roll of thunder shook the house, and there was a sudden machine-gun rattle of rain on the tin roof.

No answer. Chase keyed the mike again. "*Lily*, give me your position. Over."

Still no answer, just the unending crackle of static from the speaker.

"Oh, God!" Callie could hardly stand it. Straightening, she began to pace the room, praying to God, praying to the sea to help her brother return safely. Seconds turned slowly into minutes as Chase kept trying to raise the *Lily*.

"The storm's playing hell with the radio," he said once.

Callie didn't even answer. In her mind all she could see was the *Lily* tied up along some other boat, rolling dangerously on rough seas, unable to keep her bow into the waves because of the floundering vessel she was tied to. She could see Jeff being washed overboard by a large wave. She could see the *Lily* being hurled by the waves against the other craft and breaking up. Sinking.

All she could see was the sea taking the last of her family from her.

The minutes dragged into a half hour, then into an hour with no further word from Jeff.

The phone rang. Startled, she jumped and stared at it as if it might bite her. It had to be one of her friends, but she didn't want to talk to anyone right now. Chase keyed the mike again, and tried to get Jeff. Over and over, his voice remaining calm, he called the *Lily* and no one answered.

The phone kept ringing, and finally Callie reached for it, ready to give short shrift to whoever it was.

"Ms. Carlson?" asked an unfamiliar man's voice.

"Yes?"

"Ms. Carlson, this is Warrant Officer Hemlich of the United States Coast Guard. I'm calling about Jeff Carlson."

Her heart slammed, her eyes closed, and her brain fell silent as she waited for the awful news she was sure must be coming.

"Ma'am, Mr. Carlson asked that somebody call you and tell you he's all right. We're escorting him to harbor right now."

CHAPTER 2

CALLIE COLLAPSED. HER LEGS GAVE WAY AS THE adrenaline washed from her system in the tidal wave of relief that poured through her. She caught herself on the edge of the couch and managed to sit, the phone still in her hand.

"What happened?" Chase asked. He leaned forward as if ready to jump to her aid. "What's wrong?"

"Jeff . . . he's okay," she managed to say, her voice shaking. "He's okay. God, I thought . . . it was the Coast Guard and I thought . . ." She couldn't even finish the sentence.

Another rumble of thunder shook the house until the windows rattled, momentarily drowning the clatter of rain on the metal roof. Salt spray swept up off the inlet was beginning to cloud the windows, blurring the outside world.

Callie leaned forward, covering her face with her hands, letting herself feel the relief, letting the tension of the past hours slowly ebb from every aching muscle in her body. She wanted to cry, but she wasn't alone, so she drew deep, steadying breaths and said silent prayers of thanksgiving.

After a few minutes, Chase spoke. "You still going to kill him when he gets home?"

It was the right question, because the absurdity of it struck her, bracing her. She dropped her hands from her face and looked at him. "I'm going to sink that damn boat!"

"It's an option. Sink both of them."

She started to laugh, and for a moment she wondered

if she was going to be able to stop, or if she was going to sail off into the hysterics that had been threatening for hours now. But her laugh trailed off, and with it escaped the last tension in her body. "He's all right," she said again, making herself believe it. "They're escorting him back to harbor."

"Escorting?"

For the first time, the word struck her as odd. "That's what they said." She searched Chase's face, hoping he would explain it away.

But he didn't. "Did they say why?"

She shook her head, feeling a new tension grip her. "I should have asked. I assumed . . . I thought because the seas are so rough . . . "

He nodded. "Maybe that's it. Maybe Jeff was having a little more trouble than he let on. Or maybe they needed help towing the other boat."

She clung to that but didn't believe it. Her life had been a series of catastrophes, one after another. Why should this time be any different? But she needed to believe that word *escorting* was innocent.

Her stomach growled, unhappy that she had fed it nothing but grits since the morning. The thought of food provided a welcome distraction. "I'm going to make something to eat. Join me?" She expected him to make an excuse and go back to his solitude, but he surprised her.

"Sounds good," he said. "Can I help?"

She had fried chicken left from dinner the previous night. The argument with Jeff had started as they were setting the table, and neither of them had eaten more than a few mouthfuls. She brought that out, along with the potato salad they also hadn't touched, and she and Chase sat at the big oak kitchen table that had belonged

26

to her great grandmother.

"Thanks for helping me this afternoon, Chase."

He paused, a spoonful of potato salad between the bowl and his plate. "That's what neighbors are for." He smiled.

His smile, Callie thought, was an amazing thing. It transformed his face from piratical and dangerous to warm and welcoming. Only the diamond twinkling in his earlobe reminded her that he could look like a buccaneer.

"Well, thank you anyway," she said. "I honestly think Jeff would never have answered my radio calls."

"You may be underestimating your brother. It sounded to me like he cares about you a lot more than you think."

"I know he cares about me. He just doesn't want to listen to me." She sighed and managed a rueful smile. "Maybe I *am* a nag."

"Could be. Or it could just be that he's young and thinks he knows more than he does. That's common at his age."

"Yes, it is."

"Anyway, I think he would have answered your calls when the weather got worse. He understood your feelings enough to have the Coast Guard call you."

"That's true." The word *escorting* floated back into her thoughts, but she dismissed it, unwilling to believe it meant anything except that the Coast Guard was making sure her brother got safely back to port. "So you're a seaman, too?" In her book, that was no recommendation.

"Diver."

The word was clipped in a way that told her there was a lot of emotion behind it. Even as she was wondering

27

whether to question him, he started talking.

"I was doing deep dives for insurance companies interested in salvage."

"How deep?"

"My personal max is around three hundred feet. Most of the dives were somewhere between a hundred and a hundred seventy feet though. The deeper you go, the shorter the dive and the harder it is to actually work, so I didn't do too many really deep ones. For those they tend to use ROVs—remotely operated vehicles."

"I don't know much about it, but don't most divers stay above a hundred?"

"Usually. For recreational diving anyway. This was work."

"Specialized work."

"Very."

She hesitated, then asked, "You said you had an accident?"

His face tightened and his shoulders tensed. "Yeah," he said roughly. "I got into trouble, and they had to bring me up too fast. I got the bends."

She caught her breath. Even though she didn't know much about diving, she knew about how deadly decompression sickness could be. Air embolisms in the tissues and brain could cause permanent damage. "Bad?" she asked.

"Yeah."

That probably explained the limp and the flickers of pain she saw cross his face from time to time. She felt a surge of sympathy for him, but also a burst of anger. "The damn sea," she said bitterly.

He shook his head. "It's best not to look at it that way, Callie. You could get hit by a car crossing the street."

28

She pushed back from the table, her appetite gone, and carried her dishes to sink. "It's the sea," she said. "It's different. You *know* it's different."

Turning to face him, she leaned back against the counter and folded her arms. "I grew up in a seafaring family, and I hate the water. People come down here to the Keys and look out at the pretty aquamarine waves and think she's beautiful. They don't know her. Jeez, listen to me." She gave a harsh laugh and shook her head. "I sound so superstitious."

"Most of us who live with the sea are superstitious," he said with a shrug.

"It's illogical though, and I know it. The sea is no different than a mountain, or a hurricane, or any other force of nature. It's just an inhospitable environment for us. But . . ." She trailed off. "My dad used to talk about her like she was a living, breathing being."

"It feels that way when your life depends on it."

"He loved her. More than anything, he loved the sea. Jeff's the same way."

He nodded slowly. "That's hard on you, isn't it."

"You know, you'd make a good psychologist." She gave a little laugh and tried to shrug off her mood. "I'm being unreasonable, and you're using active listening to get me to talk about it."

"Do you analyze every conversation?"

"No, I don't. But I'm sensing you're on Jeff's side in this."

He shrugged one shoulder. "I don't know that I'd say that. He was a jerk to go out this morning. I thought so when I saw him go. But that's youth, more than anything."

"I mean about the sea. You love the sea, don't you?"

"Yeah. I do."

29

"In spite of what happened to you."

"Like I said, I could've been hit by a car crossing the street."

She had a feeling he didn't quite believe that, that he was replying with logic when his feelings were really something very different.

He cleaned his plate, then carried it to the sink. "Thanks for the meal. I need to get on back to my place. But . . . if you need anything, give me a call. I reckon I'm still good for something."

A couple of minutes later he was walking back around the inlet in the pouring rain. Callie Carlson was quite a nice armful of woman, he thought in the detached way an artist might admire a painting. She had a Meg Ryan sort of cuteness with short blond hair, and a pair of legs that were made for shorts. In another lifetime he might have checked her out seriously, but not since he'd discovered that life was a hell of a lot easier if you just left women out of it.

Even here in the protected cove the waves were battering against the seawalls and the mangroves. The heron had disappeared, and all the other wildlife was hiding somewhere in the safety of the thick tropical woods. He was sodden and dripping long before he reached his house, but he didn't care. Getting wet had never bothered him.

He was chilled, though, by the time he climbed the steps to the shelter of his porch. Going around the side to where Callie couldn't see him from her house, he stripped his clothes and left them in a wet heap on the redwood planking.

Inside he poured a finger of whiskey into a glass and knocked it back, hoping it would take the edge off the chill. Then he climbed into the shower and let the hot water beat some of the ache out of his body.

The bends had done some damage to his hip joint and to his back, and there was nothing he could do about that. But compensating for the pain caused him to move and sit awkwardly, and as the day wore on his muscles began to stiffen and shriek. A hot shower always helped that.

He had just finished toweling himself dry and was climbing into a pair of jeans when he heard an engine coming up the rutted, sandy road to his house. He hadn't had a single visitor in the three weeks he had lived here, and he wasn't expecting any now.

Tension filled him again, a different kind. The nightmare visions that plagued the darkness began to crawl around the edges of his mind in the storm-dimmed house. Unable to ignore his uneasiness, he got the Beretta out of the drawer and walked to the bedroom to watch out the back window and see who was coming.

A green Ford Explorer came around the bend, emerging from the thick growth almost as if it had sprung out of the plants. He didn't recognize the vehicle, and his hand tightened on the butt of his gun.

The car's windows were darkly tinted, and he couldn't see the driver. Licking his lips, Chase lifted the gun and waited.

What he was waiting for, he didn't know. He didn't believe in his nightmare demons, yet he was absolutely convinced he had something to fear. A hundred times a day he told himself it was just paranoia, but he didn't believe that either.

Instead he kept remembering that even paranoids have real enemies. It was an old joke, but it didn't strike him as funny at all. Not anymore.

The Explorer pulled to a stop right behind his pickup truck and the engine turned off. Not exactly a surreptitious approach, Chase decided, relaxing a little.

Then the car door opened and a sigh of relief escaped him as he recognized his old friend Tom Akers. Suddenly embarrassed to be holding a pistol, he shoved it back into his dresser drawer, grabbed a T-shirt, and pulled it on.

He stepped onto the front porch just as Tom was climbing the steps. Old salt that he was, Tom was wearing a sou'wester. He looked up, saw Chase, and broke into a huge grin. "How ya doin', man?"

"Great. How's it going, Tom?"

They met at the top of the steps and shook hands vigorously.

"You're looking a helluva lot better than the last time I saw you."

"Nobody looks good in a hospital bed."

"Ain't that the truth?" Tom shucked his rain gear and hung it on the back of a porch chair.

"Come on in. I've got a bottle of whiskey just waiting for you."

"I figured you had one with my name on it."

Chase's kitchen, living room, and dining area formed a spacious open L. He and Tom sat at the table with the bottle between them and two highball glasses. Chase poured them each a couple of fingers of whiskey.

Tom took a sip, nodded approval, and set his glass down. "So how are you doing, really?" he asked. "Is the pain getting any better?"

Chase shook his head. "That's pretty much steady. I'm learning to live with it."

"And the nightmares?"

"The same."

Tom sighed and took another sip of whiskey. "Shit, I was hoping it would get better."

"It's only been a couple of months. Maybe it will."

"Do you remember anything about what happened down there?"

For some reason, the question set Chase's teeth on edge. It wasn't just that he didn't like to remember it, it was the feeling he got that everybody was waiting for him to remember something new. And at some instinctive level, he had a strong feeling that it wouldn't be healthy for him to remember any more. "Just . . . the hallucinations. It's not very clear. It probably never will be."

Tom nodded. "Well, it was a hell of a thing, and I'm damned if I can understand how it happened. It's not like you haven't been diving at those depths hundreds of times."

"Things happen."

"Things like that don't happen to careful divers like you." Tom rubbed the back of his neck as if something irritated him. "I had a bad feeling that day. A real bad feeling. It was like they put that decompression chamber on deck because they *knew* something was going to happen."

Chase shook his head. "You know better, Tom. It's a standard precaution on a commercial dive boat, especially on a deep dive. I wouldn't have gone down without one there."

"I still didn't like the feeling, but I was damn grateful we had it." Tom dropped his hand from his neck. His face had been weathered to the patina of old, gnarled wood by a life at sea, and right now he didn't look happy. "Something was wrong out there that day."

Chase agreed with him, but he didn't want to say so

aloud. Giving voice to the fears that plagued him would only make them seem more real. "There sure was. Me. I fucked up royally."

Tom's eyes, the color of the sea on a cold day, narrowed. "You? The way you plan and consider every detail? No, I ain't buyin' it."

"That's the only explanation. I didn't do something right. I know it. It'd be nice if I knew *what* I did wrong, but I don't. It doesn't matter. I'll never dive again."

"So what are you going to do?"

"Figure out what to do with the rest of my life." *As soon as I can figure out how to sleep again.* But he didn't tell anybody except his doctor about his sleep problems. He didn't want anybody to know how far gone he was.

"Well, you'll figure out something. You were a SEAL, for God's sake. You can do damn near anything."

Chase gave him a half smile. "That's sure what they try to beat into you in training."

"And you did it. All of it. Not many make it through Hell Week, let alone the rest of it. And if you can do that . . ."

"That was a long time ago, Tom. A long time ago."

Tom snorted. "Not so long that you've lost your determination. You'll find something to do. Something dangerous, probably." He chuckled. "Yup, it'll be something dangerous."

Chase didn't know about that. He was getting awfully sick of living on the edge. He and Tom went back a long way, though, all the way back to when they'd both been in the navy, he a SEAL and Tom a boatswain's mate. They had served on the same ship, been stationed at the same base, and both had gotten tired of the military life around the same time. Tom was five years older, but that had never stood in the way of their friendship, not even when Chase had been a brash nineteen-year-old who was sure he could conquer the world.

Now, with sixteen years of friendship behind them, they looked across the table as equals. Tom could say things to Chase that no other living human being could get away with. Tom knew it, and he took advantage of that now.

"What you *can't* do," he said, "is hide away out here like some hermit. At least stick your periscope up once in a while. I start to get insulted when you don't call for a month."

One corner of Chase's mouth lifted. "I reckon I can manage that."

Tom laughed. "You reckon right. Stop acting like a wounded dog and crawl out of your den."

"Damn it, Tom." Chase wanted to laugh, but he resisted the urge. "I just managed to crawl into it. After two months in the hospital and rehab, I *need* the quiet and solitude."

"Mmm." Tom sounded doubtful. "What you need is some fun and the company of good friends."

Chase didn't answer that. He found himself looking past Tom, out at the dark, stormy afternoon, and wondering if his nightmares would be easier to handle if he lived in town. Or if they'd just be worse.

"I came out here for the quiet," he said levelly. And indeed he had. He had believed that there would be less stimulation, less to rasp his raw nerves. He'd also figured that it would be a lot harder for somebody to get at him—if somebody wanted to get at him. But he didn't want to say that out loud, not even to his oldest friend.

"Well," Tom said after a bit, "I guess you know best what you need." His tone was heavy.

Chase dragged his gaze from the window and saw how troubled Tom looked. "What's wrong?"

"You. What happened to you." Tom shook his head and took another swig of his whiskey. "Call me a superstitious old sea dog if you want, but something about this ain't right. Damned if I can put my finger on it, Chase, but something sure as hell ain't right."

Chase felt his stomach twist uneasily, but he refused to let go of his rationality. "It'd be easy to believe that, Tom. Real easy. But I have to accept responsibility for what happened."

"Responsibility? I'll lay it at your door when you tell me exactly how it was you screwed up."

"I don't know. I can't remember. But I must have done something."

"Yeah. That's what everybody wants to believe."

Silence fell between them, filled by the drumbeat of rain on the roof and the low growl of the storm. Yeah, thought Chase, everybody wanted to believe he'd made a mistake. He wanted to believe it himself, because to believe otherwise would give substance to the things he saw in his nightmares.

"I miscalculated something," he said finally.

"Mmm." Tom's response was noncommittal.

"It had to be. My first thought was that I'd gotten a nitrogen-oxygen mix in my tanks instead of helium and oxygen, but the tanks tested for the right mixture, Tom."

"That they did."

"So whatever happened probably wasn't nitrogen narcosis. Which means the doctors were probably right about me having some kind of stroke that caused my

36

hallucinations and panic."

"I never heard of a stroke doing that, but I guess it's possible." Tom's tone remained dubious.

"Transient ischemic attack, they called it. They said it might even have been caused by pressure on my carotid arteries at that depth."

"Constricting the carotid arteries causes unconsciousness and death, not hallucinations."

Chase nodded slowly, neither agreeing nor disagreeing.

"Well, I suppose the doctor knows better than I do." Tom pushed back from the table and walked around the room, checking things out. "Pretty cozy little place you got here. I wouldn't mind holing up here myself."

"So crash in the spare room."

Tom laughed. "Don't tempt me. I sure as hell haven't got anything to go home to."

"When do you sail next?"

"Not for three weeks. The *Hope* is in for some scraping and painting."

Chase knew how restless Tom tended to get when he was tied to the land, especially since his wife had died. At these times, he and Tom were usually busy planning all kinds of things to keep busy.

"Why don't you sail with me?" Tom asked suddenly. "I can always use a good mate."

For an instant, just an instant, Chase seriously considered it. The sea was in his blood, running through his veins. He needed her scents and sounds as if they were the very essence of life.

But the thought of being out there on the water again, with nothing between him and the grasping arms of the sea except the hull of a ship, made him go cold all over.

"Think about it," Tom said, as if sensing his reaction.

"Don't answer now. You might feel different in a couple of weeks."

"Thanks." But he knew he wouldn't do it. And for the first time he realized that not only would he never dive again, he would never sail again. The realization stirred the embers of rage in his belly.

As suddenly as if someone had thrown a switch, the rain stopped. Through the open windows, they could hear the waves against the shore, but not one other sound.

Tom picked up his whiskey. "Let's sit out on the porch," he said.

Chase didn't need an explanation. Tom might talk about how cozy his place was, but he hated to be indoors for long.

"That's better," Tom said, standing at the porch railing as if it were the bow of a ship, one hand stuck into his pants pocket, the other holding his highball glass.

The world was a collage of grays and dark greens, everything shining wetly. From the Carlson house around the inlet came the warm glow of lamplight falling through windows.

"Who lives over there?" Tom asked.

"The Carlsons. Brother and sister. She's waiting for him to get home. The kid sailed out this morning in a thirty-foot rustbucket. He's okay, though."

"Kid's got more balls than brains," Tom remarked.

"That's what I thought. He's probably feeling pretty proud of himself, though. He salvaged a pretty nice fishing boat, from what he was saying on the radio earlier."

Tom perked up. Salvage was a subject he was comfortable with, unlike illness, injury and nightmares.

"Yeah? That's some piece of luck."

"The kid thinks so."

"What was wrong with the boat? What happened to the crew?"

"I don't know. He found it sinking, said it had been scuttled."

"Scuttled?" Tom turned and leaned back against the railing, shaking his head. "I don't like the sound of that."

"Neither do I"

"Nobody scuttles a perfectly good boat unless they've got something serious to hide."

"The thought crossed my mind."

"You didn't tell the sister that?"

Chase shook his head. "What's the point? But it did cross my mind that if somebody had something to hide, and these boys bring it to the light of day, they could be in some serious danger."

Tom nodded.

"The Coast Guard may think the same thing. They're escorting the boys in."

Tom sucked air between his teeth. "Not good." He jerked his head toward the house. "So what's the sister like? A withered old prune?"

In spite of himself, Chase laughed. "Far from it. Cute and blond."

"Hmm. Well, with that right next door, I guess I can see why you want to hide out here. Especially after Iris dumped you." Iris, Chase's most recent on-and-off girlfriend, hadn't even visited him in the hospital. Chase didn't want to think about that, and Tom didn't seem to want to get into those dark waters either. The change of subject was swift. "Speaking of which, Dave Hathaway asked me to say hello to you."

39

Dave Hathaway was the executive at the insurance company who directed salvage operations when the company decided it was worth their while. "What's Dave got to do with Iris?"

Tom chuckled. "Brain fart. I don't know what made me think of him. But he did want me to say hi, asked me to remind you if you want a job with the company, he's got one for you. He said he could use an experienced diver to oversee deep-salvage operations."

"He mentioned that to me just before I got out of rehab. I told him no."

"Why?" Tom set his glass down on the railing and put both his hands on his hips. "Look, Chase, I know you've been through a rough time. Nobody feels great after a serious accident and weeks of rehab. But you gotta get on with life again sometime, and now's as good a time as any to get off your butt and get going."

Chase nodded.

"Don't you nod at me. Talk to me, damn it! Supervising deep-salvage operations would be just the ticket for you. There isn't a thing you don't know about the subject. You'd be a hell of a lot better at it than some white-shirted pencil pusher who's never had to salvage anything more difficult than a golf ball in the rough, because you *know* what's involved and what the risks are. You'd be a real help to the people who actually have to do the work."

"I don't want to work for that damn company again."

The vehemence of Chase's response took Tom by surprise. He stood perfectly still for a few moments, his gaze scanning Chase's face intently. Finally he said, "What aren't you telling me?"

Chase shrugged a shoulder. "Not a damn thing."

"They took care of you after the accident, didn't

40

they? Paid all the hospital bills and everything?"

"Every last dime."

"Showed proper concern?"

"Oh, yeah."

"I thought so. They sure investigated the hell out of it. At least as far as I could tell. Do you know something different?"

"I keep telling everyone, I don't know anything at all!" Chase's tone was impatient, and he regretted it instantly because this was Tom, his old friend, and Tom didn't deserve that.

But Tom had known him a long time, and it apparently didn't faze him in the least. "I'm just trying to figure out why I hear hostility in your voice when you talk about the company. You keep saying *you* must have made a mistake, and all they're doing is offering you a job, so why are you mad at them?"

Chase threw up a hand. "I don't know why I feel this way. I just do. I don't want a damn thing to do with them again."

"Okay, okay." Tom held up a pacifying hand.

"Sorry. I didn't sleep well last night, but that's no excuse for biting your head off."

"Forget it." He turned back to the rail and looked out over the choppy inlet.

Chase stared at his friend's back and saw by the way his shoulders were set that Tom was unhappy with him. Well, hell, what was he supposed to do? He had too much shit to deal with right now, and he didn't need any additional pressure about getting out and getting a life. The time for that would come, but not yet.

"Look," he said finally, hating the feeling that he'd wounded Tom, "I just need some time. I've got some problems I need to deal with before I'll be ready to start working."

"Problems?" Tom turned and looked at him. "What kind of problems . . . other than the pain?"

"I've got . . . well, I have some flashbacks. They're supposed to start wearing off in a few months. But . . ." He shrugged, not wanting to discuss it in detail.

"Flashbacks to what happened when you got into trouble?"

"Sort of." And that's as specific as he was going to be. If he told Tom what was really going on, Tom would probably want to have him committed.

"I didn't know that. Hell." Tom rubbed the back of his neck again, a nervous gesture. "I'm sorry, man. I'm really sorry. You got someone helping you with that?"

"Yeah." A bottle of sleeping pills and a Beretta. He wouldn't take any of the other drugs the doctor had suggested.

"Well, okay. But you better keep in touch, or I'm going to be showing up on your doorstep unannounced every week, got it?"

Relieved to be getting away from the difficult stuff, Chase laughed.

After that, it got a whole lot easier. They put Jimmy Buffett on the stereo and kicked back on the porch, talking about old girlfriends, distant ports of call, and the hell they had raised in younger years.

They watched as the *Lily* sailed into the cove and the two boys tied her up at the dock. Chase noticed the boys didn't have the boat they had salvaged with them, and wondered what had happened. He almost suggested going over there to find out, then remembered it was almost darkfall. No way was he going to be out after dark.

"Say," said Tom, "we've got time. Why don't we go

to the Bahamas for a few days?"

"That's a possibility. Let me think about it." He looked around and saw that the night was beginning to creep out of the shadows in the undergrowth. It would be dark in a few more minutes. The back of his neck started to crawl, and his empty glass gave him the excuse he needed.

"Let's go inside. I'm getting cold, and I need a refill."

Tom followed willingly enough, and he didn't even say anything when Chase closed all the windows and locked them. But he did look thoughtful. Very thoughtful.

Chase had a good idea what Tom was thinking, but he was damned if he was going to confirm it by saying it out loud. He didn't need for the whole world to know he was insane.

It was bad enough that *he* knew it.

CHAPTER 3

TORN BETWEEN WANTING TO GIVE JEFF THE COLD shoulder when he got home and needing to take care of him the way she had for years, Callie finally decided to at least make a decent dinner for them. Afterward she could give Jeff hell for blowing off his job and scaring her to death.

By the time she heard the *Lily*'s engines approaching, she had two chickens almost done in the oven, instant mashed potatoes ready to microwave, a sheet of biscuits, and a big tossed salad. She had even made up her mind to invite Jeff's friend Eric to join them. Maybe if she couldn't get through to Jeff, she could get through to Eric. She had often thought that of the two Eric was the more sensible and down to earth.

When she heard the *Lily* pull up to the dock and the engines cut out, she couldn't stand the suspense any longer. Instead of waiting indoors as if she didn't care, she went out onto the side veranda from where she could see the boys tying the boat to the dock. Folding her arms, she waited, determined not to run out there and demand the entire story.

Once the boat was secure, the boys jumped back aboard to get their gear. Callie tapped her toe impatiently, staring through the gloom, wondering if they were just trying to annoy her with their dilatoriness.

From across the inlet, she heard the faint strains of Jimmy Buffett, and had the sudden wild wish that she could be over there with Chase Mattingly, sipping a drink and relaxing. Instead, she was standing here being a mother to a twenty-year-old who was convinced she was overly protective. A twenty-year-old who never let her forget that she wasn't really his mother, she was just his sister, and she wasn't all that much older besides.

Of course, she believed that Jeff only said those things to irritate her, because the truth was, she was the only mother Jeff had had since the age of six, and he knew it as well as she.

Finally, Jeff and Eric were trudging up the dock through the gloom toward her, carrying bait buckets and a cooler.

"Hey, sis," Jeff said. He was a taller version of his sister, with the same Nordic blond hair and blue eyes. "Did the Coast Guard call you?"

"Yes."

"Hi, Callie," Eric said politely. He was as tall as Jeff but dark-skinned, with eyes that were a soft, warm

44

brown.

"Hi, Eric. Join us for dinner?"

"Sure!" Eric's enthusiasm was palpable. His parents were divorced, and neither one of them seemed to have any time for him anymore. At twenty, he was old enough to be on his own, but it didn't seem right to Callie, and she had a feeling Eric was pretty lonely living by himself.

When Jeff reached her, he dropped the bait buckets and grabbed her in a bear hug, giving her a big kiss on the cheek. "I'm sorry, sis. I didn't mean to scare you."

"Just . . ." She broke off, not wanting to get into it before dinner. Neither of them had eaten last night, and she wasn't going to let that happen again. "Thanks for having them call me. I was scared to death, Jeff."

"Sorry."

"Now go wash up, guys. I want to be able to smell the food."

They both laughed and hurried past her into the house. She stood on the veranda for a few more minutes, listening to the quieting waves, and smelling the freshness of the rain-washed world. Jimmy Buffett was no longer audible, and she guessed Chase had closed his windows. Too bad. Maybe she ought to get herself an inexpensive stereo one of these days. She could probably afford it now that Jeff was making some money.

That was when she remembered he probably didn't have a job anymore. Stifling a sigh, she went in to finish preparing dinner.

By the time they all sat down at the table, Callie knew something was seriously wrong. Jeff wasn't being his usual boisterous self. In fact, he was downright subdued.

But his appetite was fine, she realized with relief as she watched him take half a chicken and give the other half to Eric. That was followed by a huge heap of mashed potatoes, three biscuits, a river of gravy, and a large serving of salad. Nothing, she thought, could be all that bad if he was eating.

"What happened to the boat you salvaged?" she asked, suddenly realizing that they hadn't towed it in with them.

"Coast Guard's checking it out," Jeff said, then stuffed his mouth with potatoes.

"Checking it out? Why?"

Jeff shrugged, chewing mightily. Callie looked at Eric. "Why?"

Eric didn't try to hide behind the food. "They said it's unusual for somebody to try to scuttle a boat. They asked us a whole bunch of questions about it, like they wondered if we knew anything, but we didn't. Anyway, they want to look the boat over before they give it to us. They said something about making sure it hadn't been used to transport drugs, and something about Customs checking it out, too."

"Oh." Callie shrugged. "Makes sense."

"That's what we thought."

"How long do they think it'll be?"

"A few days," Jeff said, reaching for a biscuit. "The captain of the cutter said it seems really weird. I guess they're going to try to find out who the owner is."

"Does that mean you won't get to keep the boat?" That would certainly explain why Jeff was so subdued. He'd risked his neck to get the vessel.

"He said that since it wasn't fully sunk, if the owners want it back, they have to pay us for salvaging it. But since they tried to scuttle it, I don't think anybody's

46

going to want it back."

"Which is crazy," Eric said. "It's a really neat boat."

"Cool," Jeff agreed. His blue eyes were suddenly alight with excitement. "Wait'll you see it, Callie. It's a dream."

Eric laughed excitedly. "It's perfect. We could let two people at a time fish. More money on each trip."

Callie was enjoying their excitement but felt her stomach lurch as Eric reminded her what he and Jeff were going to use that boat for. But, she told herself, it wouldn't be the way it had been with her father. The boys would be taking tourists out on day trips for deep-sea fishing; they wouldn't be going out for weeks on end the way her dad had. At least at the end of every day she would know Jeff was safe.

"It'll be great, sis, you'll see," Jeff told her enthusiastically. "And once we've got the boat free and clear, most of what we make will be profit!"

She nodded, smiling, but the smile felt unnatural on her face. In her heart she could feel only trepidation. She knew she had to hide it, knew it wasn't fair to Jeff, but God, she didn't want to lose the last of her family to the sea.

She managed to smile and laugh appropriately until the boys were doing the dishes and she was sitting at the kitchen table with a cup of coffee. Then she couldn't hold it in any longer.

"Jeff? What about your job? You missed work today."

He shrugged but didn't look at her. "It doesn't matter. We've got the boat now. As soon as I saw that baby, I knew I wasn't going to give her up to get back here for that dumb job."

"Mmm." Her face felt frozen now. "Maybe if you call

47

Mr. Donleavy and explain, he won't fire you."

"I don't care if he fires me! I've got the boat I need to start my charter service."

Why was it, Callie wondered, that she could remain so calm at work when dealing with other people who took these attitudes, yet with her own brother her temper always flared to white heat almost as soon as they started talking?

She drew a couple of deep breaths, told herself to pretend she was dealing with a patient, and said in her calmest voice, "Jeff, you don't have the boat until you get it back from the Coast Guard. What if they find out there are drugs on it? They'd probably impound it as evidence and you'll never get it—at least not until they don't need it anymore. You need money in the meantime. Besides, you might need money to fix her up once you have her."

"I've got money," he said impatiently. "I've got all the money I was saving toward buying a boat. That's almost two thousand dollars."

And why was it, Callie wondered, that two thousand dollars sounded like so very much when you were twenty and sounded like so very little by the time you were nearly thirty? "You can always use more," she said. "And what if there's a delay getting the boat back from the Coast Guard?"

"You worry too much, Callie."

He'd been saying that to her for years, ever since he had grown old enough to argue with her when she didn't want him to do something. Her stock answer was, "I'm just concerned about you," but tonight something in her seemed to snap.

"Yes, I worry too much," she said in a low voice. "Of course I worry too much. Since I was fourteen years old

I've been responsible for you and had to worry about you. And since Dad died, I've had to worry about *everything* for both of us. So just tell me, Jeff, when are you going to start doing your own worrying so I can stop having to do it for you?"

He stood with a pot in his hands, looking shocked, as she got up from the table and walked out of the kitchen. Eric, she noted from the corner of her eye, looked as if he wanted to be anywhere else on earth.

And she didn't care. She was twenty-eight years old, and she was sick and tired of being responsible for her ungrateful brother. Sick and tired of being responsible for someone who hated having her worry about him. Let him go to hell on his own roller coaster. She was washing her hands of it here and now.

She left the house and walked down to the path, turning toward the point. As many times as she had walked out there today she was surprised she was doing it again. But somehow, despite her hatred for the sea, it was to the sea she always turned when she needed the comfort of perspective.

The storm had blown away since sunset, and the above was clear and speckled with brilliant stars. The breeze blew briskly, carrying the musty scents of the forest behind, mingling them with the richer scents of the shore.

At last she looked out toward the Atlantic, across the waves that rolled in steadily. The sea was almost phosphorescent tonight and she wondered if the storm had stirred up the phytoplankton, or if the water itself had a subtle glow. She often wondered about such things, and stubbornly refused to look them up. She didn't want to know any more about her enemy than she already did.

The steady rhythm of the waves was hypnotic as always, and little by little the tension and worry ebbed from her, seeming to slip away with the surf.

Squatting down, she wrapped her arms around her knees and watched the waves in their eternal dance.

Little by little, she began to see herself as smaller and smaller, as if her mind were lifting up above on a bird's wing, and seeing her tiny body against the vastness of the shore and sea. The perspective brought her peace as it always did.

Finally, feeling better, she stood and walked back to the house. Jeff was heedless, but he was only twenty. And he could always find another job if he needed to. It wasn't worth the emotional energy she was investing in it.

When she got back to the house, Jeff and Eric were sitting on the veranda smoking cigarettes. That was another thing Jeff had refused to listen to her about, but at least he bowed to her insistence that he not smoke indoors.

"I'm sorry, Callie," he said as she climbed the steps. "You're right. I'll call Mr. Donleavy in the morning and try to straighten things out."

She managed a shrug as if she didn't care, even though it pleased her that he'd apparently thought about it. Maybe pretending not to care would be the best way she could teach him to think for himself. "Are you spending the night, Eric? You're welcome to."

"Thanks, Callie. I think I will."

"You know where everything is. Help yourself. Good night, guys."

It was earlier than her usual bedtime, but she was exhausted from all the tension of the day. Hiding away in her room with a glass of milk and a book seemed like

50

the perfect escape.

As it turned out, it was. Twenty minutes later she was fast asleep.

Tom suspected something. Chase sensed it when his old friend suddenly announced that he was staying the night.

"No point driving back to Miami," Tom said with a shrug. It's late and it's a long haul."

"Sure. Glad to have you." Gladder than he could say. Maybe he would actually be able to sleep tonight.

Tom pulled his pipe out of his back pocket, along with a tobacco pouch. "I'll just step outside and light up."

It was almost a question, and Chase opened his mouth to tell him he could smoke his pipe indoors, but then it struck him that this might be a good time to face down some of his fears. With Tom here, maybe he could go out onto that porch now that it was dark. And maybe if he did that he'd be one step closer to banishing these insane ideas of being threatened by the night.

"Sure," he said, with more calm than he felt. "Let's get some air."

Crossing the threshold was one of the hardest things he'd ever done. It hadn't even been this difficult in SEALs training when they'd tied him up and thrown him in the swimming pool. He'd faced that with a hell of a lot less trepidation than he was facing opening the door and stepping out into the night.

But he was a man who'd long ago learned to take his fear and turn it into something useful. Once he made up his mind to walk out that door, he was going to do it no matter how hard his heart pounded or what kind of cold sweat he broke into. All the adrenaline that suddenly flooded him with an overwhelming urge to run could also be used to make him do the impossible.

He used it now to propel himself out the door and onto the dark porch.

His ears buzzed oddly, and he could have sworn he heard the shadows whispering to one another. But he made himself ignore it and walk over to the railing. Tom joined him, taking his comfortable time about packing his pipe and lighting it. Soon the familiar, comforting smell of Tom's tobacco wafted toward him, and the night seemed a little less threatening.

Then he saw shadows moving along the shoreline, coming toward them, shadows with small, glowing eyes. For an instant, Chase's heart lurched as panic slammed him in the chest. This wasn't the first time he'd seen glowing red eyes in the dark. Usually they were bigger.

Tom pointed with the stem of his pipe. "The boys are coming over this way."

Tom's reasonable tone yanked Chase back from the edge.

Forcing himself to look more carefully, he recognized the silhouette of Jeff Carlson, saw that both boys were smoking cigarettes. Not glowing eyes at all. Christ, he thought with a sudden wave of self-disgust, he had to quit this crap!

"Wonder what they want," Tom remarked.

"Probably to tell me all about the salvage today. I talked to Jeff on the radio a couple of times."

"Ahh."

The boys reached them a couple of minutes later. Jeff introduced himself and Eric, saying, "I guess I was talking to one of you on the radio this afternoon."

"Me," Chase said, shaking the boy's hand, hoping the

kid didn't notice his palm was slick with sweat. "I'm Chase Mattingly. This is Captain Tom Akers."

"Nice to meet you." Jeff looked at Chase. "I wanted to thank you for taking care of my sister this afternoon. She worries too much."

"You think so?" Even with his skin crawling from the feeling he was being watched from the shadows in the woods, Chase didn't miss the irony. "Hell, son, I thought you were an absolute fool to sail out this morning."

Jeff jerked his head as if he'd been slapped. "We didn't expect to be out for very long."

"Planning for the unexpected is what makes the difference when all hell breaks loose," Chase said unrepentantly. "I don't blame your sister for worrying. There's not much else she can do when you won't exercise your own common sense."

He wasn't quite sure what response he expected, and he wasn't sure he cared. The shadows were still whispering to one another, and they seemed to be moving in closer, as if they didn't care about the presence of other people. He felt almost as if something was breathing down his neck, but he forced himself not to look. He wouldn't give his hallucinations that much power over him.

Tom had grown very still and very quiet, and was looking intently at him. He wondered if that was because Tom sensed his fear and tension, or because he disapproved of what Chase had said to the boy.

Jeff and Eric stood frozen, too, but Jeff was the first to move, turning to toss his cigarette butt away onto the damp sand. Then he looked at Chase.

"We were only going out for a couple of hours," he said to Chase. "But you're right, sir. We should have thought about the possibility that something could go wrong."

"Damn straight," Chase said flatly. "A lot of things could have happened to delay your return, and on a bucket that size you don't want to be six or eight miles out when a storm hits. You were damn lucky today."

"Yes, Sir."

Tom puffed on his pipe and blew a smoke ring into the humid air. It was visible for only a second before the night swallowed it. "A wise captain never underestimates the sea or the weather, and never overestimates his own ability to deal with them."

"Yes, sir," said Jeff, and Eric echoed him.

The shadows seemed to be closing in even more, and Chase had the feeling that the maw of night was opening to swallow him the way it had swallowed the smoke. He could feel sweat streaming down his face and neck, and soaking his T-shirt. He had to get inside *now*.

"It's sticky out here," he said abruptly. "Let's move this discussion inside."

Tom gave him a quick look, but said nothing, merely nodding agreement. The boys hesitated briefly, but then followed.

After the warm night air, the air-conditioned cottage felt icy, but for Chase it was a relief to know all the windows were locked, and all the curtains drawn, and any shadows that got in would have a hard time finding a place to hide.

Everyone sat at the table. The boys weren't old enough to consume alcohol, so Chase dug them out some soft drinks. The dark boy, Eric, looked a little nervous, but Jeff Carlson looked downright awed. His gaze kept sliding toward Tom as if he wanted to ask a million questions.

"I'm a deep-sea diver," Chase said. "Was, anyway. Tom's the captain of a salvage vessel, the *Lady Hope*."

Jeff's eyes lit up. "Really? You spend all your time at sea looking for vessels in distress?"

Tom grinned around his pipe. "I've been known to do a bit of that from time to time, but mostly I get hired to go out and do specific jobs for large shippers or insurance companies."

"Do you ever get there and have to save people's lives?"

"Sometimes." Tom settled back in his chair, puffing on his pipe, but saying nothing more. He wasn't one to toot his own horn. "How about that boat you found today? Chase says it was abandoned and scuttled."

"Well, it was sinking. There were holes in the hull. It looked deliberate to me."

Chase's and Tom's eyes met across the table. Chase looked at Jeff.

"Didn't you find that odd?" he asked.

"Yeah," both boys said simultaneously. "It's a great boat," Eric said. "Not a thing wrong with it. Beats me why anybody would want to sink it."

"Unless maybe they were carrying drugs," Jeff said. "That's what the Coast Guard suspects. But it still doesn't make any sense to me. Once the drugs are off the boat, why sink it?"

"Maybe," said Chase, "they knew the boat had been identified as a drug runner. In that case, you'd want to move the cargo to another vessel and sink the one that had been identified."

Eric and Jeff exchanged glances and nodded.

"That makes sense," Eric agreed.

"Well, we sure didn't see any drugs on board," Jeff

said. "Except that we didn't really get to look all that close. Once we got the pumps on board we were pretty busy trying to find out where the water was coming from. It looked like somebody actually drilled holes in the hull."

"It should have sunk pretty fast then," Tom remarked.

Jeff shook his head. "It had kind of reached an equilibrium, you know? Like there was enough water in the boat that no more was coming in? But when we started pumping, we were barely getting ahead of it, so we were pretty hectic trying to stop it."

Chase looked at Tom. "The best-laid plans . . :"

Tom nodded.

"What do you mean?" Jeff asked.

Chase looked at him. "Only that somebody intended to sink that boat fast, but it didn't work the way he planned it."

Jeff laughed. "It sure didn't. It seems like there was enough air trapped in the hold to keep it afloat. Or something. It beats me. It should have been gone, but instead it was just sitting there, way too low in the water."

"Wouldn't have been long before the waves would have capsized it," Eric remarked. "If we'd been much later, what with the seas getting higher, it would've been too late."

"And if you'd been aboard her when she capsized," Tom said sternly, "it would've been too late for you."

Jeff looked abashed, and Eric looked down at his hands.

"Now I know it's not my place to be telling you what to do," Tom continued, "but salvage is a very risky business. You two are damn lucky you didn't go down with that vessel."

"Amen," said Chase. "You can justify those risks when someone's life is at stake, but nobody was aboard that boat. There was no justification to risk your own necks."

Jeff appeared mutinous, as if he finally wanted to disagree. Chase wouldn't give him the chance.

"It's simple, son," he said firmly. "Whatever your dreams, and however much salvaging that boat meant to you, it all would have been worthless if you'd drowned."

Jeff turned to Tom. "Would you have salvaged her?"

"I don't know," Tom said. His pipe was out, and he took a minute to relight it. "I wasn't there and didn't see it. But I can tell you this, if that boat was swamped and listing, I never would have boarded her until I'd attached floats so she couldn't roll over." He lowered his head and looked at Jeff from beneath bushy brows. A curl of smoke wafted up from his pipe.

Jeff nodded. "Okay. You're right."

Chase was surprised at how well the boy was taking this lecture. He'd gotten the impression from Callie that Jeff didn't listen to anyone. But maybe it was just Callie he didn't listen to.

Rising, ignoring the whispers in his ears that seemed almost like voices, he went to dig out an ashtray for his guests.

Both boys immediately lit Marlboros, adding their clouds of smoke to Tom's.

Eric spoke. "You said you're a deep-sea diver, Mr. Mattingly?"

"Call me Chase. I used to be." He didn't really care to discuss it.

But Tom wasn't going to let him off so easily. "Chase here trained with the Navy SEALS."

57

Those words had the predictable effect. Two young men looked at Chase with huge, awed eyes. He felt like an imposter. "I quit years ago," he said gruffly.

"Yup," said Tom. "Eight years ago. Then he worked as a salvage diver until recently."

Chase considered strangling his friend. Tom *knew* he didn't want to get into this. But Jeff Carlson was looking at him as if he were a superhero.

"I always wanted to do that," Jeff said.

"What?" Chase asked gruffly. "Be a SEAL?"

Jeff shook his head. "No, dive. I've always wanted to dive, but it's so expensive."

Chase was tempted to seriously discourage him from such thoughts, then realized he was just being an old curmudgeon. "It's not that expensive to take a little training and rent the equipment for a recreational dive."

"I've been saving for my boat." He suddenly brightened. "Now that I've got a boat, maybe I can take some lessons."

"Maybe," Chase agreed. It might even teach this kid some thought for consequences. Divers couldn't afford to be careless, even on relatively shallow dives. Planning and preparation were everything. No winging it, the way this kid was apparently wont to do.

"If we've really got a boat," Eric said. "But Callie's right, Jeff. If they find drugs or something on that boat, we might never get it."

"But we salvaged it. The law says it's ours."

"Not exactly," Tom said. "It wasn't fully sunk, so if the owner claims it, all you get is salvor's fees. It'll be a chunk of money, might even be more than the boat is worth."

"Really?"

"I've seen folks try to get out of paying for a salvage

58

job that saved them and their boat by claiming the cost of the salvage was more than the boat was worth. But they usually lose in court."

"Well, that's okay," Jeff said. "I wouldn't mind getting paid for salvage. Either way, I'm ahead."

The kid wasn't getting it, Chase realized. It wasn't penetrating Jeff's mind that he might wait until hell froze over to get either the boat or the payment for salvage. He found himself wondering if he'd been that blindly optimistic at twenty, and seemed to recall that he had been. Why else would he have become a SEAL?

And apparently Jeff wanted to get off this subject before he was forced to face reality, because he turned to Chase, and asked, "Was Hell Week as bad as they say?"

The question startled a laugh out of Chase. "I guess it was. I don't remember a whole lot of it. You get to a point where you're so crazy from lack of sleep, fatigue and discomfort that you kind of . . . well, zone out, I guess would be a way to describe it. That whole week is a fog in my memory."

Jeff nodded as if he could imagine it. He couldn't, of course. Nobody could. But Chase didn't tell him that.

A short while later, the boys said good night and headed back home. Chase watched them walk out the door as if the night didn't scare them at all, and he wished he could feel like that again.

When he glanced at Tom, he found his old friend staring at him from eyes that saw too much.

"How bad is it?" Tom asked.

Chase pretended not to understand him. "What?"

"The night."

Chase drew a deep, disgusted breath and looked away.

"Come on, man, you told me about it in the hospital. It's more than nightmares, isn't it? Ever since the sun went down you've been jumpier than a cat."

"It's nothing."

"Christ, Chase, cut it out! After what we've been through together, don't lie to me."

If there was any person on this planet he ought to be able to confide in, it was Tom. They'd been places together that most men hadn't. After the death of Tom's wife, Chase had been the one who'd held his friend as he wept. But he didn't want to admit his weakness to the man he admired more than any other.

"It's the nightmares, isn't it," Tom finally said. "They're not happening just when you're asleep."

Chase closed his eyes, the corners of his mouth drawing tightly down with the discomfort of having his vulnerability exposed. Some things he just couldn't bring himself to say.

"Well, hell." Tom picked up his pipe and sharply rapped it against the edge of the ashtray, knocking out the dottle. Then with his brown, gnarled hands, he packed it with fresh tobacco and lit it again. "You think you were attacked, don't you?"

"I *couldn't* have been attacked. Bill Evers and I were the only people down there."

Tom leaned back in his chair, resting his elbow on the table, cradling the bowl of his pipe in his palm as he drew on it. "There are different kinds of attacks."

Chase nodded slowly, feeling the pressure of the night beyond the walls and windows, feeling it push inward on his house the way the sea had pressed in on him down at nearly two hundred feet, as if it wanted to squeeze the life out of him. "Could be," he said finally, not believing it.

But it made him feel a little better to know that somebody else was feeling just as paranoid as he was. Maybe he wasn't *that* crazy after all.

CHAPTER 4

WHEN THE SHERIFF'S CARS PULLED UP, CALLIE WAS standing on a ladder under the eaves of the house, scraping away the peeling paint. She wore a headband, but perspiration was getting into her eyes anyway, making them sting. Even with help from Eric and Jeff, she saw no way she was going to have this painting done before her vacation was over.

All thoughts of her vacation and the paint job vanished, though, when she looked down from her perch and saw three sheriff's cars and the forensics van pull up to the house. She recognized Deputy Markell when he climbed out of the first vehicle. She had known him most of her life, but that didn't make her feel any easier. This was plainly no social call.

"Morning, Callie," Markell called up to her. "Can you come down a minute?"

Her heart was hammering so hard now she could hear it, and the dry taste of fear filled her mouth. This was not good She could read that in the number of cars, in the way the other deputies fanned out around the house, in the arrival of the forensics van. "What's wrong, Fred?" she called down to Markell. She felt frozen in place, her hands attached to the ladder in a death grip.

"Come on down, Callie," Fred Markell said again. "I need to talk to you."

She nodded jerkily, put the scraper in the pocket of her canvas apron, and climbed down the ladder, acutely aware of the way the wooden rungs creaked beneath her feet, of the way the ladder swayed slightly under her weight. The ground seemed awfully far away.

But not far enough. All too soon she was standing on it, facing Fred, feeling as if every cell in her brain was scurrying in a different direction trying to find some plausible, unthreatening reason for three police cars and a forensics van to be in her yard.

"Callie," Fred said, "it's about Jeff."

Just then, two officers came around the corner of the house escorting Jeff. His hands were cuffed behind his back.

"Jeff!" Callie cried out his name disbelievingly and started toward him, but Fred's hand on her arm stopped her.

"Don't do that, Callie."

She whirled on Fred. "What the hell is going on here? My brother didn't do anything! He's been with me!"

"He's been charged with grand theft and murder."

"Theft? *Murder*!" Shock stunned her brain. She turned and started toward Jeff again, but this time Fred gripped her elbow with enough firmness to hurt.

"No, Callie," he said sharply. "No. Don't interfere or *you'll* get arrested."

His grip on her elbow held her there while she watched in horror as her brother was put into a police car and driven away. This had to be a nightmare. This had to be. There was no way this could be real . . .

"Callie." Fred's voice seemed to come from a great distance, from down a long tunnel. "Callie, I have a search warrant for the house and boat."

She faced him, stunned almost past comprehension. "Warrant?"

He handed her some papers. "We have to search the

house and the boat, Callie."

"For what? For God's sake, for what?"

"For items belonging to the two men who owned the boat Jeff salvaged. For weapons. For bloodstains."

"Weapons . . ." This time it was she who grabbed Fred's elbow. "Fred . . . For the love of God, tell me what's going on here!"

Fred shook his head. "Your brother and Eric Block have been charged with theft and murder. If you want to know more, talk to the State Attorney, or get a lawyer. Right now, we've got a search warrant to execute. You can watch if you want, but stay out of the way."

She went inside to do precisely that, but she noticed that Fred Markell followed her, as if he didn't want her out of his sight. She dialed Shirley Kidder's number and once she explained what was happening, she was put through to the lawyer immediately.

"Hi, Callie," Shirley said. "Jeff's in trouble again?"

"Arrested for murder and grand theft, and they're searching my house right now."

"I can't do anything about Jeff until the arraignment. That'll happen tomorrow or the next day. And I can't do anything about the search warrant in time to stop them, Callie. You'll just have to let them go ahead. If there's anything wrong with the warrant, we can get anything they find thrown out of court. Other than that . . . just let them do it. I'd come out there except I have to be in court in twenty minutes. And there isn't anything I can do by being there anyway. Call me back later this afternoon and we'll get together to hash this out."

Callie's heart sank even further.

It was a nightmare. She could hardly believe she was awake. She kept wanting to pinch herself and make it all go away.

But it didn't go away. The sun rose higher, the August day grew hotter, and she watched her life get turned inside out and upside down. Finally, she couldn't stand to watch any longer as strange men poked into every nook and cranny of her life, even into her dresser drawers, handling her undergarments. She hurried outside, feeling as if she was going to throw up, and stared out toward the mouth of the inlet. She couldn't even bear to look toward the *Lily*, where the forensics team was hard at work. Her whole life had suddenly spun out of control, had become a kaleidoscope of fractured images her mind was afraid to identify.

"What's going on?"

Chase's voice startled her, and she whirled around with a soft cry. She hadn't see him in the week since Jeff and Eric had salvaged the boat. He looked bigger and more powerful than she remembered, like an anchor in the midst of her storm.

"I don't know," she told him, her voice stretched thin with tension. "God, I don't know. They came and arrested Jeff for theft and murder and now they're tearing the house and boat apart, but no one will tell me anything!"

"Theft and murder? What the hell for?"

"I don't know! It must have been that boat he salvaged."

"That's not theft."

"I know that. But I don't know what else it could be!"

He nodded, his eyes narrow slits against the glare off the water. "I don't suppose they'd tell me anything either."

"Why should they? They won't tell me, and it's my house and my brother!"

Feeling as if she might shatter into a million pieces,

64

she wrapped her arms tightly around herself and turned so that she couldn't watch what was happening at the house and boat. She had forgotten she was still clutching the warrant until it crumpled against her upper arm.

Chase reached for it. "Can I?"

She shrugged and let him have it. She hadn't even finished reading it yet. Every time she had tried, the typewritten legalese had made a cacophony of unintelligible syllables.

She focused on the splinters of light shooting off the waves in the inlet, feeling the pain of them stab her eyes, and preferring it to the pain piercing her heart. Beside her she heard Chase flip the pages of the warrant, one after another. Time passed. Seagulls cried overhead, and the waves lapped against the shore as they had for eternity and would for eternity, but nothing in her life would ever be the same again.

"It's the sea," she heard herself say. "It's the goddamn sea. It's not going to be happy until it's taken everything in the world from me." Crazy thoughts, but apt on such an insane day.

"Christ." Chase whispered the word, and handed her the warrant. "They found human bloodstains on the boat your brother salvaged. They found a tarp stuck in an equipment locker that was covered with human blood and gore. The owner of the boat and his crewman have been missing since that day. They were last seen sailing out that morning on that boat with two clients. They're looking for personal items that belonged to the two missing sailors, for bloodstains on your brother's boat, for possible murder weapons, and for a large-caliber handgun that could have been used to shoot holes in the hull."

Callie's hand flew to her mouth and covered it, as if she were trying to hold something in. The waves continued to roll in, the sun continued to shine . . . and the iciness of death seemed to settle over her. Her brain stilled, growing utterly silent.

Finally, she said into her hand, her voice broken and small, "He didn't do it."

"No, of course he didn't."

Slowly, hardly daring to believe her ears, she looked up at him. His eyes, as dark as tropical thunderheads, looked steadily back at her.

"He didn't do it," Chase said again.

Somebody in this world-gone-mad believed her, believed in Jeff. It seemed like the most natural thing in the world to turn to him for comfort, and like the most natural thing in the world when his arms closed around her.

They stood like that for a long time. Why not? There was nothing either of them could do or say right now. The tide eventually rose until it lapped around their feet, washing away the sand from beneath them so that they sank lower. Callie found herself wishing she could just sink all the way and never be seen again.

"Callie?"

She turned her head, with Chase's arms still around her, and looked at Fred Markell.

"We're done, Callie. We're going to have to seal the *Lily* for a few days, until we're sure we've got everything we need, but the house is yours again."

She opened her mouth to thank him, then realized the last thing on earth she wanted to do was thank Fred Markell for anything.

"Did you take anything from her house?" Chase asked.

Fred shook his head. "I don't believe so. I'll check with the others, though." He started to walk away, but Chase stopped him.

"What should we do now?"

Fred looked back. "Unless you want him to be represented by a public defender, get the kid a lawyer. This afternoon if you can. He's going to need representation at his hearing in the morning."

Callie closed her eyes for a moment, then broke away from Chase and marched back toward the house, heedless of the way her sneakers squished.

"What are you going to do?" he called after her.

"Go see my lawyer."

On the veranda, she kicked away her sneakers, then walked into the house, ignoring the sand that still clung to her. What did it matter anyway? The cops had messed everything up. Oh, they hadn't torn it up badly, but everything was out of place, nothing was as neat as it had been. The house felt violated, and she hated Fred for that.

"Do you know somebody to call?"

She hadn't heard Chase follow her into the house. He must move as silently as a cat despite his limp, she thought irritably. "I already called," she said.

"You need somebody who can defend a murder case."

"I know. I called the lawyer who defended him last time."

"The last time?"

"He was convicted of aggravated assault when he was sixteen."

She expected Chase's face to close up, expected him to walk away. He was a stranger, after all, and the bomb she had just dropped would have been enough to convince most people that Jeff must be guilty. And for some reason she couldn't quite put her finger on, Callie wanted Chase to walk away. She wanted him gone *now*. She didn't want him to see her pain, her grief or her shame. This was all somehow so humiliating that she didn't want him to witness it.

But he didn't budge. "What happened?" he asked steadily. "Did he wave a broken bottle at somebody in a fight?"

"It was a small knife, and it wasn't even a fight." She paused, studying his eyes. "I have to go."

She went to her room long enough to rinse the sand off her ankles and feet and change into a clean shift, then headed out for her car.

Chase was standing right there beside her car. His own was blocking her driveway, a big, black pickup with a purring engine. "I'll drive you," he said.

"I can do it myself," she said. "Just clear the way."

"I'll drive you," he repeated. "When this really starts to hit you, you don't want to be behind the wheel."

Something in the steel of his gaze told her he wasn't going to back down easily. To save time, she gave in.

An hour later they were pulling into the shady parking lot outside Shirley Kidder's office in Key West. She shared an old Conch house on a corner of Whitehead Street with three other attorneys. The lush tropical foliage had grown, Callie noticed. The flowers that had been by the walkway had been replaced with white gravel, probably to conserve water.

"I'll wait out here," Chase said. "You don't want me in there."

Callie managed to thank him, then climbed out of the car.

The office looked the same inside though. At the

68

reception desk, Nancy still had a smile wide enough to light a dark night.

"She's waiting for you," Nancy said warmly. "Just go right in."

Shirley Kidder was about thirty-five, with a lean runner's build and short, dark hair that refused to lie flat. When she looked up to greet Callie, her smile was friendly but her hazel eyes were troubled. She motioned Callie to the leather armchair facing her desk and cut straight to the chase. "What happened?" she asked.

Callie passed her the warrant she'd brought along. "Jeff found an abandoned boat four days ago and salvaged it. Now it turns out the boat's owner is missing and they've charged Jeff with grand theft and murder. All I know is what's in this warrant."

Shirley took the warrant from her and read it over with the speed of an attorney accustomed to reading such documents.

"It's in order," she said presently. "Did they take anything?"

"I don't think so. Not from the house. I don't know about the boat. They told me they were sealing it in case they needed to come back for something else."

"Hmm." Shirley leaned back in her chair and flipped to the last few pages of the warrant. "Well, once they left the premises, they finished executing the warrant. They can't keep you off the boat, or keep you from using it. If they're really worried about it, they should have impounded it. Who searched the boat?"

"A forensics team."

"My guess would be they didn't find anything suspicious on the boat." She reached the last sheet of paper in the warrant. "This is all they gave you?"

Callie nodded.

"They didn't give you a piece of paper saying what they took, or that they didn't take anything?"

"No."

Shirley sighed. "I'm going to have to call these jerks and have a few words with them. They can't do it this way. In the first place, they have to give you a signed receipt itemizing every item they took, or a statement saying they took nothing. You have to sign it, too. It's to protect them. In the second place, now that the search of the boat is completed, they can't tell you to stay off of it. So I'm going to twist some arms tomorrow and get you the use of the boat back, okay?"

Callie nodded. "But I'm mostly worried about Jeff."

"I know you are." Shirley gave her a sympathetic smile. "But all of these mistakes could wind up being really important if we have to go to trial."

"Oh, God, a trial?" Callie's heart lurched and her stomach turned over. "Do you think it will come to that?" All afternoon she had been clinging to the belief that they would find a way to clear this up fast.

"Well, it all depends on how much reasoning I can do with the state. I'll have to look at what they've got, but judging by the affidavit attached to the warrant, what they've got is purely circumstantial—unless they found something at your house or on Jeff's boat. Basically, we have evidence of foul play, at least two missing men, and your brother arriving inopportunely on the scene. It's enough for them to charge Jeff, but it's a long way from enough to take to trial, okay?"

Callie nodded, clinging to the slender straw of reassurance.

"First things first. He'll have his advisory hearing in the morning. You don't need to be there. I don't know if you recall what happened last time? But it's on closed-

70

circuit TV. Jeff will be at the jail, and the judge and I will be in the courtroom. Come if you want, but you won't get to see much of Jeff at the hearing."

"Do you think you'll be able to get bond?"

"On this case? I think so, because Jeff has ties here, and he didn't run the last time he was charged. But it's not going to be cheap."

Callie drew a ragged breath. "I don't have very much, Shirley."

"You have a house. If you trust Jeff not to go on the lam, you can get a lien on the house—or the boat, if it's worth enough."

Callie drew another ragged breath and closed her eyes. "I can't leave him in jail."

"I don't blame you. Believe me, I'll do my best to get him a reduced bond. This is a lousy case any way you slice it. His prior conviction isn't going to help any, but I'll deal with it."

Callie nodded. "Does it help any that Chase Mattingly and I were talking with Jeff on the marine radio while he salvaged the boat?"

Shirley sat up. "You were? That's good. That's very good. I'll use it to turn the screws on the State Attorney. He'd hardly have been talking to you on the radio while he was murdering two men. That would stretch anyone's imagination. Anything you can think of that might weaken the state's case, you let me know, okay?"

Twenty minutes later, Callie walked out of Shirley's office into the buttery light of late afternoon. Chase was standing beside his truck, arms folded across his chest, staring intently down at the pavement as if he had blocked out the entire world. When he heard her approaching footsteps, he lifted his head.

"How was it?"

71

"I don't know. I mean . . . Oh, God, he's charged with murder! How could anything be good? But Shirley thinks the case is weak so far—although she hasn't seen all their information, so I guess I shouldn't count too much on that. And she thinks she can get Jeff out on bail if I'm willing to put the house up as surety . . ." Her voice trailed off as her throat clogged. She had to blink rapidly to hold the tears back.

"My grandfather built that house," she heard herself say as if from a great distance. That seemed so important somehow, even though she knew Jeff wouldn't run away and she wouldn't lose it. But that house had never had a lien or a mortgage on it. Never. "God, how am I going to pay the legal fees?" It would take all of her savings, and probably a good deal more.

Chase helped her into the car. He'd kept the engine and air-conditioning running, so the interior was cool and welcoming. They drove along narrow, shady streets dappled with golden sunlight and long shadows, the time of day Callie loved best—but she didn't even notice it.

"I guess it doesn't really matter," she said presently, inviting Chase into her mental conversation somewhere in the middle. "I have to do it. I can't leave Jeff in jail."

"It's on the tip of my tongue to say, 'why not?' It might teach him something about considering his actions."

She turned to look at him in disbelief. "You can't mean that!"

He shook his head. "You're right, I don't—because he didn't do anything wrong. On the other hand, he's a grown man—or at least he'd like to be treated like one, so why should you have to go racing to his rescue?"

"Because I'm his *sister*. That's what families are for!"

She couldn't believe this man. What kind of life had he lived?

"Did he ever pay you back for the attorney's fees when he was charged with assault?"

Her teeth snapped together so hard that the crack was audible. "He was just sixteen! He didn't have that kind of money."

"And now he's twenty and still doesn't have that kind of money."

"I don't believe you!"

"What's not to believe?" He turned the car onto US 1 and stepped on the gas. "When I was twenty I was self-supporting. If I'd needed a lawyer, I would have paid for it myself. This kid has got it too easy, Callie. He works at a dead-end job when he feels like it and saves up for his dream boat. What are you saving for? His next scrape?"

"You don't know anything about it!"

"I know something about it. If he was old enough to drop out of school at sixteen and get himself into trouble with the law, he was old enough to pay you back the attorney's fees. If he's old enough to be sailing out on the ocean, risking his neck salvaging sinking boats, cutting out on his job because he'd rather go sailing, then he's damn well old enough to pay for his own attorney."

"He doesn't have the money!"

"Then let him go to a public defender. Or make him agree to pay you back starting right away. He's got to take responsibility for his own life."

"But this isn't his fault!"

"It's not your fault either."

"What is the matter with you?" She stared at him in angry disbelief. "You sound like the ultraconservative

73

party line—every man for himself."

He swore and swerved to avoid a vehicle coming onto the highway from the shoulder. "Look," he said after a minute. "I'm not saying you shouldn't help Jeff. But you've got to give him most of the responsibility, or he's never going to learn a damn thing about taking care of himself. Everyone gets hit by bolts out of the blue in life, but we can't live our lives expecting somebody else to take care of the problems for us."

She averted her face looking out blindly at the passing buildings and foliage. She knew about bolts out of the blue. They'd struck her repeatedly, starting with her mother's death. And it was true, nobody had shouldered the burdens for her. But that didn't mean she should leave Jeff out on a limb. He needed all the help he could get.

She was mad at Chase for the things he was saying, but not because of what he was saying. What he was saying made sense in its own way, although she found it harsh. What she was mad about was that he was echoing the feelings inside her, feelings she didn't even want to admit to herself, let alone say out loud.

Since their mother had died when Jeff was six, her brother had been her responsibility. Her dad had kept on going to sea to fish for weeks at a time, leaving her sole responsibility for her little brother and the house. It hadn't been easy, and she had resented the hell out of it. She had understood that her dad needed to fish to keep them fed, but she had still resented it.

Then he had died, leaving her with all the responsibilities, including keeping Jeff fed. And she resented the hell out of that, too. She resented the hell out of having had to use her savings for a lawyer four years ago because Jeff couldn't keep a lid on his temper.

She resented that she was going to have to do it again. She resented his devil-may-care, worry-free approach to life when she spent all her time being responsible and reliable. Jeff had even cost her her fiance, because Mel hadn't wanted the responsibility for the boy.

She hated all those feelings of resentment. She was ashamed of them. She wanted to bury them so deep that she could deny they ever existed. But every word Chase had spoken had echoed those feelings, and forced her to face them.

She hated him for that.

By the time they pulled into her rutted driveway, night had fallen. Callie sensed a strong tension in Chase, but she didn't care. She was still mad at him and didn't want to know why he was gripping the steering wheel so hard, or why he was breathing rapidly. She just plain didn't care.

When he pulled up to the house, he didn't get out and come around to help her out. She was glad he didn't. It made her escape all the easier. She didn't even thank him for the ride, and she hoped he noticed, because she never, ever wanted to see him again.

The shadows pressed in on the windows of the car, patterns of darkness that seemed to leer at him. Chase kept his gaze firmly pinned on the road, to where the beams of the headlights drove the shadows back, but he could still feel them all around him, laughing in whispers and scratching at the windows.

It had been like this on the dive, he remembered, and felt sweat break out on his brow. Dark. All he could see had been illuminated by his lamp, a narrow beam of light in the black, cold depths of the sea. Around him he'd felt the swirling of currents, but they weren't

75

currents. They were something else, and gradually they had taken on shape and dimension.

He forced himself to ignore the memories, to think about his outburst with Callie Carlson. Christ, he'd been a jackass.

She would probably never speak to him again, and it annoyed him to realize that had been the entire motivation behind his outburst in the car. He hadn't been really concerned about what was best for her or for Jeff, only concerned that he yank himself out of this mess before he got in any deeper.

It behooved a man to know his own weaknesses, and one of his greatest was that he was a sucker for a damsel in distress. Just let him come across a female with a serious problem, and he started to fancy himself a white knight.

Hell, that was how he'd gotten tangled up in his misbegotten marriage in the first place. Julie had waltzed into his life with sad eyes and tales about an abusive, alcoholic father—all of it true, of course, but that didn't mitigate what had happened. Right away Chase had wanted to rescue her, and within three weeks he'd married her, taking her away from her father and installing her in the safety of a small apartment just outside the base.

It had been pretty good for a while. She'd been suitably grateful, and he'd been suitably dazzled by her beauty, and a sense of his own nobility.

Unfortunately, she couldn't handle the long separations when he was at sea, or on temporary assignment elsewhere in the world. She grew bored and lonely and began to have affairs. Eventually he'd found out about them.

But what happened after the wedding was common to

navy marriages, and he'd learned to live with it. After all, a sailor really wasn't very good husband material unless you managed to find a woman as faithful as the famed Penelope, and in all his years in the navy, he'd seen only a handful who met that qualification.

What he remembered, what he had learned, was to be a hell of a lot more cautious when it came to helping a woman out. It was one thing to lend her a hand. It was another to lend her your life.

So here he was, feeling a tug toward Callie Carlson, who was certainly a lovely, beleaguered damsel in distress. And naturally he'd acted like a fool, said things he had no business saying, trying to convince both her and *himself* that this was Jeff's problem. Because he didn't want to get involved.

Christ, what a sap!

Well, he'd probably pissed her off so good she wouldn't even give him the time of day after this. And that was the way he wanted it. Absolutely. He'd come here to tunnel into the solitude and face down his own problems, not to get tangled up in some stupid kid's life because he couldn't bear to let a woman go down.

It was her brother and *her* problem. And she could damn well deal with it by herself.

Having reached that firm, unalterable decision, he told himself he was only being wise.

He didn't believe it, but he was getting used to not believing his own rationalizations. It seemed to have become a way of life.

And now he was pulling up behind his house, with the night just waiting to swallow him—and he realized he hadn't left a light on.

"Christ!" He swore under his breath and resisted the urge to hammer the steering wheel. The truck jolted to a

77

stop, and the engine choked into silence.

The darkness inhabited his house.

It was a stupid, insane thought, and he knew it, but the feeling persisted anyway. And now, like a kid who feared there was a crocodile under the bed but needed to go to the bathroom, he was considering the fastest way to reach the door, unlock it, and flip a light switch before the darkness could grab him.

He swore again, and this time he did slam his palm against the wheel. This was nuts. Crazy. Wacko. Loony. He *knew* there was nothing out there except for trees, birds, and a few deer. There were no demons; the night had no face or voice, nor any means to strike out and hurt him.

He knew that with his head, but some primitive part of his brain refused to believe it.

His back chose that moment to jolt him with a sharp jab of pain. For an instant he could do little except grip the wheel, breathe like a marathoner, and wait for it to subside.

But it had a salutary effect on him, because it reminded him of what was real. He was real. The car *was* real. The house was real. The pain that racked his body was real, and the night was nothing but the absence of sunlight. It was the same world out there now that it had been at three o'clock that afternoon.

Grabbing the keys, he yanked them out of the ignition. Then, reminding himself that he'd endured far worse in his life, he opened the car door and climbed out.

At once he could hear the quiet susurration of the gentle waves in the inlet. It was a sound he had loved all his life, and it touched him now, brushing at the fears that gnawed the edges of his mind, trying to send them back into the dark places where they belonged.

It was the same world now it had been twelve hours ago. He reminded himself of that once again, and forced himself to walk at a normal pace up to his porch, to climb the steps as if he had all the time in the world, and to unlock his door—all without giving in to the crawling sensation that he was being watched from the shadows in the woods.

When he opened his door, though, he faced something else. It was darker inside than outside. Inside there was no starlight to cast a pale light over the world. Inside the house there was nothing at all but a yawning, impenetrable blackness. Just like it had been in the sea . . .

He could have closed the door and walked away. He even considered sitting on the porch all night. But then he squared his shoulders and decided he was damned if he was going to let the night take over the one haven he had in the world.

He stepped across the threshold. The night closed around him, and for an instant he felt as if he were suffocating. But still he refused to give in to it, and took yet another step into the maw of darkness.

He stood there, forcing himself to endure the blackness, just as he had forced himself to endure the panic when they'd bound him and thrown him into the pool during Hell Week. There were some things in life that you could only master by submitting to them, and fear was one of those things.

Memory snippets from the dive circled his mind like wolves waiting to attack, but he refused to give in to them. He had survived the dive, he reminded himself, and he would survive the darkness.

That was when he heard the porch creak behind him. And that was when the night spoke his name.

CHAPTER 5

AFTER CHASE DROPPED HER OFF, CALLIE FOUND SHE couldn't hold still. She paced the house for a few minutes, but the absolute emptiness and silence were almost terrifying. Her footsteps on the plank floors echoed loudly, reminding her she was alone. Jeff would not come home tonight.

She thought about pulling out her bank statements to verify that she had enough in savings to pay Shirley's fee, but she didn't really need to do it because she knew her balance to the penny. She made a list of things she would need to take with her tomorrow, but there was only one item on it: the deed for the house, and that was in a safety-deposit box at the bank, not far from the courthouse.

Chase must be home by now, she thought. It took nearly fifteen minutes to drive between their properties even though it only took five or six minutes to walk the distance around the inlet, because a car had to go all the way back out to the street along a rutted road.

Stepping out onto the porch she looked to see if any of his lights were on. She really needed to go over and apologize to him for not thanking him for the ride. Regardless of how she felt about what he'd said, she had no right to be rude. He had made her angry, but her anger had faded as she accepted at least part of the justice of what he had said. Jeff should share this burden.

And it was as good an excuse as any to avoid spending the next half hour pacing and thinking about Jeff. Even getting angry was preferable. Besides, a brisk walk would probably clear her head better than pacing.

She set out with only the starlight to guide her. Halfway around the inlet, she began to reconsider her decision because there were still no lights on at Chase's house. Maybe he hadn't gone home. Maybe he'd gone out to get something from the store, or to visit a friend. She was just about to turn around and head home when she heard an angry shout and commotion.

Without a thought for her own safety, she broke into a dead run toward his house.

Chase whirled around in the darkness and saw the shadowy figure on his threshold. In an instant, skills that had been hammered into him years ago surged. There was no conscious thought involved, just instinctive reaction to threat.

He sprang forward with a shout, grabbing the intruder, whirling him around, and throwing him to the deck flooring. An instant later he had a knee between the man's shoulder blades, and his arm twisted up around behind him.

The man's feet kicked uselessly.

"Don't move or I'll break your damn neck," Chase growled. The body beneath him grew instantly still.

That was when he heard the running footsteps pounding toward him out of the darkness. How many were out there? He lifted his head and peered into the shadows, trying to see who was coming.

"Jesus, Chase!" groaned the man beneath him. "It's me, Dave Hathaway!"

Dave Hathaway. An old acquaintance, the guy who'd been his contact at the insurance company. He hesitated, not sure he was ready to trust anyone, not with those running footsteps still coming his way. "Who came with you?" he asked.

"Nobody. I swear. For God's sake, what's wrong with you? Just let me up!"

"Who's that running this way?"

"How the hell should I know? Damn it, Chase, you keep this up, I'm going to file charges!"

Just then, Callie burst out of the darkness. "Are you okay?" she demanded as soon as she saw the shadows on the porch.

"If I wasn't, you wouldn't be either," Chase remarked. He levered himself to his feet, releasing Dave. "You shouldn't run head-on into danger that way, Callie."

"Oh, will you cut it out! I'm sick of your damn advice. When I want it, I'll ask for it."

Dave rolled over, groaning, and pushed himself up onto one elbow.

Chase backed up, giving him more room, waiting for the hammering of his heart to slow down and the adrenaline to flush out of his system.

Turning, he stepped once more into the maw of darkness inside his house, but this time he didn't give himself a chance to feel it. Reaching for the switch, he flipped it, flooding the interior with light.

"Come on in, you two." He didn't wait to see if they followed. He went to get the whiskey bottle. "You want a drink, Dave?"

Dave, stepping through the door and rolling his shoulders as if they hurt, said, "Yeah. A beer, if you got it." He was a small, slender man with a receding hairline.

He looked at Callie, who was right behind Dave.

"Nothing for me, thanks."

He got Dave his beer, and poured himself a splash of whiskey. Tipping his head back, he downed it in one gulp, feeling the burn all the way to his belly.

Dave pulled out a chair at the table and collapsed into it, reaching for the beer bottle. He took a long swig, followed by a satisfied sigh. "Somebody should have warned me that visiting you is dangerous, Chase."

"I don't like it when people come up behind me in the dark. Especially when nobody's supposed to be there. What the hell were you doing?"

"I thought you knew I was here. I was parked on that little spur off your driveway, just waiting for you to get home."

"I didn't see you." And that didn't make him happy. He'd been too absorbed in his own thoughts to see something he should have. He was losing his edge.

"Well, I was there," Dave said. "Got there just before dark, and figured since I'd driven all the way up here, I might as well hang around and see if you came home. Tom Akers said you were spending most of your time holed up here." He rolled his shoulders again. "Jeez, you scared about ten years off my life."

Chase didn't answer. What was the point? He couldn't undo what had happened, and he wasn't going to apologize for it.

Callie's head pivoted as she looked from one man to the other, as if uncertain what to make of them. Chase couldn't blame her. He was weird enough to perplex anyone.

"Take a seat," he told Callie. She pulled out a chair at the other end of the table from Dave. Chase sat between them. "Did you want something?" he asked her.

"I was just coming over to say thank you for giving me a lift earlier."

He shrugged a shoulder. "No problem."

Dave spoke. "Well, since Chase obviously isn't going

83

to make introductions, I will. Hi, I'm Dave Hathaway. I work with Chase."

"I'm Callie Carlson, a neighbor."

His head lifted a little. "You related to Jeff Carlson?"

Chase saw the way Callie seemed to shrink a little and tense. "He's my brother. Do you know him?"

Dave shook his head. "Nah. I just heard about him on the news . . ."

"Christ, Dave, what's the matter with you?" Chase couldn't believe the man had said that to Callie. He wanted to wring Dave's neck.

"I'm sorry." Dave held up a hand and looked sheepish. "I'm sorry, you're right. I guess I'm still a little shook." He gave Callie an apologetic smile. "Really. I'm sorry."

Callie nodded, but didn't quite look at him. "Forget it."

"The story just caught my attention," Dave plunged on. "I don't think the kid did it, you know?"

Chase wished Dave would just take a hint, but Callie suddenly looked hopeful and terribly vulnerable. He had the worst urge to place himself between her and all the rest of the world.

"Why do you say that?" Callie asked Dave.

"Because it doesn't make any sense. If he killed those guys, why would he bring the evidence home with him?"

Callie suddenly smiled, and Chase realized that in all the time he'd spent with her, he'd never seen her smile that way. It unsettled him, somehow.

"That's right," she said. "Jeff isn't stupid. Besides, somebody had tried to scuttle the boat. Why would he kill the people, scuttle the boat, then salvage it?"

"Good question." Dave was nodding agreement.

"They're just looking for a scapegoat."

"Don't they always?" Chase asked.

"Seems that way," Dave replied. "Anyway, I figure it was just some drug deal gone bad, and those kids happened to stumble on it, you know?"

"That's what I think," Callie agreed fervently.

"It happened what . . . seven miles out?"

"About that," Callie agreed. "I'm not sure exactly. It's probably on Jeff's log."

"See?" Dave said, spreading his hands. "Somebody was running drugs and something went wrong. If you want to take a boat out just to scuttle it, you want to get outside territorial waters so nobody can come after you for polluting. I bet somebody was there to pick up a drug shipment from Mexico and instead they got killed."

Callie nodded. Chase reserved judgment. He was having a little problem, wondering why Dave knew so much about the case and why he was so interested. Although it was not really that big a deal, he told himself. The arrest had probably been headline news even in Miami, where a huge population of boaters made piracy a hot topic, and Dave was just trying to cover his mistake of mentioning it in the first place.

"They'll figure it out," Dave said reassuringly. "Once they really start looking over what they've got, they're going to know it doesn't make sense."

"I hope so." She smiled warmly at Dave, then rose. "I really need to be getting home. I didn't mean to intrude, Chase. I just realized that I hadn't thanked you for your help this afternoon."

He again waved away her gratitude. "Let me walk you home, Callie. It's dark, and it's getting late." The offer came automatically, something he would once have done without a second thought. Now, as soon as he spoke, nervousness settled in the pit of his stomach.

"It's not necessary. I walk along the inlet all the time at night. See you."

He hated to admit how relieved he was that she didn't want his company. Because truth to tell, he was about as keen on stepping out into the night again as he would have been to put his hand in a buzz saw. He even found himself tensing when she opened the door, as if he expected something to come springing through it. When it closed behind her, a long breath escaped him.

"You okay, Chase?" Dave asked.

Chase looked across the table at the man who had sent him on the last, fateful dive. They had worked together frequently in the eight years Chase had been a salvage diver, but Chase still didn't feel he knew him well enough to be answering questions like that. "I'm fine," he said shortly.

"Well, I know about the nightmares . . . I mean, the company's been kept informed of your recovery. Since we're paying for it."

A reminder, Chase thought, and it hadn't been accidental. His antennae started humming as he realized that this was no haphazard social call on Dave's part. "What's the point?"

"I'm just concerned about you. And we'd really like it if you'd come to work for us full-time."

"I was happy being a contractor. I'm not sure I want to get chained to a desk."

Dave laughed. "I can understand that. Just think about it, okay? It wouldn't be a full-time desk job anyway. You'd have to go out to supervise recovery operations."

Chase nodded slowly, watching the man closely. "I'll think about it."

"Good. That's all I can ask. The company feels real bad about what happened to you, even though it wasn't our fault."

"I never said it was anybody's fault."

Dave gave another laugh. "No, you sure haven't. Anyway . . . we're still wondering, though. Did you remember anything about the dive?"

They kept asking that question, and every time they asked it, Chase's paranoia increased another notch. "I told you what I remembered. What does it matter anyway? Bill Evers was there. He told you what he found. What difference does it make whether I ever remember anything? And even if I do, my memory would be suspect after what happened. Why? Is someone suing?"

Dave shook his head. "I'm just curious. We'd like to know more about what happened to you down there. It would be nice to actually pin it down, you know? Instead of being stuck with vague possibilities put together by the medicos."

"Some things can never be known."

Dave sighed, then sipped his beer. "You're right about that. I hate uncertainty. I've always hated it."

"Funny for a man who's in the insurance business."

Dave threw back his head and laughed. "Hey, we only bet on sure things. Don't you know that?"

Chase's hip poked him with another fiery spear, so he stood up and began pacing around the room, trying to work off the pain. "I'd like to remember what happened down there just so I could figure out what I screwed up. But it's all a blank except for wisps of the hallucinations. I don't even remember most of the descent."

"I understand that's normal."

"That's what the docs say. Traumatic amnesia. I'll probably never get much of anything back."

"Maybe just as well."

Chase nodded. "Probably. Except for not knowing what I did wrong. I guess it doesn't matter, though. I'll never dive again."

Dave was silent for a few minutes, sipping at his beer, drumming his fingers absently on the tabletop. "I feel responsible. I sent you out there."

Chase snorted. "You didn't *make* me go. And anyway, nothing should have gone wrong, if I'd done everything right. So whatever happened was my fault. End of discussion."

"Okay." Dave stood and stretched hugely. "Guess I oughta be heading home. I just wanted to see how you were doing."

"I m fine."

Dave gave him a crooked smile. "I guess that's all I'm going to get out of you, hmm?"

"That's all that's worth saying."

"It's a damn shame about that woman's brother," he said as he walked to the door. "I take it he didn't notice anything unusual when he boarded the boat?"

"Apparently not. Other than that somebody put a bunch of holes in the hull. But he didn't have a whole lot of time to look around. He was too busy keeping it from sinking."

Dave shook his head. "I can't imagine climbing onto a sinking boat. Not for any reason." He paused at the door. "But I also can't imagine why he was charged. What the hell did they find on that boat to make them think that kid killed two people?"

"A bloody tarpaulin in an equipment locker would tend to lead to the conclusion that someone had been

88

killed."

Dave shook his head. "You're right about that. But only a lunatic would shoot the bottom of a boat and then try to rescue it." He said good night and stepped out the door.

Chase listened to him drive away, then listened to the night settle in again, still and unbroken. The whispers were still there but not quite as loud or ominous as they usually were. Maybe the night was no longer so sure it could overwhelm him.

He locked the door and headed to the kitchen to find something to put into his stomach. He hadn't eaten since breakfast, and the whiskey was gnawing a hole in his belly.

So the bottom of the boat had been shot out, he thought, remembering what Dave had said. The affidavit on the search warrant hadn't said that, just that there were holes in the hull. Apparently they'd found out what had made them. Or maybe the news was just speculating.

But Dave was right. Nobody but nobody would shoot holes in the hull and then try to salvage the sinking boat, and most especially not when it was loaded with evidence of a murder.

He ate his dinner, a thick ham sandwich with Swiss cheese, tomato, and lettuce, then took up his usual station at the table, waiting for the night to be over. The hours crept by on leaden feet while he strained his ears, listening to every sound as if it was a potential threat. After what had happened earlier, he felt stupider than ever for getting this tense just because it was dark outside.

But stupidity didn't put him to sleep, or ease the tension that filled his body. At least tonight he didn't feel the need to get out the Beretta. The pain in his hip and back had settled down to a dull roar, and the edge even seemed to be off his fear. Maybe he was getting better?

He nurtured the hope for a while, turning it around in his mind. It was possible. The doctor had said he would gradually improve. For the first time in months he felt the stirrings of hope.

Then he heard it. It was soft, stealthy, almost inaudible. He strained his ears, trying to make it clearer, trying to pick out what it could he. It moved across his front porch, he realized.

His heart slammed. Something was out there. Just a raccoon, he told himself. Just a raccoon.

He didn't believe it.

He had a choice. He could sit there and try to tell himself it was a racoon, and not believe it, or he could go outside and look.

It should have been easy, but he found himself paralyzed with trepidation. God, he hated this. It was so simple to get up and look. And if he'd known for sure there was some human agent out there, even one that was bent on killing him, he could have moved forward.

It was not knowing that was killing him and making him helpless. A sudden surge of bile rose from his stomach, and fury filled him. He was not a coward, and was not going to act like a coward.

With a supreme effort of will, he pushed back from the table and headed for the door. He hesitated again when his hand touched the knob. He could feel the night on the other side of the door, a huge, breathing, hungry entity, pressing inward, trying to reach him.

Stupid! With a violent yank, he pulled the door open.

The night shrank back before the lamplight that

90

spilled forth. Reaching out, he found the switch for the porch light, and flipped it on.

There was nothing out there. Nothing. Not even a startled raccoon. Furious at himself for his sick imaginings and his fear, he turned to go back into the house.

That was when he saw that a chair had been moved halfway across the porch, so that it stood right under the window.

As if something had been using it as a ladder.

Callie slept poorly and couldn't face the thought of breakfast, so she set out early for the Monroe County Courthouse.

At eight o'clock she was in the courtroom as the judge began the hearings over closed-circuit TV

Jeff's case didn't come up until nearly nine-thirty. As soon as the bailiff recited his name and the charges, she leaned forward, straining to hear every word, her stomach twisting into tight knots. She listened to Shirley's argument, but in the end what she heard, all she really heard, was that Jeff's bail had been set at a quarter of a million dollars.

Shirley argued for a property bond, but the judge said that would have to be dealt with in a separate hearing.

The sum boggled her mind, and she had to keep reminding herself the house and land were worth more than that. Much more than that. She slipped out of the courtroom and met Shirley in the hallway.

"A quarter million," Shirley said immediately upon seeing her.

"I heard."

"Damn good for two charges of murder. Charges that might well become capital murder."

Callie's heart stopped, and she felt hot and cold wash over her in sickening waves. "Capital murder?" she repeated, her voice a croak.

Shirley nodded somberly. "Two murders committed during the commission of a crime, namely grand theft."

"They want . . . they want the death. . ." She couldn't even finish the sentence. Reaching out, she grabbed at the wall to steady herself. It didn't offer a whole lot of support.

Shirley took her other arm, tucking it through her own and steadying her. "The death penalty," Shirley said flatly. "They're sure as hell thinking about it. But they didn't push it that far today, which is the only reason bail was set."

Giving a gentle tug, Shirley pulled Callie toward the door. "I don't know if you heard most of what I said."

Callie shook her head, feeling too stunned to speak, or even to remember exactly what Shirley had argued.

"Well, I argued the weakness of the case, Jeff's prior good behavior—basically, Callie, the judge wasn't much more impressed by the state's case than I am."

"How do you know that?"

"He gave your brother bail. A very small bail, considering the charges."

"Oh." Callie tried to tell herself this was good news, but she couldn't believe it, not when the death penalty was being considered.

"Anyway," Shirley continued, "I asked for a property bond and the judge refused to discuss it in advisory, which is what the hearing today was. So I've set another hearing for tomorrow morning, for a full bond hearing."

"You mean I can't get Jeff out today?"

"Well, you can if you've got twenty-five thousand dollars in cash to pay a bail bondsman."

92

"I don't have that kind of money!"

"I didn't think so. Listen, Callie, here's how it works. You pay a bail bondsman ten percent of the bail—which you never get back, because that's his fee—and he'll take your house as surety for the rest. Or you can hang in a couple more days, and we'll get you a property bond from the clerk of court. They'll still put a lien on your house for surety, but at least you don't have to pay the bail bondsman twenty-five thousand to do the same thing. It'll take two or three days to get it straightened away, but it appears to me this is the only way you can do it."

Callie nodded, feeling almost numb as the news kept getting grimmer. But only one thing truly mattered. She turned to face Shirley. "And Jeff? Is Jeff going to be okay?"

"I can't make any promises as to outcome, Callie. You know that. Jeff should never have been convicted of aggravated assault four years ago, but he was, primarily because the victim was a wealthy doctor and your brother was a nobody. I still haven't seen all the state's information on this case, and I still don't know what information I'll be able to put together on Jeff's behalf, so I don't want to even speculate on the outcome. But I will tell you this. I don't believe Jeff did it."

That wasn't much help, but it was the only straw Callie had to cling to. At least Jeff's attorney believed in him. Getting in her car, she drove straight to Stock Island to the jail.

The new Monroe County jail was set on stilts like most of the newer buildings in the area, above the floodwaters that could occur from a tropical storm or hurricane. Underneath was a paved parking area that was still roped off by construction fencing. The sheriff's petting zoo was at one end of the building, but Callie hardly noticed the animals. Her mind was fully focused on how she was going to give Jeff the bad news.

An elevator took her up from the parking level to the reception area, a large, softly lit room floored with blue, black, and beige tiles. Blue-plastic chairs were clustered in a couple of places, some of them occupied. Everyone in the room sat with their heads down.

A woman in uniform sat behind a glass window under a sign that said INFORMATION. Callie walked over to her and asked to see Jeff.

The lady checked her computer and shook her head. "He's having a hearing this morning."

"I know, I just saw it. It's over."

"But he's with a group of prisoners, ma'am, and he won't be returned to his cell until everyone's hearings are done."

"Do you know how long that might be?"

The woman shook her head. "That depends. I really couldn't say."

Callie took her seat with the others and found herself sitting with her head down, staring at the tile on the floor. She told herself to lift her head, that she had nothing to be ashamed of, but somehow she couldn't bring herself to do it. She was ashamed even to be there.

Two hours later, divested of her purse, she was allowed in to see Jeff. The instant she laid eyes on him, her heart started to break. He gave her a smile, but she could tell how hard it was for him. He looked pale and exhausted.

But he insisted he was okay, that no one was hurting him.

"Just tired," he said, giving her another wan smile. "I didn't sleep much last night. I was too scared."

She wanted to reach out and hug him, but she wasn't sure that was permitted, and they were being watched by a guard. "Shirley's got a bond hearing set for tomorrow," she said, trying to encourage him. "I won't be able to get you out right away because it takes a couple of days to put the house up. Two or three days, Shirley said. Can you make it?"

He nodded. "Sure. I can make it." But the skin around his eyes was even tighter now than when she'd first seen him. "I'm sorry, Callie. God, I'm so sorry!"

"You didn't do anything wrong! You didn't kill those men."

"No . . . but if I'd just been responsible enough to come back in time to go to work, I never would have tried to salvage that boat."

She shook her head because her throat was suddenly tight, and she didn't think she could speak. Finally she managed to say hoarsely, "You didn't do anything wrong, Jeff. Certainly nothing that deserves a murder charge." Daring, she reached out and covered his hand with hers. The guard didn't say anything, but she could feel his eyes burning into her head, so she drew her hand back quickly. "Do you need anything?"

"Cigarettes." His mouth twisted. "I know, you probably think this is a great time for me to quit."

Right now that didn't seem very important to her. "How do I get them to you?"

"There's no point, sis. They don't let me smoke in here . . ."

This time she was the one who forced the smile. "Good."

He gave a choked laugh at that. "Yeah, I got three or

four days to quit, right? Say, are you going to see Eric? He was at advisories this morning, too, but they wouldn't let us talk."

"I guess I can do that."

"Thanks. I don't know if his folks will come visit him."

"I love you, Jeff. We'll beat this thing."

"Sure. I didn't do it. They can't execute me for something I didn't do, right?"

He didn't sound any more confident than she felt. She hung around for another hour, and got a few minutes with Eric. He had a public defender, he said, and no, he hadn't heard anything from his parents.

"Do you want me to call them?" Callie asked.

He shook his head. "I already did. I left a message. They'll come see me."

Callie hoped he was right. Five minutes later she was taking the elevator down and feeling even worse than she had before she came here.

Jeff was released on bond three days later at one-thirty in the afternoon. Callie spent the intervening time scraping the peeling paint off her house like a madwoman, finding her only relief from worry and fear in keeping busy. The phone rang frequently, but she soon realized it was mostly reporters looking for a story, or friends who seemed more curious than sympathetic. Before long, she stopped answering it. Every day, twice a day, she called Shirley to learn what was happening.

In all that time she didn't see Chase, not even sitting on his porch, and vaguely she wondered if he'd gone away. As focused as she was on her concern about Jeff, however, she didn't even think to go knock on his door and see if he was all right.

As soon as the clerk of court finished verifying the tax and property records, and approved the bond, she was off like a shot to get Jeff.

When Jeff stepped out of the sally port, Callie felt her heart sink. He looked even more exhausted and frightened than the day before. His shoulders were slumped, and his step had none of the cocky assurance he usually displayed.

"Did they hurt you?" she demanded the instant they got outside. For the last three days, she had worried about that constantly, plagued by all the horror stories of what could happen to people in jail, fearing that he was lying to her when he said everything was okay.

He shook his head. "It was scary, but nobody hurt me. I slept on the floor, though . . . " His voice trailed off. "I'm sorry, Callie."

She looked up at him quickly, hearing the thickening in his voice, and saw to her horror that her brother was about to cry. His eyes were red and watery. "Jeff . . . "

"I'm sorry, Callie," he said again, and drew a shaky breath. "You had to put the house up . . . I'm so sorry. . ."

He looked quickly away and took a couple more shaky breaths. "God, I'm sorry."

"You didn't do anything wrong, Jeff."

"Yes, I did! I shouldn't have gone off half-cocked that morning just 'cause I was angry at you. I shouldn't have sailed when the weather was going to be bad, and I shouldn't have cut out on work."

"Maybe not, but what you did wasn't bad enough to warrant a murder charge, Jeff. We've been over this already, and I want you to stop beating yourself up over it. As for putting the house up to get you out—we do what we have to do. That's life. As long as you don't

97

skip out, it won't matter anyway, so don't even think about apologizing."

He looked at her, his eyes burning. "I won't skip out on you, Callie. I'll do everything they said I have to. I swear."

"I know you will." Reaching out, she hugged him tightly. "I love you, Jeff. I don't say that enough, but it's true."

"I love you, too, sis." His voice was muffled, awkward with embarrassment.

She stepped back, her own throat tight with feeling, and tried to give him a bracing smile. "Now let's get you home."

He didn't say much during the hour-long drive home. Jeff usually had plenty to say about everything, and was rarely repressed for long. Apparently getting charged with murder had shaken him to his very core. She wondered if he would ever be the same again and feared that he wouldn't.

For some reason she hadn't expected it to hit him this hard this quickly. Nothing had ever seemed to hit Jeff very hard, not even his conviction for aggravated assault when he'd been immediately released into Callie's custody and sentenced to probation. He'd lost a little of his cockiness for a while, but it had all come back eventually. She had expected to get treated to some of his youthful bravado when he came out of the jail, to hear him talk about all of this like it was going to blow away in the next breeze. A little denial, maybe some anger.

Not this total dejection, as if he had given up hope.

When they got home, he headed straight for his bedroom, saying he hadn't gotten much sleep the previous night, lying on the floor of the cell. He didn't say whether discomfort or fear kept him awake, and she didn't ask. His youthful male pride had taken enough dings in the last few days. She certainly wasn't going to ask him if he was afraid.

While he slept, she started cooking a big old-fashioned dinner of the kind her mother had used to make when her dad came home from the sea. Even though Jeff had only been gone for a few days, she had a feeling that he had traveled a lifetime. A homecoming celebration seemed in order, even if there was little to celebrate.

While she was peeling potatoes for the pot roast, she glanced out the window and saw Chase Mattingly walking along the path toward her. Wherever he'd been the past few days, he was back. After a moment's indecision, she decided that if he'd come to ask about Jeff, she would invite him to stay for dinner. It was the neighborly thing to do. Besides, it might be good for Jeff.

But she found herself hoping he would keep on walking. She wasn't at all sure she liked him. He was abrupt and sometimes blunt to the point of rudeness. Worse, he was an attractive man, and once or twice when she'd thought of him, she had felt her body stir in ways it hadn't stirred in years.

And that wasn't good. Not at all. Never, ever again was she going to get involved with a man that way. Every man in her life had abandoned her eventually. The way she figured it, if she never let a man get that close again, it would be too soon.

But her hands fell still as she looked out the window and watched Chase walk along the narrow beach, climbing up to disappear among the mangroves, reappearing when the path returned to the shoreline. His limp was bad today, and something about the stiff way he was holding himself spoke volumes for the pain he must be suffering. Despite it, he kept on walking, never once pausing to give himself a break.

Whether she liked him or not, she respected him for that. At her job, she dealt with women who had suffered terrible experiences, either as rape victims or the victims of spousal abuse. They were women who had a lot to feel bad about, women who had every reason to complain and feel sorry for themselves. And some did. But she always most admired the ones who refused to think of themselves as victims. The ones who were determined to find ways to deal with what had happened to them, and were determined to put their lives back together.

Chase had that kind of spunk, she thought. So why was he hiding out here like this?

Suddenly remembering the potatoes she was peeling, she dragged her attention from the window and back to dinner preparations. A few minutes later, she heard the knock on the front door.

Wiping her hands on a dish towel, she went to answer it. Chase stood there.

"Sorry to bother you," he said. "I've been in Miami visiting a friend, and I was just wondering if Jeff got out?"

"He's out on bail." She hesitated, really reluctant to invite this man into her life again. Yet it was possible Chase would know something to say to make Jeff feel less crushed. For all her training in psychology, Callie didn't feel she truly understood the male ego. "He's sleeping now, and I'm making dinner. Would you like to join us?"

He shook his head quickly, taking a step back. "I'm

not trying to intrude. I was just wondering about Jeff."

She felt strangely rejected. Silly considering how she felt about him. "Well, if you change your mind, I'll be serving around six. And I know Jeff would like a chance to talk with you."

"Thanks." He backed up another step. "I might come over later. Thanks."

Then he turned, limped down the steps, and continued his walk.

Strange, she thought. Why had he stopped to ask about Jeff, then lit out like he thought he might catch something?

Shrugging, she went back to work on dinner. She would never understand men.

CHAPTER 6

HE COULDN'T GO ON LIKE THIS.

The thought struck Chase as he stood looking out at his nemesis, the sea. She was unusually beautiful today, dappled in a variety of greens and blues, the water clear enough to see the seaweed beds on the bottom. He still felt a chill creep along his spine when he saw the water, but that was gradually lessening.

A few weeks ago, when he'd been released from rehab, he'd thought it would do him good to be absolutely alone for a while. He'd figured he'd be able to face his demons and get on with life.

Instead he felt as if he were mired in quicksand and going nowhere. His problem with the darkness didn't seem to be improving much. He'd thought he'd made a great stride when he came home the other night and was able to get out of his car in the dark and walk to the house, but Dave's unwelcome appearance had put paid to that. All Dave had done was reinforce Chase's paranoia. There really *had* been someone waiting for him in the dark.

Then later, finding the chair moved . . . well, it was probably another example of how he was losing his mind. In the daylight he was convinced he must have moved that chair himself, somehow, during the scuffle with Dave. In the dark, he had been convinced that something else had moved it.

And no amount of talking to himself seemed to be making it any better. He was sitting up night after night, like some lunatic, keeping company with his pistol again and listening to the voices in the night wind.

This was bad.

And even worse, he was starting to feel like a useless, unproductive slug. Never before in his life had he been utterly without work, utterly without goals, utterly without plans. He was drifting in the sea of his paranoia like a boat without sails or rudder. Hell, he was even withdrawing from the society of his friends.

This was all so unlike him that it was making him seriously uncomfortable with himself. Somehow he had to get on the stick again, pick up the pieces of his life as best he could, and start *doing* something with himself. The longer he remained in this isolated cove in the company of his nightmares, the worse he was going to get.

The solitude thing had been a stupid idea.

Maybe he ought to reconsider Dave's offer of a job at the insurance company. He didn't like the idea of a desk job, but he could live with it. Or he could open a dive shop of his own. He certainly had enough savings to front the costs. Or he could really face his nightmares, and take that job that Tom had offered aboard the *Lady Hope.*

Deciding that it was time to take control of his life again made him feel better than he had in a while. All he had to do was take a first step.

And the easiest first step was to be neighborly to Callie and Jeff Carlson. Instead of refusing Callie's offer to join them for dinner, he ought to accept it. Instead of sitting around in his cottage brooding about his problems, it would do him some good to think about other people's.

Besides, Callie appealed to him. He figured she was ruining her brother by mothering him too much, but otherwise he found her very attractive. While he was bound and determined never to get seriously involved with a woman again—one bad marriage was enough—it wouldn't hurt to make a friend.

His mind made up, he headed back toward the Carlson house.

The roast was cooking, filling the house with delicious aromas. With nothing else to do until Jeff awoke, Callie found herself getting out the family photo albums. There weren't a whole lot of photographs. Her parents had taken them in haphazard fashion during their early years together, and when Callie and Jeff had been small. Callie sometimes thought most of the photos had been taken by her mother to share with her father when he came home from the sea, particularly when she and Jeff were little and changing so rapidly.

There were very few photos of her father. Most were of Jeff and Callie, but there had been a handful of times when her father had turned the camera on her mother. If she had wanted to reciprocate, it was difficult to tell from the albums.

And after her mother had died, no one had taken any photos at all. After that, the only pictures of Jeff were school photos.

Sitting at the table, with the overhead light on, Callie went through the albums, watching Jeff grow up, watching herself grow up. Watching her father age.

There was one particularly good picture of him, apparently taken by her.mother as he sat on the veranda one evening, smoking his pipe. Wes Carlson had been a good-looking man. Captured as he was in a contemplative pose, he was an enigma.

Callie sat staring at that photo for a long time, trying to read it for answers to questions that would always remain unanswered now. She hadn't known him very well—what child ever really knows a parent?—but with each passing year she felt that lack more and more. She had been twenty-four when he died, and they had been strangers to one another.

After her mother's death, Wes Carlson had become a quiet and withdrawn man. He still fished as he always had, vanishing out to sea for weeks on end, but Callie suspected he did it only because he had children to feed. When he came home, he said little and spent long hours sitting on the veranda, staring into the distance as if he were waiting for something.

Sometimes Callie thought he'd been waiting for death to take him to Lily. She'd cooked his meals and washed his clothes, but deep inside she felt her father had died along with her mother.

Many times in the last four years, she had wished he were still here. What would he have said when Jeff was charged with aggravated assault? Maybe he would have known how to handle things better than she had, and maybe Jeff wouldn't have been convicted at all. And now . . . what would he do now that Jeff was charged with murder?

She told herself she was an adult, and as capable of dealing with this as her dad would have been. It wasn't as if either of them had any experience with this sort of thing. Sometimes there was no choice except to rely on common sense and competent advice such as Shirley's.

But she still wished her dad were here. She wished she could smell his cherry pipe tobacco, and feel his powerful arm around her shoulders, and hear his rough voice say, "It'll all work out, Calypso. You'll see."

As rarely as Wes Carlson had been home, he had still managed to make her feel safer than anyone else ever had, including her mother.

Blinking back tears and trying to swallow the lump in her throat, Callie turned to a photo of her mom. She hardly remembered Lily. That made her feel terrible, but after fourteen years, all that was left of Lily Carlson was an occasional snatch of remembered song or a wisp of perfume.

And a horrible, vivid image of scarlet blood pooling all over the white tile of the kitchen floor. It was as if every other memory of her mother was in black and white except that final one. Even after all this time, that image was still seared into her brain in horrifying detail, and had become her main memory of her mother.

Lily had been killed by an ectopic pregnancy, and the doctor said she had probably bled to death so fast that nothing could have saved her. But Callie still felt somewhere inside that if she hadn't been out with her friends, if her father hadn't been out at sea, if Jeff hadn't been staying over with a friend, maybe one of them could have gotten her help in time.

She still lived with that fear and guilt, and suspected her father had, too. Maybe that was part of the reason he'd become so withdrawn. Maybe in his heart of hearts he believed he could have saved Lily if he'd been home.

Callie wondered if he had ever guessed how much she had blamed him. Probably. She had only been fourteen, and it had probably been obvious in a million ways.

It'll all work out, Calypso. Her dad had been the only person in the world who called her by her given name rather than her nickname, and right now she would have given anything in the world to hear him say that just once more.

It'll all work out, Calypso.

She was on the edge of tears, and breathing raggedly as she tried to hold them in. Jeff might wake up at any time, and she didn't want him to find her like this. But one by one, errant tears dropped onto the album, and one by one she wiped them away.

Chase rapped on the Carlson's door, and when Callie answered, he gave her a crooked smile. "If the invitation's still open, I'd like to join you for dinner."

Her eyes were reddened, he noticed, as if she'd been crying, and now they widened with surprise. "Uh, sure," she said, as if he'd caught her totally unawares. "Come on in. Jeff just got up a little while ago. He ought to be out of the shower soon."

He nodded and followed her into the kitchen. She told him to have a seat at the table while she checked the pot roast.

"It sure smells good in here," he remarked.

"Pot roast always smells delicious," she agreed.

As a conversation it had nowhere left to go, and

Chase found himself at a loss for what to say next, especially since he was acutely conscious of Callie's reddened eyes. The sight made him feel awkward and intrusive.

Jeff appeared, wearing jeans and a T-shirt with a towel around his neck. "Smells good, sis," he said. Then he saw Chase and paused awkwardly.

"Hi," Chase said. "Callie invited me to join you for dinner. Do you mind?"

Jeff shook his head, and after a moment's hesitation came to sit at the table. "It's nice to have company," he said. It sounded as if he was relieved not to have to be alone with his sister.

Chase glanced at Callie, wondering what she might have said to Jeff. Not that he could blame her for saying almost anything, given the parameters of the problem. She had her back to him, and he couldn't help noticing her bottom, cradled very nicely by a white pair of shorts, and her long, smooth legs. Uncomfortable with his reaction, he returned his gaze to Jeff. "I'm glad you're out of jail."

Jeff colored to the roots of his hair and looked utterly miserable. "I didn't do it!"

"I know you didn't."

The young man's face grew hopeful, and his blush began to fade. "You must be the only person on the planet who believes that."

"Well, I think your sister believes it, too."

"Of course I do," Callie said vehemently.

"They think I did it because of what happened with that doctor on the boat when I was sixteen," Jeff said. "I know they do because one of the cops said so. He said any guy who would pull a knife on a man would just as soon kill him. But I didn't pull a knife on that guy,

107

either!"

"What exactly happened?" Chase asked.

"I was crewing on a fishing boat. We took this group of doctors out for a day of fishing, and this one guy just kept getting more and more obnoxious. He kept telling me how stupid I was. You know, picking on me. Finally, I was trying to cut his line because he got it caught on something, and he told me I was just a chickenshit fag who wouldn't even stand up for myself. So I turned around and told him to shut the fuck up or I was gonna punch him."

"And you had a knife in your hand."

Jeff nodded miserably. "I was cutting the line. I forgot I had the knife, but I swear I never waved it at him or anything. He told the cops I'd jabbed it at him."

Callie spoke. "The prosecutor wanted to plead it down to a misdemeanor, but the doctor wouldn't let him. So Jeff got a felony conviction and two years' probation."

She handed Jeff a stack of plates and some flatware, and he started setting the table. "I've got water, juice, cola, and milk for beverages. Nothing stronger, I'm afraid."

"Water for me, thanks," Chase said. He realized his eyes were following Callie as she moved around the kitchen, and he dragged them away, only to find Jeff giving him a speculative look. Needing to find a safe subject to discuss, he returned to the immediate problem.

"What you need to do," he said to Jeff, "is write down everything that happened out there for your lawyer. And Callie and I should write down how we talked to you on the radio. If we put all of it together, it might help."

Jeff nodded almost eagerly. Apparently he was glad

108

to have something to do about the mess he was in. "I can do that. I think they took the boat's log, though."

"Did they?" Callie frowned. "They didn't tell me that. And Shirley said they were supposed to give me some paper saying what they took, but they didn't."

"Great," said Chase. "Slipshod police work. Really helpful."

Callie glanced at the clock. "It's too late to call her."

"She probably didn't find out anything yet, sis," Jeff said. "You know how slow things go."

Callie looked down at her hands and nodded, looking so sad that Chase had the worst urge to reach out and hug her. *Whoa*, he told himself. That was a good way to get into trouble.

After a moment, she lifted her head and set her chin. "It'll all work out," she said, as if she were repeating a mantra. "It'll all work out."

"Oh, man," Jeff said, his face twisting, "I sure hope so. Shirley said they're thinking about asking for the death penalty and I didn't even do anything!"

He jumped up from the table and hurried out of the room. Callie looked at Chase, her expression reflecting anguish. "I don't know what to say to him."

"I don't know what you *can* say, Callie."

She gave a little laugh that sounded almost like a sob. "You're right. What can you say to make a charge of murder look any better?"

"Life is a bitch sometimes." And sometimes there wasn't a damn thing you could do to mend things. He made a lame shot at trying to distract her. "You know, I could really use a cigarette."

She drew a deep breath, closed her eyes a moment, then said in a pleasant hostess's voice, "I'll get you an ashtray."

"Forget it. I haven't smoked in years. But I could sure use one right now. I've got half a mind to drive to the store and get some. In fact, why don't I bring back a carton, and we can all sit around and smoke until we turn green."

She looked at him as if he'd lost his mind, then a small laugh escaped her. "I've got half a mind to drive off the Seven Mile Bridge." She turned away quickly, showing him her back.

He didn't need to read her face, though. He could read the slump of her shoulders, and the way her hand covered her mouth. In spite of himself, feeling almost as if he were moving in six fathoms of water, he rose and went to her, turning her around to face him, then wrapping his arms around her. She fit against him as if she'd been created to do so. The feeling almost overwhelmed him, but he forced himself to ignore it.

"You won't," he said grimly. "You're not going to give the sea the satisfaction."

A shudder passed through her, but she didn't make a sound. He held her tighter. After a little while, she spoke in a small, strained voice.

"The sea's taken everything from me," she said, her voice breaking. "Everything. And now it wants my brother."

"It does seem that way." Another man might have thought she was crazy, but not Chase. He'd wrestled with the sea too many times to think Callie had gone off the deep end.

"It sounds crazy," she said, her voice shaky. Pulling out of his embrace, she pressed the heels of her palms to her eyes a moment, then dropped them. "It just seems that the sea did this, too. I mean . . . it's like it wouldn't take that boat, just so Jeff and Eric would find it and salvage it. Just so they could be . . . could be . . ."

"Don't let yourself think that way, Callie. Jeff's going to be okay."

She looked up at him, anger sparking in her gaze. "You can't know that! I have every right to be worried."

Christ, he just kept putting his foot in it. He was beginning to think that the diving accident had stolen his ability to deal with people. "I didn't say that. What I mean is you can't afford to give up hope. You can't afford to think there's no way out of this. Because if you start thinking that way, you'll miss opportunities to do something about it."

"What opportunities? They think my brother killed these men because he salvaged their boat! I can't prove that he *didn't* do it!"

He didn't know what to say to that, but it was wholly against his nature to assume there was no way to avert a catastrophe. There had to be something to do that would help Jeff. He just wished he knew what that might be.

All he knew was that as a white knight he was failing abysmally. Finally, he said, "I'm going to talk to Jeff. How long till dinner?"

"Um . . . fifteen minutes, I guess."

Turning, he went to look for her brother. It seemed safer than dealing with her—which made him a coward, but what the hell. He *knew* he was a coward these days.

Callie watched him go, feeling angry beyond words that there was nothing she could do, and worried almost to the point of despair. There was no way she could prove Jeff hadn't killed those men, and the knowledge terrified her. It was like a nightmare, where no matter how fast you ran, you couldn't outpace the monster coming after you.

Needing to keep busy so she didn't start screaming

111

like a wild woman, she pulled glasses out of the cupboard and filled them with beverages.

She couldn't prove Jeff didn't do it.

Unless she could find out who had.

Turning the idea around in her head, she felt her heart begin to accelerate. Maybe she *could* find out what had happened on that boat that day before Jeff had found it. Maybe she could find out something about the victims, about the fishermen who had gone out on the boat with them. Maybe she could find a clue there as to what had gone wrong.

At this point, she decided, anything at all was worth a try. First she had to learn everything Shirley had been able to get from the cops. She also had some contacts through her job. Maybe they could point her in the right direction. Those men hadn't been killed for no reason at all, and if there was a reason, maybe she could find out who was behind it.

Just the thought of taking action, any action, made her feel better. With a new sense of determination, she put dinner on the table and called Jeff and Chase.

Feather wisps of orange and fuchsia clouds spread across a turquoise western sky as the sun set. Chase stood on the Carlsons' veranda, looking up at the clouds, aware that night was encroaching once again. He could feel the tension returning, burgeoning in every cell of his body.

"It's beautiful, isn't it?" Callie said.

"Florida sunsets are the best." And he needed to be getting home before it got much darker. He wasn't at all keen on the idea of walking around the inlet once night fully ruled, of passing through the dark shadowy places among the reaching arms of the trees. In fact, he wasn't sure he could make himself do it, even though he'd managed to walk from the car to his house the other night. Any gain he might have made against his fears seemed to have evaporated when he found that chair moved out of place. As the shadows closed in, he felt the pressure of dread.

"Thanks for dinner," he told her. "It was great. I need to be getting back now, though."

"I'll walk with you," she said unexpectedly. "I need to stretch my legs."

He wouldn't mind her company at all, but he didn't like the idea of her walking back alone in the dark. On the other hand, he reminded himself, she'd done it the other night without any problem. He found himself envying her fearlessness.

Hell, maybe he was the one in need of a white knight. The sour thought made him grimace.

"Sure," he said to Callie, feeling small. "I'd enjoy the company."

They descended the steps together, and began to walk toward his cottage.

"I'm glad there was something on TV that Jeff wanted to watch," Callie remarked. Overhead, the tangerine clouds were turning pinker.

"He needs the distraction. You could probably use some, too."

"No, I don't want to be distracted. There's too much to do."

He glanced down at her, and saw that her face was a shadowy blur in the deepening twilight. Unconsciously, he quickened his pace. "What's that?"

"I figure the only way I can help Jeff is to try to find out why those two guys were murdered. If I can do that, I can probably figure out who was behind it."

"Good thinking." He hesitated, reluctant to upset her newfound sense of purpose, then decided he might as well call the shots the way he saw them. She needed to be wary. "But have you considered how dangerous that might be? We're talking about hunting for murderers here. If this was worth killing over once, it's worth a hell of a lot more now."

"I don't care," she said defiantly. "I can't just sit back and watch my brother go to the electric chair."

"It won't do him a hell of a lot of good if you get yourself killed."

"I won't get killed. I'll be careful."

"Yeah, right. You have a whole lot of experience in detecting, I suppose. You have a background as a private investigator, right? Come off it, Callie. If you start nosing around this thing and word of it gets back to the killers, they'll be dumping you off a boat somewhere."

"It's a risk I have to take. Jeff's life is on the line."

"So put yours on the line, too. Makes great sense."

She stopped walking and faced him. He stopped, too. "Well, what do you suggest, Mr. Know-it-all?"

The instant he stopped walking, he felt the pressure of the night increase tenfold, taking his tension of a minute before and putting the screws to it. It wasn't fully dark yet, but it would be soon. He didn't know how long he could stand here before he turned into a gibbering idiot. "Listen," he said, his voice rasping. "Could we just keep walking?"

Her head jerked, but it was dark enough now that he couldn't read her expression at all. He didn't know if she was angry with him or if she'd picked up on his fear. He was male enough, and she was pretty enough, that he hoped it wasn't the latter. Christ, he didn't need

114

these complications right now!

He turned and started walking briskly, struggling not to break into a run.

She caught up with him. "What's wrong?"

"Nothing." *Liar.*

"Something's wrong." She looked quickly around. "Did you see something?"

"Nothing."

"Chase . . ." She grabbed his arm. "What is wrong with you?"

Suddenly furious, as angry as he'd been in many, many years, he rounded on her. "I'm scared shitless of the dark, okay?" Then he gave in and broke into a trot, figuring he'd reach his house before the last of the twilight faded. At least tonight he'd had the sense to leave a light on. It beckoned to him through one of his windows, and he headed straight for it.

Moments later he heard Callie's running feet right behind him. Damn the woman, why couldn't she just leave him alone?

But even worse than his frustration was the twisting, unmanly awareness that he was glad she was behind him, because while she was behind him, nothing else could be.

He reached his porch at last, threw open the door and stepped inside, flicking the switch that turned all the lights on. A dozen bulbs blazed, driving the night back to where it belonged.

He stood for a minute, catching his breath, ashamed of himself and angry all at the same time. He wanted to find a hole—a brightly lighted hole—to just crawl into and never come out of again.

He heard the cottage door close and whirled around to find Callie had entered behind him. He hated her just

115

then, because she was seeing him at his worst, helpless in the face of a nameless fear. He felt stripped bare to the most shameful part of himself.

"Look," he said, squeezing the words between his teeth. "Just go home."

"I'm not going anywhere." Crossing the room, she sat at the table and folded her arms. "Have you always been afraid of the dark?"

"What are you going to do? Analyze me? I don't need that from you. I've got a shrink of my own, thank you very much."

She ignored him. "You couldn't have been afraid of the dark all your life or you'd never have been able to deep dive. I hear it's darker than night down there."

"Shit." He said the word under his breath, but she heard it anyway.

"So, you've been afraid of the dark since your accident? That seems perfectly reasonable to me. It must have been very dark down there."

He faced her, setting his hands on his hips. "Look, it's not just the dark. It's the things *in* the dark. So lay off and leave me alone, lady. I'm crazy."

She nodded slowly. "I imagine you think so."

"No, I *know* so! I sit here all night, wide-awake, and I listen to the darkness whisper. I wait for it to pounce. The things that attacked me in the sea are here. They're outside right now, just waiting for me. That's how crazy I am."

She just sat there, continuing to look at him, her gaze steady and her expression—hell, what was her expression?

It wasn't sympathetic, it wasn't pitying, it was . . . it was *attentive*. Nothing more or less.

Finally she spoke. "I have a patient who was brutally

116

attacked by a stranger when she was sixteen. She nearly died. Today she's twenty-seven and has a child of her own. She lives behind an eight-foot fence, in a house with a security system, keeps the lights on all night, and has four attack-trained Rottweilers. She sits up all night, listening to every little sound, terrified that someone might break in."

"Christ! Is that supposed to make me feel better?" Eleven years and the woman was still suffering from this stuff. The Beretta was looking good again.

"All I'm trying to say is that what you're suffering is perfectly normal."

"Is it? Well, I've got news for you. I wasn't attacked. I had an *accident*."

"Accident victims have the same post-traumatic stress. Some of them can never get in a car again. Or drive down certain streets. It's not unusual, Chase."

His tone was angry, bitter. "How many of them populate the night with demons, though?"

She shrugged a shoulder. "When you're afraid of something, the mind is good at making up excuses for it. Since there's no water outside the door, demons will do for a reason."

He swore and turned away from her, throwing up his hands, feeling that he just wasn't getting through.

"I'm sorry," she said presently. "I suppose it helps to feel you're unique."

Her sarcasm surprised him, even as it felt like a lash on his soul. "Do you work at being a bitch?"

He heard nothing but silence from her, but refused to turn around. He wanted her out of there, now, because she was making him feel as if she could read his soul.

"Well," she said after a moment, "I suppose you could call me that. It can't be pleasant to be told you're magnifying your problems."

"I'm not magnifying anything. I sit here night after night and tell myself I'm imagining things, that there's nothing out there, that I'm just crazy. Then something as small as a chair being out of place throws me over the edge again."

His face twisted as a searing bolt of pain shot through him from his hip all the way down his leg. Cursing quietly, he yanked a chair back from the table and sat, waiting for it to pass, feeling icy beads of perspiration break out on his brow.

"Is the pain ever going to get any better?" she asked softly. He looked at her and for the first time saw genuine concern in her blue eyes.

"Who the hell knows." Little by little, the fiery pain ebbed, returning to its usual dull ache.

"I'm sorry, Chase," she said presently. "I wasn't minimizing your problem. I was just trying to tell you that it's normal. And most of the time it eases up."

He didn't answer. Part of him was still angry that she was seeing him like this, but part of him was as grateful as hell that she was here. Her presence seemed to be as effective as the lights in holding the darkness at bay. Maybe even more so, because even when he closed his eyes he didn't hear the mocking whispers of the shadows, didn't hear things scraping against the windows or the side of his house. The night had fallen silent.

For the first time in a long time, he let go of the tension while shadows still lurked outside. For the first time in a long time, he felt the tension seep out of his muscles while darkness still ruled the world.

He looked at Callie and wondered if she had any idea that she had just become a talisman.

The silence that stretched between them suddenly seemed fraught with possibilities, and he felt himself straining toward them and recoiling from them all at once. This is dangerous, he told himself. At any time in his life, this would have been dangerous, but right now with all the problems he faced, and with all the problems she faced, this was downright perilous.

Her gaze continued to meet his steadily as the air in the room seemed to thicken. Then, to his amazement, her cheeks colored faintly, and she looked down.

"I'd better be getting back," she said. "I don't want Jeff to be alone too long."

That shocked him back to reality, dispelling the moment of near enchantment. "You don't think he'd hurt himself?"

She shook her head. "No. Not really. But . . ." She left it incomplete, giving him a look that said that regardless of what she believed, she wasn't taking any chances.

Rising, he limped into the kitchen and pulled the magnetic memo pad off the refrigerator. Returning to the table, he scribbled a number, tore off the sheet, and passed it to Callie. "If you need any help at all, call me. I mean it."

She looked up at him, her eyes wide and blue, and somehow they seemed to reach out to him, to touch him someplace deep inside. And for an instant, just an instant, he trembled on the cusp of something at once important and terrifying.

An electric tingle filled him, and he realized he could almost feel her silky skin against his palm, could almost taste her mouth beneath his, could almost hear her sighs in his ear. For an instant, just an instant, desire crashed over him like the breakers of a stormy sea.

If he didn't step back now, he was going to step forward. Afraid of what he was feeling, of what she might not feel, he stepped back.

She took the paper with a nod. "Thanks, Chase."

Then she walked out of the cabin into the night, as if there was nothing at all threatening out there.

Nor was there, Chase told himself. And for a little while he actually believed it. But later . . . later he heard the scratching at the windows again, and saw something shadowy move past one.

He might not believe there was anything out there, but there damn well was.

He thought about going outside to check on it, but remembering the chair, he hesitated. Which would be worse? To go out there and find nothing, or go out there and find something?

Damned if he did, damned if he didn't. Giving in, he went to get the Beretta. If there was something out there, he was damn well going to find it *now*.

He waited until the scratching started again, at the rear of the cabin. Then, with more fortitude than he'd shown in a while, he flipped the switch, casting the cabin into darkness.

For an instant he could hardly breathe. For an instant he felt as if he were drowning, as if the shadows were as thick as the water at thirty fathoms. He forced himself to ignore the feeling, made his leaden limbs move, reminded himself that once the night had been his friend.

He opened the door slowly and stepped out of the cabin. The scratching was still coming from around back, and as soon as he stepped onto the porch, he felt the breeze that was probably causing it. A stiff wind blew tonight, rattling the palms, causing the mangroves

120

to sigh like lost souls. He smelled the sea and felt his heart leap with a yearning he hadn't allowed it to feel in months.

The sea called to him even as the night threatened him. He had told himself they were one and the same, but they were not. Listening to the gentle lapping of the waves in the inlet and the creaking of the dock to which the *Lily* was tied as the boat tugged at her moorings, he felt the whisper of the peace he had once found in the sea.

Almost as if drawn by a force outside himself, he climbed down from the porch, and walked around the seawall to the water's edge. The waves sparkled dimly in starlight, murmuring a soft, liquid lullaby.

She called to him, and he wanted to go.

Squatting, he forgot the night and listened to the sea's siren song. Responding to it, he reached out a hand and felt her warm waters kiss his fingers. Peace began to fill him, and the night seemed to lose its fearsome grip.

Then, sounding like the crack of a gun, the door of his house slammed shut.

At the loud crack, Chase instinctively rolled sideways until he was on his back, pointing the gun toward the house. Nothing moved except the breeze and the swaying trees. No darker, thicker shadow had coalesced out of the night.

It had to have been the breeze, he thought. The breeze had caught the door and slammed it.

But he didn't quite believe it.

Rolling once again, he came to a crouch and began to make his way closer, keeping low, hugging the shadows that now promised safety with concealment. His training came back to him instantly.

He reached his porch and still saw nothing. The

breeze had gentled some, and the palms were whispering rather than clattering. Step by step, keeping crouched, he climbed to the porch. Nothing.

Finally, deciding it had to have been the wind, he straightened and went to open his door. He swung it inward and peered into the dark maw inside his house.

There could be something in there. He almost sensed that something was. Feeling his heart pound, he weighed his options and decided that whatever was in there couldn't possibly do any worse to him than his own fear did. If he let fear cripple him, he might as well be dead.

Stepping into the yawning blackness, he felt for the light switch and threw it.

The sudden blaze from all the lamps was painful, but it revealed that the darkness inside had concealed no secrets. There was nothing there. Carefully, though, he made his way back to the bedroom, the one part of the house he couldn't see from the front door. Nothing. He was alone.

Turning, he went back to close his front door. Just as he was about to swing it shut, he caught sight of something glistening. Reaching out, he turned on the porch light.

There, draped across the planks of his deck and leading down to the water, was a trail of wet seaweed. For the first time, he considered that the demons he feared might not all be in his mind.

CHAPTER 7

CALLIE CALLED SHIRLEY KIDDER FIRST THING IN THE morning. "What's happening on Jeff's case?"

"Very little I'm afraid. I don't have full discovery yet, just what the State Attorney and sheriff are willing to share. The Monroe County sheriff says they're going to deliver a paper to you telling you what they took during the search. Apparently it was just the boat's log and some clothing."

"So they didn't find anything else?"

"Not a thing. And you can use the boat anytime you want. I told them to either impound it as evidence—which considering they didn't find anything at all on the *Lily* would be a very hard thing to justify—or release the boat. They released it."

"Good."

"With regard to the clothing, they took Jeff's clothes out of your hamper. Did they tell you that?"

"No. They said they didn't take anything!"

"Well, someone took four pairs of undershorts, three pairs of tennis shorts, one pair of jeans, five pairs of socks, and six T-shirts out of the hamper. You can get irate that they didn't tell you about this after you get the good news. All of the clothes, dirty though they were, including the pair of jeans that was soaked with salt from seawater, proved to be perfectly free from bloodstains. So as it stands now, they haven't got one direct link between your brother and the dead men, other than that he happened upon a sinking boat."

"Thank God!" Callie's spirits soared.

"This doesn't, however, mean that we're out of the woods."

And just as quickly her spirits plunged. "What do you mean?"

"They've still got a strong circumstantial case. Strong enough to press this charge. And unless somebody comes up with another suspect, this is probably going to

123

run through to the bitter end. Have you been reading the papers?"

"No." They were still lying wrapped in plastic in a pile on the veranda. She'd picked them up from her box out at the highway, but since Jeff's arrest she hadn't even wanted to open them.

"Well, your brother and his friend made the front page when they were arrested, and the papers aren't letting the story quiet down. Which means the State Attorney's office isn't going to turn loose its two best suspects unless they get something better to replace them with. For now, the status is quo, Callie. The sword is still hanging there. Or whatever other lousy metaphor you prefer."

"God." She closed her eyes, struggling against an overwhelming sense of despair.

"It could be worse. They could have found something on the boat or in his clothes. What I'm saying is, this isn't going to go away quickly."

After she hung up the phone, Callie went out to get the newspapers. Her hands were shaking, and she felt as if she were taking a violent roller-coaster ride. She didn't want to read the stories in the paper, didn't want to see how her brother was being cast in the press, but it was the only way she could find out enough information to start her own investigation.

And she was damn well going to start one. She couldn't wait for the state to get around to looking for someone else. It sounded as if their minds were pretty well made up.

Jeff was outside, standing on a ladder, scraping the last of the flaking paint from the gables.

"Mornin', sis. I'll start painting this afternoon," he called down to her when he heard her come outside.

Callie stepped to the edge of the porch and looked up at him. He was high on a ladder, wearing nothing but stained denim shorts and deck shoes.

"You don't have to, Jeff."

"I want to. It'll keep me busy."

She hesitated, then asked, "Did you ever call Mr. Donleavy?"

"Yeah, when I got up this morning. I guess he doesn't want a murderer working for him."

"Oh, Jeff . . . " Her heart ached for her little brother.

He shrugged a shoulder. "Can't blame him. Say, are you making breakfast this morning?"

"Thinking about it. Are you hungry?"

"I could eat a horse."

"Okay, I'll make something."

Back in the kitchen, Callie dropped the papers on the table and resisted the urge to smash something, or at the very least to call Donleavy and give him a piece of her mind. Right now she didn't know who she was angrier with. The State Attorney or Mr. Donleavy. She could have cheerfully throttled either one.

Instead she started making skillet potatoes. Busy. She *had* to keep busy. And she wasn't ready yet to look at the papers.

Fifteen minutes later, she thought she heard Jeff talking to someone. Her heart slammed, wondering if it were the police come to take him back to jail. At this point she wouldn't have been surprised if they'd found something *else* to charge him with.

Dropping the potato she was dicing, she wiped her hands on a paper towel and hurried out onto the veranda to see Chase standing near Jeff's ladder, talking to him. When he saw her, he smiled faintly. "Morning," he said.

"Good morning."

125

He was wearing a white T-shirt and cuttoff jeans, and in the bright sunlight he looked strong and powerful, like a bulwark against life, not at all like the disturbed man she had met last night. She had the worst urge to dump all her problems on him and ask him to deal with them.

And for an instant, just one small instant, she had the self-pitying wish that just once in her life she wouldn't have to face everything alone.

"I thought I'd come over and help with the paint job," Chase said. "If you don't mind."

"Callie's making breakfast," Jeff said from his high perch. "There'll be enough for Chase, too, won't there, Callie?"

"Sure. There'll be plenty. It'll be ready in about an hour."

Back in the kitchen she threw a couple more potatoes in the microwave to cook while she finished cubing the ones she had cooked earlier. Fifteen minutes later, the potatoes were browning in the frying pan, and she was dicing scallions, green peppers, and ham to throw in with them.

The cooking gave her an excuse to avoid looking at the stack of newspapers on the table. Much as she needed to glean information so she would know where to start her own investigation, she was mortally afraid of what she was going to read there and how it was going to make her feel. No matter what they said about Jeff and Eric it was going to make her angry, and there was no way the paper could even begin to reflect the truth about the young men who were accused.

All she could do was promise herself that she would skim over the parts about the boys and concentrate on the information about the men who were missing.

Jeff and Chase came in when she called them and took turns in the bathroom washing up.

"Oh, man, skillet potatoes," Jeff said approvingly as he came to the table.

"Not without a shirt, you don't," Callie told him sternly.

He made a face at her. "I don't see why I can't eat without a shirt. I can work without one."

"It's different. When I'm eating I don't want to see your hairy underarms and chest. Now get a T-shirt."

Jeff looked at Chase as if for support, but Chase shook his head. "I'm with Callie," he said.

Grumbling, Jeff went back to his bedroom.

"You'd think," Callie remarked, "that this rule hasn't been in effect all along. I *never* let him eat shirtless."

Chase chuckled. "I think he was trying to pull a fast one."

"You mean because you're here he thought I wouldn't scold?" She shook her head. "He knows better now."

Chase saw the pile of newspapers that she'd moved to one end of the counter. "You're not going to read those."

"Yes, I am."

He shook his head. "I don't think you want to do that."

"How else am I going to find out who was killed so I can start trying to find out what happened?"

"Well, we could find out who the boat was registered to.

Or you could ask me to read that crap so you don't have to see it."

"You'd do that for me?"

"Sure."

127

She felt a smile, a genuine smile, stretching her mouth for what felt like the first time in ages. His offer touched her and made her feel a little less alone. "Thank you."

He shrugged. "No problem. It seems like the least I can do."

The least he could do? This man didn't understand the word least, Callie thought. Helping paint her house, and reading through those newspapers was a lot more than "least."

On a sudden impulse she asked Jeff to say the blessing when he rejoined them. To her surprise, Chase immediately reached out and took her hand and Jeff's, bowing his head for the prayer. It had been a long time since she had clasped hands with others while saying grace. Not since her mother had died. For the first time in days, a sense of peace stole over her.

"Amen," she heard Jeff and Chase say, and echoed it herself. When she lifted her bowed head, she felt as if the meal had indeed been blessed.

Both men piled their plates high with the skillet potatoes, and filled their glasses full of orange juice. Callie took a smaller portion, not really feeling hungry.

At first the conversation revolved around the food—Chase asked for her recipe—and the painting, but inevitably, as the meal drew to a close, it began to swing back around to the charges against Jeff.

"It's weird," Jeff said, "to have people believing I killed those guys. I don't even know their names or what they look like."

Callie looked at him. "Do you *want* to know?"

"Sort of. I mean, this is affecting the rest of my life."

"It's in the paper," Chase said with a nod toward the stack on the counter. "I've suggested to Callie that I

128

read the articles, though. Neither of you really needs to know what the press is saying about you."

The corners of Jeff's mouth drew down, and he pushed his plate aside. "You're probably right. I probably sound like some kind of monster."

Callie reached out and covered his hand with hers. "You're not a monster. *We* know that."

"But no one else does. And Eric's still in jail. His parents won't help him make bail."

Callie felt her heart squeeze. "Maybe they can't, Jeff."

"Maybe not."

"We were lucky that this house is all paid for. Otherwise, I couldn't have bailed you out either."

"I know." He looked down at the table. "Do you think I can visit him?"

Callie looked at Chase and he shrugged. "I don't know," she said. "Let me ask Shirley. There might be a reason why you shouldn't."

"What reason?" he asked bitterly. "Are we going to make up a new story? Why would we? They don't even believe the *truth*."

"Easy, son," Chase said quietly. "Getting angry and bitter isn't going to help anything. You need to keep your head clear."

Jeff jumped up from the table. "I need to do *something*." He grabbed dishes and carried them to the sink.

Callie started to reach out to him, but stopped, acutely aware that there wasn't anything at all she could do to make Jeff feel any better. She hadn't felt this helpless since she had found their mother dying in a lake of blood on the kitchen floor.

The same kitchen floor that Jeff was pacing across

now. For an instant, time shifted, and she saw again the scarlet pool spreading around her mother.

Chase spoke, jerking Callie back to the present, "Why don't we talk about what happened out there that day? In detail. We'll write down every last thing you can remember about it, and we'll write down everything Callie and I can remember about talking to you on the radio. Maybe there'll be something there that'll be useful."

Jeff shrugged, saying nothing, and finished clearing the table.

Chase looked at Callie. "Do you have a pad or a tape recorder we can use?"

Grateful for something to do, Callie went to the desk in the living room and returned with a yellow legal pad and a pen.

"Okay," Chase said. "Callie, will you take notes? Or do you want me to?"

"I'll do it."

"All right. When exactly did you first see the boat, Jeff?"

The boy leaned back against the counter, folding his arms across his chest. "I don't know. I guess it was sometime around two. We'd been fishing but hadn't had much luck, and it was right around then we realized that we'd drifted out a whole lot farther than we'd planned to go. I was checking our position when Eric saw the boat."

"Do you remember what your position was?"

"Sure." He closed his eyes a moment and recited coordinates. Callie scribbled them down quickly.

"How sure of that are you?" Chase asked, his heart beginning to pound. In his mind he carried a mental map of where he did his salvage diving, and what he

130

was seeing in his mind's eye right now didn't seem possible.

"Pretty positive," Jeff said. "I was using the global positioning system. Why?"

Chase took the pad from Callie and read the coordinates again. "Do you have a navigational chart?"

"Sure, on the boat."

"Get it, would you?"

Jeff hurried out and Callie looked at Chase. "What's wrong?" she asked.

"Maybe nothing. Probably nothing. Let me check a chart before I say anything, okay?"

She nodded reluctantly. "Okay."

Chase waited impatiently, telling himself that he'd misremembered the coordinates, but he was sure he hadn't. All looking at the navigational chart would do was confirm what he already suspected, and his suspicions were tightening his stomach until it felt like a ball of lead.

Jeff returned a few minutes later with a plastic-covered chart. He spread it on the table and they all helped hold down the corners.

"Here," he said, pointing to a red X. "I marked the spot when I got the reading."

"I'm surprised they didn't take this chart during the search," Callie said, eyeing it uneasily.

Jeff shrugged. "Maybe they didn't think it was significant. It's just a chart. Thousands of boats have the same one."

Chase hardly heard them. He was bent over the map, looking for coordinates where *The Happy Maggie*—the boat he had almost died trying to salvage—had gone down, his fingers tracing the contour lines.

It wasn't hard to find the place. The Florida Keys sat

131

on the southern edge of the Florida Escarpment, a piece of the continental plate that extended westward from the Florida coast for around a hundred and fifty miles. The escarpment ended abruptly just a few miles south of the Keys, dropping away rapidly into the deep waters of the Atlantic. In the area where Jeff had found the boat, the average depth was about ten meters, too shallow for the dive he had been on. But little more than a mile farther out, and slightly to the east, was exactly the position where he had dived at fifty-seven meters. His heart began to pound. It was too damn close for coincidence.

"You say you found the boat around two o'clock?"

"Yeah. Somewhere around then."

Chase sat back in his chair and thought about it. Trip time out, dive time, recovery time. It was possible. It was too possible, and he didn't believe in coincidences this big. No way.

"Chase?" Callie said. "What is it?"

He looked at her, then back at the chart. He stabbed his index finger at the spot where he had gone on his last dive. "This is where I had my accident." The corner of Jeff's red X touched his index finger.

Callie leaned over, closer to the map. "That's amazing. Quite a coincidence."

"It's no coincidence," Chase said. "It can't be."

She looked at him; her eyes wary and doubtful. "Why couldn't it be? Or better yet, what else *could* it be?"

His hand tightened into a fist then relaxed. "I find it very hard to believe that I nearly died here"—he stabbed the map with his finger—"and then two months later a scuttled boat is found *here*, and there's evidence that at least two men were killed."

"Things happen. It's just a coincidence."

"No," Jeff said suddenly. "It's too much of a

coincidence to ignore. Eric and I were drifting out there. We were getting carried slowly landward, and from time to time I corrected and took us farther out. Nobody was correcting the boat we found. She would have drifted just that way that day."

"No, it's just a coincidence," Callie said flatly. "It's a leap to link these two things. In the first place, Chase had an *accident*. There's no reason to think that could be tied in any way to the murder of these charter-boat operators. No reason at all!"

"No reason," said Chase heavily, "except ten million dollars in uncut diamonds."

CHAPTER 8

"TEN—" CALLIE BROKE OFF IN AMAZEMENT, ASTOUNDED beyond words. "Wait a minute! Where did the diamonds come from?"

"From *The Happy Maggie*."

Jeff sat down again and looked at Chase with all the eagerness of someone who expected to hear a great story. "That's what you were diving for, wasn't it?"

Chase nodded. "The boat's owner claimed he was transporting ten million dollars in uncut diamonds when he hit an underwater obstacle and the boat sank. He was covered by insurance, but naturally the insurance company didn't want to pay if they could find a way out of it."

"I imagine not," said Callie, still amazed by the thought of such sums.

"So I was hired along with another diver to go down there to find out what happened to the boat, and see if we could find the diamonds. They were supposed to be in a safe in the owner's cabin. The insurance company was hoping either to recover the diamonds or to find out they weren't there. They suspected a scam."

"I can sure see why," Callie said. She glanced at Jeff and saw that his eyes were sparkling. At least this story was getting his mind off his own problems.

"Either way," Chase continued, "the company would be happy, because either way they wouldn't have to pay for the diamonds. So Bill Evers, a guy I often dive with, was supposed to get the diamonds, and I was supposed to check out the boat and find out why it sank."

"Did you?"

Chase shook his head. "I don't remember anything about it. I started hallucinating, and they had to yank me up. Bill reported that there appeared to have been a bilge fire on board—which directly contradicted the owner's version of events—and there were no diamonds. I guess the company didn't pay the owner a dime."

"My God, the things people dream up," Callie said. "Did the owner really think he could get away with both the diamonds and the insurance money?"

"I don't know what he thought. But that's not the point here. What if someone else thinks there are still ten million dollars' worth of uncut diamonds out there on that boat?"

Jeff slapped his hand down on the table, startling Callie. "Man oh man!"

"Whoa," Callie said. "Wait a minute. There could also be a lot of other reasons those men were killed."

"Sure there could," Chase agreed as if it didn't matter. But it did matter, to *him*. Because if someone had been willing to kill two men for those diamonds, they sure as hell wouldn't have hesitated to try to kill

134

him somehow.

Except, he reminded himself, reining in his own sense of excitement with difficulty, Bill Evers had said there were no diamonds down there. And Bill hadn't run into any trouble.

No, it didn't fit. Turning it around in his mind, he could see a dozen holes in the theory.

But somehow that didn't shake his conviction that the two incidents were linked.

If he could find out what had happened to those two men who were killed, he might possibly find out what had happened to him. It was a slim possibility, but it was one he wasn't willing to pass up.

He looked at Callie and Jeff. "We're going to find out what the hell happened on that boat that day."

"Well, I'm all in agreement with that," Callie said, "but I'm not at all sure it's going to be tied in to what happened to you."

"If it is, it is," Chase said. "But it might well be tied in to the diamonds. At least then we'd have a motive for what happened out there."

"Drugs could have been the motive," Callie argued.

"Except," Chase pointed out, "if they'd found any sign of drugs on that boat, Jeff would probably be charged with trafficking, too."

She hadn't thought about that. And suddenly the diamonds didn't sound like such a remote cause for the murders as they had. Anything would be better than having drugs dragged into this mess, she realized. Her brother was exactly the age where people would believe he'd be stupid enough to get involved in trafficking. A twenty-year-old with a boat. A suspicion of drug involvement was the *only* thing that could make this mess worse than it was right now.

"All right," she said. "It's a theory. It's the only theory we've got. But we have to go back to basics anyway. We've got to find out about the guys who owned the charter boat, and whether or not they took someone else out with them that day. And if so, who and for what reason."

"Agreed," Chase said. "I'll start with the newspapers."

An hour later he had compiled the bare bones. Callie sat beside him, taking down everything he discovered in the Miami paper and the Key West paper. Jeff, who'd gotten impatient, went back to scraping, but came in for a drink of water right about the time they were finishing with the papers.

"Okay," Chase said when Jeff joined them at the table, "let's go over what we've got."

Callie picked up the pad. "George Westerlake was the owner of the *Island Dream*, the boat that Jeff salvaged. He was fifty-three, a former pharmaceutical rep who retired to the islands five years ago and started a charter service. With him was his partner, James "Jimbo" Rushman, also fifty-three, a displaced commercial fisherman. Apparently when the net ban got passed, Rushman gave up on commercial fishing and bought into Westerlake's idea for a charter service. The two men had been friends since high school."

"Not likely they killed each other then," Jeff remarked.

"I don't know about that," said Chase. "Partnerships can make enemies out of the best of friends if the business starts to go bad."

"No financial problems," Callie reminded him. "That was mentioned."

"No *known* financial problems. Something might yet

136

turn up."

She nodded and returned to reading. "They both lived on Big Coppitt Key, so I guess that's a good place to start looking into things. The papers also said that Westerlake's wife was under the impression that her husband had a charter that day for deep-sea fishing."

"Which means he took a party or parties aboard," Chase remarked.

"So there are other missing people?" Jeff looked horrified. "I could be charged with their murders, too?"

Callie didn't know what to say to that. She couldn't lie, but short of a lie there didn't seem to be a single soothing thing she could say.

"The papers aren't exactly clear on this," Chase said. "All they said was that the victims *may* have taken two other men out on the boat."

"But why wouldn't the cops know that already?" Callie asked. "I mean, somebody must have seen them set out. Somebody must know *something*. And if they knew that for sure already, why wouldn't Jeff be charged with their murders, too?"

"I don't know," Chase said. "I'm assuming they're not sure there were any other people on the boat."

"Or maybe," Jeff said bitterly, "if they find out there were two other men on that boat it becomes really unbelievable that Eric and I could have boarded and killed all of them."

Callie looked at Chase. "The prosecutor couldn't possibly withhold that kind of information."

"Hell, I don't know," he answered honestly. "I wouldn't think so, but maybe they're not above stacking the case. Or maybe they just don't have enough information to make two additional murder charges."

He rubbed his chin, feeling the bristles of the beard

137

he'd forgotten to shave that morning. "It's not a whole hell of a lot of information, is it?" He didn't want to look at Callie, didn't want to see the fear that never left her blue eyes anymore.

"It's more than we had earlier," she said firmly. "So where do we start?"

"In Key West, bright and early in the morning. We'll check the marinas there and see what we can find out about these guys."

"Not today?" Jeff asked, disappointed.

"I want to make some phone calls first. I might be able to find out a little additional information before we start asking questions people aren't going to want to answer."

Callie's eyebrows lifted. "Why shouldn't they want to answer?"

"Because we're nobody, Callie. Because you're related to the man who's been charged with the murders."

The look on her face ripped his heart, but he forced himself to ignore it. He was getting involved in this for his own sake, he told himself, not for hers. He couldn't afford to get involved for hers. He didn't have enough left in him to pay the cost for that.

"I'll go with you," Jeff said.

Chase shook his head. "That would be a big mistake."

Jeff's expression grew thunderous. "Why?"

"Because you don't want to get accused of witness tampering."

Jeff swore and stood up so quickly that his chair tipped over. He left it there as he stormed outside. Moments later they heard the sound of the scraper removing the last paint flakes from the eaves.

"He does have a temper," Chase remarked.

"He's under a lot of strain. As bad as this is for me, it's got to be a lot worse for him."

"I suppose." Chase rose and went to pick up the chair Jeff had knocked over. "He needs to learn to control his anger better, Callie, or it'll get him into more trouble."

She snapped then herself. "Who made you so almighty perfect? Who gave you the right to tell other people what they need to do?"

He looked into her angry blue eyes, and felt as if he were losing something, but that was so ridiculous he refused even to consider what it might mean. "I never claimed any right," he finally said. "I just call the shots the way I see them."

"Well, clean up your own act before you start telling us how to clean up ours."

That was low, low enough that he felt his own temper flare. But unlike Jeff Carlson, he'd learned to rein it in a long time ago, so he never uttered any of the retorts that sprang immediately to his mind. Instead, he spoke quietly.

"I'm going to go make phone calls now. I'll let you know what I find out." Then he turned and walked out, letting the screen door slap closed behind him.

He heard Callie follow him onto the veranda, but he didn't look back until he was halfway around the inlet. She was still standing there, staring after him, and she looked so alone and frightened that he felt his heart ache.

No, he told himself. None of that. Just do what you have to and forget everything else.

He kept walking.

And Callie kept watching.

A half hour later he was on his way to Miami.

Like most insurance companies, Vantage Maritime, Inc., owned a huge, brand-new office building. Maritime's Miami offices were on the top three floors, and the lower floors were rented out to various tenants, mostly lawyers and doctors. The building reeked of money, with rose-marble pillars and floors, and brass appointments everywhere. Chase supposed the building was intended to convey that Maritime was financially solid. To him it just announced that Maritime was raking in huge profits on its policies.

Dave Hathaway kept him waiting twenty minutes. Chase supposed he shouldn't have been surprised, but he *had* called to make an appointment, and had driven nearly a hundred and fifty miles to get here. The secretary finally motioned him to go in.

Dave wasn't at the top rung of the company, or anywhere near it, but he did rate an office with a window and carpeting, even if it was a small office. Chase had always thought Dave deserved more than that, considering how much his oversight of salvage operations must save the company every year. But Dave seemed content, and Chase kept his opinion to himself.

Dave greeted him with a big grin and came around the desk to shake his hand. "So you decided to take me up on the job?"

"I'm still thinking about it." Which was true enough, even if it wasn't at the top of his list of concerns right now.

Dave motioned him to a chair, then settled back behind his desk. "I suppose you want to know more about what we're offering."

"It crossed my mind."

"Good. Given your experience, I think I can offer you seventy a year. Plus full benefits, of course."

"Sounds good." It compared favorably to what he'd been making as an independent. Unfortunately, it meant being chained full-time to a desk.

"I figure you can oversee deep-salvage operations on both coasts for us. You know who the best people are, you know how to evaluate the dives and whether they're at all practical to make. The kind of thing we've been leaving to the individual contractors to decide."

"So why do you want to hire somebody to do it when the contractors already do it?"

Dave flashed another grin. "In the long run, this is the cheaper way for us to do it."

It made sense.

"Besides," Dave continued, "you're a recognized damage expert. I don't know anybody else who's as good as you at looking at a sunken boat and determining what happened. Remember that case two years ago when they claimed an accidental bilge fire and you showed it was arson? Saved us a pretty penny on that one. There's nobody else as good at that as you, Chase. We don't want to lose you."

"But I won't be diving anymore."

Dave sat forward. "I know that. But we can bring you photos and samples to examine. And you know exactly what to tell divers to look for. You'd be invaluable to us."

Chase nodded, but something about this was troubling him, though he couldn't say exactly what. The proposal, as Dave was putting it, sounded perfectly reasonable. It was probably just his damn paranoia again.

"You don't have to decide right now," Dave said. "But think about it. Meantime, I haven't had lunch today. Join me?"

Chase hesitated. If he went to lunch with Dave right now, he might not get back up to this office. "Sure," he said. "But first, could you do me a favor?"

"Anything within my power."

"I'd like to see the report on that last dive I took."

Dave paused mid movement and looked at him. "You know those reports are confidential. What do you want to see it for anyway? You already know what Bill found down there."

"I just need to see it in black and white. The questions are driving me crazy, and I got to thinking that maybe Bill had put in more detail than what I've been told."

"I see." Dave was hesitating visibly, and Chase understood why. Violating company policy could get him into serious trouble. He considered withdrawing his request for Dave's sake, then decided to stick to it.

There might be more information in Bill's report on the dive, and that information might be useful to him, either to cure his damn nightmares or give him a clue as to what was going on out in those waters, something which had not only affected him, but had affected Callie and Jeff, too. Admittedly, the connection was a tenuous one, but he was damned if he was going to overlook any possibility.

"Just don't ever tell anyone I did this for you," Dave said, and hit the intercom switch. "Lettie? Could you bring in the Bruderson salvage report, please?" Dave sat back in his chair and looked at Chase.

"Thanks, Dave."

"I can't show you the whole file, you know. Some of it would breach client confidentiality in a way I could never justify."

"I only want to see Bill's report on the dive. You can justify that. Hell, I was there."

"But you can't remember anything." Dave's gaze was suddenly intent. "You *don't* remember anything, do you?"

"Not a damn thing. How many times am I going to have to answer that question? I can't even remember getting my equipment on. Everything's a big blank." Except for the demons in the darkness. He remembered those every time he closed his eyes, dark shapes that seemed to coalesce out of the very water, something like the movie *The Abyss*, only darker and more threatening. He sometimes wondered if that film had laid the groundwork for what his mind had imagined in the depths of the sea.

Lettie came in with a thick file and handed it to Dave. "That's everything we've got," she said.

"Thanks, Lettie. I'll be going to lunch in a few minutes, so hold my calls, okay?"

"Sure thing." The door closed quietly behind her.

Dave opened the file and began flipping pages.

Chase spoke as he watched the pages turn. "Why was Bruderson carrying all those diamonds anyway?"

"He owns jewelry stores in Miami, Tampa, and New Orleans. He said he was carrying the diamonds to his Tampa store."

Chase shook his head. "I'd have thought there'd be safer ways."

"Apparently he does it all the time. Gives him an excuse to take a nice long sail and deduct the cost." Dave looked up with a half smile. "Business people have all kinds of ways to turn their pleasures into deductible expenses. It must give the IRS fits."

"You'd think so. I'm surprised the company would insure him, though."

"He paid enough for the coverage, I'll tell you." Dave

143

flipped a few more pages. "Here we are." Releasing the clasp, he lifted out a stack of pages, then passed three of them to Chase. "Take your time . . . but no more than fifteen minutes. I've got a meeting at three, and I want time for lunch beforehand."

Chase nodded, then bent to read the report. It was typed, of course, with a header that said it had been compiled from Bill's written report of the dive and subsequent interviews. For the first time since the dive, he found himself wanting to talk to Bill. He looked up at Dave. "You don't have the raw report?"

Dave shook his head. "I don't know what they did with that. The investigators who looked into your accident took everything, and all I got back was this. It's probably in the file on your accident."

"Can I see that?"

"Not from me. I'd have no excuse to ask for it. You could try the legal department, but considering they've been worried you were going to sue, you'd probably have to get a lawyer to shake the file out of them. Is it worth the trouble?"

"I'm not going to sue."

"You and I know that, but the legal eagles aren't taking any chances." He gave a laugh. "You know lawyers."

"Yeah." Giving up, Chase read the report. Everything seemed to be there—a description of the boat's damage, which would seem to support an explosion or fire in the bilge, Bill's report that the safe was empty, and even a description of Chase's erratic behavior.

Chase handed the report back. "Thanks, Dave."

"Did it jog your memory any?"

Chase shook his head. "Nope. Doesn't even ring any little bells."

"Funny the guy would claim to have hit an underwater obstacle when there was an explosion and fire."

Chase shrugged. "He might not have been able to tell the difference. They'd probably feel pretty much the same to him, and he could have put the fire down to damage caused by impact."

"I'd be quicker to believe that if he'd mentioned a fire at all, but he didn't. Add that to there being no diamonds, and it gets suspicious as hell."

"It sure does."

"The legal guys are thinking about turning it over to the state attorney as insurance fraud. I don't know whether they've got enough to go on, though. So, are you ready for lunch?"

Dave selected a nearby seafood restaurant where the late-lunch crowd was just beginning to thin out. They were given a table near a window with a view of a baking parking lot. Dave ordered a grouper sandwich, and Chase asked for the captain's plate, a mix of broiled seafood.

"So how's life on the Keys generally?" Dave asked.

"I like it."

"There's a lot of weirdos out there on Key West."

"Some. Depends on what you think is weird."

"It's probably the only place on earth that ballyhoos that gays, lesbians, and cross-dressers are welcome."

Chase started to smile. "Mayberry RFD meets Fire Island. What's wrong with that?"

"It's not natural, that's what's wrong."

"Mm. Well, I kinda have the attitude that anything that nature produces is natural. It may not be to my taste, but I can't see giving anybody a hard time over something that isn't hurting anyone else."

Dave shook his head. "I wouldn't expect that attitude from a former SEAL. You guys are the most macho men on earth."

"Maybe. I used to think so. Then I realized we were just crazy. It's a useful craziness at times, but it's still crazy."

Dave laughed at that. "Well, you've got me there. I sure wouldn't volunteer for it."

"Most people wouldn't."

"So you're happy down there just soaking up the rays, huh?"

Happy wasn't the word Chase would have used. He hadn't been happy in a while. "I always planned to retire there."

"You're kinda young for retirement."

"I sure haven't been feeling that way lately."

"So what about the job?"

"I'm still thinking about it, Dave. I'll let you know."

Forty minutes after failing in an attempt to reach Bill by phone, he was heading down US 1 for home and feeling amazingly eager to get there. He'd never liked Miami, but given his recent psychological problems, he was surprised to discover he was glad to be heading back to the Keys.

Living on an island, even an island as big as Lower Sugarloaf Key, seemed like an insane choice for a man with his problems. But he'd bought the cottage last year, with an eye to spending his vacations here, and it had seemed like a much better place to hole up than his apartment in Tampa. He had been craving solitude, convinced that if he just locked himself away somewhere, he'd be forced to make peace with his demons. If he'd stayed in Tampa, he could have continued to ignore his problems. Or so he had believed.

But truth to tell, the sea had called him the way she always did. Even when he was terrified of her and uncertain whether he could even sail a boat again, he was drawn to her. And the Keys were as close to one with the sea as it was possible to get while still standing on solid ground.

The sea had always been in his blood. As a boy he'd grown up along Tampa Bay, watching the oceangoing vessels come and go. There'd never been a doubt in his mind that he was going to join the navy just as soon as he was old enough.

His dad had owned a gas station, and had never understood his son's urge to go to sea. His mother, not wanting him to be gone so far for so long, had tried to talk him out of it.

But the sea's grip was unbreakable. The day he turned eighteen, Chase Mattingly had joined the U.S. Navy. A year later he had volunteered for the SEALs, a decision he still sometimes wondered about. Not that he'd ever regretted it, but he sometimes wondered what had propelled him, whether it had been some kind of insecurity he'd been trying to overcome, or merely the arrogance of a youthful male. If it had been arrogance, the SEALs had taught him more of it. He knew what he was capable of, and knew his limits were far beyond most people's imaginings.

Which only made his current predicament all the more disturbing. He wasn't accustomed to seeing himself as weak, but lately he'd been embarrassingly so.

Traffic was heavy and sluggish all the way to Tavernier, but then began to lighten. There was a jam on a narrow bridge where a driver had apparently braked hard and the boat he was towing had slipped forward off the trailer and rear-ended the car. Since the bridge was only two lanes, and there was no shoulder, traffic backed up badly. Chase and a couple of other men helped get the boat back on the trailer and secured so the driver could pull the rig out of the way.

The exertion felt good after spending so much time cooped up in the car. By the time he resumed the drive, Chase was in a better frame of mind, able to admire the vistas of the Gulf to the right and the Atlantic to the left. In the late-afternoon light, the water almost looked as if it had been painted in varying shades of green, ranging from olive to light, minty green, to lime, to deep blue-green farther out in the Atlantic. The patchy color always reminded him of camouflage, except that it was much more beautiful, at times almost iridescent.

It had been a while, he realized, since he had last truly noted the beauty of the sea.

Somehow he had to find the key to making peace with himself so he could start enjoying life again, enjoying moments like these. Somehow he had to find a way to get a handle on these nightmares and strange fears so that he could get on with the business of living. And getting to the bottom of what had happened on that boat just before Jeff found it might be the key he was looking for.

Bill Evers's report hadn't said a damn thing useful, and that bothered him. Of course, the legal eagles had already taken their turn at it, and had probably sanitized it considerably. But there was a woodenness to it that troubled Chase considerably. He knew Bill from a dozen dives. Nothing about the man was as flat and dry as that composite report made him sound. There was no way, even in a written report, that he would have been as clinical as that.

Not that he knew Bill all that well personally. They'd

done a dozen or more dives together, and had gotten along well enough, but they weren't close. And since his accident, he hadn't wanted to see Bill at all, or even talk to him, because he hadn't wanted to open that nightmare up. He'd been on strict avoidance of anything that reminded him of what had happened.

But that had changed. Now he had a burning urge to speak with the man, and intended to try to reach him again just as soon as he got home.

And somehow thinking of Bill and his report got him around to thinking about tomorrow, and going around to the marinas to ask questions. He wished to hell Callie would let him do it by himself, but he had a feeling she would probably want to kill him if he didn't take her along. Not that he couldn't understand that. After all, her brother's life was on the line, and there was no way she could be sure he'd ask the right questions if she wasn't with him. But hell. He supposed he could suggest that *she* might get charged with witness tampering, but would she even listen?

Callie was another complication in his already complicated life, he realized. Part of him wanted to move to another county just to get away from her, and part of him just plain couldn't stay away. Well, it was nothing to worry about, he assured himself. Every time he turned around, she was blowing up about something he said. If he'd had to make a bet on it, he would have bet she hated him.

The sun was low in the west when he at last reached Sugarloaf Key. The trip had taken longer than he'd anticipated, and the shadows were working their way out from the thick undergrowth. Remembering the seaweed he'd found on his porch last night, he felt his uneasiness spring to life again. There was something going on that didn't have anything to do with hallucinations. He sure as hell hadn't hallucinated that seaweed.

But he also hadn't hallucinated the fact that there was no one and nothing around his house, and other than the seaweed no sign of anything disturbed. So where the hell had it come from? And when? At this point he couldn't even be certain that it hadn't been there when he'd come out his door. He hadn't looked for it. He'd been too preoccupied looking for threats at eye level.

Hell. Maybe he was just utterly and completely losing his marbles. Maybe he was falling into some weird kind of fugue states and had put the seaweed there himself. He'd heard about crap like that. Maybe he was a hell of a lot further over the edge than he realized.

The thought killed his mood completely.

Turning off the highway, he drove down the narrow paved road that led to Lower Sugarloaf Key, passing houses until finally the road narrowed to a single lane and there was nothing on either side of it except the thick growth that covered this part of the island, a hammock full of tropical hardwoods and thick vegetation. There his driveway turned off, plunging through the dense trees and bushes until it opened up right behind his house.

Golden sunlight slanted across the inlet and splashed against the side of his A-frame. It looked so inviting he found himself thinking of getting into his swim trunks and spending a few minutes paddling around in the water. He hadn't done that since before the accident, and getting into the water again would probably be a big step in the right direction.

Making up his mind, he went inside to change. When he came out wearing only his trunks and carrying a

150

towel, Callie was approaching. He descended the porch steps and waited for her, feeling wary. Every time he saw her, it seemed, she was either getting deeper into trouble or mad at him for his opinions. The sight of her approach didn't exactly fill him with joy.

But it did cause a deeper, more primitive reaction in him. His body didn't seem to care that she was a pain in the butt; all it seemed to notice was that she looked good enough to devour. He had a sudden, very unwelcome image of this woman lying naked on the sheets of his bed and smiling up at him.

This would, he thought, be a very good time to remember an urgent errand elsewhere. But he didn't. Instead he stood glued to the spot and awaited his fate.

"Hi," she said, as she drew near.

"Hi." He wondered what new catastrophe had occurred.

"Going for a swim?"

"Thinking about it." Stupid reply when he was standing there in swim trunks, holding a towel. This woman was killing his brain cells.

"Good evening for it." She gave him a tentative smile. "Look . . . I wanted to apologize for getting mad at you earlier. I'm not usually so . . . quick to anger. This whole thing has really got me on edge."

"That's understandable."

"So, I'm sorry."

"Apology accepted."

She nodded, and her smile widened a little more, causing a curious tightness in his chest. "Thank you. Do you have snorkeling gear?"

"Uh . . . no." He usually got in the water with tanks on his back and a regulator in his mouth or a helmet on his head. It had been years since he'd last snorkeled.

"I have some stuff. Why don't you come over, and I'll

get it for you. This inlet is a great place to snorkel."

He followed her. There was something inevitable about this, he found himself thinking. As inevitable as the waves coming ashore. It was as if the sea, having failed to kill him, was now determined to throw him into the riptide she had made of Callie's life.

Any sane man would have told him these thoughts were pure lunacy. Unless, of course, that man had lived with the sea.

CHAPTER 9

CALLIE GOT THE SNORKELING GEAR OUT OF THE BACK room and brought it out to Chase, who'd insisted on waiting on the veranda.

"Thanks," he said, as she passed him the snorkel and mask. "Where's Jeff?"

"He went to a movie with a friend. It's better than sitting around here wondering if he'll go to jail for the rest of his life."

"A lot better. I went in to Miami today to read the report on the dive to *The Happy Maggie*."

Callie's heart jumped. "Did you find out anything?"

"Only that I was right about the coordinates. Jeff found the *Island Dream* less than a mile from the *Maggie*."

She shivered, feeling suddenly cold despite the warmth of the evening air. "I feel like a goose just walked over my grave."

"Yeah. It had that effect on me earlier." He turned toward the water. "Why don't you join me?"

She thought about it as she watched him walk down to the water's edge. It was late enough in the day that there wasn't much good snorkeling time left, but the water looked so inviting.

And so did Chase. She'd been resolutely ignoring how he looked since she'd first set eyes on him in those swim trunks, but she couldn't ignore it any longer. He had a beautiful, powerful body, tanned from long years in the sun, strong from hard work and lots of swimming. He was dusted with fine golden hairs that caught the late-afternoon light and almost seemed to glow, as if he were carved out of bronze.

She recoiled from the attraction even as she felt it. Mel had taught her the price of being attracted to a man, not only by the way he had wanted her to abandon Jeff, but also by the way he had abandoned her.

That episode had effectively chilled her remaining interest in men. And Chase was just another man, she reminded herself. He'd already made the major mistake of telling her Jeff ought to be taking care of himself—as if he could in these circumstances. Men, she reminded herself, always disappeared when you needed them most, and Chase would be no different. Not if he thought Jeff ought to be handling a murder charge by himself. As soon as the going got tough, Chase would vanish, the way every other man in her life had.

Feeling anger turn her stomach over, she pivoted sharply and went back into the house, intending to start a load of wash. Instead she found herself changing into her blue maillot and getting out another mask and snorkel.

Part of her wondered if she'd lost her mind, but part of her felt drawn to swim in the water as if the sea were sending out a silent siren call she couldn't ignore. Step by step she walked across the porch, along the seawall, and down the steps to a narrow strip of sandy beach.

In the late sunlight, the water was a deep green, the surface nearly as smooth as glass. It was warm, too, and when she put her foot in, she could feel the tickle of the surface tension, but no discernible difference in temperature.

It was easy, so easy to walk in deeper, rinse the mask, put the snorkel on, and give herself up to the sea.

She had been swimming since childhood, but she no longer trusted the sea, so she stayed in the shallows, gliding over the sandy bottom, pausing to check out shells and watching small fish swim. The day was dying, though, and before too long she began to notice the shadows were growing. Rotating, she put her feet down and stood, looking around the inlet.

The sun was low now, so low it almost glided over the top of the water. The breeze had stirred up little wavelets that splintered the golden light, giving the water a dappled appearance.

Chase was only a few feet away, gliding smoothly along facedown. She wondered if his fear of the dark was beginning to trouble him. It was certainly beginning to seem too late in the day to her to be swimming. Turning, she headed for shore.

Before she had taken three steps, Chase rose out of the water beside her. Shoving his snorkel mask back, he flashed her a big smile. "That was great! Thanks for lending me the snorkel."

His smile was irresistible and she had to smile back. "You're welcome." The golden rays of the sun glanced off the jewel in his earlobe, and without thinking, she reached out to touch it with a finger.

For an instant, time seemed to stand still. She stopped breathing, and found herself looking into his stormy gray eyes. Almost, just almost, he seemed to lean into

154

her touch, and his eyelids drooped.

She caught herself and drew her hand back, regretting the loss of contact, even though she knew it was wise. Men could not be trusted. "Does that mean something?"

"What?"

"Your earring."

"Oh. Yeah, it does. SEALs all wear them. It's an old diving tradition to wear a valuable jewel in your ear. The oldtimers figured it was a way to be sure somebody would come after their bodies if they got into trouble."

"Mmm. Gruesome thought."

He shrugged.

"So you were a SEAL?" That, she thought, probably explained some of his arrogance.

"For nearly ten years."

"And the navy let you wear earrings in uniform?"

"Yeah."

"I wouldn't have thought that." She was beginning to feel cold as the air brushed over her wet skin, so she walked up closer to the shore, to where the water was shallow enough that she could sit in it. It just covered her breasts, and kept her warm. Chase came to sit beside her.

"It'll be dark soon," she remarked.

"Mmm."

"If you want to go home, feel free."

"No, I don't think so. I think I'm going to stick it out for a while."

"Desensitization?"

"Maybe. I don't know. I just know I'm getting damn tired of being trapped by fear."

"I can understand that." She was also impressed that he was so frank about his fear. In her experience, men tended to skirt around such things, at least when talking to women. She wondered if it was part of his arrogance or just that he was honest. Either one could cause him to say things most people wouldn't.

The water was moving gently, lifting Callie just a little, then letting her settle onto the sand again. It was soothing, almost like being rocked in a cradle.

Chase spoke. "Is Callie short for something?"

"Calypso."

He looked at her. "I like that."

"So did my dad. He never called me Callie. And nobody else ever called me Calypso."

"Which do you prefer?"

"I'm used to Callie. I'm not sure I'd answer to anything else."

"What happened to your folks? I know you said the sea took your dad . . ."

"He was washed overboard during a squall. I was standing out there on the point waiting for him. They were two days late, and I knew something was wrong, but I was so wrapped up in Jeff dropping out of school and telling Dad about it that . . . well, I had myself convinced that Dad had just decided to stay out a little longer because the fishing was good. Finally, I saw the boat coming, and I was so impatient to tell him about Jeff . . ."

She trailed off and drew a deep breath. "That was four years ago. I still miss him."

"I know. I still miss my dad, too, and it's been ten years. He had a heart attack."

"I'm sorry."

"That's life. Sooner or later, we lose the people we love."

It was on the tip of her tongue to tell him that was a very bitter outlook, but the words died stillborn because the truth was, that was how she looked at life, too. Except that when she heard someone else say it out loud, it sounded bitter, cynical, and very unpleasant and still very true.

"What about your mom?" he asked.

"She died when I was fourteen. I was out with some friends, and when I came in, she was lying in a pool of blood on the kitchen floor. Tubal pregnancy." Picking up handfuls of water, she ladled it over her shoulders, enjoying its comparative warmth. "The doctors said it happened fast, and there was next to no chance of saving her, even if anyone had been with her when it happened. But for a long time I blamed my dad for not being there. He was at sea."

"And he went back to sea?"

"Of course. He had to feed us." She raked her wet hair back from her face, determined to leave the subject there. But from some well deep inside where she kept them buried, the words burst forth on a tide of long-buried pain.

"I was fourteen and became a full-time mother to a child of six. I resented the hell out of that. I couldn't spend time with my friends anymore, I couldn't date. I couldn't do anything because I had to look after Jeff. And when Dad came home, I pretty much had to keep on doing it, along with all the cooking and cleaning because he was always busy getting ready for the next fishing trip, working on the boat, mending the nets . . ." She unleashed a long breath and closed her eyes, trying to silence herself. He didn't want to hear all this, and she sounded like such a whiner. Never mind that the memories still tightened her chest until she could hardly breathe. "Well, you do what you have to."

"Sure. That doesn't mean you have to like it."

The water lifted her a little higher this time, warning her that the tide was coming in. The inlet was in twilight now, the last of the sun's golden rays gone. Overhead, the subtropical sky was beginning to blush a fiery red.

"Time to get out of the water," she said briskly. "It's getting dark, and I'm getting cold."

She felt him follow her, but refused to look back. When, she wondered, was the last time she had dumped on somebody like that? Had she ever told anyone about how she felt about having to take responsibility for Jeff? No, she'd never told a soul because she was ashamed of the feelings. Not even Mel, whom she had once honestly believed she loved.

She turned to look at Chase as he reached her side. "You're easy to talk to."

"Maybe that's because I listen."

That was true, she realized. He might infuriate her with his arrogant comments on the things she and Jeff chose to do, but he always heard everything she said. That was an unusual trait in anyone.

He threw his towel over his shoulder, and helped her drape hers around herself. "So, you've been raising Jeff for the last . . . fourteen years, right?"

"Basically, yes."

"You never had a chance to be young."

His bald statement of something she felt deep in her heart suddenly tightened her throat until it ached, and made her eyes prickle with tears. It was true. Before she'd left childhood, she'd been turned into an adult. A mom.

"Self-pity," she said finally, "is a loathsome thing."

"True, but what you're feeling isn't self-pity, Callie. It's *hurt*. And you're entitled to that."

Which only made her throat tighten more, until she

158

couldn't even speak. He astonished her by putting his arm around her shoulder, and she wondered if the contact comforted him as much as it comforted her. It was getting dark after all, and while she was being assaulted by old sorrows, he was probably being assaulted by his fears. Justifiable fears.

The sky was blazing with red and pink as they climbed onto the veranda. When she invited Chase in, he accepted. In the chilly air-conditioning of the house, however, her wet swimsuit felt like ice, and his couldn't feel any better.

"Let me get you a blanket or something," she said. "You're going to freeze. Then I'll make us something hot to drink."

She dug an old army blanket out of the linen cupboard and gave it to him. Then she went to her bedroom to change. Peeling off the wet maillot was a relief, and she toweled herself briskly. She needed a shower but that would have to wait. She felt uneasy at the idea of bathing with a strange man in the house. About the only way to get really cold in the Florida Keys, she thought, was to go swimming, then step into air-conditioning. Right now she felt so cold that she half expected to see snowflakes coming out of the air ducts.

She pulled on a pair of jeans and a sweatshirt and headed for the kitchen to make hot chocolate. Chase was already there, standing on his towel with the blanket wrapped around him. "I'm dripping," he said. "I probably ought to go home before I ruin something."

But she didn't want him to go. The thought of sitting here alone as night gathered, waiting for Jeff to come back at some distant hour, didn't seem at all attractive.

"Maybe something of my father's would fit you," she offered impulsively. "I kept a few of his things." A few

159

that she couldn't bear to part with. He'd always worn white at home when he wasn't working, because it was cooler, and she'd saved a pair of his white slacks and one of his loose white shirts. It only took her a minute to get them out of the clothing bag where she'd stored them, and she offered them to Chase.

He took them, but looked at her. "You're sure you don't mind?"

"Really, it's okay. It was silly to hang on to them anyway. And help yourself to the shower."

They fit well enough. Chase was an inch or so taller, but the pants had been too long for her dad anyway, and he'd always rolled the cuffs up.

"Much better," he said when he emerged from the bathroom freshly showered. "I'm no longer in danger of becoming an icicle."

She caught her breath and could hardly look away. He had been handsome in swim trunks, but dressed all in tropical white he awakened some long-forgotten romantic image in her heart, especially with that piratical earring. She quickly turned her attention to the cocoa she was making. "I hope you like hot chocolate."

"Sounds good."

He'd rolled up his swimsuit in his towel, and he set it on the end of the counter. "What can I do?"

"Not a thing. This is the instant variety."

The teakettle finally sang out, and she poured boiling water into two mugs, over the cocoa mix. "Marshmallows?"

"Really?" He laughed. "I haven't had a marshmallow in my cocoa since I was a kid."

She pulled out a bag of them from the cupboard. "Jeff loves them. Sometimes when we cook over the grill, he still roasts a couple for himself."

"Did you ever do that? Sit around a campfire and roast hot dogs and marshmallows?"

She put the cups on the table and they sat facing one another. "Sure. Dad used to build a fire on the beach from time to time. He said it was a good way to get rid of the brush he cleaned up from around the house, but we always had a great time cooking over it, toasting marshmallows, singing songs. And he always, *always* told us the story of the monkey's paw."

He smiled. "And the man with the golden leg."

"Of course! And no matter how many times I heard them, I always jumped and screamed."

"We used to go camping, and my dad always built fires. He claimed the smoke kept the mosquitoes away, but I think he just enjoyed the fire."

"I know my dad did. Heck, we all did."

They exchanged smiles of understanding, and for the first time around Chase, Callie felt herself relax fully. Maybe he wasn't such a bear after all, she thought. Maybe he just had an unfortunately blunt manner at times.

"Why don't we go into Key West for dinner?" he suggested suddenly. "Or to that seafood place on Stock Island?"

She found herself hesitating, and only partly because of her own fears of involvement with men. It was getting darker by the second out there, and she wondered how he was going to handle it. But maybe he could handle it better when he wasn't alone? Maybe this was an opportunity to try to desensitize himself?

A counselor as much by nature as by education, she couldn't say no to that possibility. She understood being a prisoner of fear, and if she could help him even a little, there was no way on earth she could refuse.

161

"Sure," she said. "Just let me change into something cool." Because no matter how cold she felt right now, it was warm and humid outside.

She pulled on white shorts and a bright blue polo shirt, ran a brush through her drying hair, and added a dab of lipstick.

"I need to get some shoes," he said, as she rejoined him. "Why don't we walk around the inlet to my place, and I'll drive."

"Sure."

She left a note for Jeff on the refrigerator and stepped out into the warm evening air. It felt good, humid though it was, after the chill she'd gotten from swimming. The tide had swallowed up most of beach, and was lapping at the seawall now. They walked on the narrow path between buttonwoods and mangroves, guided by starlight. The red mangroves appeared eerie in the dark, with their long roots that looked like thin bowlegs rising out of the water. Since childhood, Callie had fancied that they looked as if they were walking out of the sea.

If the dark was making Chase nervous, he didn't show it until they neared his house. Until then his strides had been long and purposeful, but now they shortened and became quieter. As if he were trying to creep up on something. Callie watched him with concern, wondering if his fears would overwhelm him.

But they didn't. They reached his house and climbed the steps to his porch. Chase walked to the door to unlock it, and Callie stepped to the side to stay out of the way. As she did so, she stepped on something soft and slippery, and a startled sound escaped her.

Chase whirled around. "What's wrong?" His voice was tight with suppressed tension.

"I stepped on something . . ."

"Let me flip on the light."

He finished unlocking the door and threw it open, reaching inside for the porch light. When it came on, they both blinked. Then Chase swore.

"It's just turtlegrass," Callie said, stepping away from it. The same stuff that washed up along the shore in long ridges, looking as if someone had just mowed a lawn. This was green and glistening, still fresh.

"Yeah," Chase said tautly, "but how the hell did it get there?"

She hadn't thought about that, but she did now, looking down at the trail of turtlegrass. It led from the middle of the porch down to the seawall, where it apparently ended.

"Somebody put it there," she said finally. "There's no other explanation."

"Yeah," he said, "but who? And why?"

Slowly she looked up at him, a very unpleasant thought occurring to her. "Maybe you've got good reason to fear the dark."

"What do you mean?"

"Maybe somebody's out to get you."

He almost snorted. "This is a juvenile trick, Callie. If somebody wants to get me, all they need is a gun."

"Unless they want to prey on you until you go crazy."

He didn't answer that. A few minutes later they were driving toward Key West, the seaweed lying unmentioned between them. Callie wondered if Chase had dismissed it completely, or if he was just keeping his thoughts to himself. She didn't like the idea that someone was actively trying to disturb or frighten Chase, nor could she believe it wasn't making him uneasy, given his fear of the dark. Denial. This had to be some kind of denial on his part. And there was nothing she could do about that without being obnoxious.

"Let's go to Billie's," she suggested. "Unless you don't want to drive that far."

He glanced over to her. "It's only a few miles farther than the place I mentioned. Besides, it would be fun to walk down Duval Street. I haven't done that in years."

"Why so long?"

"I've been busy. I only bought the house a year ago, and this is the first time I've spent more than a day here. You know how that goes. How much time off do you take to play tourist?"

"Not much," she admitted. If she had her way, she'd move somewhere as far as possible from the sea, but there was Jeff, there was the house, and there was her job. She couldn't justify it.

Parking was terrible in Key West, even though tourist season was over. They did manage to find a county resident's spot available about three blocks from Duval and from there walked to Billie's. It was a lovely evening with a balmy breeze blowing. People walked the lighted streets everywhere, and the shadows remained at bay in the deep tropical foliage that surrounded many of the old homes.

"I've always loved Old Town," Callie remarked, feeling reluctant to admit that there was anything about the Florida Keys that she actually liked. Awareness of her own contradictory reactions made her feel silly. She *did* love Old Town. And until she had lost her father at sea, she had even loved living in a tropical climate surrounded by dropouts from mainstream society.

She hoped Key West could always remain this way, but doubted it. More homes were being built every day in the Keys, and they weren't all being sold to

164

fishermen, musicians, writers, and artists. The conservative mainstream was gradually moving in, and that was bound to impact the lifestyle.

But she could forget all that here in Old Town. Here things moved slowly. People moved slowly. Everyone was out to have a good time, wandering in and out of shops after the sunset celebration at the dock. Tourists and locals commingled up and down the streets and in the bars and restaurants. Mopeds skittered by in huge numbers, as did bicycles. Most people who lived here found it was easier to walk or bike than to try to drive on the west end of the island, and over the last few years, the number of mopeds had grown phenomenally because they could weave through the narrow streets more easily, and be parked almost anywhere.

There were few street signs. Most were marked by painting on the corner lampposts. There were few stop signs, either, and most people cheerfully navigated by yielding to other cars and pedestrians. It was one of the few places in the world where a car or a moped would actually halt without a stop sign to let pedestrians cross the street.

And every time she came here, Callie forgot everything she hated about life and got caught up in the wonderful feeling of relaxed energy.

They were seated immediately at Billie's. Like many businesses here, the restaurant kept the doors wide-open to the streets while air-conditioning blasted inside, inviting passersby to step into the coolness. Surrounded by windows, they were able to watch the people coming and going from Mallory Square.

Chase ordered a beer, she ordered a margarita, and they both ordered the captain's platter.

"You know," Chase remarked, "Jimmy Buffett could

walk these streets and nobody would even notice."

"He probably does. He has a house here."

"I know. I just mean there are dozens of people who look just like him."

She laughed; he was right. Shorts and ball caps and topsiders were nearly a uniform. "Have you been to his store?"

Chase shook his head.

"I hear there are enough Jimmy Buffett T-shirts and ball caps to keep any Parrothead happy."

It was his turn to laugh. "Maybe we should check it out after dinner. I'm sorry we missed the sunset party."

Callie shook her head. "I'm not. We've got as good a view at home, and we don't have to put up with the crap."

"What crap?"

"The sidewalk performers. Oh, some of them are really good. There's one musician I really like. But some of them—well, their huckstering is offensive. I happened to stand next to one of them when he wasn't performing, and trust me, if the tourists heard what he thought of them, they'd probably shove him into the water rather than put money in his duffel bag. And I've watched a couple of them get downright nasty when they didn't collect enough money to suit them."

His gray eyes crinkled at the corners as he smiled. "So you're down on the sunset celebration?"

She shrugged one shoulder. "Not really. Just at some of the attitudes. If you want to be a sidewalk performer, that's your choice. It doesn't give you a right to demand that everyone pay you as they walk by."

"So what's different about the one musician?"

"He plays requests and never asks for a dime. Never. And he's so nice to everyone. Some of the others could take lessons from him. Of course, to be fair, there are others who are pleasant, too."

"You're the first person I ever heard complain about the sunset celebration."

"Probably because the last time I went was with my ex-boyfriend." The words were out before she even knew they were coming, and once they emerged she wished she could snatch them back. It suddenly seemed as if there were a cone of silence over their table, blocking out the sounds of the diners around them. God, she didn't want to go there.

"I take it the experience wasn't pleasant," he said slowly, as if feeling his way with care.

"Not very." She looked away, staring out the window at the colorful parade of tourists and locals. Mel had all but ruined the Key West experience for her, she realized. She hadn't come back to Old Town in the four years since.

"What happened?" he asked.

His tone was gentle. It wasn't just a casual or curious question; she could tell by the way he asked. And that was probably what brought it all spilling out.

"He'd been complaining for weeks about my having to take charge of Jeff. I mean, he was all sympathetic in the weeks right after the funeral, but then he started pushing me to find somewhere else for Jeff to stay, someone else to look after him. I refused." She shook her head and looked down at the table, noting the British coin that was embedded in the acrylic layered over the wood. It gave her something to focus on, and she stared intently at it, trying to control her breathing, hoping the pressure in her chest would ease.

"I'll be the first to admit I wasn't thrilled with the responsibility," she continued. "But Jeff is my baby

167

brother. I practically raised him myself. I felt as if Mel was telling me to give my child up for adoption."

"I can understand that."

"We fought about it." She shrugged a shoulder as if it didn't matter.

"And that's when you broke up?"

"Pretty much. It was an ugly scene. We were here for the evening, and we stopped in one of the bars on Duval. He drank too much. I guess he was feeling pretty rotten that night, because he didn't usually drink heavily. But he had enough that night that he didn't really care what he said."

"It must have been bad." He reached out and covered her hand with his.

Instinctively, she turned hers over and clasped his fingers. God, it felt so good to have someone hold her hand like this, to feel that comforting contact. His grip was strong, reassuring, and she found herself furtively aware of the warmth of his skin. She had the worst urge to rub her palm against his, but resisted. Instead she forced herself to remember what had happened with Mel because it reminded her of why she wasn't going to give in to the mixture of almost irresistible feelings Chase awoke in her. Feelings of yearning, feelings of desire. Too many dangerously attractive feelings for a woman who was determined to remain alone.

She spoke, making herself focus on Mel. "Did you ever see *Virginia Woolf*?"

"Yeah."

"Well, it was like that. Uglier and uglier. Louder and louder. The dangerous thing about letting someone get too close is that they know what will really hurt you. Mel knew all my buttons, and he pushed every damn one of them. By the time he was done I felt raw to my

168

soul."

"I'm sorry." His hand squeezed hers. "Nobody should be able to do that."

"But they can. If you let them get too close, they can." Even as she spoke, she knew she was being childish. Wasn't this the very thing she warned her clients about, the making of rules based on one bad experience, or one bad person? "Of course," she added, "that's the risk you have to take to let anyone into your life."

"True."

"Anyway it was ugly. He said horrible things about Jeff—and I don't mind telling you, I get a motherly reaction to that. I seem to remember wanting to go for his jugular in Jeff's defense."

"Understandable."

"Well, I said some pretty unforgivable things myself. That thing about knowing which buttons to push? It's a two-way street."

There was a sudden twinkle in his eyes, and she was amazed to feel herself responding to it, as if the ugliness she was remembering was so long past it wasn't worth wasting anything but amusement on.

"Seeing as how you're a psychologist," he said, "I imagine you were better at pushing his buttons than he was at pushing yours."

She almost laughed, but was too embarrassed to let it out.

He was right. "Let's just say we were both pretty bruised and bloody by the time we got thrown out of the bar."

"Some fight, huh?"

"Verbally, yes. I guess I gave tit for tat. Which I'm not proud of. Anyway, that was the end. Right there and

169

then."

"Probably for the best."

"Oh, it was. I suppose I could have been more understanding about his problems with Jeff, but after all the counseling I'd done, my warning bells were clanging big-time."

"How so?"

"If a man wants to cut you off from family and friends, he's trouble. Maybe I was overreacting a little—I mean, his main problem seemed to be Jeff—but my entire family *is* Jeff."

He nodded. "You were right. He was wrong. Period."

The waiter appeared with their dinners: conch fritters, stuffed crab, fried shrimp, fried scallops, and the fingers of the fish of the day, mahimahi. Delicious aromas rose from the plate, and Callie felt her appetite kick in for the first time since early that morning. The only downside was the way she felt when Chase drew back his hand. His touch had been wonderfully comforting.

It was time, she decided, to change the subject. "So you drove all the way to Miami to read the diver's report? Didn't someone give you the details already? I'd think that would be the first thing you wanted to know after your accident."

"It was. And they gave me the details. Mainly, I wanted to read the report in Bill's words to see if it jogged my memory at all. Instead, all I got was the sanitized final report. My friend at Maritime told me I'd have to get a lawyer to get the original report out of the legal office because they're afraid I'm going to sue them."

He shook his head. "With rare exceptions, any accident on a dive is the diver's fault. If they'd found something in my air tanks instead of the proper mixture, that would have been one thing. And I wouldn't have sued the company anyway, I'd have gone after the guy who filled my tanks. What else could the insurance company be responsible for? *My* mistake, whatever it was?"

She liked his attitude. "So you're really sure *you* did something wrong?"

"It had to have been me. I just wish I could figure out what I did. Diving was something I was *always* very careful about. It's not a place to take chances or cut corners, and especially not when you're going that deep."

She nodded, watching as he speared a scallop with his fork. "That undermines your confidence, doesn't it?"

He looked at her, a faint smile lifting the corners of his mouth. "Analyzing me?"

"No, just wondering. It would undermine my confidence."

"Of course it does. So does the feeling that there's something in the darkness just waiting to pounce on me. That's nothing but a nightmare, but I can't convince myself of that."

She hesitated. "Well . . . there's the turtlegrass on your porch."

He shook his head. "Like I said, that's juvenile. Maybe one of the kids up the road did it."

"I don't know if I could ignore it that easily if it were on my porch." No, she'd probably feel really uncomfortable, wondering who wanted to bother her and why.

"I didn't say I was going to ignore it. I just don't think it adds up to a real threat." What he didn't tell her was the niggling doubt he'd started having last night that maybe he'd done it himself in some kind of fugue

171

or split-personality thing. That worried him far more than the possibility that some kid up the road was having fun at his expense.

He couldn't imagine why anyone would do such a thing, but there was no explaining kids. Unless . . . He suddenly wondered if the seaweed was directed at Jeff and had just wound up on his porch by mistake. With all the news coverage of Jeff being arrested for the murders of a couple of well-liked charter-boat operators, it was entirely possible someone was trying to scare him.

Maybe some jerk was trying to create the impression of a dead man coming up from the water, to scare Jeff and Callie.

At the thought, his stomach twisted, and anger began to burn in him. He could blow it off if someone was trying to mess with him, but if they were trying to hurt Callie and Jeff, there was going to be hell to pay.

CHAPTER 10

AFTER DINNER, THEY WALKED ALONG DUVAL STREET, peeking into shops. When Callie's hand brushed Chase's, he thought, What the hell, and clasped it. She didn't pull away. Instead, her fingers curled around his.

They were, he thought, like flotsam being tossed in the waves of an uncertain sea, and for the moment they were clinging to one another, until the next wave came along and sent them on a new course. It was just nice, for now, to have the contact with another soul.

But the thoughts he'd been determined to avoid seemed to be equally determined to come to mind as they walked around Old Town, listening to music pouring out of the open doors of bars and clubs, and the cacophony of voices, accents, and languages in the swirling crowds.

He had enough problems of his own, he told himself. Lest he forget, his back and hip stabbed him regularly with fiery pain, and once he avoided turning down a street because it looked too dark. Still, he found himself worrying about Callie and Jeff.

They had no one but each other, and. both of them desperately needed someone to lean on right now. Jeff seemed to be leaning on Callie, but she had no one to turn to. Her role as mother to Jeff made it all but impossible to lean on him—and Chase wasn't sure Jeff could have handled it anyway. Not because he thought the boy was particularly weak—although he was typically heedless for his age—but because Jeff was facing a situation so overwhelming that it was unlikely he had anything to offer anyone else right now.

Sometimes, Chase thought, problems could be sufficiently overwhelming to justify utter selfishness, and facing a murder charge certainly fell into that category.

By comparison, his own problems were piddling. What did he have to worry about, after all, except some pain, some disappointment, and an irrational fear of the dark?

Pain he could live with. Day by day he was coming to terms with a future that involved hurting every minute of every day. His fear of the dark—well, as bad as it sometimes was, he could learn to live with that, too.

He had a sudden memory of himself, only a few days ago, sitting at the table with the Beretta and thinking about suicide, and he felt such a wave of self-revulsion that he almost pulled his hand away from Callie's, for fear of sullying her.

Christ, what a weakling he'd become! He hated self-pity, and lately he seemed to be drowning in it. He needed to get his head out of his fucking ass.

Sitting around in magnificent isolation with a pistol and a bottle of whiskey might make a great artistic image for a three-minute song, but as a way of life it sucked, and it was inexcusable. Shame over his own behavior made him want to find a hole to crawl into.

Except holes were dark. The unexpected humorous twist of his own thoughts made him laugh out loud. Callie looked up at him questioningly.

"Don't mind me," he said. "I just realized I'm a grade-A jerk."

"Why?"

"Nothing important. A breath of fresh air just blew through my head. About damn time. Want to stop and get a drink somewhere?"

"Sure."

They entered a place that was open onto the street, little more than wide double doors fronting a long curved bar. Callie ordered iced tea, and Chase asked for club soda with a twist of lime. Reggae was playing over the speakers, and everyone was talking loudly and laughing.

Chase spoke, and Callie had to lean over to hear him.

"We could plan a crime here, and nobody would hear us," he said.

She laughed. "I was thinking practically the same thing." But the reggae beat was infectious and she found her foot tapping in time. Cold air blasted downward from the air conditioners, but the crowd was so dense it battered uselessly on the tops of their heads.

Somebody bumped into Callie's back, shoving her hard up against Chase. His arm came out immediately to

174

steady her, holding her close to him.

Time stood still. Callie had always hated that cliche, but that's exactly what she felt as her entire length was pressed to Chase's hard muscularity. She had never thought of herself as a carnal person, but in that instant she discovered she could be weakened by desire.

She couldn't move, she couldn't breathe. Everything else in the world faded away until all she was aware of was the man who held her and an almost unbearable yearning for him to hold her even closer. A longing unlike any she had ever felt before filled her, leaving her feeling heavy, soft, weak, and needy. God, she had never ached like this before!

The suspense was nearly as unbearable as the need, filling her with fear that he would let go of her and longing to be held closer still. The tension reached every cell in her body, imprisoning her in the moment.

Slowly, slowly, she tilted her head until she looked up at him, and the heat and awareness she saw in his gaze suddenly filled her with panic. *No*!

The word was like a thunderclap in her head, and she stepped swiftly back, not caring that she bumped hard into someone else.

"Are you okay?" Chase asked swiftly. Was it her imagination, or did his voice sound thick?

"I'm . . . I'm claustrophobic."

"Then let's get out of here." He used his body like the prow of a ship, cutting a path for her through the waves of the crowd. Moments later they were out on the street again, where the balmy night air was far easier to breathe.

He reached for her hand, but she yanked it back. It was almost as if her skin felt raw, and she couldn't bear a touch right now.

"It was close in there," he said, not commenting on how she had pulled back from him.

"It was awful." A lie, but convenient. She despised herself for not being able just to be honest about it, to tell him that something was wrong with her, and that if he was at all interested in her, he'd better just run now, because she absolutely panicked when he got that close.

But she was surprised by the force of her own reaction to the closeness, and as they wandered along Duval Street, she found herself pondering it. It was, she thought, an overreaction to something that happened between men and women all the time. It wasn't as if he had threatened her in some way.

But she *had* felt threatened, and for the first time she found herself considering the possibility that she had a hangup about men, something that went far beyond simple reluctance to get involved again because she had had a relationship fail badly.

It was, she realized, something deeper. An unwillingness to trust anyone to come that close. As if some kind of betrayal were the inevitable outcome of caring.

The thought jolted her. Maybe she had been spending too much time trying to sort out other people's problems, and had been too busy to realize just how mixed up her own head was getting. Because something in her was certainly mixed up.

And now she had the worst urge to get home, to find a quiet corner where she could be alone to think about just where she was messed up.

"It's almost midnight," she said. "I need to get home."

They found their way back to the car, and drove the twenty-five miles home in silence.

Jeff was waiting for them when they pulled into the Carlsons' driveway. He stood on the edge of the veranda and waved, looking entirely too happy for Callie's peace of mind.

"You don't have to get out," she said swiftly to Chase. "Thanks for a great evening."

His face was shadowed, but she could tell he was looking at her. She felt a pang when she realized she was sending him back to his empty house and the darkness that troubled him so much. She hesitated, then said, "Unless you'd like to come in?"

He didn't move, and for a moment he didn't speak. "Which would *you* prefer?" he asked finally.

"I . . . " She trailed off, uncertain herself.

"Did I do something wrong?" he asked.

"No. *Really*."

"Then why have I been getting the deep freeze ever since we stopped for a drink?"

"Look, I don't want to get into this now. It's late."

"I have a feeling that with you it's always too late."

"That's not fair." And she was getting angrier than she ought to because she was on the defensive. Being a psychologist had disadvantages, she thought sourly, the primary one being that she knew exactly what games she was playing. "Look, I'm sorry. I'm . . . having a problem with myself. It really doesn't have anything at all to do with you."

She wished she could read his face, but it was too dark. Jeff was coming down from the veranda toward them, and time for private conversation was drawing to a close.

"Come in," she said, almost desperately, realizing that she needed to make amends for a lot of reasons. "Come in for a few minutes. We need to discuss what

177

we're going to do tomorrow anyway."

Silence. Then, "All right."

They climbed out of the car. Jeff had turned the porch lights on, and puddles of golden light held the night at bay. Callie was surprised to realize she was noting such things out of concern for Chase. Never before had she paid any mind to the darkness, but tonight she did. Glancing up at him, she searched his face for signs of strain or tension, but saw nothing.

"Hey, sis. Hey, Chase." Jeff stood grinning at them, his hands in the pockets of his shorts. He lifted onto his toes, then rolled back onto his heels.

"I guess you had a good time tonight," Callie said, returning his smile.

"Oh, yeah. I met a girl."

Callie's heart plummeted as fast as an elevator with a broken cable. "A girl?"

"She's really neat, Callie." Jeff was simply beaming.

"Great." Her enthusiasm was weak, but her brother didn't seem to notice as they climbed the porch steps and went indoors.

"I knew her in high school," Jeff said, as they gathered at the kitchen table. "Her family moved up to Tavernier, but she came back here last month to take a job."

"Really." Callie looked at Chase, wondering if he felt this was as potentially bad as she did. Then she wondered why it should even matter what he thought. "So she knows who you are?"

"Sure." Jeff looked at her, his brow creasing. "Didn't I just say so?"

"That's right. You did." Callie felt the limpness of her own smile. She didn't want to do this, but she couldn't stand by and watch a disaster in the making. "Does she

178

know about . . ."

"About the murder charges? Yeah, she does. And she doesn't care. When I told her I didn't do it, she believed me."

Worse and worse, Callie thought, her stomach sinking to join her heart. But Jeff was giving her a wounded look and she didn't want to say any more. There was a limit to what she could do to protect him, much as she hated to admit it. "Neat," she said.

But the smile was gone from Jeff's face. "I thought you'd be happy for me," he said. He rose from his chair and walked out of the house.

"Damn it, damn it, damn it," Callie said tightly when she heard the front door slam behind him. "Damn it, I always say the wrong thing."

"Maybe you try to micromanage," Chase said. "Maybe you just need to let him take his knocks."

This time she didn't flare at him. "Am I crazy?"

"About what?"

"About this girl. What kind of girl wants to date a guy who's been charged with two murders?"

He nodded. "I agree, it doesn't sound good. But you're not going to convince Jeff of that. She said she believes he's innocent. He needs that desperately, Callie. And maybe, just maybe, this girl is naive and nice. Maybe it's not that she's just scum who doesn't care about these things."

"Maybe." She sighed. "Maybe. You're right. But how can I get enthusiastic? Even if she *is* a perfectly nice girl, this is hardly the time for him to get involved."

"This is exactly the time. He *needs* something hopeful, Callie. He needs someone besides the two of us to believe in him. He's growing up hard and fast right now, and he needs the support. It'll also do him some

179

good to have somebody else to worry about."

"You're right." She gave a sad laugh. "I'm the psychologist, but you see it all so much more clearly. I'm falling down on the job here."

"The thing is," he said kindly, "this *isn't* your job. This is your life. It's easy for *me* to be objective.

"Right again." She sighed and looked toward the front of the house. "I guess I should go find him."

He shook his head. "He'll figure out that you're just afraid he'll get hurt. But let him figure it out himself, Callie."

"Are you trying to tell me I'm smothering him?"

A crooked smile appeared on his face. "I'm saying you probably don't need to worry nearly as much as you do."

"You're probably right. I'm thirsty. Would you like something?"

"Ice water, thanks."

She got two large glasses of ice water and rejoined him at the table. "I'm sorry about tonight," she said. "I didn't mean to give you the freeze."

"No problem. I overreacted."

Reflecting on how silent she'd been on the way home, she wasn't sure he had, but she was willing to let it go for now, for the sake of peace. "Apparently," she said, "we press each other's buttons a lot."

His smile broadened. "Apparently. No big deal." He took a long drink of his ice water. "And I'd better be heading home now. I want to get an early start in the morning."

"How early?"

"Early enough to talk to some of the boat owners at the marinas before they set out for the day. I'll pick you up at . . . oh, five-thirty? That ought to be early enough."

She walked with him out onto the porch. Jeff had turned off the porch lights on his way out, and Callie was relieved to feel the darkness close around her, as if it could conceal her failings from Chase. But he couldn't possibly feel the same, given his fear of the night, and she felt guilty for the comfort she was taking from something that disturbed him.

But if he was disturbed, he didn't show it. He turned to face her, his face a pale blur in the starshine. "I had fun this evening," he said. "It did me good to get out at night. Thanks."

"Sure." But even as the humidity wrapped around her, dampening her skin, the warmth of the tropical night seemed to creep into her every cell. That heavy yearning was awakening in her again, that magic that Chase's mere presence seemed to summon. Everything else, all her worries, seemed to fade into distant background noise as a deep, silent need filled her. "I'm sorry I was so flaky," she said again, finding it hard to draw enough breath for speech.

"No problem. Really." But he didn't move. The night coccooned them, and the sea sang a soft love song to rhythms as old as time. And to Callie, it suddenly seemed blindingly obvious that the best way to overcome a fear was to face it.

So she faced it. It was as good a rationale as any for making herself step closer to Chase. It was as good a reason as any to reach out and take his hand, to feel his warm skin against hers. It was as good an explanation as any for why she was giving in to a magnetism she had been determined to fight.

Then she stopped worrying about reasons. Because whether she liked Chase Mattingly or not, whether she had hangups and neuroses or not, all that mattered right now was the siren song in her blood, and it was calling her to the man who looked like a buccaneer.

With a gentle tug of his hand, he drew her against him, until they met breast to chest and thigh to thigh. The whisper of the waves nearby seemed to grow until it was a rushing sound in Callie's ears. Fear and hunger filled her until she was helpless to move.

Then Chase kissed her. Some part of her realized he had meant it to be a gentle, friendly gesture, but it didn't stay that way for long. She never knew who moved first, but suddenly she was wrapped around him and he around her, their arms straining as if they could meld by sheer pressure of will, their mouths hungry, almost hurtful as they sought to drink.

This was need at its most elemental, and never in her life had Callie felt anything like it. It swept past her defenses, demolishing them as if they were made of air, and conquered every hesitation and resistance almost before she was aware of them.

Her body came to pounding, throbbing life, telling her that nothing else whatever mattered. And she believed it. Believed for these few, insane moments that if she could just have this man everything would be all right.

But then Chase released her, stepping back into the night. He was breathing heavily—or maybe it was her—and the sound seemed to keep time with the heartbeat of the waves.

"Good night," he said huskily, and went to get into his car. She watched him drive away, feeling raw and shaken to her very core by the violence of the feelings that had consumed her but had been left unconsummated. She felt bereft.

Once again, said a bitter little voice in her brain, a man had walked away when she had most needed him. It always happened that way.

Then she told herself not to be ridiculous. Chase had done what was best for both of them. Firmly, she closed her mind to the episode. She didn't want to think about it at all. Thinking would only make it hurt worse.

Across the inlet, a light shone in the window of his house. She wondered how it must be for him to get home after dark alone, especially with his fear.

Then she went back inside and got ready for bed. Everything, she decided, could just damn well wait for tomorrow.

Coming home alone in the dark was a bitch. Just as simple as that. All evening long he'd been fighting his awareness of shadows in the dark places along the streets in Key West, along the road as they drove, and now he was pulling into his own backyard and noticing how the shadows pressed inward, as if they wanted to swallow the car and its headlight beams.

God, he had to beat this thing. It was ruining his life.

The seaweed was still on his porch, he realized. He wondered if he would find more. And if he did, it meant he hadn't put it there himself, because he knew exactly where he'd been since he had discovered it.

That was a hopeful thing, he decided. *Someone* had to have put it there. It didn't just crawl up out of the water by itself. And if it wasn't him, it meant he wasn't crazy. At least not *that* crazy.

Suddenly buoyed, he switched off the ignition and lights, and climbed out of the car. Around him the night breathed. Something stirred in the brush to his right.

He was being watched. He felt the gaze of someone

or something boring into the base of his skull. Animals, he told himself. Just some animal.

But it didn't feel that way. Trees rustled in the breeze, and the forest seemed to come alive. A twig snapped somewhere. Something was out there.

With his scalp crawling, he walked around his house to the door. The breeze gusted suddenly, and he could taste a storm on the air as the trees swayed and leaves whispered.

He climbed the porch steps, fighting a powerful urge to look over his shoulder. The only way he could get over this, he told himself, was to face the night again and again until he could fear it no longer.

At the top of the steps, he looked over to see if there was more seaweed. There wasn't. In fact, there was no seaweed at all.

Something, or someone, had carried it away. And that made him suddenly certain something or someone was watching him.

A cold chill ran down his spine, and he moved swiftly, unlocking his door and hurrying inside. When he slammed the door behind himself, he locked it, holding the demons outside at bay.

There was one lamp burning, but it wasn't enough. Reaching out, he flipped the switch that turned on the rest of the lights, driving the shadows back into the darkest corners. Cold sweat dampened his forehead, and his heart was racing.

Christ, who moved the seaweed? he wondered. The things he feared wouldn't have done that. Hell, the things he feared didn't even exist. He could see a prankster putting the seaweed out there, but coming back to clean it up?

Had it.even been there at all? For an instant he felt

reality slip as he wondered if he had imagined the whole thing. But no, Callie had seen it, too. He hadn't imagined that Callie was with him, and hadn't imagined their discussion about it.

He wasn't *that* crazy.

For an instant, he thought of Jeff, wondered if the boy had done it. After all, the kid had been home alone, and he'd been angry earlier. Maybe this was his way of getting even.

But somehow that didn't strike him as right, either. He might not know Jeff all that well, but he didn't believe the young man would do this.

So who did that leave? Demons out of the sea?

The darkness was closing in again, pressing at the walls and windows of his cottage. He thought of the Beretta and went to get it.

But where before he had sat up all night thinking about using the gun on himself, tonight he sat up with it for protection. Something was out there, and he was no longer sure it was a figment of his imagination.

The night was endless.

The day lightened without fanfare. No blazing streamers of color arced across the sky. Morning simply came, dim and gray at first, brightening steadily. Chase and Callie waited at the Key West Municipal Marina, and with the light the docks began to stir. A few people who had spent the night on their boats appeared on deck. A few others pulled up in cars and walked to their boats. The day had begun.

"Let's go," Chase said.

He and Callie climbed out of the car and approached the nearest boat, where a man was standing at the stern watching the activity around him.

"Morning," Chase said when they reached the dock at the *Osprey*'s stern.

"Morning," the man replied. He was wearing shorts and a tank top, and needed a shave. A sign announced his boat was for charter. "You folks looking for a charter?"

Chase shook his head. "Sorry, not today. I just wanted to ask you a couple of questions, if you don't mind."

The man scratched his chin. "Depends."

"Well, I'm trying to find out what happened to George Westerlake and Jimbo Rushman."

The man stared at him. Then he turned and spat over the side of the boat. Callie felt her gorge rise.

"They know what happened," the man said. "Them two boys killed 'em."

Callie's heart turned over, and she found herself wondering if Jeff could even get a fair trial around here, if this was the way everyone was thinking.

"Actually," said Chase, speaking in an easy tone, "they're not real sure *exactly* what happened."

"Nobody's ever gonna know exactly," was the reply. "Ain't nobody but those boys was there."

"Maybe." Chase sat down on the piling and rested his elbows on his knees. "But we can sure find out more about it than we know already."

"You're some kind of investigator." It wasn't a question and the man hesitated. "You ain't from the paper?"

"Nope."

He nodded slowly, thinking about it. A boat farther down pulled away from the dock, and the wake caused the *Osprey* to rock. The man hardly seemed to notice.

"Maybe you can tell me what slip George and Jimbo

186

used," Chase said. "Then I can talk to the boat owners to either side."

"What are you aimin' to find out?"

"Who went out on the boat with them that day."

The man nodded again. "Nobody's turned up missing?"

"Not yet."

"Mmm." He rocked back on his heels. "Come on aboard. I've got some coffee brewing." He turned and went below.

Chase stepped onto the stern and jumped down onto the deck. Callie hesitated. She hated boats. She hadn't been on one since her father's death, despite getting the *Lily* for Jeff so they could "go fishing from time to time." Jeff had asked her more than once, but she'd always managed to come up with an excuse.

There was no reason to be afraid, she told herself. The boat was tied to a dock, the water wasn't deep, and it was mirror-smooth this morning, except for the diminishing waves from the other boat's wake. Chase turned and held out a hand to help her, and it took all her willpower to reach out and grasp it.

"You don't look so good," he said.

"I hate boats."

"You don't have to . . ."

But before he could finish, she took the two steps that brought her aboard the *Osprey*. She might hate boats, but she wasn't phobic. At least she didn't think she was, although when she felt the deck bob beneath her, a tendril of panic snaked itself around her spine.

She took a deep breath, steadied herself, and looked at Chase. "I hate boats," she said flatly.

Chase laughed.

"What's so funny?" she demanded, feeling annoyed.

"Between us we got enough hangups for twenty people." He laughed again.

In spite of herself, she laughed, too. "A real pair."

He stood with his feet braced apart and drew a lungful of the fresh sea air. "It smells better here than any coast I've ever been on."

"Really?"

"Really." He took another deep breath. "God, I love the sea." And feared it. And sometimes even hated it. But mostly he loved it. He felt the boat sway gently beneath him, and a fierce ache suddenly filled him. Maybe he should quit worrying about the dark, and face off with the sea again. Maybe what he really needed to do was take a boat out until he couldn't see land on the horizon, and go one-on-one with the only thing he'd both loved and hated his entire life.

"I don't think I like what you're thinking," Callie said, drawing him back to the present.

"What am I thinking?"

"I'm not sure, but you look like an acolyte at the foot of an altar."

He shrugged. "The sea's in my blood."

Another reason to keep clear of him, Callie thought. She wanted no part of a man who was having an affair with the water. Sooner or later the sea took everything.

The boat's owner returned to the deck carrying three mugs of coffee. "It's black," he said as he passed them around. "Got no milk or sugar. Sorry."

"I like it just this way," Chase said, and Callie murmured agreement. "I'm Chase Mattingly, by the way. This is my . . . assistant, Calypso."

The man nodded to both of them. "I'm Ben Haverstock. Been running charters out of here for the last twenty-three years."

"That's a pretty successful business."

"It does me well enough. Mainly it keeps me where I want to be."

Chase nodded. "It's as good a reason as any to do something."

"Hell, man, it's the best reason in the world."

Another boat pulled away from the dock, and Callie felt her stomach roll as the wake hit them, lifting, tipping, and dropping the deck beneath her feet over and over. She managed to keep her balance, though, and managed to keep her coffee from spilling. Apparently she hadn't completely lost her sea legs.

"So," Chase asked, "where did the *Island Dream* tie up?"

"Other side of the street. See that empty slip? That was George and Jimbo's. They was doin' okay. George was pretty much a landlubber, but Jimbo kept him straight. 'Course, during the season, just about anybody with a decent boat can make some money."

Chase nodded.

"Lotsa chickens to pluck," Ben said. "Not that I think of them as chickens, mind. But some do."

"Was George one of them?"

Ben shrugged. "Coulda been. Jimbo was, but he was fairly mad about the net ban. Had his reasons. It was the damn retirees and tourists, he claimed, who caused the net ban, wanting to be sure they could keep their sport fishing."

"Some think that's true, all right."

"Maybe it is. I reckon Jimbo figured they'd screwed him so making money off taking 'em sport fishing was a good way to make it even." Ben turned and spat over the side again. "Not that he ripped 'em off. He didn't. Charged going rates for the usual trip. But he sure didn't like 'em."

"So the day he disappeared, was he taking some fishermen out?"

Ben shrugged. "I don't know about that. I was out on a two-day charter to the Tortugas. Left the day before."

Just then another boat pulled away from the marina, and when Chase saw it was one of the ones beside George and Jimbo's slip, he cursed.

Ben Haverstock laughed. "Guess you'll have to talk to Ray another day."

"Guess so."

"So . . ." Ben said, drawing the word out. "You think them boys did it?"

Chase shook his head. "I absolutely do *not* think those boys did it."

Ben nodded slowly, bobbing from the waist. "Well, maybe they didn't. And if they didn't, you'd better find out who was on that boat. Tell you what. Give me a number I can call, and I'll ask around for you. Folks know me and might be more willing to talk."

Callie decided she liked this man, even if he did spit over the side. At least he was willing to keep an open mind.

"What changed your mind?" Chase asked.

Ben sucked air through his teeth. "The fact that the two guys who supposedly went out on the *Dream* ain't turned up missing."

"A very good point," Chase said to Callie a few minutes later as they waited at the light to cross Palm Avenue to the other side of the marina. "There ought to be a couple of fishermen reported missing by now."

"I've been wondering about that. But if the two guys were here on an extended trip and didn't know anybody locally, maybe nobody knows they're missing yet."

190

"Possible, I guess." Chase sounded thoughtful.

"I mean, everybody seems to know they took a couple of people out with them that morning, so it must be that nobody knows who they were yet."

"Or it could mean they're not missing or dead."

"That would be too easy." The light changed, and they started crossing the street.

"What do you mean, too easy?" Chase asked.

"Too easy. Things in my life never work out that way. If these guys aren't dead, then they probably killed the boat owners. Too nice and tidy."

They reached the other side of the street and Chase halted, looking down at her. "You're getting bitter."

"I guess so. Why not?" She turned from him and waved an arm toward the water. "Beautiful isn't it? Look at it. Smooth and clear and peaceful-looking. But it's a killer. One way or another it kills. I hate it."

Chase took a chance. "The sea didn't kill George Westerlake and Jimbo Rushman. And it didn't charge your brother with murder."

"No, I realize that. Factually, that's true. But emotionally . . ." She trailed off and tightened her mouth.

Emotionally, he understood exactly what she was saying. The sea was at the root of it all. He had felt that way at times. But right now, standing this close to boats and the water in the daylight, all he could feel was the call of the ocean.

A deep well of pain opened inside him, a pain that went far beyond what his body inflicted on him, far beyond the fears he experienced in the dark. It was a yearning for a lover that had been lost to him, and for a minute he could neither move nor speak.

When he did speak, his voice was thick, and he

191

couldn't even look at her. His gaze fixed itself to the water, his ears heard only the gentle lapping of it against the sides of the boats nearby as the morning breeze ruffled its surface.

"Ever since I can remember, I wanted to go to sea. I can't explain it. It just always was. I belonged to the sea."

"Like Jeff," she said.

"Maybe. The sea is alive. You can feel her presence even on the shore. She has happy days, she has sad days and she has angry days, and she's very much alive. The connection I feel to her is almost . . . mystical. Her tides are in my blood. I feel her ebb and flow and her moods as strongly as I feel my own. Without her, I'm half-alive."

Now he turned and looked at Callie. "Does she exact a price for her tolerance of us? I sometimes think so. Does she actually move events?" He paused. "Damned if I know, Callie. But sometimes I feel she does. Lately I've been feeling that I cheated her, and she wants something more from me. Crazy? Maybe. But if you say you feel the sea is after Jeff, I believe it's possible, because I can feel her still wanting me."

She caught her breath, then spoke in a hushed voice. "What can we do?"

"Exactly what we're doing. The sea is a force, Callie, but she's not a god. She's also mysterious. Jeff may not be what she's after here. If she's after anything at all."

He shrugged, then gave an uneasy laugh. "There, that's my craziness for the day."

She could tell he felt a little embarrassed—or maybe it was uneasy—about what he had just said, but right now she felt incredibly close to him. He had validated a feeling she had been struggling to put into words, a feeling that had been born in her.

Her family had always belonged to the sea, and now she wondered how she had ever thought she would escape its clutches. It would take what it would, when it would, just as it had taken her father. At least Jeff had a fighting chance—if they could learn something.

Two middle-aged men dressed in shorts and tank tops were approaching them along the dock. Lovers, Callie thought. There was something in the way they moved, the way they talked to one another that reminded her of an old, comfortably married couple. They climbed aboard a boat two slips away.

"Let's go talk to them," Chase said. Callie followed a few steps behind.

The men were friendly.

"We knew George and Jimbo," the taller of the two said. "George was a great guy. Jimbo was . . . well . . ." He looked at his partner.

"A gay basher," said the shorter man. "We avoided him."

The taller one nodded. "Exactly."

Chase spoke. "I'm not getting a very flattering impression of Jimbo."

The taller one smiled. "He was probably a great guy, too. In his own circles. Just not . . . cosmopolitan."

The shorter one laughed. "Generous, Tom. That's very generous."

The taller man shrugged a shoulder. "What's the point. He had his worldview, and it didn't fit with ours. But he didn't bother us unless we got too close, and that's about the best you can expect from people."

"Sometimes it is," agreed Chase. "You wouldn't happen to know anything about the two men they took out with them the day they were killed?"

"Not a thing," said the taller man. "Did you notice anything, William?"

"Not really. Except I thought it was strange they were going out on a sportfisherman for a dive."

Chase and Callie exchanged quick looks. "A dive?" Callie said.

"Yeah. At least that's what I thought. Why else would they be carrying aqualungs aboard? Well, maybe they couldn't find a dive boat to charter. I guess it doesn't make a whole lot of difference what you go out in."

"That depends," Chase said. "Did you notice anything else about their equipment?"

"No, afraid not. About the only part of diving gear I recognize is the air tanks."

"So many people want to dive the reefs," Tom said. "We ought to try it sometime, William."

"I don't think so. Snorkeling is as deep as I want to go."

Chase spoke. "You wouldn't happen to know who owns that boat?" He pointed to the one that was on the other side of Westerlake's slip.

"Some stockbroker from Miami," Tom said. "He owns a house in Old Town and comes out on weekends and holidays."

"So he wouldn't have been here that day?"

"I don't have a clue. Probably not. It was a Wednesday, wasn't it?"

Chase thanked them, then he and Callie went back to the car.

"What now?" Callie asked. The sun was beginning to get warm, and she could feel it prickle her skin.

"Dive shops," Chase said. "Somebody filled those cylinders."

CHAPTER 11

"WHAT GOOD IS IT GOING TO DO TO GO AROUND TO ALL the dive shops and ask questions?" Callie asked. "We don't know who these men were. We don't know what they looked like. Nobody is going to know who we're talking about. Why would they remember anyway? They probably fill lots of air tanks for tourists."

"Probably." Chase drummed his fingers on the wheel. They were still sitting in the parking place while he thought things over. "Most of the dives people take around here are in thirty feet or less of water."

"Of course. You have to go oceanside of the reefs to find water deeper than ten meters."

"Exactly."

"So?"

"It would be interesting to know what these guys filled their tanks with."

"I'm not following."

"It's simple. If they were diving in the reefs, they probably got the standard compressed air in their tanks. They could get that anywhere around here."

"But?"

"If they were going to dive much over a hundred thirty feet, and if they expected to be down a while, they'd probably want a heliox mixture. Helium and oxygen."

"But why?"

"The helium and oxygen mixture prevents the narks."

"You're going to have to back up here, Chase. I haven't got a clue what you're talking about."

"Okay. Let's go get some breakfast, and I'll explain. I need time to think about what tack to take with this anyway."

She was more relieved than she wanted to admit that they weren't going to go around to shops asking for two men they couldn't name and couldn't describe. Without more information it would be a big waste of time.

They found a small restaurant near the harbor that served breakfast with a view. Chase sat looking out the window, watching the boats putting out for the day.

After they ordered, he spoke. "What don't you understand? Nitrogen narcosis?"

"I've heard of it, but I don't really understand it."

"I'm not sure anybody really does, to tell you the truth." He flashed her a smile. "They know something about it, but not everything. There are a lot of assumptions made in this area."

"Okay. I can live with that."

"Not much choice." His smile broadened a shade. "Nitrogen narcosis, also known as the rapture of the deep or narks, is the effect of the nitrogen in our blood on our central nervous system when the pressure increases. You *do* know that the pressure increases as we go deeper in the water, because of the weight of the water above us?"

She nodded.

"Okay. The air we breathe on land is mostly nitrogen, about eighty percent, actually. That stuff is in our blood all the time. For some reason, and this really isn't understood, nitrogen has an anaesthetic effect on us when the pressure increases. It starts to interfere with the functioning of the central nervous system. For a diver this means you might start to get dizzy or euphoric, or even extremely paranoid. If you're on the alert for it, and recognize it, you can usually deal with it, though."

"That's what happened to you?"

"It seems to be. I got wildly paranoid, started hallucinating. Classic narks. I've never had a case that bad before."

"And that was from the compressed air in your tank?"

"Actually, I was on heliox. Helium and oxygen. The helium's an inert gas, too, but it's less likely to cause the narks." He was frowning, and shook his head, as if dismissing a thought. "So maybe it wasn't narcosis. Maybe the docs are right, and I had some kind of stroke. Anyway, something must have been seriously out of whack in my body that day, because I went over the edge. Full-blown hallucinations. I've never done that before. Never."

"What happened?"

"I don't remember. I do know they pulled me up too fast because I was trying to pull my helmet off, and that's why I got the bends so bad."

Callie saw the flicker of agonized self-doubt in his face. "What went wrong?"

"I don't know," he said, shaking his head. "Narks. Bends. Everything. I don't know. But I sure as hell must've done something wrong."

Impulsively, she reached across the table and squeezed his hand. "Maybe you didn't do anything wrong at all."

He averted his face. "I must have," he repeated. "Because everything else was right."

She was surprised to feel herself aching for him. Self-doubt could be a destroyer. Not knowing how to reassure him, she decided to shift the focus of the conversation. "What are the bends, anyway?"

He shook himself visibly, and looked at her again. "Gas bubbles. You have air dissolved in your blood and

197

tissues all the time, you know. When you dive, those bubbles get compressed by the pressure, becoming small, small enough to get into places they couldn't ordinarily fit, like the brain and the joints. Now when oxygen and carbon dioxide bubbles get into your tissue, the body can take care of them. And even with nitrogen or helium there's no problem while you're down there because the bubbles stay small enough to pass in and out of tissues without hurting anything. But when you come back up too fast, they expand before they can get back out into your bloodstream. I've seen divers with bubbles visible under their skin.

"Anyway, you have to ascend slowly enough that the body can reabsorb the gases into the bloodstream before the bubbles get stuck and expand enough to do damage. We're talking serious damage, Callie—ruptured tissues, blood clots. We pulled a diver up one time, he was coughing up blood because the bubbles were tearing his lungs open. I was lucky. It just messed up my hip joint and some of my spinal nerves."

She had the worst urge to hug him. "Will it ever get better?"

"Who knows? Most likely not, though." He leaned back to let the waiter serve them fresh-squeezed orange juice. "Did you know high-altitude pilots can get the bends? They reduce the likelihood by putting them on pure oxygen."

"I never would have imagined that." Callie thought over what he'd told her. "So you think these two divers might have been diving the same place where you were hurt?"

He sighed. "I don't know. It crossed my mind. The coincidences are starting to get deep."

Something in Callie rebelled. "We don't have any

more than coincidence, Chase. And it's not much of a coincidence. There are an awful lot of boats on those waters out there. To try to draw a link between the sunken boat you investigated and the boat Jeff found is really stretching it."

"Until you think about ten million dollars' worth of uncut diamonds, two men who were killed in the vicinity of the first wreck, and two divers who have disappeared in the same area."

"But we don't know that they did! Maybe those men got off the boat somewhere else. Maybe they were just out there to dive the reefs and they got left out there by the murderers. Maybe George Westerlake and his partner were smuggling drugs. God knows these waters are full of drug runners even now." Although it wasn't nearly as bad as it had been back in the seventies.

Chase's gaze settled on her, his stormy gray eyes measuring. On his earlobe, the diamond winked. All he needed, Callie suddenly thought, was a cutlass, and to let his dark hair grow.

"What's wrong?" he asked.

"Wrong?"

"I thought you agreed with me this was worth checking out."

"It *is*. I'm not saying it isn't. But I'm leery of clutching at straws, and I feel that's what we're doing. If we knew anything about these divers—"

"Hold that thought," he interrupted her. "You just gave me an idea. I'll be right back."

She watched him get up and cross the restaurant. He spoke to a waiter, then disappeared around a corner. Call of nature, she decided. Although it would have been politer if he hadn't interrupted her.

Turning her attention to the harbor beyond the

window, she hardly noticed that the waiter brought their breakfasts. Sometimes she wished she lived as far from the sea as it was possible to get, maybe in the upper Midwest, where she heard the only waves were those the wind sent rolling across endless acres of wheat and corn.

But part of her knew she wouldn't be happy there. Much as she hated the sea, she loved it, too. And she resented the hell out of that.

The harbor was peaceful this morning, boats rocking gently on the swells caused by the wake of other boats. Picture-postcard perfect. Some part of her wished she could let go of the tension inside her, the feelings and fears that had been born with her father's death, and just relax into the beauty she saw.

But some essential trust in her had been destroyed with her father. She no longer trusted the sea, and she no longer trusted men. And Chase was probably no different, she thought. He was as changeable as the sea, and probably no more reliable. And like most men, he'd be out of here when he was no longer getting what he wanted, when he no longer needed anything from her. Or when the going got too tough.

This last thought, crossing her mind with such bitterness, astonished her. She didn't think her father had abandoned her because things got too tough, did she? Mel, yes, but her *father*?

Feeling almost frightened by the direction of her thoughts, she was glad to see Chase making his way back to her.

"Great timing," he said as he slid into the seat across from her. "The eggs are probably cold."

"He just brought them."

"Well, I've got good news, maybe."

"What's that?"

"Pearl Rushman has agreed to see us."

"Pearl Rushman?"

"Jimbo Rushman's wife. She says she dated your daddy years ago. So she's going to talk to us about the men who chartered the *Island Dream*."

Pearl Rushman lived on big Coppitt Key, off a narrow road that wound past battered mobile homes and small cinder-block houses. The money that was gradually reshaping the Keys hadn't reached this enclave yet. Pearl's house was down near the water, her small yard scattered with hubcaps, car parts, and other trash. Beside it rested a boat so old it looked as if it was ready to crumble.

Inside, though, the house was meticulously tidy. Callie guessed the yard had been Jimbo's doing.

Pearl was a pleasant-looking woman of fifty, with steel gray hair cut short and dark eyes that peered from behind thick glasses. Her skin was tanned and weathered, and her hands showed a lot of hard work and arthritic joints.

She invited them in and offered them iced tea. They sat in a living room furnished with pieces that were probably older than the house by far.

"They're my things," she said when Callie mentioned them. "Handed down." She pointed to a small table. "That there is about a hundred and fifty years old. Abel Rushman made it with his own two hands when he settled here back in 1842." A smile creased the corners of her eyes. "But you know all about that, don't you Callie? Your family goes back about that far, too, don't it?"

"Nearly. My people came here right after the Civil

201

War."

Pearl began to rock her chair gently. "Not many of us left, us old Conchs. When life gets hard here, it gets too hard. The hurricanes blew us into the sea, the pineapple trade died, the sponge trade died—it's always something dying. I told Jimbo not to get so upset about the net ban. It's the way of things, I told him. We'll just find another way to survive. We did, too. At least until he got hisself killed."

She said it with such surprising calm that Callie felt almost startled. She searched the woman's face, wondering if she were suffering some kind of dissociation or severe denial, but saw nothing in those dark eyes except resignation.

Chase spoke. "I don't think he wanted to get himself killed, Mrs. Rushman."

She snorted. "You don't know my Jimbo. Now take your father, Callie. There was a good man. If your momma hadn't turned his eye, I'd'a dragged him to the altar with me. But Jimbo . . . " She shook her head. "If there was trouble on that boat, my money says he was part of it."

"But . . ." Callie hardly knew what to say. She'd come here in dread, expecting this woman to say horrible things about Jeff.

"Your brother, you mean?" Pearl nodded her head. "I don't think he killed my Jimbo or George. Natalie Westerlake thinks those boys done it, but I know better. The Carlson family don't go 'round killing nobody. They was always better than that, and the twig don't fall far from the tree. I always knew Jimbo was gonna get hisself killed. That man couldn't keep his nose outta what was none of his bidness. Never could. And some folks' bidness in these parts ain't healthy to go pokin'

202

your nose into. That's what I told them deputies when they come askin' questions. That Carlson boy didn't do nothin'."

Callie wanted to jump up and hug Pearl, but all she could do was say, in a voice husky with emotion, "Thank you."

"No need to thank me." Pearl shook her head. "I say it like I see it. Always have, always will. Jimbo got hisself into somethin', and that's all there is to it."

Chase spoke. "Do you know anything about the two men who chartered the boat that day from Jimbo and George?"

"I know they paid cash the day before, and they paid extra because they wanted to go out past the reef. Deep-sea fishing I thought, but Jimbo said they was a couple of crazy divers."

"Why crazy?"

"What's the point of diving out past the reef? Not much to see, is there? Jimbo said they just wanted to dive deep, say they had. Men." She shook her head.

Callie felt her heart beating faster, and she looked at Chase. The intensity in his eyes was almost frightening.

"Did Jimbo tell you anything else about them?"

Pearl cocked her head, thinking about it. "Only that they knew exactly where they wanted to go. Usually tourists let the captain guide 'em, you know, but these guys had a chart and marked the place they wanted to dive. Said it was some kind of contest with a coupla friends, and they had to go to the same place. Jimbo didn't care."

Callie leaned forward, so tense she could hardly stand to sit. "Did Jimbo mention their names, Mrs. Rushman?"

The older woman shook her head. "Not that I recall.

Now he mighta written it down on the account books, but I doubt it. They paid cash, and Jimbo didn't like to record cash sales."

"Where are the account books?"

"The cops took 'em. Reckon they want to know who those two guys are as much as you do."

"Somebody knew about those diamonds," Chase said. They had left Mrs. Rushman's house, and were driving back to US 1.

"Can we stop at the cemetery?" she asked impulsively.

He glanced at her. "Sure. Where is it?"

She gave him directions, and three minutes later they were pulling into a cemetery with a view of the Gulf of Mexico. It was a quiet little place off a narrow road, with a few above-ground crypts, a few headstones, and a lot more flat marble markers.

Chase pulled the car to a stop and Callie climbed out, walking across the grass to her mother's marker. It was simple, flat in the ground. Her dad hadn't been able to afford anything bigger, but it was fine as it was, she thought. *Lily Pendrick Carlson* was all it said. Thirty-three years old. So young. Not much older than Callie was herself now. There'd never be a marker here for her dad. Impossible as it seemed, his body had never washed ashore.

She stared at the stone for a few minutes, thinking of her mother and remembering so very little. That hurt. Why couldn't the memory claim more of the past than a few snatches?

Lifting her head, she looked out to sea. The water was mint green, and the sun was hot on her face. Her mom would have liked the view. Lily Carlson was as tied to the sea as her husband. "It makes the rhythm of my days," she'd told Callie more than once. "I couldn't live anywhere else." Fishing was good, and food was plentiful, and everything else, from mosquitoes to hurricanes, was just something to be endured.

Callie shook her head, and wondered why she couldn't be as accepting.

"Your mother?" Chase had come up beside her and was looking down at the marker.

"Yes."

"Pretty name."

"She was a beautiful woman."

"You take after her?"

"I guess. Except I got my coloring from my dad. Mom was dark-haired and dark-eyed."

"If she looked anything like you, she was a knockout."

All of a sudden the heat in her cheeks was not entirely from the sun. "Thanks," she said awkwardly.

"Just telling the truth."

She stared at her mother's marker a few minutes longer, wishing she could talk to Lily about this mess, and about Jeff. But some wishes couldn't come true. Finally, she sighed and turned for the car. "Thanks for bringing me. I don't come often enough."

"Glad to do it."

He still looked like a pirate, she thought as she glanced his way. Today he wore a white shirt with rolled-up sleeves and khaki shorts along with a blue ball cap, not a pirate's costume at all, but she still felt he needed a cutlass.

Back in the car, he turned to her. "The diamonds," he said, bringing them up again. "Somebody knew about the diamonds."

"I'm beginning to agree with you."

"So unless there's something else you want to do, I'm going to go home and start calling places I know that can provide heliox. There aren't a whole lot of them, and they don't do it all that often. Maybe somebody will know something about these guys."

"Sounds good. And I'm going to call Jeff's lawyer. I want to know what they found in that account book."

Chase headed them homeward. "Of course," he said, "they might have simply used compressed air, in which case I'm not going to find out a damn thing."

"But what you told me . . . it would be stupid to use straight air, wouldn't it?"

"Depends on what they were expecting, and how much they intended to do. The wreck is marked by a buoy because the insurance case isn't settled yet, so they wouldn't have to spend any time searching for it. All they'd need to know is exactly where the safe is. If they did, they could use compressed air because they'd be planning on being on the bottom for only a few minutes. They'd still have to face narks, though." He shook his head. "I think it's stupid, especially since you can't be sure nothing's going to go wrong and keep you down longer, but people do it. For really short trips."

"Oh." She felt a burst of frustration. "Damn it, I wish there was just one thing that was clear-cut and obvious to follow up on."

"There is. Two divers went out on that boat. Two divers didn't come back. If they were left out there, or killed out there, somebody ought to be raising a cry by now. Ergo, those divers aren't missing."

"Which is all well and good, except we don't know who they are."

"We'll find out something, Callie. One way or

another, we're going to find out something. Because I'm not going to rest until I find out what the hell is going on here."

She should have been reassured by his determination, except that it was easy to talk about solving this mess and entirely another matter to actually *do* it.

When they got home, he dropped her off and went to his place, promising to come over after he'd made some phone calls. Inside, Callie found Jeff lounging at the kitchen table, wearing nothing but shorts, his arms and chest speckled with paint. He was drinking water and eating a peanut butter sandwich.

He scowled at her when she came in.

She tried smiling, although she didn't at all feel like it. "Hey," she said. "You started painting?"

"Nothing else to do," he grumbled.

"I appreciate it."

"Where were *you*?"

"Out trying to discover who went out on the *Island Dream* the day Westerlake and Rushman were killed."

He straightened and, as she'd hoped, his scowl faded. "Did you find anything?"

"Two divers went out with them, but we couldn't find out who they were. Chase is making some calls."

"Divers?" He straightened even more, and his tone became excited. "Chase was right about the diamonds?"

"Maybe. We don't know for sure." She tossed her purse on the counter and grabbed a glass from the cupboard, filling it with ice and water. "We talked to Jimbo Rushman's widow. She said she doesn't believe you killed anyone."

A flicker of appreciation passed over Jeff's face, then gave way to sour gloom. "She must be the only person in the Keys then."

"Uh . . ." She hesitated, then decided to take the bull by the horns. "What about Chase and me? What about the girl you met last night?"

Jeff tossed his sandwich on the plate. "What about her." His tone was truculent.

Callie sat beside him. "What happened, Jeff?"

"Did I say anything happened?"

"You don't have to. Or are you still mad at me about last night?"

"Oh, come off it, Callie. You're not the center of the universe. Why would I waste all this time being mad at you?"

She didn't know quite how to take that. Jeff had sometimes, even in recent memory, stayed mad at her for days. "So something else happened," she said, deciding to ignore the implied insult he'd just thrown at her.

"Nothing that matters."

"Okay." If he didn't want to talk, she wasn't going to push him. He'd probably get around to it sooner if she pretended disinterest anyway. "I'm going to call Shirley. Is there anything you want to ask her?"

"Oh, I don't know. How about when am I going to get my life back?" He shoved back from the table and left. A few moments later she could hear the sounds of him working on the far side of the house.

She felt a strong urge to throw something. His attitude stank, and while she could understand he was suffering from a lot of stress and fear, so was she. If he could have a minor temper tantrum, why couldn't she?

Except that no matter what she threw, she'd have to clean up the mess. Instead she settled for throwing Jeff's sandwich in the garbage and rinsing his plate and glass. It wasn't as satisfying, but at least it wasn't destructive.

Then she called Shirley's office, and to her surprise was put right through.

"I was just about to call you, Callie," Shirley said. "I got the paperwork from the sheriff, and all it lists as being taken are Jeff's clothes and the logbook from the boat. Have you noticed anything else gone?"

"Nothing."

"Good. Okay. I'll need you to come by here in the next few days and sign this so I can get it back to them. I raised Cain about you being told they hadn't taken anything at all, but they said it was a miscommunication with the officer who spoke to you. Things happen."

"Sure. I'm not really worried about it, Shirley."

"Well I am. Mistakes are my meat and drink. Meantime, I'm working on the state attorney. I pointed out to them that until they could prove the other two people who went out on that boat have turned up missing, they've got a paper-thin case against Jeff. I mean it wouldn't take much to raise a reasonable doubt in a jury's mind about who actually killed these two guys. The fact that the guys who chartered the boat haven't been reported missing is as suspicious as hell."

"I agree with you. And that's what I called about, Shirley. I talked with Pearl Rushman this morning. She says the men who chartered the boat were divers. I was wondering if anybody has their names."

"Divers?" Shirley was silent a moment. "You know, that boat was found three or four miles out beyond the reef. I could see a fisherman wanting to go out there, but what the hell was a diver doing so far out?"

"Treasure hunting maybe?" She didn't want to mention the diamonds to anyone, not until she had something more than a string of coincidences. She didn't want Shirley to think she was going off the deep end, especially since they had *no* proof that those diamonds had ever been on the boat. "There are an awful lot of wrecks out there that have never been found." Which, she realized suddenly, could well account for the divers without Chase's ten million in diamonds. Her stomach lurched and sank. Nothing, absolutely nothing, was getting them anywhere with this.

"Well, it wouldn't be the first time," Shirley said. "I wonder why the state attorney didn't mention they were divers."

"Maybe he doesn't know."

"If *you* found that out, and he doesn't know, I'm going to give him hell over the quality of his investigation." Sylvia suddenly laughed. "It'll make my day. Let me get at it."

"But wait, Shirley. Does anybody know the names of the men who chartered the boat?"

"Nope. Dead end there. And that's making me really suspicious, Callie. These missing guys are like phantoms. Nobody's looking for 'em, nobody knows who they were . . . Most people don't go through life leaving such a thin trail. You'd at least expect one of the hotels to report that a client had overstayed his reservation without making arrangements, and the bags were still in the room."

"You would expect that."

"See what I mean? There ought to be *something*. An abandoned hotel room with luggage, a relative calling frantically, something. And the state attorney knows it, too. That's the reason Jeff and this other kid haven't been charged with four counts of murder instead of two."

"*One* count is more than enough," Callie said grimly.

"Well, I'll badger them for the names of these two guys, Callie. It'll make 'em nervous. And by the way, don't talk to Pearl Rushman again. I don't want there to be any hint of witness tampering, okay?"

"Okay. I didn't think." Butterflies fluttered uncomfortably in her stomach. "Jeff wanted to know if he can visit Eric in jail."

"Absolutely not. Don't even think of it. Anything he and Eric discuss will be listened to and noted, and you'd be amazed how even the most innocent statement can be twisted in court."

"All right. I'll tell him. Do you know if there's any chance that Eric will make bail?"

"He's not my client. If you want to do something about that, call the public defender's office. As far as I know, the kid's still in his cell."

Callie tried to call Chase, but his line was busy. Needing to keep herself occupied, she made a pitcher of lemonade, then carried two glasses outside. Jeff was high on a ladder, painting beneath the eaves at the peak of the roof. Creamy white paint was rapidly replacing the old, chalky white.

"Lemonade?" she called up to him. "Then I'll help you paint."

"Sure." He climbed down from the ladder, bringing brush and paint can with him. He took a moment to tap the top onto the can, then wiped his hands on a rag. "Thanks."

She watched him drain the glass in one long draft, so she passed him hers. "I can get more," she said.

"Thanks. Listen, I want to paint the shutters black instead of green this time. Okay?"

"Sure." She nodded agreeably. It was a small enough concession to make him happy. The shutters on the

211

house were real ones, designed to let air circulate through while keeping the sun out, and designed to withstand high winds. Painting them was a job all by itself. "Did you get the paint for it?"

"No, I wanted to make sure it was okay with you first."

She smiled at him. "Thank you, Jeff. But it's fine with me. I'll even paint them while you do the rest of the house if you want."

He smiled back at her. "Great. I hate painting those things."

"You certainly complained loudly enough about it last time."

He laughed and drained the second glass of lemonade. "What did Shirley say?"

"Not much. You can't visit Eric, though. She said they'd be listening to everything the two of you said, and things could get twisted. She also said she doesn't think he's going to make bail."

"How could he? A quarter of a millions dollars is a lot of money. If we didn't have this house and land free and clear, I'd still be rotting there, too." He sat on the porch step and wiped his brow with the back of his arm. "Life's unfair, Callie. And don't give me that crap you always do about my birth certificate not guaranteeing life is fair."

"Okay, I won't." She sat beside him and watched as he took an ice cube and popped it into his mouth to suck on. "Want some more lemonade? I'll get it for you."

He tucked the ice cube up in his cheek. "Maybe in a minute. So you and Chase didn't find out anything useful this morning?"

"Only that these guys were divers and wanted to go out past the reef into deep water. And apparently

212

nobody has turned up missing yet." She hesitated, then decided Jeff was old enough to share her concerns. "There are a lot of reasons divers could have gone out beyond the reef, though, Jeff. There are a lot of wrecks out there."

"Yeah, I know. I used to dream about being a diver and hunting for a sunken treasure ship like the *Atocha*." He rolled the ice cube around in his mouth and bit on it, crunching it.

"I imagine a lot of kids dream about that. And be careful. You don't want to break a tooth."

He grinned and crunched again. Callie didn't have the heart to scold once more. At least he was smiling. Finally. "Yeah, and some even grow up to do it. I really thought about it. But then I figured that was too much of a long shot. I mean, I could hunt for years and never find anything. Fishing is more practical. At least I bring home something to put on the table, or to sell at the market."

Callie was surprised, and ashamed to admit it. She'd always seen Jeff's desire to fish as willful and selfish. Never, ever, had she viewed it as a practical choice he might have made so that he could help out at home. Never had it occurred to her there might be something he wanted to do even more, but was out of his reach.

"Do you still want to hunt treasure?" she asked almost hesitantly.

"You better believe it. Eric and I found a couple of places that look really promising from reading stuff at the library. But it'll have to wait until we can afford the gear and everything." He shrugged. "Those wrecks have been down there for four hundred years. They're not going anywhere."

Somewhere along the way, Callie thought, she had

213

missed the fact that Jeff had grown up. Treasure hunting might sound wild, but his approach to the practicalities of it was fully mature.

Not that she liked the idea of his diving any more than she liked the idea of his fishing. Either way he was going to be at the mercy of the merciless sea. But regardless of how she felt about that, she was mortally ashamed to realize that she had never guessed her brother cherished bigger dreams, or that he and Eric had actually been researching the subject. She had honestly thought Jeff hadn't opened a book since his G.E.D., except for his studies for his captain's certificate. Now she found out he was researching the distant past at the library.

"I wish you'd use your brains on more than that," she said.

"I know." He shrugged. "Let's not get into that again, okay? I've heard everything you have to say. But *this* is what I want to do."

"You can always come back to it after college."

"If there *is* a college," he said grimly. "What if I get the death penalty?"

Her breath stuck in her throat, and she wished she'd never said anything about him wasting himself. She was never going to win that argument. Why couldn't she just leave it alone? "It doesn't matter," she said finally. "You'll do what you want."

"Damn straight I will." He stood up and put the glass down on the porch. "I'm getting back to work."

The brief moments of connection between them were shattered again. Shattered, as usual, by her own inability to keep her mouth shut.

Callie wanted to cry. She just wanted to curl up in a ball somewhere and sob her eyes out until she could cry no more. Instead she picked up the two glasses and went back indoors. She decided she'd try Chase again, then go out and start painting.

Hard work might keep her from losing her mind. Nothing else possibly could.

CHAPTER 12

CHASE MADE HIS PHONE CALLS AND DIDN'T GET anything useful. A couple of people said they would check around and get back to him. Since it was daylight, he curled up on the couch and let himself sleep. Sleep was a precious commodity these days.

The nightmares came as always, but somehow in the daylight his body knew they were just dreams, and the panic didn't set in as strongly. He was able to see the darkness and the demons but felt the terror from a distance.

But there was a difference this time.

He found himself at depth, in the dark, cold water as he always did. In all his other nightmares, though, he'd been alone except for the shadows that were trying to kill him. Nothing at all had been visible.

This time he still felt the lurking things around him, but he could also see the glow of light from his arc lamp. This time he could see the boat he had come to look at. This time he was aware of his diving partner, Bill.

The Happy Maggie lay on her side in the silt, a hole in her bow. He moved toward her, feeling the sea resist, feeling the pressure of nearly six atmospheres working against every movement he made. Things darted in the darkness outside the beam of light. Bill was nearby, and

215

in his earphones he could hear the voice of the dive master. When he answered, his own voice was distorted by the helium in his air mix. He didn't know if they could understand him on the surface. He could hardly understand himself.

The hands of the sea reached out for him, as they did every time, and he struggled to evade them, but he could hardly move. He heard Bill's helium-affected voice in the headphones, but couldn't make out the words. The light he carried seemed to bob wildly, and he could feel something tugging at it, trying to tear it away from him.

Currents, he told himself, but there were strange sounds in the water, sounds that didn't come from him. He turned his head and could barely make out Bill's shadowy shape, only slightly more solid-looking than the other shadowy shapes that were coalescing out of the water.

Fear pounded in him, but he tried to ignore it. He was imagining things, he told himself in the dream. Just imagining the feeling that hands were pulling at him, trying to drag him deeper, that fingers of water were plucking at his mask trying to tear it from his head. Just imagining it.

He looked down at the *Maggie* and saw the boat drifting farther and farther away. Something was carrying him off into the cold dark depths of the sea. He couldn't breathe. He was suffocating . . .

Chase jerked awake, drenched as always in a cold sweat. He jumped up off the couch, needing the solidity of the floor beneath his feet, needing to move to shake off the nightmare.

Evening was falling, he realized. Golden late-afternoon light was pouring through his windows, announcing the lateness of the hour. He'd slept longer than he had planned to. The phone hadn't rung. Apparently no one had learned anything.

He had a whopping headache, and he felt sticky from the dream-induced sweat. Deciding to take a swim, he stripped, climbed into his trunks and grabbed a towel.

Christ, he hated those dreams!

Down at the water's edge he looked across the inlet and could see Jeff on a ladder. Painting? He couldn't really be sure from here, but the gable of the house was fresh white. He felt a twinge of embarrassment that he hadn't been there to help the way he'd promised to on more than one occasion.

Christ, he was fucking up everything in his life. Since he'd screwed up that dive, he couldn't seem to do a damn thing right.

Then he cannonballed off the seawall and sank in the warm water until his butt touched bottom. Coming back up, he knocked the water out of his eyes and started swimming. Across the inlet and back, he promised himself. He could manage that much without letting his fear overtake him.

The other day with Callie had been different, because he hadn't been alone. But today he was alone, and going into somewhat deeper water—although the inlet was not really that deep. Uneasiness tickled his spine anyway.

He refused to listen to it. It was time, he told himself, to stop listening to his fears. Time to take a grip on life again. Time to be a man about this.

It wasn't that he was ashamed of being afraid. Fear was a good thing, and a wise man listened to it unless he was certain it had no basis. But being crippled by fear was something else altogether, something shameful, something he never would have believed possible of himself in the past.

217

He had discovered it was possible, but possible and inevitable were two different things. Reaching inside himself for the can-do stamina and sheer pigheaded arrogance that had gotten him through his SEALs training, he struck out across the inlet.

The water embraced him, buoying him as he swam, very different from what he had felt at fifty-seven meters below the surface, where he had been absolutely certain the ocean was going to crush and drown him. And it wasn't as if he'd never been at those depths before. Hell, he'd been down to nearly three hundred feet. Ten atmospheres of pressure. A man could hardly twitch down there.

Why had it gotten to him so badly this time? And why couldn't he get over it?

And why had his nightmare changed this time? Was he beginning to remember what had happened? But his dream image of the damage to the boat didn't match the damage report from Bill. No, he wasn't remembering. His nightmares were just changing their mode of torment.

He'd always been a strong swimmer, but two months out of the water had slowed him down. By the time he was halfway across the inlet, the only thing he was thinking about was his tiring muscles. That filled him with further disgust. Christ, he'd let himself go to hell.

He pressed on, pausing from time to time to breathe deeply and be sure he expelled all the carbon dioxide from his lungs so he wouldn't cramp. The inlet wasn't all that deep, and he could have walked the rest of the way, but he refused to give in. There was only one way to deal with being out of shape.

When he reached the other side and stood up, he found Callie waiting for him with a towel on top of the seawall.

"Are you trying to prove something?" she asked.

He felt stung. "I used to swim that distance and more all the time."

"Not lately. I saw you out there. I don't think you were taking frequent rest stops to admire the view."

He had to laugh. He took the towel from her and scoured his face and hair with it. "I'm out of shape. There's only one way to get back in."

"Next time, don't do it when nobody's watching. Even you could drown in the five or six feet of water out there if you cramp."

He slung the towel around his shoulders. "I know how to avoid cramping."

"Mmm." Her expression didn't agree with him. "Come up on the porch. I'll get you something warm to drink."

He had the worst urge to tell her to piss off—he wondered if this woman had any idea how bossy she could get?—and just start swimming back, but while he might be a macho meathead, he wasn't a fool. If he tried swimming back right now, he probably would cramp from the buildup of exertion by-products in his muscles.

"Thanks," he said, feeling a whole lot of sympathy for Jeff.

Jeff was washing out paintbrushes in an outside sink near a shed. A sink outside was something Chase had never seen before—at least not that he'd noticed—but it occurred to him it would be a really handy thing, especially for a fisherman. There were some things you didn't want to do inside the house. And it sure was a great place to wash paintbrushes.

With the towel still draped over his shoulders, he strolled over that way.

"How you doing, Jeff?"

The boy straightened and looked at him. "Could be better."

"What's wrong? Apart from the obvious, that is."

That drew a faint smile to Jeff's mouth. "Callie. It's always Callie. I think she's afraid to let me grow up."

"I think she's afraid that the sea is going to take you the way it took your father."

Jeff nodded as he went back to rinsing the brushes. "Yeah. She's bound and determined I'm wasting myself, though. Well, I coulda wasted myself worse. Instead of fishing and making some money, I could be out there trolling for treasure."

"Ahh." Chase leaned his shoulder against the shed. His legs still felt rubbery, but they were getting better. His hip was shrieking at him, too, but he was determined to ignore it. "Did you tell her that?"

"Sure. I don't think it made an impression."

"People very rarely respond well to the if you think it's bad now, how about this' approach."

"I don't know. All I know is, she's not going to be happy with me unless I go to college."

"How do you feel about that?"

"Shit." Jeff turned and snapped the brush he had just rinsed, flinging water off of it. He snapped it a couple more times, then hung it on a nail over the sink and reached for another brush that was soaking in a bucket full of paint-whitened water. He began running it under the tap, working the water through the bristles.

"Shit?" Chase asked. "Shit what?"

Jeff laughed. "I don't know. I'm not going to college. I made up my mind about that. I can't stand being cooped up in a classroom all the time."

"College isn't as cooped up as high school."

"Doesn't matter. I also don't like studying things that bore me. *That*'s a waste. If I want to know something, I go to the library or buy a book. Why should I let somebody *tell* me what I have to learn?"

Chase wasn't quite sure what to say because he sensed he might be getting on thin ground. He hadn't gone to college himself, but had done quite well. At least until lately, and no college education could have saved him from what he was going through. On the other hand, he understood why Callie considered it important.

"The idea of college," he said carefully, "is to open you up to ideas and possibilities you might never discover otherwise."

"I don't see how reading Jonathan Swift or studying sociology is going to help me captain a fishing boat."

Chase decided to let that go. There was no logical, concrete response he could make to that. Nor was he of the mind that everyone had to have a college education. Besides, if Jeff ever decided he wanted or needed one, it was never too late to go.

"So you've thought about treasure hunting?"

Jeff looked up, his eyes suddenly alight. "Oh, yeah. But like I told Callie, it's not practical. I mean, it costs a ton of money, and there's no guarantee you'll ever make a dime."

Chase was impressed that Jeff had considered the practicality of it. Callie had given him quite a different impression of the boy. He'd expected a heedless dreamer. "Well, most treasure hunters have investors," he agreed.

"I know. And I don't know anybody. There's no way I could get that kind of backing. But Eric and me, we figure we might be able to get enough money eventually

221

to at least take a stab at it. There's a lot of wrecks like the *Atocha* out there that have never been found."

"And a lot of people looking for them," Chase reminded him.

"Sure. But a lot of people looked for the *Atocha* before she was found, too."

"And it took Mel Fisher what . . . sixteen years or so? Even after he got some really good information out of Spain."

"But it's out there," Jeff said stubbornly. He shook the brush out and hung it on a nail beside the first one, then pulled yet another brush out of the bucket and started rinsing it. "There must be close to fifty wrecks out there that still haven't been found."

"Some estimates say only twenty-five. And that's a *lot* of area they're talking about."

"I know." Jeff sighed as he worked water through the bristles. "It's a long shot. Probably one of the longest shots in the world. But man, I'd love to do it."

"You'd have to do a lot of research on land, too."

"I know. I'm already doing it. I've even got contacts in Spain who are helping with research."

Chase was impressed. "How'd you do that?"

Jeff suddenly grinned. "The good old Internet." Then he shrugged. "Well, it'll be years before I can afford even the most basic equipment I'd need. Then there's a problem with getting a permit from the state. Only a handful of people are getting them anymore."

Chase nodded, but his thoughts had drifted to Tom Akers and the *Lady Hope*. Tom had most of the equipment. And Tom was likely to be interested in something like this, given good information. For the first time in over two months, Chase felt a real spark of excitement.

222

"I used to think a lot about treasure hunting, too," he said.

Jeff finished the brush and looked at him with new interest. "Really?"

"Yeah." But he didn't want to commit to any more than that, not yet. But even as he had the thought, he realized that this boy needed something more to hope for than an acquittal on murders he hadn't committed. He needed something good to look forward to. Hell, who didn't?

"You know," Chase said, "if you've got some time, I could start instructing you on diving. There's a lot to learn before you even put a flipper in the water, if you want to do it right."

There was no mistaking the light in Jeff's eyes. "Wow! Great! When can we start?"

Chase shrugged. "Right now if you want."

When Callie came out of the house a few minutes later with a tray of beverages, she found Chase and Jeff hunkered together on the porch chairs, talking intently about diving. Chase thanked her for the mug of hot cocoa, and Jeff seemed equally pleased by the lemonade she'd brought for him.

"Chase is going to teach me to dive, Callie."

She saw the eagerness and excitement in Jeff's eyes, saw the happiness in his smile. Her heart plummeted, and she had the worst urge to start screaming. Teach Jeff to dive? Chase knew how she felt about the sea, he knew how much she wanted Jeff to go to college. How could he possibly do this to her? Diving was even more dangerous than boating!

Then she looked into Chase's eyes and saw a challenge there, which only confirmed her conviction that he was aware she would be angry about this. Damn

223

him to hell!

Instead of shouting, though, or objecting, she managed a pallid smile and went back into the house. There she sat in the darkening living room in the cool air-conditioning, listening to their muffled voices, hearing the happiness and excitement in Jeff's tone, and wondered why it had been years since anything she had done for him had made Jeff as happy as he was at that moment.

"Callie?"

The room was dark. Callie stirred and saw her brother's shadowy figure in the front doorway.

"I'm going to walk Chase back now," Jeff said. "He's going to give me a diver's manual to study."

"Great."

"Wanna come?"

She didn't want to spend another minute in Chase's company. However, going along might give her an opportunity to put a lid on this new enthusiasm, an enthusiasm that was seriously dangerous. Dropping out of the loop wouldn't help anything at all. "Sure," she answered. Reaching out, she turned on a light so they wouldn't come back to a dark house.

Chase was waiting on the porch, wearing nothing but his trunks. He'd hung the towel she'd given him over the railing to dry.

"You don't have anything for your feet," she said. "Maybe I should drive you back."

"I'll be okay."

"Wait a minute," Jeff offered. "I've got a pair of flip-flops . . ." He dashed inside the house and came back with them a minute later.

Chase slipped them on. "Thanks. I never think of flip-flops without thinking of *Margaritaville*."

Jeff laughed and sang the stanza. Chase joined him, and Callie found herself tagging along after a couple of Jimmy Buffett wannabes through the dark along the path around the inlet.

She was in a terrible mood, and she resented the closeness that had evidently sprung up between Jeff and Chase. She resented their being able to walk along singing at the top of their lungs like a couple of drunken sailors while she followed behind wanting to shake them both.

What was the matter with her? she asked herself. Yeah, there was a lot wrong in her life at the moment, but it was wrong in Jeff's life, too, and he was doing a whole lot better job of handling it than she was.

And why should she resent the fact that Jeff had found a friend in Chase? There really wasn't anything about Chase that she could object to—other than his association with the sea and his morbid fear of the dark. Jeff needed a halfway-decent role model, something he hadn't had since their father's death.

So what was the matter with her? Did she think she could keep Jeff all to herself? Was that why she'd been difficult about that girl he'd met last night? Because she was terrified someone might take him away from her, the same as she was terrified the sea might do?

God. That was sick.

So maybe that wasn't true. But somewhere deep inside, she knew that it was. She could feel it in her heart of hearts. She was terrified of losing Jeff, whether to the sea or to his own life. He'd been her anchor and her purpose almost since childhood, and losing him would leave her empty of purpose. Empty of direction.

Hell, if Jeff left, she wouldn't have a life.

Sick, Callie, she told herself. Very sick.

Glum reflection followed her all the way to Chase's house. The walk did her good though, and by the time they reached his porch, she was feeling better anyway.

"Come on in while I get the book," Chase said.

They followed him inside. From Jeff's demeanor, Callie guessed he would have been glad to stay with Chase the rest of the evening, but he didn't want to let his sister walk home alone.

And why not? she wondered. She'd walked around the inlet alone many times after dark. Feeling frustrated and restless and just generally unhappy, she stepped back out onto the porch. The door was open, so she could hear Chase give Jeff the book, and tell him a little about it. She could hear the hero-worship in Jeff's voice.

And she hated it. Wanting to get away from it, she walked to the far edge of the porch and looked into the woods.

Her heart stopped. Two red glowing eyes were staring back at her from the woods. Too high to be a deer, too big to be any animal she knew of in these parts. God, it looked like some kind of monster . . .

But almost the instant she saw them, they winked out.

Something must be reflecting the light, she told herself. She moved, trying to see them again. Nothing.

Maybe she had imagined it?

"Jeff? Chase?" Her voice was little more than a croak.

As soon as she spoke, the lights winked on again, farther back in the hammock, higher up. Then they were gone. Her heart was thundering now.

"Chase?" Her voice was louder this time. "Jeff?"

Jeff's voice came from the doorway. "What is it,

226

Callie?"

"Come out here, please?"

"What's wrong?" Chase asked as he came up beside her. "You sound scared."

"I am. I saw red lights flickering in the woods." She pointed. "Right out there. They looked like eyes, except they glowed. But they were too high and too big to be a deer, or anything else I know about around here. As soon as I called you, I saw it higher up the rise . . ."

Chase swore. His hands gripped the railing until his knuckles were white. "You saw it, too?" he asked tautly.

She looked at him. "Too?"

"I've seen it before. I thought I was imagining it."

With that simple sentence, he told Callie exactly what kind of hell he'd been going through. She had to stifle an impulse to reach out to him, as she thought what it would mean not to be able to trust your own senses.

"Well let's go catch whatever it was," Jeff said excitedly. "Do you have a flashlight?"

But Chase shook his head and Callie said a vehement "No!" at the same instant.

"Why the hell not?" Jeff demanded.

"Because," Callie said. "Because whatever's out there could be dangerous." She looked at Chase for confirmation.

He was still staring into the woods, clinging to the rail, his face as tight as a wound spring.

"It could be," he said. "It could be."

"But I want to know what it is," Jeff argued.

"Well," said Chase, turning to look at him, "if it's not a monster from the sea, it was some person who might get really unpleasant if he got caught."

"You know how to handle that, Chase. You're a SEAL."

"I don't go running after unknown dangers in the dark, Jeff. It might just be a prankster, but it could be somebody whose armed with a gun, or worse. It might even be an attempt to lure us out into the woods in the dark."

But Callie's thoughts were running in a different direction. "I don't think you should stay here," she said.

He looked at her. "I'm not going to be run off."

"I'm not talking about being run off. I'm talking about staying at our place tonight. We've got plenty of room. But whoever was out there . . . Chase, between this and the seaweed, I've got the feeling that whoever is doing this is . . . well, it's more than just a prank. A prank happens once. The only kids who live around here live too far away to want to pull something like this over and over again. It's ridiculous even to consider it, and why would they want to pick on you anyway? They don't even know you."

He nodded slowly and looked toward the woods again while Callie continued.

"What I saw out there takes some effort. And it must be somebody who knows about your . . . problem with the dark. Otherwise, they're expending an extreme amount of effort just to annoy you, and I don't think that's very likely."

"You're probably right," he said. "I've been seeing stuff like this and the seaweed on and off for weeks. Some of it I thought I imagined."

"You didn't imagine the seaweed."

"No."

"And I didn't imagine those eyes. Lights. They *had* to be lights. I've seen animals' eyes in the dark, and they don't look like that."

"What problem with the dark?" Jeff asked Chase.

228

He hesitated, then said, "Since my diving accident I've had a problem with darkness. It . . . scares me."

"Oh." Jeff shrugged it aside as if it were of no importance. He certainly didn't look as if his idol had been toppled. "I guess I can see that. It gets pretty dark down there where you were, right?"

"Pretty dark," Chase agreed.

"I got locked in a closet once by accident," Jeff said. "It was a long time before I could be alone in my bedroom at night without the light on."

Callie, feeling a burst of pride at her brother's understanding, broke one of Jeff's cardinal rules and reached out to hug him. "You're pretty special, Jeff," she told him.

He wiggled away, looking embarrassed. "Nah," he said. "But I'll tell you, if somebody's trying to scare you at night, Chase, then you don't want to stay here. Callie's right about that. Come stay at our place. We can check out the woods for clues in the morning."

Chase started to shake his head, and Callie could well understand why. He could hardly like the idea of being protected by a woman and a youth. His pride had suffered enough blows lately without adding another one. Again she felt that tug in her heart, an ache for his pain. She pushed it aside, not wanting to feel anything for him beyond superficial, safe friendship.

"You know," Callie said, "the truth is, if there's some jerk creeping around in the woods, I'd feel a whole lot better tonight if *both* you and Jeff were there with me. So if you don't want to come to our place, I'll just camp on your couch tonight."

He startled her with a sudden grin. "You're a lousy liar, Callie."

"I'm not lying!"

"She's not," Jeff said. "I'm not ashamed to admit it. I'd feel a whole lot better if you were around, too."

"Why don't you stay here, then? I'd kind of like to know whether anything else happens tonight."

Jeff went inside to read the diver's handbook Chase had given him, but Chase and Callie remained on the porch.

"Are you okay?" she asked him. "I mean, with being out here in the dark? You seemed more comfortable when we walked over here, too."

He was still standing at the railing, gripping it, and she stood beside him, her eyes scanning the woods constantly for another glimpse of the eyes.

He spoke. "I learned a long time ago that the only way to deal with fear is to face it. I forgot that for a while."

"Don't give yourself a heart attack."

A snort of laughter answered her.

"No, really, is it getting better?"

"I'm not sure. I *am* getting madder."

"At what?"

He looked down at her. "At myself. At whoever is doing this to me. Shit."

"What?"

"My damn hip. It feels like Attila the Hun is jabbing it with a red-hot poker."

"Maybe you should sit down?"

He shook his head. "That's something else I'm damned if I'm going to give in to." Although he remembered the nights when the Beretta had seemed like an option. Remembered them with shame.

Something inside him was changing, he realized. A few weeks ago he'd felt whipped. Now he was getting mad. Mad enough that he'd begun to talk about it. The

230

anger somehow helped ease the embarrassment that usually kept him from discussing his problem.

"I started having the nightmares when I was in the hospital," he said. "They weren't so bad, though. Not as bad as they got eventually. They were just nightmares, and I'd wake up in a cold sweat with my heart pounding. I figured they'd stop."

"But they didn't."

"No. They got worse. After I got out of the hospital, it got so I couldn't even go to sleep at night. I had to stay awake just to avoid the dreams. For some reason they're not as bad when I sleep in the daytime."

"I wonder why?"

"I don't have a clue. Anyway, I went home to Tampa, and then . . . well, it got to be more than nightmares. More than just being afraid to sleep. I started feeling . . ." He halted, then said, "This is going to sound crazy as hell."

"I've heard some pretty crazy things in my day."

"I guess." He sighed, and his grip on the railing tightened. "I started feeling like I was being watched. Not all the time, just sometimes. I'd be walking down the street and get the feeling so strongly that I had to go home. Or I'd be sitting in my apartment and I'd be sure I wasn't alone. I was having a nervous breakdown, I guess."

"Mmm." Callie's reply was noncommittal.

"I started seeing a psychiatrist about all this stuff. He said it was post-traumatic stress, that it ought to let up in a few months. He offered me pills to help, but I didn't want to take them."

She dragged her gaze from the woods and looked at him. "You're not the kind who gives in easily, are you?"

"No. Are you?"

231

She had to laugh. "No. I'm like water on stone, I guess. Drip, drip. So how come you came out here?"

"Two reasons. One, I thought that if I got away from people, the feeling of being watched would have to stop. I mean, I couldn't tell myself it was happening because there were other people around. So I figured, get away from people and the feeling will go away. Either that, or I'd at least be able to talk myself out of it."

"Did it help any, coming out here?"

"Not a bit. Anyway, my other reason for moving here was pretty straightforward: face the fear." Face the fear or die. "It didn't work. It just seemed to get worse."

"That happens sometimes. Worse before it gets better. Your doctor was right though. When post-traumatic stress shows up early, within the first six months, it usually goes away more quickly. Not always, but usually."

"Well, what's going on here is a little more than that, apparently."

"You mean the seaweed and the lights in the woods?"

"Exactly. Two nights after I got here, I saw a shape at the window, a shape with glowing red eyes. It looked something like what I'd hallucinated when I was diving. I ran outside to investigate it, but there was nothing there. And that's—well, that's when I started to get afraid of the dark. Started to feel as if there were demons out there. Everything got all twisted up in my head. My accident, the hallucinations I had under the water. . ."

She reached out and gripped his arm. "Did you ever describe those hallucinations to anyone?"

"Sure. To my doctors." He thought about it. "To my friend Tom, and to Bill Evers, my buddy on the dive. Bill wanted to know what the hell had freaked me out so bad. Poor guy. I can imagine how it felt on his end, watching me go nuts at fifty-seven meters down, seeing me try to pull my helmet off."

"Scary. I'm surprised *he* isn't having nightmares after that."

She gave up scanning the woods, figuring that the show was probably over for the night. After all, if you were going to gaslight someone, overdoing it could ruin the effect. Still, they kept their voices lowered, so they couldn't be overheard. Turning so that she leaned her hip against the rail, she folded her arms and looked up at Chase.

"So lots of people know what you saw down in the water?"

"A few. I don't know how many. I see what you're getting at, Callie."

"And?"

"I'd trust Bill and Tom with my life. Tom's an old friend and Bill and I dived together a few times. We're not exactly friends, but you don't dive with someone you don't trust. Neither of them would do this." He sighed and rubbed his hip absently. "I've got to sit." He limped his way to one of the wicker chairs and dropped into it, stretching his aching leg out in front of him. Callie came to sit in the chair beside him.

"I've been thinking about it," he said presently. "Ever since we both found that seaweed on the porch. I've been trying to figure out why anyone would want to pull a prank like that. I even considered the possibility that it was directed at Jeff, but that they got the wrong house."

"At Jeff? Why on earth . . ." Then she understood. "God, that would be *cruel*."

"Yeah, it would. But if you link it with the lights, it doesn't fit anyway. The lights started before Jeff got into all this mess. I saw them a couple, three times."

Callie leaned forward, resting her elbows on her knees and propping her chin in her hands. The night was so beautiful, she thought, with the breeze rustling the trees, and the water lapping peacefully at the shore. Light from a crescent moon dappled the water.

"On nights like this I used to sit out on the veranda with my mom," she said. "When the mosquitoes weren't too bad. We'd sit together on the porch swing, rocking back and forth, and she'd tell me stories. I can remember the stories, but I can't remember what she looked like, sitting there in the shadows, talking. I can't even remember what her voice sounded like."

"I'm sorry," he said. He reached out and cupped her shoulder.

The sensation sent a warm shiver running through her. It was a warning, and she should have jumped away from his touch, but she didn't. She couldn't.

"So am I," she said. "It kills me that I can't remember it more clearly. But that's not what I'm getting at. What I was going to say was that after she died, the evening never felt the same to me again. In all these years, I never sat on that porch swing again. The chain's so rusty now I'd be afraid to, but it wouldn't matter even if I put up a new chain. I couldn't sit there."

He squeezed her shoulder. "Maybe if you tried sitting on it, you'd remember more about what she looked like and sounded like."

"Maybe. And maybe I don't want to. Maybe that's why I won't. Maybe I'm afraid of remembering any more clearly because it'll hurt."

"Could be." He withdrew his hand and she felt the loss instantly. How could a simple touch be so comforting?

"Anyway," she said, "there was a point to all of this."

"Which is?"

"Maybe you remember more from your dive than you think you do."

The silence was suddenly profound. It was as if the sea grew still and the night held its breath. Chase didn't move a muscle or speak for a time that seemed endless. Finally, he said, "I *don't* remember."

"Maybe someone is afraid that you do. Maybe someone doesn't want you to. If you doubt your own sanity, or are so distracted by nightmares and terrors, how likely are you to remember anything?"

"But I don't remember. Everyone knows that."

"Except that you remember the hallucinations you had down there. Everyone knows that, too."

He turned to face her. His expression was unreadable, a mask in the yellow glow of the porch light. "Why in the hell would anyone want to do that?"

She straightened and stared right back at him. "You said it yourself. Ten million dollars in uncut diamonds is a lot of motivation."

CHAPTER 13

"But the diamonds weren't down there."

"How do you know that?" Callie demanded. "Did you check the safe yourself?"

"Bill did. And Bill said they weren't there."

"What if Bill lied? What if somebody *paid* Bill to lie."

"No." He stood up quickly, his entire posture rejecting the idea. "I've worked with that man on and off for years. There's no way he'd lie about something like that."

"Has he ever had that much motivation before?"

"Jesus Christ, Callie."

He strode away to the far end of the porch and stood with his hands on his hips, his back to her. "Look," he said evenly. "I know I told you that Bill isn't a close friend. And he's not. But you don't do the kinds of dives I do unless you trust your diving buddy. I put my life in Bill's hands more than once, and I never ever saw a single thing that would make me distrust him, or think he might lie. And if it weren't for him, I wouldn't be here talking to you right now."

She waited a minute, then followed him.

"Listen," she said to his back. "Bill's your friend. I understand that. But look at what we've got going on here. You already think that those men my brother was accused of murdering may have been killed by divers going to look for the diamonds. It's slim, you know it's slim. *I* know it's slim. It's also a hell of a coincidence, considering that we're neighbors. But if you accept that, are you going to pile another coincidence on top of it, and say somebody just happens to be harassing you and taking advantage of your fears by tormenting you this way, but it has nothing at all to do with those diamonds? My God, Chase, that's just too much to be believed. The *only* way all of this fits together is if it's *all* tied to the diamonds."

"The diamonds weren't down there," he said flatly.

"Fine!" Callie threw up her hands. "They aren't down there. The insurance company said they weren't down there. Anybody who heard about the case would know that. So why would a couple of divers go down there to look for them anyway, unless they knew that somebody

236

lied?"

He stiffened even more, but he didn't speak. She was getting tired of talking to his back, and tired of his stubbornness.

"Loyalty is all well and good, Chase. But don't let it blind you."

"You're right," he said. "Those divers weren't looking for the diamonds. There's no link to your brother at all."

She felt as if she'd been punched in the stomach. All of a sudden, it was hard to breathe. He was washing his hands of the whole thing, she thought. The only reason he'd been trying to help her find out what happened on the *Island Dream* was because he thought it was tied to what had happened to him. Now that he was dismissing the link, he wouldn't help her anymore.

Like every other man in her life, he was abandoning her. Well, what had she expected? Men were never around when you needed them. Never.

"I'm going home," she said tightly. "Do you want Jeff to stay?"

He whirled around. "You're not going anywhere alone. You don't know who might be out in those woods."

"Just some damn demons from your nightmares," she said acidly. "What could they want with me? I don't have anything to do with *your* problems."

"Goddammit, Callie. If this is all tied together the way you just said, you damn well *do* have something to do with my problems."

"You just said none of it's linked." She turned and started to walk away, but he reached out and caught her arm. Her anger grew to white heat. "Don't you *dare* manhandle me."

"Then quit acting like a jerk. You don't know who's out in those woods, and you don't know what they're after. There's no guarantee they only want to bug *me*."

"You think I'm afraid of a little seaweed and some crazy red lights?"

"Anybody with half a brain is afraid of a threat when they don't know what it is."

"I know what it is. But you won't listen to me."

"Jesus." He glared at her.

He was still gripping her arm, and the look on his face frightened her. Instinctively, she started to swing at his arm, hoping to make him let her go.

In an abrupt movement that caught her totally by surprise, he wrapped his arms around her, pinning her hand to her sides so she couldn't hit him.

"Don't hit me," he said in a low voice.

"Then let go of me!" She tipped her head back, meaning to return glare for glare, but in the instant their eyes met the world careened wildly off its axis. All of a sudden, she could think of nothing except the way their bodies were pressed tightly together. The heat of him so close.

Her breath locked in her throat. He no longer looked as if he was furious with her. Instead she saw hunger. Yearning. She felt the same awakening in her, needs so strong that she didn't recognize what they were because she'd never felt them before.

Then his mouth swooped down and claimed hers in a kiss that was nearly violent with desperation.

At first she was utterly still. Then she felt her body leap in response, dizzying heat running along her veins. The sensation panicked her, and she hammered wildly on his shoulders.

He let her go so swiftly that she stumbled and would

have fallen if he hadn't steadied her.

"Christ," he said raggedly. "Christ, Callie, I'm sorry. I shouldn't have . . . Jesus." He turned his back again and gripped the porch railing. Even in the poor light she could see the tension in him, and the whiteness of his knuckles. "I'm sorry," he said again.

She felt weak, trembling from head to foot, but she gathered what dignity she had left and turned away. Not caring what might be out in the woods, she descended the porch stairs and headed along the path home.

He was no better than Mel, she thought numbly. Hot tears began to run down her cheeks, but she hardly felt them. *No better*.

What was it with men anyway? she wondered. Why did they all feel so *entitled* to do what they wanted any way they wanted? Even Jeff, and God knew she had tried to raise him to be better. But he thought nothing of ignoring her wishes and running off in his damn boat anytime he felt like it. Thought nothing of depending on her to take care of him when he hit a rough spot because he couldn't take care of himself.

And her father, thinking nothing of going back to sea and leaving his fourteen-year-old daughter to mother his six-year-old son for weeks on end with scarcely any help. Maybe it was different in his generation, maybe girls were expected to do that—but that didn't make it right. He could have found a job on land. He *could* have been around more. Could have been there to help her, to ease the burden, to ease the *fear*.

Because what she had given up to become Jeff's caretaker was small potatoes beside the fear she had felt all those weeks when her dad was out at sea and Jeff was her sole responsibility. God she had been *terrified*. What if she did something wrong? What if Jeff got hurt?

What if she was doing a lousy job of raising him?

At the age of fourteen she had been standing beside a little boy's bed while he slept, overwhelmed with guilt and grief because she wasn't doing enough, she wasn't loving enough, she wasn't patient enough, because she had shouted at him over nothing, or because she just hadn't known how to do it right.

No fourteen-year-old should have to go through that, especially when the child wasn't hers.

But she had. Those terrors still haunted her. Every time Jeff did something crazy or heedless, she wondered where she had failed. She lay awake nights, wondering where she had gone wrong, and feeling so horribly guilty for all the things she had failed to do.

If she had done things right, Jeff wouldn't be in this trouble. He'd be in college. He never would have been charged with that first assault.

She had failed, and her failures might cost her baby brother his future—or even his life.

She started walking again, feeling more hopeless than she had felt in a long time. Chase had at least given a direction to her search for the truth about what had happened on the *Island Dream*. What was she going to do? She didn't know enough about diving, enough about where the boat had been found, to continue to look.

The more she thought about it, the more convinced she became that this was all connected, what had happened to Rushman and Westerlake, what had happened to Chase, the crazy things with the seaweed and the red eyes in the woods—they all had to be connected because it was just too damn many strange things happening all at once for them not to be related.

She heard footsteps pounding behind her on the path,

and she whirled around, her heart slamming. It had to be Jeff, she assured herself. The person creeping around in these woods after dark wouldn't approach so noisily. At least she hoped not.

But she stepped off the path anyway, and hid behind a tall, elderly buttonwood.

It was Jeff. She recognized the way his shadow moved as he came around the bend in the path. She stepped out from behind the tree, and he drew to a sharp halt.

"Jesus, Callie! What are you thinking, running out all by yourself like that? And what the hell is Chase thinking, letting you go alone?"

"We had a fight. Besides, there's nothing out here for me to be afraid of."

"That's a pretty big assumption."

"Big assumptions seem to be the order of the day," she said acidly, and started striding rapidly down the path again. "Everyone else is making them. Why shouldn't I?"

He caught up and walked beside her. "What happened?"

"We fought. Basic disagreement." Through the mangroves, she could see the silvery sparkle of the moon-dappled water. Ordinarily she would have been enchanted. Tonight she hated the whole world.

"What assumptions?" Jeff asked.

"Never mind."

His footsteps grew sharper, angrier. "I'm not a kid anymore, Callie. Will you quit trying to cut me out of things? You're upset, and I want to know why."

"It doesn't matter, Jeff." The last thing on earth she was going to do was tell him that Chase had manhandled her. Jeff would probably get furious and go

241

after Chase, and just get himself into more trouble. "It'll blow over."

"Was it about him teaching me to dive?"

"No." Although now that she thought about it, that was another reason to be angry with Chase. He knew how she felt about Jeff and the sea, yet he was still doing this. "We never even got around to that."

"You don't approve, do you."

"Not really."

"Damn it, Callie, just butt out of my life."

She was shocked. She and Jeff had argued before, but he'd never once said that. "Butt out? Jeff, I raised you! That gives me some rights."

"I know you raised me, and I'm grateful for it, but that doesn't give you the right to tell me what to do for the rest of my life."

All of a sudden, Callie found it impossible to breathe. Her lungs seemed to have stopped working, frozen in shock. Then her heart slammed and she drew in an agonized breath. "Jeff . . ."

"I'm not kidding, Callie. You're always on my case about something. You're never, ever happy with me. Just stay out of my life. Get a life of your own."

They reached the end of the path and emerged into their own yard as he spoke. He gave her one last angry glare, then ran up the steps and into the house.

She stood alone in the moonlight, realizing that her entire life was crumbling around her.

And all of it was her own fault.

After Chase sent Jeff to follow Callie, he retreated to the fortress of his house and locked all the doors and windows.

Why not? It was one thing to say he was going to face

242

this thing down, and another actually to do it. And whether a human agency made those eyes in the woods or put the seaweed on his porch, there was still the whispering, rustling pressure of the darkness that rose out of the sea every night to torment him.

He got the Beretta and put it on the table, but he didn't sit down with it, didn't pour himself a glass of whiskey. Although he *was* tempted to reach for the gun.

He couldn't believe he'd grabbed Callie that way. Never before in his life had he grabbed a woman in anger. He was appalled at himself, and he didn't blame Callie for being furious.

He wondered if his accident had not only given him nightmares and strange fears, but if it had changed his personality in some essential way. It seemed he couldn't even trust himself not to do something stupid when he was angry.

Christ.

What in the hell had possessed him?

He passed on the whiskey and got himself a glass of ice water. His hands were trembling, he realized. He was shaking in reaction to his own violence. That had happened to him once before, a long, long time ago in training, when he'd been deliberately provoked by an instructor. But not once since then had he allowed himself to be angered to violence.

Jesus H. Christ, he was coming apart at the seams.

Remembering the look on Callie's face, he knew he had done more than shock her. He'd wounded her.

The night was battering at the walls of his cottage. He could feel it, but he didn't give a shit. There were more important things to worry about, like his own disintegration.

Self-pity was waiting in the wings, and moved

suddenly to center stage. There wasn't a hole deep enough to bury himself in, he thought. Nothing he'd tried was making anything better. He might as well just barricade his doors and windows and hole up forever, never seeing another living soul. Just pack it all in and become a hermit until he died, because he was sure as hell never going to be useful to anyone again.

He paused in his pacing to stare at the Beretta. Or, he could just pull the trigger.

But he'd never been a quitter, and he hated self-pity. Listening to his own thoughts made him want to gag. Christ, there had to be a way out of this hole he kept digging deeper for himself. There *had* to be a way.

Callie's face swam into the view of his mind's eye, her appalled, stricken expression after he kissed her, the look of disappointment. He couldn't let that lie. He had to apologize to her. Get down on his damn knees if necessary.

He strode to the door and touched the knob, suddenly once again aware of the pressure of the night outside. He could wait until morning. She might be more amenable then anyway, after she'd calmed down.

In his heart of hearts, though, he knew an apology alone wasn't going to do it. But if he walked over there in the dark, that might prove to her how sincerely sorry he was.

And he needed her to understand that. He recognized the selfishness in his need for forgiveness, but he needed it anyway. And she needed to know he was truly sorry, even if it didn't ease her wound any. He owed her that.

Taking a deep breath, he opened the door. The rustle of the breeze in the trees greeted him, along with the gentle lapping of waves against the seawall.

The sea was not the threat, he realized suddenly. She was trying to tell him something. He just couldn't understand.

It was an insane thought, but it stayed with him as he took his courage in his hands and set out for Callie's. And it seemed to him, as he walked, that the gentle lapping of the waves held the night at bay, as if the sea created a cocoon around him, guarding him.

More insanity. He was losing the last of his marbles, and he was past caring.

Callie was sitting on one of the wicker chairs on her porch, curled up as tightly as she could get, her knees drawn to her chin and her arms wrapped around them. Her eyes and throat burned with unshed tears. Not since her father's death had she felt so alone and lonely.

She honestly didn't know what to do about Jeff. Maybe he was right that she was being too controlling, but he wasn't as grown-up as he thought, either. What was she supposed to do? Keep her mouth shut when she saw him doing something that could get him hurt?

The idea of his diving terrified her. She realized she was being ridiculous. People dived all the time without any problems. Most of the people who went diving around there didn't even go deep enough to need to decompress on their way back up. She'd heard that somewhere, years ago. The depths simply weren't great enough until you got well out past the reefs into the ocean. How much trouble could Jeff get into in thirty feet of water? If he suddenly ran out of air, he'd still be able to reach the surface. There were moray eels, of course, and sharks, but they weren't a major concern.

So he was right. On this, at least, she ought to butt out. As long as he followed the rules of diving and used common sense, he should be perfectly all right.

But then she remembered Chase. He'd done everything right. He'd been diving for years, and look what had happened to him. It was small comfort to remember that he'd been five times deeper than Jeff would ever be likely to go.

She was losing Jeff, she realized. One way or another, he was going to leave her. He was going to carve out his own life, make his own decisions, and . . . he wouldn't need her anymore. God, how that hurt.

She swallowed hard, trying to get rid of the lump in her throat. She was almost strangling on grief, and no matter how much she told herself that this was the normal course of events, that every mother eventually had to let go, she didn't know how she was going to stand it.

These feelings couldn't be normal, she thought. They were too strong. All mothers felt trepidation and loss, but they let their children go. She was clinging so hard to Jeff that it was unnatural. Apparently she needed him even more than she thought he needed her.

But if she didn't stop this, she was going to destroy their relationship. God, she had to learn to let go.

She bit her lip, trying to hold in a welling tide of grief. Shouldn't she be feeling proud? Jeff was ready to stand on his own two feet. He *wanted* to. That was far better than him wanting to stay with her forever.

All of a sudden she wondered if he was still living with her only because he was aware that she needed him. Her heart skipped a beat at the thought, and she found herself staring blindly out over the water. Was *he* in his own way trying to take care of *her*?

She hadn't thought of that before, and the notion made her feel even more pathetic. God, had he known all along what she was just discovering, that she was leaning on him? Probably. Hadn't he just told her to get a life?

Cruel words, but they went straight to her heart because they were true. She had no life aside from Jeff and work.

"Oh, God," she whispered, "what am I doing?"

It was all too much. The murder charges, watching Jeff start to break loose, discovering what a spineless wimp she was. It was just too much. One scalding tear ran down her cheek.

She heard Chase's approach before she saw him. It never entered her head it was anyone else. Already she recognized the rhythm of his limping walk. She waited uneasily, wondering what could be momentous enough to make him journey through the night alone, not really wanting to see him after what had happened between them.

His shadow emerged into the yard from the path, and he came to the foot of the stairs, looking up at her. After a moment of silence, he said, "I'm sorry."

"You came all the way here to say that?"

"Yeah. I'm sorry, Callie. I can't believe I did that. I just can't believe it."

He had walked through the night that terrified him to apologize. Her heart skipped again, differently this time. "Are you okay?"

"To hell with me," he said. "I'm worried about you. What I did . . . God, I'm sorry."

Something inside her, something she hadn't been aware had frozen, thawed just a little. "I made you mad," she said tentatively. And it was true.

"That's no excuse. That's never an excuse. What I did was plain wrong. I should never have laid a hand on

247

you, and I sure as hell shouldn't have kissed you in anger. That was disgusting and reprehensible."

She didn't know quite what to say. It *had* been disgusting and reprehensible. She also knew that *anybody* was capable of doing things he or she shouldn't in the heat of anger. Something else concerned her more. "Are you . . . inclined to do things like that?"

"No. *Never.* I never did anything like that before in my life. Not even when I was married, and God knows that if I was looking for excuses to act like a Neanderthal, my wife gave me plenty of them."

"Um . . . why don't you come up here and have a seat," she suggested. Warning bells were going off in her head, reminding her of what this man had done, reminding her that abusers were great apologizers, but she refused to listen to them. Some deep-rooted instinct told her Chase wasn't an abuser. And she was impressed and touched that he'd faced his fear of the dark to come apologize. That had to have been so hard for him.

He took the wicker chair next to hers. They sat quietly for a while, as the night deepened and the waves continued to lap at the seawall.

"Are you . . . comfortable out here?" she asked finally.

"Hell, no." He gave a harsh laugh. "But that's okay. I'll just sit out here until the darkness suffocates me or morning comes. There doesn't seem to be any other way to get around it."

"Maybe not," she admitted. "Would you rather go inside?"

"No. No, I've got to face it."

"Sometimes that's the only option," she agreed. "So you were married?" The idea bothered her, though she

248

couldn't say why. Nor did she especially care. Whatever effects Chase had on her, she wasn't going to waste any time analyzing them, because she wasn't going to allow him that degree of importance in her life. Or so she told herself.

"For about four years."

"Not happy?"

"I thought I was. *She* wasn't. But maybe that was my fault. I was always away training, or at sea, or on some kind of a mission. Not much of a marriage."

"She found someone else?"

"She found a half dozen someone elses. Finally, somebody clued me in."

Callie's heart ached again for him. "I'm so sorry, Chase."

"I'm not good husband material."

"You know that from one marriage?"

"I don't generally need to be beaten over the head with an idea before it penetrates."

"Mmm." She made the sound as noncommittal as possible.

He turned to look at her. "Are you saying I do?"

"I'm just not sure you got the right lesson, that's all. My mom didn't fool around on my dad, and he was gone for long stretches, too."

"Who the hell was she going to fool around with out here?"

"This may surprise you, but she had a car. She went to town, she went to visit friends. She had an entire life when my dad was at sea. But she didn't cheat."

"Hmm."

"As for nobody to fool around with out here . . . well, there was the guy who built that ridiculous A-frame of yours."

"What's ridiculous about it?"

"It looks like somebody lifted it off a snowcapped mountain somewhere. Let's just say it doesn't fit the local decor."

"Matter of taste I guess. So what about the guy who built it?"

"He wrote mystery novels for a living. Lived up in Detroit and came down here in the winters. He made more than one pass at my mom when dad was away. She used to make me answer the door so she wouldn't have to talk to him."

"Sounds like a pest. What happened to him?"

"I don't know. One day the house was sold to a couple from Miami who liked to come out on weekends. Then you."

He sighed. "Some neighbor I've turned out to be. I really am sorry, Callie."

"I believe you." At least talking to him was easing the tightness of grief in her chest, distracting her from all her concerns about Jeff.

"I suppose," he said, "that you're mad at me for offering to teach Jeff to dive."

"I was."

"I guess I can see that. My last dive hardly makes a good recommendation for a teacher."

"I wasn't even thinking of that. It never crossed my mind."

"Maybe it should have. Anyway, Jeff and I were talking about treasure hunting, and it suddenly occurred to me the kid really needs something to look forward to right now. So I figured I could give him some instruction. I'm not talking about showing him how to use a regulator, putting a tank on his back, and throwing him into the water. I'm talking about learning to do it right. All of it."

"That's good." She felt a little better realizing that.

"I honestly don't believe people should go diving just for a lark," he said. "It's important to know what you're doing, and important to know how to do it safely. A half hour of instruction might work for a tourist who wants to go just once, but it doesn't make a good diver."

Her mood was lightening as she listened to him. "Sounds good. If Jeff is willing to put that much into it."

"I think he is. But if he's not, I can promise you *I* won't put him in the water."

"Thank you." She was warming to him again, and glad of it. She didn't want to be angry with him, she realized. Another warning bell sounded, and again she ignored it.

"No need to thank me," he said. "There are too many divers who don't know what they're doing. I'm not going to add to the number. Hell, recreational divers even get careless about using dive charts and computers. You've got to treat the sea with more respect than that."

"They're probably the same people who get behind the wheel and drive by faith."

"Drive by faith?"

"Sure, faith that everyone else on the road is going to look out for them."

He chuckled. Callie thought his laugh sounded a little strained, but given that he was sitting in the dark with her, determined not to give in to a fear that had been keeping him a virtual prisoner for weeks, it was hardly surprising.

She felt an impulse to reach out to him, to take his hand and offer him the comfort of touch, but she was afraid how he might mistake that. Afraid of how she might respond if he *did* mistake it. She couldn't forget the astonishing surge of desire she had experienced when he had kissed her in anger. How much more might she respond if he touched her with simple need?

She had a feeling that she was walking through a swamp here, on a barely visible path, where one misstep might land her in serious trouble. She didn't want to get involved with a man, and she most certainly didn't want to get involved with one who had Chase's kind of problems. She was, however, beginning to doubt her ability to be friends with this man without getting involved. Something about him kept tugging at her heart, drawing her closer.

Until tonight, she had believed that he wasn't seriously interested in her. Now she wasn't so sure. Kissing her in anger had opened up a whole pile of unpleasant possibilities. It had also made it impossible for her to ignore what she was feeling.

A sigh escaped her, and slipped away on the breeze.

"Something wrong?" he asked.

"Life in general. But nothing new."

"Mmm. Same here." He moved, and the wicker creaked a little. "I was thinking about what you said."

"Which what I said?"

He chuckled again. "About my buddy, Bill Evers. You're right. Ten million is a lot of motivation. Maybe even enough to get Bill to lie."

"It would take an awful lot less than ten million to make most people lie."

"Probably." He rubbed his chin with his hand, and his beard rasped. "But there's a problem, Callie."

"Which is?"

"He might lie for ten million, but I honestly don't see him killing two guys for it."

Now she understood why he'd reacted so strongly to

252

her suggestion. It wasn't so much that Bill might have lied, but that he couldn't believe Bill was a party to murder. She twisted in her seat and tried to read his face. It was a dim blur, though, so she had to guess. "So maybe he didn't. Maybe somebody paid him to lie, and somebody else went back to get the diamonds. Maybe he was out of the picture once he told the lie."

He thought about it for a few seconds, then nodded slowly. "That's possible. That falls within the range of believability. I don't like what it would say about him, and I never figured him for the type, but it's at least possible."

He stood and began to pace the porch. "There's just one problem with this, Callie. If he lied, then dropped out of the picture, he's still a loose end. And the guys who killed Rushman and Westerlake obviously don't want to leave any loose ends."

Callie's stomach fluttered nervously. "I didn't think of that. Maybe you'd better call him, Chase. Maybe you'd better warn him. Right now." She stood up and started toward the door, then had a thought that froze her on the spot.

"Chase?"

"Hmm?"

"Don't forget. You're a loose end, too."

CHAPTER 14

"IT'S LONG-DISTANCE," CHASE SAID WHEN THEY GOT to the kitchen and she pointed to the phone.

"Go ahead."

As he was punching in the number, Jeff came out of his bedroom, diving instruction manual in hand.

"What's going on?"

"Chase and I just thought of something. He's making a call."

Jeff looked at Chase, then back to her. "I thought you were pissed at him."

"I got over it."

Jeff started to smile. "You never could stay mad for long, sis."

"Only for as long as you keep shouting back at me."

He laughed. "So what's up?"

"Tell you in a minute."

Jeff pulled out a chair and sat at the table. Chase hung up the phone.

"He's not answering." He glanced at the dive watch on his wrist. "It's not that late. He could be out somewhere, or maybe he's out at sea on a contract." He looked at Callie. "Mind if I make another call? To Miami?"

"Go right ahead."

Callie waited impatiently, hoping that this time Chase could at least talk to someone. Now that the idea had occurred to her, she didn't want to wait indefinitely to get whatever answers they could.

"Tom." Chase's voice was warm as he spoke into the phone.

Callie found herself wishing his voice would sound like that when he said her name. It would be nice to have that kind of friendship.

"Tom, you got a minute? I want to talk about the dive back in March . . . yeah. You said something didn't feel right to you . . . mmm . . . well, I was wondering. How did Bill seem to you that day? Was he okay?"

She tried to read his face but couldn't. All she could do was sit on the edge of her seat and wait.

He listened for a while, then said, "Thanks. Thanks for telling me. Yeah, why don't you?" Then he hung up.

He turned to face Callie, his expression grimmer than she'd ever seen it.

"Bill is dead," he said. "They found his body early this morning. Apparently he'd been dead for some time."

Callie felt ice wash over her. "How?" she asked. Her voice was little more than a croak.

"They don't know yet. Tom just heard about it on the news. He was going to call me . . ." He trailed off and looked away.

Callie didn't know what to say. Part of her was feeling icy tendrils of fear wrapping slowly around her spine and touching the base of her skull, and part of her was feeling sympathy for Chase. He and Bill had shared a special bond. They had relied on each other for safety.

She was moving before she really thought about it, crossing the kitchen to wrap her arms around Chase and hug him.

He was so much bigger than she that it seemed almost pointless, but then his arms closed around her and held her tightly, and she could feel just how much he needed to be held.

"I'm sorry," she said.

"Yeah. Me too. We didn't have a whole lot in common, but he was the best diving buddy I ever had."

Jeff cleared his throat. "I'm sorry, Chase."

"Thanks."

Reminded of Jeff's presence, Callie suddenly felt embarrassed and backed away from Chase. He let her go instantly.

"So," said Chase after a moment. "This puts a kink in things. Tom said he's going to look into what happened

255

to Bill. He'll let me know what he finds out."

"If he's been dead for a while, it'll be hard to find out what killed him."

"Maybe. Maybe not." Chase limped over to the table, pulled out a chair, and straddled it, resting his arms over the back. Callie returned to her seat.

"What's going on?" Jeff asked. "I get the feeling there's more than just that your friend died."

Chase looked at Callie. She motioned him to explain.

"Callie suggested that maybe Bill was paid to lie about the diamonds not being on the boat. Then she pointed out that if he did that but wasn't involved with plans to recover the diamonds, he became a loose end."

"Man!" Jeff's eyes grew huge. "You think somebody killed him?"

"I don't know. Nobody knows yet. It could have been some kind of accident or something." But Chase didn't sound as if he believed it.

"It's too coincidental," Callie said. "There are entirely too many coincidences running around here, Chase."

"I'm beginning to agree with you."

"And let's not lose sight of the fact that you qualify as a loose end, too."

He shook his head. "Maybe. Maybe not. I don't remember anything about the dive, so they don't need to worry about me."

"Except that you *might* remember."

His gray eyes met hers. "Well, there's your theory about the lights and the seaweed. Keep me off balance, keep me doubting my sanity, and I won't trust my memory even if it *does* return."

She nodded. "It's been working, too, hasn't it."

"I guess so. I was actually wondering if I'd put the turtlegrass on my porch myself, in some kind attack of

256

craziness."

"Jeez," Jeff said. His eyes were still big.

"And now that you went back to check out the dive report," Callie said, "they could be even more worried about you."

Chase's eyes narrowed, and he nodded. Theoretically, no one but Tom, Dave, and Callie knew he'd checked that report. Still . . . "Do you know how paranoid we sound right now?"

"I saw the lights and the seaweed, too, Chase. And for all my flaws, I'm pretty stable psychologically."

"She is," Jeff agreed. "Look what she's been through."

Callie looked at him in surprise. "What are you talking about?"

"Losing Mom and Dad."

"You lost them, too."

"But I didn't have responsibility for my kid brother." He gave her a smile. "I *do* notice, Callie, even if you think I'm an ingrate."

She felt her throat tighten, and felt tears well in her eyes. "Enough mush," she said huskily. "You'll make me cry."

"Nah. Wouldn't want to do that. I always panic when you cry. Okay, so Callie saw the seaweed and the lights. Which means Chase didn't imagine them. Am I following here?"

Chase and Callie nodded.

"Of course," Jeff said, "that still doesn't mean you didn't put the seaweed there yourself, Chase. But you couldn't have done the lights."

"No lights," Chase agreed. "And it's logical to think the seaweed was done by the same person who does the lights."

"Which means you probably didn't do it yourself," Jeff said. "I can buy that. Especially since you don't seem all that crazy to me. Now, Callie thinks someone might be doing this to you to make you think you're crazy? Did I get that right?"

Chase nodded. "What you don't know is about my nightmares and my fear of the dark. I've . . . been pretty close to the edge since my accident. Callie thinks someone has been playing on that."

"And that's intended to keep you from believing anything you might remember about the dive?"

"Or," said Callie, "to make Chase unbelievable if he does remember something and tells someone."

"Better yet," Chase agreed. "Ruin my credibility. That would work even better than pushing me over the edge."

"Sure. And didn't you say lots of people know about your nightmares and your fear of the dark?"

"Apparently Maritime knows about it," Chase said, suddenly remembering. "When Dave stopped by to visit me, he said the doctors had been keeping him posted, and he did mention my nightmares. From that I took it that he even meant my psychiatrist is keeping them informed."

"So lots of people probably know. Whatever happened to medical confidentiality?"

Chase shook his head. "I don't know. Maritime was paying all my bills. Maybe it was necessary to keep them informed to justify their payments. I'm sure there's some loophole there somewhere. Maybe even something I signed. I don't remember."

Jeff spoke. "It doesn't matter how they know. Just that they know. So a lot of people could have known that you were seeing a psychiatrist, and could have guessed that with a little help you might not be credible if you remembered something."

"Exactly," Callie said. "Imagine Chase trying to tell someone he had remembered something from the dive, and these guys come along to say he also sees red eyes in the woods in the dead of night, and finds strange seaweed draped all over his porch."

"Seaweed that disappears," Chase said. "Let's not forget that part. It was gone later."

"Sheesh!" Jeff rolled his eyes. "These guys aren't too good at this. Callie saw the seaweed, and she saw the lights."

Chase shrugged. "Maybe they paid some kid a few bucks to do it for them. Or maybe they're just not as bright as they think."

"So you think," Jeff said, "that all of this is related to the diamonds?"

"Well, Callie said something interesting earlier. She asked me just how many weird things could be going on at one time and not be related. It got me to thinking. We have the coincidence of you finding a boat a short distance from the wreck of *The Happy Maggie*, a boat on which two people were killed, a boat which had taken two divers out there. Then you have the two divers nobody can find anything out about. Which reminds me, what did your lawyer say about that?"

Callie answered. "Only that the cops haven't been able to find the divers. Nobody's been reported missing, nobody vanished from a hotel room. Phantoms, she called them."

"That's weird," Jeff said.

"Even weirder when you connect all this to the proximity with *The Happy Maggie*."

Jeff leaned forward eagerly. "Then this stuff at your

259

place. Yeah, I see what Callie meant. Too much weird stuff, and all of it could be connected to the *Maggie*."

"About the only coincidences the connection won't explain is me living next door to you and Jeff finding the *Island Dream*," Chase said.

"Well, coincidences do happen," Callie said. "They just don't usually pile up. A woman I work with went to Washington last winter on a vacation, and as she was walking up the steps of the Capitol, she ran into an acquaintance she hadn't seen or heard from in a dozen years, not since she left Michigan. It happens. You just don't usually get a whole string of them like this."

"Sometimes," Jeff said soberly, "you get the feeling things were meant to be."

It was true, Callie thought. Sometimes you just got that feeling, and she was having it right now, looking at Chase and Jeff across the table. She definitely had the feeling that events were moving in a destined direction, that currents were carrying her, Jeff, and Chase to some preordained place. She didn't know if she liked that. A shiver ran through her.

"Actually," she said, needing to banish the feeling, "the only real coincidence would be Jeff finding the *Island Dream*. Without that, none of the rest of this would seem like a coincidence."

Chase agreed. "That's true."

Jeff made an impatient sound. "What does it matter? When you start looking at things in hindsight you can see all sorts of coincidences that made things happen."

That was a remarkably perceptive comment from her usually devil-may-care brother. Callie looked at him with new respect.

"I can do that with anything in my life if I want to," he said. "What really concerns me right now is, how do we use this to get me out of these murder charges?"

"That," said Chase, "is the question."

"Did you find out anything from the dive shops?" Callie asked.

"I was waiting for callbacks. Didn't get any yet. But I have an answering machine, so if anyone calls, I'll know about it."

"Why did you call dive shops?" Jeff asked.

"Actually, I called around to places that supply gases to commercial divers. Some deal with the public; most don't."

"How come?"

"It's hard to get a good gas mixture," Chase explained. "It takes skill to mix the helium, oxygen, and nitrogen into a safe blend, and it's too easy to screw up. Every now and then some diver dies because his mixture is off, and he's breathing nearly pure helium or nitrogen."

Callie's heart turned over. "Jeff's not going to breathe that stuff, is he?"

Chase shook his head. "Most places he'd want to dive around here, all he'd need is regular compressed air. He can get that at any dive shop. Anyway, I was hoping somebody would remember a guy, or a couple of guys, who paid cash for Trimix or heliox within a day or two of the murders. Of course, if these guys were working for a commercial dive company, we're screwed. They wouldn't have stood out, and nobody will remember them."

"If they were commercial divers," Callie said, "wouldn't they have had their own boat?"

"I doubt they would have used a company boat for this expedition regardless. What I meant was that if they frequently get gas mixes for dives for a commercial

261

venture, no one would have noticed them." Chase sighed and rubbed his eyes. "I gotta think about this. Everything's turning up a dead end, but I keep getting this feeling that the answer is right there, almost in reach."

"One thing for sure," Jeff said with a remarkable amount of firmness, "you're not going home tonight."

Chase looked at him.

"If somebody was willing to kill your buddy because he was a loose end, they'd be willing to kill *you*, Chase. Especially now that you've been nosing around."

"He's right," Callie said. "Jeff's absolutely right. You've asked a lot of questions. Who knows who may have heard about that."

He looked at the two of them, then surprised them with a laugh. "Christ," he said. "And I thought I was paranoid before."

Callie had lit up the whole house, Chase noticed. In a quiet, unobtrusive way, she'd turned on the living room lights, the bedroom lights, the veranda lights, driving the shadows back from the house. The gesture touched him.

It also made him feel small and shameful. His fear of the darkness troubled him in a way few things had. It wounded his self-image, wounded his self-confidence. His marriage had done that, but nothing else until this had affected him quite so much.

He made himself go out onto the veranda again, reminding himself that only a couple of hours ago he had managed to walk through the woods, through the shadowy, reaching shapes of the mangroves and the buttonwoods. If he could do that, he could stand on the veranda for a while and fight the darkness some more.

262

The thing about fear, though, was that even if you faced it, it didn't necessarily go away. Stepping through Callie's front door was a difficult thing to do. He could feel the night trying to close in again.

But he could also see the crescent moon, and the silvery water. The breeze had quieted, and the inlet was as smooth as glass, looking like a dark mirror. He stared into that mirror, trying to remember his last dive.

The ocean had been unusually calm that day, he remembered. A beautiful day for a dive, with bright sun, no clouds, and very little wave action. He and Bill had suited up, double-checking each other's equipment— and then he remembered nothing, not even going over the side. What had happened after that had become the stuff of nightmares he couldn't trust.

But in his dream earlier, he'd seen the hull of *The Happy Maggie*. It had been a dim blur, outside the brightest halo of his lamp, and it might only have been the creation of his dream—in fact, probably was since the hole he had seen in his dream in no way matched Bill's damage report. But he focused on the image anyway, trying to jog his subconscious into remembering more.

"Chase?" Callie came out onto the porch. "I wanted to show you your room. I made up the bed."

"Thanks. Don't be offended if I don't sleep in it. I don't sleep much at night."

"It's there if you want it." She came to stand beside him at the railing. "It's beautiful tonight. When I was a kid and dad was home, sometimes he'd take us out on the water on nights like this. I'd usually fall asleep from the rocking of the boat. I always figured he did it because he and Mom found it romantic."

He looked down at her. "That *would* be romantic."

"Sure. If you don't hate the sea."

She looked ethereal in the pale moonlight and shadows, and he felt something catch in his chest. Callie was, he thought, as elusive as the sea. You might reach out and touch her, but you could never hold her. Every time he started to feel close to her, she drew even further away. The realization stayed his impulse to reach out.

"You don't hate the sea," he said quietly.

"No? How would you know?" Her tone challenged him as much as her words.

"You hate the things the sea does. But if your dad had died in a car accident, would you blame the road? Would you refuse to ever drive again?"

"Don't use logic on me. This isn't logical."

He had the worst urge to laugh, but bit it back because she'd probably misunderstand and think he was laughing at her. Laughing at her was the last thing he wanted to do.

What he wanted to do was laugh at himself. "Listen to me trying to talk you out of your hangups. *Me*. As if I haven't got a million of my own that won't yield to reason."

She glanced up at him and laughed. Only then did he feel it was safe to let out his own laughter.

Presently, though, after their laughter died, she sighed. "Look, about Jeff's diving . . ."

"I know you don't want him to, Callie. But it has to be his decision."

"I know that. That's what I was going to say. I realized a few things about myself today, and I didn't like them. So I won't say anything more about college or diving."

"Good for you."

"It won't be easy." She sighed again. "I guess I've gotten into a bad habit of thinking I know more than he does. But that's not really true. In the first place, I'm not all that much older. In the second . . . well, if I could manage to raise him from the time I was fourteen, I guess he's probably better equipped for life at twenty than I'm allowing him to be."

"He's as well equipped as anyone his age."

"Yeah, I was thinking about what you said about being on your own at twenty. Eric—his friend—has been self-supporting for the last two years. It occurred to me that Jeff might have moved out on his own already—except for me. I think he's hanging around here because he thinks he has to take care of *me*."

"That wouldn't surprise me. But you *do* have a dock . . . "

She laughed again. "There *are* a few attractions around here. But mostly I think he just doesn't want to leave me alone. He said something tonight that really hurt."

"Which was?"

"That I need to get a life. He's right."

"I imagine a lot of women discover that when their kids grow up. Being a mom is pretty life-consuming, I'd think. Then one day they don't really need you as much."

"That day arrived a while back. I just didn't want to face it."

He gave in to impulse and slipped his arm around her shoulders. Something akin to amazement and wonder filled him when she allowed herself to lean against him, when she relaxed into his embrace. After what he had done earlier, he wouldn't have blamed her for jerking away. When he felt her arm lift and wrap around his waist, he stopped breathing.

God, it had been so long! The ache that filled him then had nothing to do with fear, and everything to do with an unending loneliness that not even the sea and his friends had been able to assuage.

This was dangerous territory, and he knew it, but he decided he could risk it for just a little while. He and Callie were worlds apart, and there could never be any more between them than this moment. Besides, he was never going to trust anyone with his heart again. But just for now he could have the illusion of not being alone in the world.

"I'm really scared," she said. "That's part of the reason I've been acting so crazy. These murder charges are real, and they aren't going to just vanish no matter how much I wish it. So I'm ragging on Jeff when I know I shouldn't. Distracting myself from the stuff I can't fix by getting on him about college and anything else that comes to mind."

"Maybe you're feeling a little resentful of him, too. He's caused some serious trouble in your life with this murder charge."

"But *he* isn't the cause. I know that." She stirred against him, then leaned even closer. "You're right, though. I guess at some level I've been blaming him."

"You're only human, Callie. You can't expect to be perfect."

"Mmm."

Was it his imagination, or was she leaning even closer. His heart accelerated a little as he tightened his hold on her. God, he needed her closeness.

"I'm sorry," she said.

His heart plummeted. He was sure she was going to pull away, and he didn't know if he could stand that.

Right now, holding her, even the dark didn't seem threatening. "For what?"

"The way I've been acting. I've been on some kind of tear, haven't I? I've been just awful to you and Jeff."

"Awful is a little extreme, don't you think?"

"No." Another sigh escaped her. "Lately I've been feeling I'm losing my grip on everything, that every last thing is getting out of my control. Jeff's growing up and pushing for independence. Then these murder charges. Then you."

"Me?"

She was silent a long time. A very long time. Finally, she spoke, her voice hushed. "You terrify me."

His heart thudded. "What I did earlier . . ."

"Not that. I've already forgotten that. It's . . . I'm just scared of you. Part of me . . . part of me wants things . . ." She trailed off.

His mind scrambled around, trying to complete that sentence, afraid he might put the wrong meaning there. Afraid of him? Wanting? Wanting *what*?

She spoke again, and unconsciously he leaned close to hear. "I swore I'd never get involved with a man again."

His heart skipped into high gear. Now *he* was scared. "Me too," he said. "Me too."

She tilted her face up, and silvery moonlight kissed her. "Your wife hurt you."

"Mel hurt *you*."

They stood, not moving, understanding filling them and drawing them closer even though neither of them moved a muscle.

Callie spoke, her voice little more than a whisper. "*You* make me feel out of control."

His heart beat heavily, and he had the feeling that the

267

next few minutes might shape his life in ways he'd never imagined.

"Jeff makes me feel out of control, too, lately," she said quietly. "But you . . . terrify me."

Right now she was terrifying *him*. His white-knight impulse had never been stronger. She needed help, and he wanted to give it, but there was danger here. Potential catastrophe. In the first place, he was nearly paralyzed by his own problems. How could he possibly help anyone else?

But worse, he wouldn't help Callie at all if she seized on him as a substitute for Jeff. He couldn't become her life simply because she needed one.

He should back away right now, he told himself. Let go of her, step back, and return their conversation to safer grounds.

But he could no more have let go of her than he could have stopped the beating of his heart. He felt almost as if he were welded to her, and ripping away would cause terminal damage.

But the night had other ideas. A breeze moved, skimming over the water and stirring its surface, shattering the mirror of moonlight. It caught the back of his head, ruffling his hair and gently pushing him toward Callie. Carrying away his last sane thought.

He bent his head, saw her face lift toward him, recognized that she wanted this as much as he. A small flame of warmth began to glow in his heart, and gently began to spread to all the other cold, lonely places.

He lowered his mouth to hers, felt their lips touch again, but this time the touch was so very different. Instead of anger and a desire to silence her, this time he wanted her to speak to him in a language older than words.

His lips moved gently against hers, coaxing her to answer his question. The warmth in him grew, settling lower, becoming a hot, heavy ache in his loins.

She kissed him back, and it was unlike any kiss he had ever known. There was a freshness, an uncertainty, and an eagerness that acted like an intoxicant on him. Drawing her around so that she faced him, he tucked her into the curve of his body and felt delight splinter through him as her other arm closed around his waist.

He deepened his kiss, sensing her inexperience and taking great care because of it. He should have called a halt, but there was some essential need in him that she was answering, overriding his caution and common sense.

She trusted him, he realized with an explosion of delight and wonder. She trusted him, or she wouldn't be holding him like this and kissing him like this. Her trust was a scary thing, because it would be so easy to hurt or disappoint her. But it was also a healing thing, a balm to wounds so old he had forgotten they existed.

Making a little sound deep in her throat, she pressed herself tighter to him, and her palms climbed his back, stroking him longingly. He began to have visions that went far beyond a comforting kiss, visions of their bodies twined, his hands and mouth on her, of the two of them rolling around in a big bed in a search to appease the fires of passion.

His hands followed his thoughts, and one of them slipped between them, finding the fullness of her breast and cradling it with a hunger. She arched into his touch as if it delighted her every bit as much as it delighted him.

Oh, man. Thunder began to roll in his head, and lightning to shoot through him to his loins. He was hardening for her, and with an instinct as old as time, he pressed himself to her, seeking release.

And all of a sudden she tore herself away from him, backing up until she was five feet away.

He stared at her, battling the waves of desire that were demanding he go to her and bring her close again. He couldn't do that. He realized it as strongly as he realized that he wanted her more than he had ever before wanted a woman.

"I'm sorry," he said hoarsely. "I shouldn't have let that get out of hand."

"It's not you . . ." Her voice broke. "It's just . . . I never . . . I'd only disappoint you." Turning, she fled into the house.

Leaving Chase on the porch with his enemy darkness and an empty ache as big as the Atlantic Ocean.

CHAPTER 15

CALLIE AWOKE IN THE MORNING WITH THE FEELING that some kind of dark cloud had vanished, leaving her head clear and her heart filled with determination. Looking back at her behavior over the past few months, she wondered what had been wrong with her. She'd been making life hell for Jeff, and had projected her fears outward on Chase Mattingly in a way that embarrassed her to death. She almost felt as if she'd been caught in some kind of dark bag, and had been flailing in every direction trying to find a way out.

There *was* no way out. That knowledge settled over her, calming her. Jeff was growing up and was going to leave. The murder charges weren't going to vanish no matter how she railed against them. And Chase wasn't

Mel. Whatever his problems, he didn't deserve the way she had been acting toward him. Maybe she was entitled to her fear of men and her doubts about their reliability, but she wasn't entitled to treat individual men according to her generalized fear.

She looked in the bathroom mirror and grimaced. "Psychologist heal thyself," she said sternly.

Well, why should it surprise her that she'd been blind to her own failings? She was only human, after all, and psychologists were no better at analyzing themselves than the general population. It was one thing to be objective when you were dealing with someone else's problems, and entirely another to be objective about your own.

Which was why, when psychologists needed therapy, they turned to their colleagues. So maybe she wasn't an utter failure just because she'd been so blind to her own problems. Maybe.

When she walked out to make breakfast, she was determined to treat both Jeff and Chase better, and to stop letting her fears rule her.

However, she couldn't make breakfast. Chase and Jeff were already doing that.

She looked around at the pancake batter, the frying bacon, the freshly baked biscuits and the beaten eggs. "How many stevedores are we expecting for breakfast?"

Chase chuckled and Jeff laughed. When her eyes met Chase's she felt a blush creep into her cheeks. Something in his expression gentled infinitesimally, and she felt a huge relief that he wasn't upset about the way she had acted last night.

"I'm hungry, sis," Jeff said, flipping a pancake on the griddle. "You know how I always love those breakfast buffets? Well, I figured we could have one at home."

271

"I trust you're going to eat all that?"

"Nah. I'll leave a little for you and Chase."

She felt herself smiling, and it was the most natural smile that had come to her face in ages. Why, she wondered, did she feel so much better when nothing at all had changed? The murder charges were still hanging over her and Jeff like a cloud of doom.

But she felt better anyway, almost as if a dreaded moment had arrived and she had found herself ready to face it. One thing for sure: She was ready for action.

"I'll even clean up," Jeff said. "See how good I am?"

"I'll do it," Callie offered. "You're cooking."

"Hey, it's a good excuse not to start painting right away."

Jeff was feeling better, too, she realized. Maybe because she and Chase had included him last night when they discussed their suspicions and the little information they had. Maybe he was just glad to feel he was going to be part of the solution. She could understand that.

Jeff waved her to the table, so she sat, then thanked him when he brought her a glass of orange juice.

"You know what we haven't done in a long time?" Jett said as he flipped the pancake onto a plate, then poured more batter. "We haven't had a cutup."

"I'm not sure anybody does that anymore," Callie said. "It's been years since I even heard of one."

"Well, we ought to do it. I'll bet some of the people from church would come."

If they didn't think Jeff was a murderer, she thought with trepidation.

"Maybe after I get this murder thing gone," Jeff said. "I'd like Sara to come."

"Sara?"

"The girl I met. She called this morning."

That explained his mood, Callie thought. "I'm glad." It was hard to say, but at least today she meant it. Yesterday she probably wouldn't have. God, what a bitch she'd become.

Jeff looked at her. "Really?"

"Really."

"Good, because she's coming out this afternoon to help me paint."

"Now that's really good," Callie said. "I'm all for extra helping hands."

"What in the world is a cutup?" Chase asked when he could get a word in.

"Oh!" Callie turned to him. "It's an old Keys tradition. A bunch of people get together. Everybody brings a piece or two of fruit from their own yards. I've got limes and guavas out back, somebody would bring papayas—you get the idea. Everybody helps cut it up into small pieces in a bowl, we squeeze lime juice all over it, and let it soak for a few hours while everyone plays and gabs."

"Then comes the fun part," Jeff said. "When the cutup is ready, we draw numbers from a hat. Then everybody in order gets to take one piece of fruit until it's all gone. The last person gets to drink the juice." He smacked his lips. "It's really good."

He looked at Callie. "We used to do that all the time with the folks from church. But lately we haven't been going very regularly."

"I know. I guess we should start going again." Thinking about it, she realized it had been nearly six months since she'd gone to church, and before that, her attendance had been spotty for a couple of years. It was as if she'd been withdrawing from everything,

273

especially since Jeff had started to become so headstrong lately. Depression. Jeez, she'd been suffering from depression.

And now it was gone. For no reason at all. But that was depression.

"Sounds like fun," Chase said. "You'll have to invite me."

"Sure," Jeff agreed.

"If anybody else even remembers what a cutup is," Callie remarked. "They even stopped having them at church five or six years ago. Too many new people from out of the Keys, and not enough old Conchs left, I guess."

"So let's start the tradition again."

She smiled at Jeff, feeling her heart lift at his good spirits.

Even if it killed her, she was going to be nice to Sara, if the girl could make him feel this good.

Jeff loaded the food onto the table while Chase put out plates and flatware. Everybody dug in, and both Chase and Jeff made a fair-sized dent in all the food.

"When did you learn to make biscuits this good?" Callie asked her brother.

"I read the directions on the biscuit-mix box."

"Well, you can do it from now on. I hate making them."

"It's easy, sis."

"It's messy."

"It's still easy."

Chase was smiling at the two of them, and for a few minutes it honestly seemed as if there was nothing wrong in the world.

But inevitably the conversation came back around to the murders. Jeff was the one who brought it up, speaking to Chase.

"If those gas suppliers don't call you back, what do we do next?"

"I'm not even going to wait that long," Chase said. "I'm thinking about calling the jeweler who owned *The Happy Maggie*."

Callie looked up from her plate. "How come?"

"I want to ask him what happened. It occurred to me last night that he might have been telling the truth about how the boat went down. The report didn't give a whole lot of details, just that he claimed he hit an underwater obstacle. Bill said it looked like there was a fire and explosion in the bilge. Now, if someone was willing to lie about those diamonds being there, why wouldn't he lie about the damage to the boat?"

"But what would be the point in that?"

"To build an even stronger case against Bruderson for insurance fraud. If he got convicted for fraud, nobody'd ever look any further for those diamonds."

Callie put her fork down and leaned back from the table. Her scalp was beginning to prickle. "I don't like the sound of this, Chase. I mean . . . if they're willing to go to these lengths to tie up loose ends, even loose ends like Bruderson, then maybe the three of us are loose ends, too. What if they've heard we're poking around about this? What if one of those places you called yesterday calls these divers and tells them you're asking about them? They'll know we've made the connection."

"The thought crossed my mind. Which is why I'm not going to let any more moss grow under my feet over this. For now, I need to get back to my place to see if anyone's called and get a change of clothes and a shower. Then I'm calling Bruderson. You can come with me, if you want."

275

Callie wanted, and so did Jeff. They did a quick job of cleanup, everyone pitching in, then they walked briskly over to Chase's house.

At his door, he started to put the key in the lock when he noticed the door wasn't fully latched. "Well, hell," he said.

"What's wrong?" Callie asked.

"I thought I locked this damn door last night." He gave it a push and it swung open.

Callie's heart took a plunge. "Chase, be careful. Somebody might be in there."

He glanced at her and nodded. "You two back away in case somebody comes running out. Just get clear."

"You shouldn't go in there alone," Jeff argued in a whisper.

Chase shook his head. "I've had training for this kind of thing. You haven't. I don't want to have to look out for you, too."

"Come on, Jeff," Callie said. "The best way we can help is to stay clear."

Jeff's expression was mutinous, but he went with Callie around the side of the house.

Chase noticed two things as Callie and Jeff moved away. The first was that all the lights were out. He knew damn well that he'd left them on last night.

The second thing was that the Beretta was no longer on the table where he'd left it. *Shit.* If someone was in there, they probably had the gun. And by now they knew he was coming in, because he had to have heard the three of them talking at the door.

Armed and dangerous. The words floated through his mind as he stepped into the house. The morning sunlight alleviated some of the gloom inside, but not all of it. He could feel the pressure of the shadows, as if they were

276

trying to break free of confinement, but he forced himself to ignore it. He had a far more serious problem right now than any his neurosis could present. And a far more serious threat than the darkness.

Now he feared what might be *in* the darkness of the shadowy places in his house.

Moving as silently as he could, keeping near the walls, he scanned the open living area, the living room, the dining room, the kitchen. Nothing there. He made his way down the hallway to the bedroom and found the door wide-open. At least there were some mercies, he thought. At least he didn't have to open that door wondering what was behind it.

Nothing. A check of the closets and the bathroom revealed the same thing. Nothing.

Outside again, he walked around the house, looking for some indication of where his visitors had come from, but the caprock was hard where it was bare, and the dead leaves on the ground revealed nothing. As dry as it had been, his driveway didn't show evidence of tire tracks. Remembering his intention to search the woods for evidence of the person who was doing the red eyes thing to him, he wandered a way up into the hammock, but found the ground too hard and too thick with dead leaves to reveal anything.

"Hell," he said as he came back to the house.

Callie and Jeff, who had been watching him from the seawall, joined him.

"Was anything taken?" she asked.

"My gun."

She drew a sharp breath. "You'd better call the police."

Back inside, that was the first thing he did.

"I'd better go," Jeff said when Chase hung up the

phone. "I'm going to be the first person they suspect."

Callie looked at him. "Why? You were with *us* all night. You don't have to run and hide from the cops just because you've been charged with a crime you didn't commit."

"You're not going anywhere," Chase agreed. "Never, ever hang your head in shame for something you didn't do."

Jeff's chin came up, and Callie thought he straightened. "You're right," her brother said. "I didn't do anything wrong."

While they were waiting for the cops to arrive, Chase decided to go ahead and try to locate Olaf Bruderson, the jeweler who owned *The Happy Maggie*.

Bruderson's Jewelry in Miami had four stores. He tried them one after another, but no one seemed very eager to tell him how to reach the owner. On the last call, Chase pressed harder.

"Look, just tell Mr. Bruderson I have reason to believe the missing diamonds *were* on his boat. Have him call me if he's interested. He can either talk to me or Calypso Carlson." He left both his number and Callie's.

"You know," he said when he hung up the phone, "I'm glad I'm not a cop or a private investigator. Trying to get a little information is turning out to be the most frustrating thing I've ever done."

Jeff and Callie were standing in the center of the living room, being careful not to touch anything.

"I'd make us some coffee," Chase said, "but I don't want to move anything."

"Maybe we should just wait on the porch," Callie suggested. "The less time we spend in here, the less likely we are to disturb something."

Ten minutes later, Fred Markell pulled up in his white-and-green patrol car and climbed out. Callie was less than thrilled to see him come around the porch and look up at them.

"Hi, Callie," he said. "Hi, Jeff."

Jeff wouldn't even look at him. Callie returned his greeting coolly. They might have been friends in high school, but she didn't much like him since the day he'd served the warrant on her, then lied to her about nothing being taken. Although, she admitted fairly, maybe Fred hadn't known that Jeff's clothes had been taken. There had been five or six deputies searching the house.

Chase explained about the missing gun and the unlocked door. Fred wrote it all down.

"Anything else missing?" he asked.

"I don't think so," Chase replied. "Not that I checked everything. I didn't want to disturb things."

"Good." Fred nodded approvingly. "Nothing messed up?"

"Not that I could see."

"Well, it was probably a crime of opportunity then," Fred said. "Somebody happened along, saw no one was at home, saw the gun on the table, broke in and took it. Probably all they wanted."

"Looks that way," Chase agreed.

"You happen to have the gun's serial number?"

Chase went into the house to get it, while Callie and Jeff remained on the porch. Nobody said anything.

Fred rocked on his heels, looking seriously uncomfortable. Finally he cleared his throat. "I don't think you did it, Jeff."

Callie looked at Fred in astonishment, and saw that Jeff was doing the same.

"Uh . . . thanks," Jeff said finally.

Fred shrugged. "You just aren't the type. Besides, there's a lot of unanswered questions on that case. You hang in there, boy. We're still looking for those divers."

Callie felt herself warming to Fred. "Thanks, Fred. I thought you'd close the case."

The deputy shook his head. "Too many questions. This is just my personal opinion, mind you, but they couldn't convict you on that load of crap they got right now. You got nothing to worry about."

Callie didn't agree with him there. As long as her brother was charged with murder, they had plenty to worry about.

Chase returned with the papers for the gun, and Fred took down the full description and the serial number.

"They'll be someone out later to dust for prints and stuff, but they probably won't find anything useful," Fred said. "Some kid probably took it and'll sell it quick. Five or six people later, it'll turn up in a crime somewhere, I reckon."

"I'll leave the place unlocked," Chase said. "In case I'm not here when the crime-scene guys come. Just tell them to come right in."

After Markell left, Chase spoke. "I wish I could believe that."

"What?"

"That five or six people later it'll turn up in a crime somewhere."

"It probably will." She looked at him curiously. "Why? What do you think is going on?"

"I'm just thinking how easy it would be to use that gun to link *me* to a crime scene."

"Oh, God! But they couldn't now, Chase. You've reported it stolen."

"There was still last night."

"But you were with *us*."

"But whoever took the gun doesn't know that." His expression was grim. "I'm liking this less and less, and I didn't like it very much to begin with."

"I've got to go back to the house," Jeff said suddenly. "Sara will be here soon."

"Go ahead," Callie said. "I want to wait here to see if the jeweler calls back."

"Okay."

Callie listened for the phone while Chase showered. When he emerged twenty minutes later, he was toweling his dark hair and wearing a white shirt and white shorts. From the start Callie had noticed how good he looked in shorts, but after their kiss last night, she found herself noticing him in an entirely different way. Her hands were absolutely itching to touch him, and she had to remind herself that she had enough problems in her life without taking on Chase's.

But the heat of the tropical day seemed to be creeping into her bloodstream, making her feel heavy, almost sleepy, except for a tingling down low that reminded her she was a young, healthy woman with all the needs of one. What a direction for her thoughts to take in the midst of all this! It embarrassed her, and made her feel ashamed somehow.

The phone rang and Chase grabbed it, letting the towel drape over his shoulder. "Mattingly," he said into the receiver.

Callie sat on the edge of her seat, then deflated as he continued.

"What's up, Tom? Yeah? Christ . . ." He listened for a few minutes. "Yeah, I will. And you, too, buddy. You were there, too." He hung up and turned to Callie. "That was Tom Akers."

She nodded.

"Bill was murdered. The cops say he was shot in the back of the head."

Callie's hand flew to her mouth. "Chase . . ."

"I know, I know. Tom said the same thing. He told me to watch my back. I told him to watch his. He was there, too."

She rose from the couch, suddenly feeling icy cold, and began to pace. "Too many coincidences," she said, her voice tight. "It's just too damn much, Chase."

"It sure is."

She stopped pacing and looked at him, feeling the worst urge to have his arms around her, as if they could shelter her from all of this. But nobody's arms could do that, and she knew it.

He must have read her expression, because he closed the small distance between them and drew her into a hug. She felt his chin come to rest on the top of her head as they wrapped their arms around each other. Neither of them said a word, but words wouldn't have helped a thing.

"I'm uneasy about leaving Jeff alone," she said finally. "He found that boat. They might be wondering if he knows something, especially since you live next to us and you've started asking questions."

"You might be right. But he ought to be okay with Sara over there. Besides, they ought to realize that if he knew anything, he would have told the state attorney to get himself off. That ought to be as obvious as the nose on their faces."

"That's true." She felt a bubble of tension within her collapse, but it was only one of the many bubbles of tension that were keeping her on edge.

Part of her knew she ought to step back from Chase

right now, but she wasn't able to. He smelled so good after his shower, a heady mix of man and soap. And he *felt* so good, so powerful and strong. It was also about the only comfort she had found in days and she didn't want to give it up. When his hands started stroking her back, she felt herself relax into him, tension seeping out of her muscles . . . only to be replaced by a new tension, a more delicious one.

The phone rang. She felt Chase stiffen, and after a reluctant moment, he let go of her. She couldn't remember ever having felt so bereft just from having someone step away from her.

"Mattingly," he said into the phone. "Yes. That's correct. I was one of the salvage divers who went down to *The Happy Maggie*. Uh-huh. Right. Yes, I can do that. I'll be there."

He hung up and looked at Callie. "That was Olaf Bruderson's attorney. He wants me to meet with him and Bruderson this afternoon at five in Miami."

Callie felt her heart accelerate. "I'm going with you." Then she remembered Jeff. "No, I can't leave Jeff."

"Yes, you can. You're not going to be able to do much to protect him even if you stay, Callie. Maybe he has some friends he can stay with? Or maybe he and Sara can take the afternoon and evening to do something fun in Key West. We'll be home by ten at the latest. Or maybe he can come with us."

But Jeff didn't want to go with them. When they got over to the house, they found that Sara had arrived. She was a lovely young woman with hip-length black hair and smoothly tanned skin, enough to turn any young man's head.

Callie started to explain about having to go to Miami, and not wanting Jeff to stay by himself at the house, without going into the reasons. But Jeff understood. "I'll hang out in town, sis," he said. "There's lots of stuff for Sara and me to do. Maybe I'll spend the night at Phil's place." Phil was a high school friend of his whose parents owned a bar on Duval Street. The two had been inseparable until Phil had graduated from school and had gone to work in his parents' business.

"That would be good. Do me a favor and call Phil to see if that'll be all right. Otherwise, I think you ought to come to Miami with us."

But Phil thought it was a great idea, and the plans were made. An hour later, Chase and Callie were on US 1, headed for Miami.

The offices of Barton, Barton, and Wilhelm were located in a posh high-rise, but inside the offices were decorated to look like something out of a gentleman's club. The leather chairs, leather tabletops, and hunter green damask wallpaper reeked money. It was a room for men, not for women. The only sign of the present era was a small window through which one could speak to the receptionist. Her office, in startling contrast to the waiting room, was full of gleaming modern equipment from the PBX to the latest model of collating copier.

Promptly at five, Chase and Callie were ushered into a large office with a view of the city. It, too, was appointed in leather, damask and brass. A wiry, sun-bronzed man in a suit sat on a sofa, smoking a hand-rolled cigar. A tall, grayhaired man in a blue pinstriped suit rose from behind the polished desk to greet them.

"Mr. Mattingly," he said in the well-rounded tones of an orator. "And this is?"

"My assistant, Calypso Carlson."

"I'm Peter Barton, Mr. Bruderson's attorney," he

284

said, shaking their hands. "And this is Mr. Bruderson."

Bruderson rose from the couch and shook their hands. "Do you mind my cigar?"

"Not me," Chase said. Callie quickly shook her head, though she'd much have preferred not to smell it. She felt, though, that it wouldn't be politic to object.

As soon as they were all settled in chairs, Barton took charge of the meeting. "Mr. Bruderson is naturally interested in your claim that the diamonds were still aboard *The Happy Maggie*."

"Actually," said Chase, "I believe they were still there at the time I made my salvage dive. I think they're gone now."

"Then what's the point of this interview? I thought perhaps you might have the diamonds and be considering making a deal with us."

Callie saw Chase's cheeks darken. "I'm not that kind of person, Mr. Barton. If I had those diamonds, I'd *give* them to you."

Barton studied him a moment, then nodded. "I still don't see the point, then. Mr. Bruderson's claim was denied by the insurance company. Without the diamonds, this is a total loss."

"There's more involved here than the diamonds, Mr. Barton. First, I don't know if you're aware of it, but Maritime is considering pressing charges against Mr. Bruderson for attempted insurance fraud."

Barton lifted a brow, and Bruderson paused with his cigar halfway to his mouth. Barton spoke. "Where did you hear this?"

"From someone at Maritime."

"They'd have a very weak case."

"Maybe. But in addition to insurance fraud, there's the matter of two young men who've been falsely

285

charged with murder."

"Why should that interest us?"

"Because I believe the murders were committed by two salvage divers who went down to Mr. Bruderson's boat to get the diamonds. You might also be interested to know that Bill Evers, the diver who was assigned to get the diamonds on the original dive, has turned up murdered."

Barton and Bruderson exchanged looks. Bruderson spoke for the first time since they had exchanged greetings. "What do you want, Mr. Mattingly?"

"What I want is to find out what's really going on here. I want to get those two young men off the murder charges, and if I can find out what happened to your diamonds in the process, you can get your money out of Maritime."

Bruderson nodded. "How much do you want?"

"I don't want anything except information."

Bruderson searched his face. "An honest man, hmm?"

"That's my reputation, Mr. Bruderson. I tend to guard it."

"So what information do you want?"

"I want to know exactly what happened when your boat got into trouble. Before I went down there, all I had was a statement that you said the boat hit an underwater obstacle. I wasn't especially interested in what you *said* because I was going down to look at it myself. My specialty is figuring out exactly what happened to cause boats and ships to sink. Unfortunately, the dive got interrupted."

"I heard," Bruderson said. "What happened?"

"I don't remember. All I know is what I was told. But I'll tell you something, Mr. Bruderson. I'm beginning to have serious doubts that it was simply an accident of

286

some kind."

The lawyer and the jeweler exchanged looks again, and Bruderson nodded.

Barton spoke. "We've been having a few qualms ourselves about what we've been told. In the first place, Mr. Bruderson didn't sink his own boat. In the second place, he *knows* those diamonds were aboard. At first we thought maybe somebody had gotten down to the wreck before you made your dive, but we've started wondering."

"Why's that?"

"Because their description of the damage doesn't fit with Mr. Bruderson's recollection of events."

"I felt the boat hit something," Bruderson said. "Then we started taking on water really fast."

Chase nodded. "An explosion could feel that way."

"But there was no *fire*. They said there was a bilge fire."

"I believe you. Did you tell anyone you were carrying those diamonds?"

"I was required to let the insurance company know every time I did. So yes, they knew I was carrying diamonds, and they knew exactly what course I was planning to follow. They said they needed to know in case something went wrong. So they'd know where to look."

"How come you didn't stay in the Intracoastal Waterway?"

Bruderson shrugged. "I wanted to do something different. I wasn't all that far out beyond the reefs. Nobody objected. It wasn't as if I was planning to sail into really deep water."

Chase nodded. "How long did it take the boat to sink?"

"About as long as it took us to figure out we were taking on enormous quantities of water and get the life raft inflated and over the side. By the time I had my wife and daughters on the raft and was thinking about going to get the diamonds, it was too late. I figured if I stayed aboard any longer, I was apt to get sucked down when she went under. By that point her stern was rising out of the water."

"So the damage was in the bow?"

"Apparently. Like I said, it felt exactly as if we'd run into something."

"That's a strange place for a bilge fire."

Bruderson leaned forward and stabbed the air with his cigar. "That's what I thought. I'm no weekend sailor, Mr. Mattingly. I knew that boat inside and out. There's no way I could have built up fumes in the bow of that boat. And it had to be damage to the bow, because she didn't heel over as she was sinking."

"The bilge exhaust was working?"

Bruderson nodded. "Up to that point."

"Interesting. I assumed the conclusions in the report I saw were from Bill's observations down there. I'm not so sure anymore."

"I'm convinced he lied," Bruderson said flatly. "Barton and I have been discussing this for weeks now, but we haven't been able to come up with any way of challenging the report, short of hiring our own divers. We've been discussing ways to do that that wouldn't just turn this all into a swearing contest. However, since this is your area of expertise, and since you usually work for the insurance companies, you might be just the person we need. Mr. Mattingly, would you like to dive down to the *Maggie* and find out what really happened?"

"If I do that," Chase said, "I'm going to do it on my own. I'm not going to be on anybody's payroll, not yours or Maritime's."

Bruderson nodded. "I can understand that. Free agent. That's fine by me. What do you want me to do?"

"Don't tell anybody at all we've had this discussion. I have reason to believe that someone is getting nervous about what I might remember, or what I might find out."

"Not a word outside this room," Bruderson agreed. "Anything else?"

Chase looked at Callie. "Yeah," he said. "You could hire some investigators. We need to find out who the two divers were who went out on the *Island Dream* the day George Westerlake and Jimbo Rushman were killed. If you can find them, you might find your diamonds."

Bruderson's eyebrows lifted. "I read about that. So you think it's related?"

"Absolutely. Coincidences are getting deeper than manure in a cow barn."

The expression brought a faint smile to Bruderson's lips. "Consider it done. Just give us all the information you have."

On the one hand Callie was elated that Olaf Bruderson was going to hire a private detective to find those divers. A full-time investigator with money and resources behind him could do a lot more than she and Chase could.

But on the other hand, the thought of Chase diving again made her blood go cold. "You can't seriously be thinking about making that dive again," she said as they wended their way along a seemingly endless two-lane stretch of US 1, where signs in sequence periodically

announced, "Patience Pays. 3 Minutes to Passing Zone."
It always took longer than three minutes, and traffic
always seemed to back up behind some slow vehicle
that for whatever reason couldn't do more than forty.
She was used to it by now and hardly noticed it.

"I *am* thinking about it," he replied.

"No," she said. "No. I've heard you're not supposed
to dive again after you've had the bends really bad."

"You're not supposed to dive again too soon. It can
take a long time for all the bubbles to get out of your
system. It's been over two months, Callie."

"I still think it's insane."

"Maybe."

"How can you even be sure you'll find the boat?
Even with the exact position, it's got to be like looking
for a needle in a haystack out there."

"There's a buoy attached to the boat. Or there should
be."

"Oh, God." Fear and horror were welling inside her
combined with a sense of impending loss. "Chase,
please . . ."

"I said I'm thinking about it. And right now that's all
I'm doing, Callie."

"What's the point of even going down there? So what
if you find out that Bill's description of the damage was
a lie. What good will that do for you?"

"It might answer the question of what went wrong
down there, Callie."

She looked at him. "What do you mean?"

"Maybe I didn't do anything wrong after all. Maybe
somebody did it *to* me."

"Meaning?"

"Maybe somebody tried to disable me. Maybe I
didn't have heliox in my tanks at all."

CHAPTER 16

THEY STOPPED FOR DINNER AT A FAST-FOOD PLACE along the way, and reached home at about ten in the evening.

"My place or yours," Chase asked as they drove down the narrow road leading to their houses.

Her heart thudded. "What do you mean?"

"I mean you're not staying alone tonight. There's too much craziness going on."

Now that she thought about it, she had to admit she didn't really want to be at home alone. What's more, she really didn't want Chase to be home by himself either, not after having his house broken into. In fact, she realized suddenly, she was as afraid for him as she was for Jeff. More afraid than she was for herself.

"Let's go to my place," she said. "As far as we know, nobody's been creeping around there."

They stopped at his house, though, so that he could get a change of clothing and his toiletries. Nothing was out of place, and other than the fingerprint dust left in a number of places by the crime-scene team, everything was as it should be.

"Cleaning this stuff up is going to be a job," Callie remarked, touching the black powder.

"It's not so bad," he said. "They were kind of half-hearted about it, don't you think? They could have made a real mess in here."

"It was like they didn't expect to find anything and didn't even want to."

"What would they do with the fingerprints anyway? Unless they already have them on record, they're virtually useless."

"Unless they catch the guy. It would prove he broke in here."

"Right. But they don't think they're going to catch the guy. And they probably won't unless he pawns the gun somewhere around here."

It felt odd, though, to have Chase in her house when Jeff wasn't around. She was used to the place being silent and empty when her brother was gone, used to being able to racket around however she wanted. Having company was not something she was really comfortable with anymore.

It made her feel awkward, and she didn't know quite what to do. Finally, she settled on making a pot of decaffeinated coffee so she at least felt she was fulfilling the role of hostess.

Chase put his things in her parents' room, where he had spent the previous night, and joined her. "You don't have to treat me like a houseguest, Callie."

She gave him a forced smile. "Southern hospitality. Nobody ever crossed this threshold without being offered food. That's what Momma taught me."

He leaned against the counter and folded his arms, watching her make the coffee. "That's what my momma taught me, too. I always noticed that while every guest was greeted like long-lost kin and stuffed with food, that didn't keep anyone from talking nasty about them when they were gone."

Callie laughed, and her awkwardness began to ease. "That was the best part of having company, wasn't it? All the things you could say after they were gone?"

"Sometimes I got that feeling. My mother was a wonderful woman, but I swear she lived for gossip and talking about other people. She knew everything about everybody in the neighborhood and had a memory like a steel trap. None of it was malicious. Humanity was just her favorite parade, and every individual was a float to be talked about and critiqued."

"That was about the size of it." She paused, feeling wistful for her lost parents. "I never knew if my dad was as interested, but I can definitely remember Mom filling him in on everybody when he came home from sea. She'd tell stories over dinner, and he'd sit and listen and ask questions, and then linger after dinner while she kept on talking and I did the dishes. It usually took the better part of a week for her to catch him up on everybody in church and in the family."

"He probably enjoyed it. She was the way he kept in touch."

"Maybe. I never thought about it like that." Her wistfulness was growing into an ache. "I miss them," she said simply. "And I wish I could remember my mother better. I remember things she did, things she said, but I can't see her."

"Maybe all you need to do is look in the mirror, Callie."

Startled, she looked at him. "What?"

"I have a feeling you're very much like your mother."

"How would you know?"

He shrugged a shoulder. "Who taught you to be a mother to Jeff?"

"That's true." She grimaced. "I don't seem to be doing such a good job, though."

"I don't know about that. You got him growed up in one piece."

She hadn't heard that Southern "growed up" since her dad had died. He used to say, "You'll get growed up soon enough, Calypso." Or "Wait'll you get growed up, Jeff. Life gets better." So far it hadn't, but as she

293

remembered him saying that, she wondered how he could have told Jeff that after his wife died. And yet he had said it countless times during Jeff's early teen years, when her brother had been rebelling over almost everything.

Chase's voice interrupted her thought. "You just remembered something," he said almost gently. "You looked . . . sad."

"I was just thinking of my dad. He used to say 'growed up,' too. I haven't heard that colloquialism since he died."

"My folks always used that expression, too. My dad was always telling me to slow down, I'd get 'growed up' soon enough."

Callie laughed, feeling her heart lighten a little. "I heard that one, too. But I think Jeff heard it a whole lot more than I did."

"Sure he did. You got growed up real fast."

She laughed again and realized it was such a relief to laugh, just laugh. It eased the tension in the pit of her stomach that hadn't left her since Jeff's arrest.

"Let's take the coffee onto the porch," he suggested when it was ready.

"Are you sure?" It was dark out there, and she didn't think he'd been exaggerating his problems.

"I'm sure. Facing it may not conquer my fear, but the more I face it, the more confident I am that I can."

The tropical breeze was balmy and soft. The moon was brighter tonight, silvering the world, and the lap of waves was soothing.

Callie sat in one of the wicker chairs, far from the swing that hung at the far end of the porch. She could feel the tension in Chase as he took the chair beside her, but she didn't say anything.

"A couple of weeks ago," he said, "I couldn't even make myself go outside when it was dark."

"You've come a long way."

"I guess. But not far enough. I still have the feeling something's out there watching and waiting."

Callie felt her scalp prickle. "Maybe that's not such an irrational fear."

"Maybe not. It doesn't seem like it after the last few days. But there was a time when I considered the darkness a friend. Back when I was a SEAL."

"I can imagine. Cover of darkness would be a great aid. Why'd you leave the navy?"

"I got tired of it. Maybe I grew up." He gave a quiet laugh. "Yeah, that was probably it. As the years start encroaching, playing those games starts to seem pointless. And foolhardy. Of course, not everyone would agree with me."

"Foolhardy? What do you call what you're proposing to do here?"

"What do you mean?"

"Diving back to *The Happy Maggie*. That doesn't strike you as foolhardy?"

"Not if I'm in control of everything."

"Weren't you last time?"

He shook his head.

Callie sat up straighter, feeling the back of her neck prickle again. "Why not? Who else was in control?"

"There were two dive masters. Required by OSHA, the agency that oversees occupational safety. I'll bet you didn't know there are OSHA standards for commercial diving."

"No, but it makes sense."

"Well, we had a stand-by diver, and somebody to manage communications and so on. Sort of a dive manager. Anyway, I'm not the only person who handled my air tanks. And I didn't supervise filling them. The standby diver handled that."

"Is that unusual?"

Chase shook his head. "Nope. These salvage dives are big, expensive operations. Everybody's got a job to do. I checked my equipment, but I didn't test my tanks. Bill did that for both of us. So somebody else took charge of getting them filled, and Bill tested 'em before the dive."

"So somebody could have put something else in your air tanks?" The thought chilled her to the bone.

"It's possible. What I can't figure is why they didn't just give me a bad mix. I'd've been dead, and it would have been put down to a tragic accident."

"My God!"

"Of course, giving me a bad mix would have left a trail. The way it fell out, I had the narks and that *could* have happened from helium. Or maybe from that stroke the doctor was talking about. It was all so messed up by me having the bends anyway—I mean they had to put me in the decompression chamber, fill me full of oxygen. By the time I got to a hospital, it was probably anybody's guess what mixture of air I was on."

"But surely somebody checked your tanks?"

"Bill took 'em in for analysis."

"Oh."

"Yeah. Oh. He could have emptied 'em and had 'em refilled by then, for all I know. Things sure look different after all that's happening."

"They sure do."

"What made sense before isn't making sense now." Chase sighed. "Dollars to doughnuts I had Nitrox in my tanks instead of heliox."

"But what would be the point?"

"To incapacitate me and let Bill falsify the report. Maybe they didn't want to kill anyone, because the authorities might start looking too closely at what happened. So they give me the narks—which are a common enough problem in diving—I can't remember a damn thing, and Bill says what they want him to. Except, I don't think they were expecting me to get as bad as I did."

Callie was beginning to feel indignant. "Why not? That was a dangerous thing to do!"

"Admittedly. But most divers have dealt with narks and know how to handle them, at least to some degree. They probably figured I'd get euphoric and would have to be brought back up in the normal way, but I'd probably forget what happened down below. That's common with narks, not to be able to remember. I don't think they expected me to go over-the-edge paranoid and try to rip my mask off."

"I'm supposed to be excusing them?"

"No, I didn't say that. I'm just trying to figure their reasoning. That's all I can come up with that makes sense. A diver getting the narks raises no eyebrows. A diver getting killed by bad air on a dive for ten million dollars would raise a whole lot of eyebrows."

"I guess." She wished she could get her hands around Bill's throat. "I'm feeling violent."

"Not toward me, I hope?"

She looked at him, and wished she could read his expression better, but she hadn't turned on the porch light, so his face was shadowed. "Not at you. At Bill."

"Well, he's already gotten his. And I didn't tell you this to upset you, Callie. I just wanted you to see why I'd have confidence about making the dive by myself.

297

That's one of the reasons I didn't want any help from Bruderson. That would get too many people involved, and offer too many opportunities for something to get fucked up."

"I can see that." She wanted to accept his reasoning and accept his confidence, but fear had a life of its own, and it was clawing at her right now, making her aware that the thought of something happening to Chase scared her at least as much as the thought of anything happening to Jeff. "Can't you get someone else to do the dive?"

"Why?"

"Because then you don't have to take the risk."

He was silent for a while, staring out over the inlet. Callie waited, trying to silence the twisting terror that was beginning to fill her. If she had realized that he might do something this insane, she would never have allowed him to get so close to her and Jeff. She would never have allowed herself to *care*.

The realization that she did care for him exploded in her like a thunderclap. God, how had she let that happen? But even as she wondered, she realized that all the while she'd been fighting him and trying to keep him safely away from her emotionally, she had been getting in deeper and deeper until it was too late. She cared what happened to him.

And now the sea would take him, the way it had taken everyone. The way it was trying to take Jeff. The soothing sound of the gentle waves was no longer soothing. All of a sudden it sounded like evil laughter.

"I can't send someone else, Callie," Chase said presently. "I have to go myself."

"Some stupid macho notion, I suppose." Her tone was bitter, bitter enough that it made *her* wince at the sound of it.

"There's nothing macho about it. It's something I have to do."

"Right. And what makes you so damn sure you didn't get the narks from helium? And what if you did? Doesn't that mean you're more susceptible, and you shouldn't do this at all?"

"I've never had narks from helium, Callie. Never."

"Until this dive."

"It wasn't helium."

"You don't know that!" Frustrated almost beyond words, she jumped up from her chair and began to pace the porch rapidly. What could she say? she wondered wildly. There had to be something to say to dissuade him from this.

But all her life no one she had cared about had ever been dissuaded when the sea called. Who was she kidding? Callie Carlson could stamp her feet and yell until the cows came home. She could get down on her knees and weep and beg—and still her men would go to the sea.

God damn the ocean and God damn men!

After a bit, she heard Chase rise from his chair and cross the porch to stand behind her. She refused to look at him, even though she longed to turn and throw herself into his arms and beg him to forget this insanity. She'd begged her father to stay home with her and Jeff after their mother died, and he hadn't listened. She'd begged Jeff not to take to the sea, but it was the only thing he wanted to do.

Why should Chase be any different? If her father wouldn't ignore the siren call for his children, why should Chase Mattingly ignore it for the sake of a couple of neighbors?

She wrapped her arms around herself, feeling cold in a way the night's warmth couldn't touch. She wished Chase would go away, just vanish into the night, so she wouldn't have to know what happened to him.

She felt his hands touch her shoulders lightly. Tentatively.

As if he feared she might consider his touch a trespass. Which she ought to, she thought. She really ought to tell him to get his mitts off her. Except that there was little on this planet she wanted as much as she wanted his touch. She craved it, and no amount of fear could swallow that craving.

"Calypso . . ." He said her name softly, so that it almost seemed to be whispered by the breeze. "Such a beautiful name. I love the way it rolls on the tongue . . ."

"Don't get poetic on me, Chase. It won't work."

He answered her with silence. She half expected he would walk away, which was what she wanted, wasn't it? That's why she was being such a bitch, wasn't it? Except that she felt so relieved when his hands remained on her shoulders.

"I wasn't getting poetic," he said. "I don't have a poetic bone in my body."

Not true, she thought. When he talked about the sea he loved, he became poetic.

His hands tightened a little on her shoulders, and she found herself leaning back into him, feeling the hard wall of his chest against her shoulders. It would have been so easy to relax against him, to ignore all her fears and anger and give in to the feelings he awoke in her so easily.

But she refused to do that, remaining stiff and unyielding even when he began to massage her shoulders gently.

"Life's a bitch," he said quietly.

She had to swallow a harsh laugh. Some part of her was unwilling to dispel the mood that was beginning to wrap them in a soft cocoon. "No kidding," she said just as quietly.

"Have you ever noticed that every time we don't want to do something, or swear that we never will, life grabs us by the throat and makes us do it?"

"Is that your excuse for making this dive? That life is forcing you?"

"It's not an excuse."

"Sure it is."

"No, it's not." His hands paused on her shoulders, then resumed their gentle rubbing.

"It's an excuse," she repeated flatly. "No one is forcing you at gunpoint."

He sighed. "Calypso, if I don't do this, I'm going to be a cripple for the rest of my life."

"If you do it, you might wind up dead. God, Chase, how are you going to do this by yourself? Can you afford to get a decompression chamber and a boat big enough to carry it? Are you going to hire someone to dive with you? You can't possibly afford all of that. So what are you going to do? Dive alone? You must be out of your mind!"

"Maybe I am. God knows I've felt like it for a couple of months now."

A pang pierced her heart, and with it came one very clear thought: Was she being selfish about this? Her breath caught in her throat, and her heart nearly stopped.

"Look, I promise you if I feel narks coming on, I'll come right back up."

Somewhere deep inside, she realized he was willing to make a promise to her, and that meant he wasn't indifferent to her. She held the feeling close even as a small voice in her head said he couldn't possibly care at all for her, or he wouldn't be thinking about doing this.

"You didn't feel the narks in time on your last dive," she said finally.

"I wasn't expecting them. If you're looking for them, they can't creep up on you. Besides . . . that was different. I've never had 'em hit me like that before." He sighed. "I wouldn't be surprised if there was something *else* in that mixture besides Nitrox."

She closed her eyes, feeling a resurgence of horror at what someone had tried to do to him.

"Anyway, I'm convinced I couldn't have had a straight mixture of heliox. I've never had a problem with the narks on a dive like that as long as my mixture was right."

She wanted to believe him, but she was afraid to. Believing him meant too much. It meant approving of the risk he was going to take. She wasn't ready to do that. Wasn't ready to invest even that much of herself in something that could wind up hurting her more than anything since the death of her parents.

"Why?" she repeated. "Why do you have to do this? It won't prove anything, Chase."

"It'll prove that I can still dive. It'll prove I didn't screw up. It'll prove that Bill lied about everything . . :"

"And that'll do what?"

"Give me my confidence back. It might even help Jeff."

"Oh, come off it. There's no way it could help Jeff. The only thing that's going to help him is finding those divers and getting a confession out of them."

"If I can prove that Bill lied about the damage to the boat, I can go to the insurance company, Callie. They'll be as eager to find those divers as you are, and so will the cops. They have a lot more resources than we do. And it might be enough to get the state attorney to drop the case against Jeff."

It was a slender hope, but it was one she couldn't refuse. Never had she felt as torn as she did right then. Frantically, she considered alternatives, trying to find a way to reach the same ends without Chase having to risk his life.

Nothing occurred to her.

She opened her eyes and turned to face him. "Chase . . . get someone else to do it."

He shook his head. "If I do that, I might help Jeff, but I won't help myself."

He touched her cheek gently with his fingertips, and she couldn't help it. She needed that touch so much that she leaned into it, pressing her cheek into his palm. Her eyes closed again, and she fought against a surge of feeling so strong it nearly overwhelmed her. What was happening to her?

"Calypso," he said, his voice quiet, husky. "Calypso, if I don't make this dive, I'll never heal. I'll never be whole again. I don't have to tell you that."

She felt his plea all the way to her soul, and wondered why he should be asking for her understanding. Her eyes opened, and she looked up at him. The shadows were deep, but moonlight reflecting off the water caught his eyes and made them silver. "Don't ask me for that, Chase. Please don't ask me to approve."

After a moment, he nodded and let go of her. The loss of his touch ripped something deep within her, and grief began to fill her. But she couldn't do what he asked. She couldn't.

"I'm going to bed," he said. "Good night."

She stood alone in the night; knowing she had failed him in a very essential way. And it didn't help to realize that he had asked too much of her. It didn't help at all.

Sleeping when it was dark was still beyond Chase. He tried to tell himself he was doing pretty good. After all, he'd just spent a half hour on the porch in the dark with Callie. He still felt the darkness closing in, felt that there were things lurking out there, but at least he was facing the feeling and not letting it get the better of him.

But the nightmares were something else. What was the point of going to sleep anyway, if he was just going to wake up every few minutes in the grip of a nightmare?

But it had been a long day, and he hadn't gotten his usual nap. Sitting in the armchair in the bedroom with the light on, he felt himself nodding.

And his thoughts kept going back to Callie. The woman was an emotional mess, whether she realized it or not. And he didn't know why he couldn't just keep clear of her. Helping Jeff out, helping himself out—none of that had to include getting involved with Callie and her damn prickliness.

God, she was a rose with some serious thorns. Every time he thought they were beginning to come to an understanding, she turned all spiky.

He ought to be glad she'd showed her true colors on the porch just now. He'd been close to wading into dangerous waters with her, and it was best to know beforehand that he couldn't count on her.

Of course, with the exception of Tom Akers, when had he ever really been able to count on anyone? Especially a woman? Thoughts of Julia came swimming to the fore, and he sighed. Come on, he thought. I don't need to dive into those waters tonight.

The story with Julia was simple, after all. He'd ridden in on his white horse to rescue her, and she'd taken advantage of him. That was the danger in playing the white knight. You laid yourself open to being used.

At least Callie wasn't pretending to be all dewy-eyed over him the way Julia had. No, Callie was being up front. She'd probably have sent him to the devil if she could have.

Callie was no different from the rest, really, except that she wasn't playing any games. When the going got tough, in Chase's experience, women tended to bail out. Julia had bailed out on him because navy life was too tough. She had said so. How, she had asked, could he expect her to live like that? The loneliness was too much. Never mind that he'd been lonely, too, when he was away.

And he hadn't seen his most recent on-again off-again girlfriend since his diving accident. She could at least have visited him at the hospital, but instead she'd called him, and said, "I'm no good with this stuff, Chase. I can't stand sickness." And she hadn't even apologized for it.

Not that he'd been in love with her or anything. He hadn't made that mistake since Julia. But . . . well, it just confirmed his opinion. They were there as long as there was something in it for them, and gone just as soon as the ground got rough.

Now here was Callie doing exactly what he would have predicted. Willing to hang around with him if she thought it would help her brother, and ready to bail out the instant he was going to do something she wasn't happy about.

They were all the same.

But this time it didn't feel the same. He wasn't shrugging it off. Instead he sat in the armchair and tried to figure out a way to solve his problem without doing what Callie didn't want him to do.

He supposed he could hire another diver to go down. If *anyone* went down there and found the damage was consistent with Bruderson's report, and not with Bill's, he could at least be reasonably certain that he hadn't screwed up his own dive. And they'd still have enough to go to the insurance company, and enough for Jeff's lawyer to make a case that the missing divers were the murderers. Anybody, even a state attorney, ought to be able to understand the motivation of ten million dollars in uncut diamonds.

But he wouldn't have made the dive himself, and as long as that was true, he'd still be a cripple.

Sighing, he rubbed his eyes and yawned, and tried to stay awake. The nightmares were lurking at the edges of his mind; he could feel them waiting to pounce and shred him. He wondered if diving would cure him of that, or if he was doomed to wake up drowning every night for the rest of his life.

Grim prospect. His back and hip were starting to throb mightily, so he got up to move around. Maybe, he thought, he should try to take a walk around the outside of the house. It would stretch his leg and loosen up his back and maybe he could put a few more of his demons to rest.

He was just opening the bedroom door when the phone rang. Callie hurried by him into the kitchen. He followed her, hoping it wasn't some new catastrophe.

"Hi, Jeff," she said into the phone. "Yeah, we're back okay . . . no . . . Don't worry. Chase is staying here tonight. I'll be fine." She paused. "Yes, he's right here.

Just a minute."

She passed the receiver to him and Chase took it. "Hi, Jeff."

"I was just making sure she wasn't lying about you being there," Jeff said, amusement wrinkling his voice. "She lies to me all the time to keep me from worrying about her."

"She does a lot of that, huh?"

"You bet. And she thinks I don't know it. Anyway, I've got to look out for her, you know?"

"You bet." He felt himself beginning to smile. Another white knight in the making. "Don't worry about it. I've got a handle on tonight, anyway. You at your friend's?"

"Phil's? Yeah. Just got here."

"How's Sara?"

"Oh, man . . . ." Jeff's voice trailed off. "I gotta get off this murder charge, Chase. I gotta. Sara's . . . well, Sara is . . ." He trailed off. "I can't describe it."

Chase was definitely smiling now. "I hear you. Just take it slow, okay? Give yourself a chance to really get to know her."

"Not much else I can do right now. It wouldn't be fair to her."

"Well, that's my best advice. I wasted it, huh?"

Jeff laughed. "I wanted to ask . . . is Callie pissed about something? She sounded funny on the phone."

Chase looked at Callie. She was busy keeping her back to him and washing the coffee mugs. "She's pissed at me."

"Why?"

"Because I'm thinking about diving down to the *Maggie* again."

"No kidding? I'll bet she's already measuring you for

307

a casket."

"Not quite."

"Give her an hour or so. She's convinced that anytime anybody gets more than twenty feet from shore they're never going to come back again."

"Well, she's got some reason for that fear."

"What? That my dad died at sea? He could have been hit by a truck, struck by lightning or—or had a heart attack."

Chase had to smile again, hearing Jeff use the same logic he'd once offered Callie. The young man had more good stuff in him than his sister realized. "That's the logic of it. But logic doesn't always win over emotions, Jeff."

"I guess not."

"After all, I know there's no reason to be afraid of the dark, but it still gives me cold sweats to step outside at night."

After he hung up the phone, Chase stood looking at Callie's back.

"I'm sorry," he said.

She didn't quite glance over her shoulder. "For what?"

"For asking you to approve of me making a dive. I should have realized I couldn't ask you that."

"Why should you even ask me?" She scrubbed at the counter with a dish sponge. "It's none of my business what you do."

"Then how come you got so upset about it?"

"I didn't say I didn't care. I just said it was none of my business."

"Mmm." She kept right on scouring that counter and he kept right on studying her back. There *had* to be a way around this, he thought. There had to be. Because for some reason he didn't think he could stand it if they couldn't heal this breach.

"Calypso . . ."

She turned around and he was shocked to see tears running down her face. "You can't do this," she said. "You can't. If something happens to you . . ." She threw down the sponge and ran from the room.

He thought about following her, but he didn't. Not right away.

Because there was nothing he could say. Not a thing. He *had* to do this for himself as much as anything. He couldn't spend the rest of his life crippled by fear and self-doubt. He couldn't.

And he couldn't see any way around it.

CHAPTER 17

CALLIE SAT ON THE SEAWALL, HER TOES DANGLING IN the warm water, feeling the tickle of the surface tension as the gentle waves rose and fell. The water was getting ruffled, she noticed, and the breeze was stiffening. A storm in the making? If so, there was hope that Chase wouldn't make his insane dive tomorrow.

And it was insane. After what had happened to him last time, and with no proof whatsoever that he'd had the wrong air mixture, he had to be utterly crazy even to consider going back down there.

A snuffling sound from the water caught her attention. A manatee, she thought. They sometimes came into the inlet hunting for seaweed The first time she had seen one, she'd been eight years old, and she had been on *The Wind Drifter*, her father's fishing vessel. The *Drifter* had been tied up to the dock, and her

309

dad had been scraping the hull, diving down below to scrape, and resurfacing every minute or so to take a breath. At least four times that afternoon he swore he was going to get an aqualung for doing this miserable job.

He never did. Probably never could afford it, she thought now. There'd always been something she and Jeff had needed more, or the boat needed more. And so he had kept diving the hard way.

That afternoon, he'd had Callie brushing flecks of paint off the bow railing, scouring it smooth for a fresh coat of paint. In retrospect, she wasn't sure how much she'd really helped him, but she'd *felt* she was helping, and her dad had believed that kids were never too young to learn useful tasks.

All of a sudden he'd surfaced beside the boat, shaking the water off his face.

"Calypso," he'd called quietly. "Calypso, come look. There's a manatee momma and her baby . . . ."

The inlet waters had been nearly as clear as glass that day, with the beds of seaweed visible on the bottom. Leaning over the rail, Callie had watched in awe as the big manatee had grazed on the seaweed and nursed her baby from the nipple under her armpit. The manatee hadn't appeared to be disturbed by the human in the water, and when she had drifted close to Wes Carlson, she had even seemed to enjoy the gentle pats he gave her.

Remembering that magical afternoon now, Callie felt tears rolling down her cheeks. God, how she missed her dad! For a few minutes her throat was so tight with grief that she could barely breathe.

But as grief began to ease, she remembered something else. There had been a time when the sea

310

hadn't been her enemy. A time when the sea had been full of wonder and promise. A time when she had wanted to grow up and become a fisherman just like her dad. There had been a time when she had begged to go fishing with him, and all she had wanted for her birthday was a trip on a glass-bottomed boat to see the reefs.

And then her mother had died, and it had begun to seem that the sea was taking her dad away from her. "Find some other job," she'd begged.

"I can't, Callie," he'd replied. "There's nothing else I can do as well, nothing else I can do that will keep us fed."

So she had begun to hate the sea. Her father's death had only hardened her hatred. The sea had kept him away from her for weeks on end, claiming what should have been Callie's by right: her father's time and emotional support.

Looking back, she could see the selfishness in her demands and needs. Her dad had been doing the best he could, and thrusting early motherhood on his fourteen-year-old daughter had been necessary. It also hadn't been unreasonable. In Wes Carlson's generation, a lot of girls who weren't much older got married and had babies. His sister had been a mother at fifteen. Why would he think he was asking too much of his daughter?

Prolonged childhood didn't exist in her father's world. Wes Carlson had had his first job at the age of eleven, and had gone to sea at twelve as a fisherman, during school breaks. He'd owned his own boat by the time he was twenty. No, he hadn't seen anything wrong in asking his daughter to care for his younger son while he went to sea. That's how it was done.

He'd been wonderfully proud of Callie for going to

college and graduate school. "Bustin' my buttons," he'd used to say. But would he be proud of her now?

The question tightened her throat again, and made her chest feel heavy. No, she thought, he wouldn't be proud of her. He'd say, "The sea gives life, Calypso. I can go out on my boat and cast my nets and bring up enough fish to feed us all and pay the bills. The sea is our mother."

And if she argued that the sea had killed him, he'd shake his head sadly and say, "No, Calypso. It was *my* fault. I wasn't wearing a safety line."

That's what he would say, and she could hear it as clearly as if he were sitting here right beside her. Wes Carlson had never blamed anyone or anything but himself for his problems. Never.

And he'd be very ashamed of Callie for blaming everyone and everything she could for her own misery.

So what if life had made her a mother at fourteen? Given the opportunity, would she have put Jeff in someone else's care all those years? Of course not. She wouldn't have allowed it. So maybe it was time to stop blaming her father and the sea, and start accepting her own responsibility. She could have refused the task. If she had, her dad would have found someone to take Jeff in while he was at sea. But she hadn't done that. It had never entered her head to do that. Instead she had cherished the idea of herself as put-upon.

Her mouth suddenly tasted bitter, and she decided she didn't like herself very much. Instead of drowning in self-pity, maybe she ought to try being proud of herself for having done what was necessary to give her brother a stable home life.

And instead of trying to keep Jeff from growing up, maybe she ought to devote herself to getting a life of her own.

As for Chase—her heart ached painfully, and her mouth went dry. She didn't think she could stand the fear.

But what right had she to beg him not to do this? Did she really want him to spend the rest of his life mired in self-doubt and nightmares? As a psychologist she damn well knew that what he was proposing would be the best possible cure for all that ailed him. Facing his demons, conquering them, and returning triumphant would heal him in a way nothing else could.

So what was the matter with her? Could she actually be this selfish? Yes, he might die, but if he didn't do this, he might as well be dead. That Beretta that had been stolen from his table—she didn't think he kept it for protection. She didn't think it had been sitting on his table so that he could shoot his nightmares.

No, she would bet he'd actually contemplated suicide more than once since his accident. Heck, she'd been trying to avoid involvement with him because he was so psychologically wounded, and now that he'd devised a method of curing himself, what right did she have to stand in his way? How could she?

Since when had her feelings become so important that she considered everyone else's needs to be secondary?

Little by little the tightness in her throat and chest eased, and a calm began to steal over her. She knew what she had to do. It was the only right thing to do. And for Chase, dying in this dive would probably be better than continuing to live the way he'd been these past few months.

Otherwise, he wouldn't even be suggesting this.

Given that, she had absolutely no right to stand in his way.

After a while, she rose and returned to the house. She was surprised to find Chase sitting on the porch.

"I was watching you," he said simply. "Lately I'm not all that sure what might be creeping around these woods."

"Thank you." She stood looking at him, filled with yearnings and fears that nearly locked her in place. "I . . . um . . . You're right. You need to make that dive."

She blurted out the words fast, needing to say them before fear stopped her.

"What changed your mind?"

"I . . . did some thinking. I was being selfish."

"There's nothing wrong with being selfish."

"Sometimes there is. This time there is. You're right. You need to do this or you'll be crippled for the rest of your life. So . . . just do it. Just . . . just . . . oh, God, be careful."

Chase didn't know what to say. Even in the moonlight he could tell Callie was shaking like a leaf. He had some appreciation of how difficult that had been for her to say, and he felt something inside him begin to unlock for the first time in years. "You're sure about that?"

"I'm not sure of anything! I don't *want* you to do this, but you *have* to. Even I can see that. And I'm just not selfish enough to try to stop you. Even if . . . even if . . ."

He had an idea what that cost her. This woman had been wounded by enough loss in her life, and he could hardly blame her for fearing more of it.

But he also realized something else. If she didn't give a damn about him, she wouldn't be so upset about this. If she didn't care a lick for him, she'd be eager to have him make this dive because it might help Jeff.

But she cared enough for him to let him do it. She

hadn't phrased her acceptance in terms of Jeff, but in terms of what *he* needed.

Something inside him swelled, making it nearly impossible for him to breathe. It had been a hell of a long time since anybody had cared enough about him to put themselves second. Certainly no woman in his life ever had.

"I'll be careful," he heard himself saying. "I swear I will."

"I know," she said raggedly. "I know . . . "

Somehow he was off the chair and across the porch. He started to wrap his arms around her, but hesitated, remembering her fear last night. Then he felt her reach for him, and all his qualms vanished.

"It'll be okay," he said, or tried to, as the rhythm of the sea in his veins became a pounding surf of need and hunger. Her caring was reaching him at levels that hadn't been touched in a long, long time, and he needed to hold her more than he'd needed anything in ages.

When he held her tightly against him, he closed his eyes and let the intense feeling of warmth wash over him. God, had an embrace ever felt this *good*?

Bending his head, he pressed his face into her hair and smelled coconut. She filled his senses, and filled his soul, and he knew he wasn't going to be able to let her go. Not this time.

But he remembered her fear, and the memory of it nearly paralyzed him. He didn't want to say or do the wrong thing, didn't want to scare her. She'd been scared too often and too much in her life, and he didn't want to give her any more of that.

He felt her stir against him, and for an instant he thought she wanted him to let go of her. His heart took a tumble, falling into a dark pit, then soaring again as her hands clutched at his back, as if she wanted him even closer.

Then she tilted her head back, and her mouth sought his. Joy burst in him, a nearly blinding white light that reached the mustiest corners of his soul. She was *asking* for his kiss, and he gave it willingly, covering her mouth with his as if he could take her very essence into himself.

She responded eagerly, her tongue meeting his and engaging in a teasing dance that thrilled and delighted him. He couldn't remember a woman's kiss ever having seemed so precious.

Her hands were all over his back, stroking, clutching, as if she was seeking something more. Finally, he lifted his head, tearing his mouth from hers, and said huskily, "Callie, if we don't stop now, I'm not going to stop."

Because if he took one more step down this road, stopping would come close to killing him. Hunger was hammering at him, and her closeness was driving him to an edge he had seldom reached. But it wasn't that he *wouldn't* be able to stop; it was that if he had to stop later, they would both be left feeling bruised and frustrated, and he was damned if he was going to allow that to happen to either of them.

She nodded, and he was sure she was going to back away. He forced himself to loosen his arms, to give her room to take that step, even though he couldn't stand the thought.

But she didn't back away. Instead she looped her arms around his neck. "I know," she whispered just before her mouth found his again.

His blood was pounding like the surf before a storm. Bending, he slipped his arm behind her knees and lifted her against his chest.

"This is it," he heard himself mutter. "Say no now."

But she didn't say no. She let her head fall into the crook between his shoulder and neck, and damned if he didn't feel her tongue run along his skin.

He fumbled at the door, got it open, kicked it shut. He carried her to the bedroom he was using and laid her down on the coverlet. The lights were on, and she blinked as if they bothered her. He wished he could turn them out, but he wasn't sure what would happen if he did. What if his terrors took over and ruined this? Despite all the progress he'd made, he still didn't trust himself.

But she was probably shy, and he had the distinct impression she had never made love before. The way she had talked about her boyfriend, he was almost sure that Callie was a virgin. If the lights bothered her . . .

No, he couldn't. He just had to hope she wouldn't become too embarrassed.

And that gave him pause yet again. He couldn't remember the last time he'd made love with a sexually inexperienced woman—if ever. Even his wife had been experienced when he met her. He knew the idea would excite many men, but all it did was fill him with trepidation. Talk about pitfalls and minefields.

"Chase?" She was looking up at him, her expression confused, the early signs of hurt around her eyes. His dawdling was making her unsure.

Dropping to his knees beside the bed, he caught her face between his hands and kissed her deeply. "Just be sure," he said huskily. "Just be sure . . ."

"I am. Very sure."

And she *was*. Because the peace that had filled her when she accepted that Chase had to do this dive or his life wouldn't be worth living now told her how precious every moment had become. There was a new strength in her, a strength born of resignation.

All her life she had thought that resignation was weakness, that a strong person fought against things they didn't like, and fought for what they wanted. But tonight she had discovered that resignation could make her strong. That accepting what could not be changed and dealing with it was a different kind of power.

And she felt powerful now. More powerful than she had ever felt. Chase might die on his dive, he might be gone forever in a day or two or three, but she had the power to take what she wanted from these precious few hours. The power to give herself and give all the feelings she had for him, feelings that she had fought hard to deny. The power to accept his feelings for her. The power to make memories that she would regret only if she refused them.

The lights bothered her eyes, but only her eyes. She didn't want to cast him into darkness for these priceless hours. She wanted what was between them to be as far removed from the darkness as was humanly possible. Light and life and love. That was all that should mark this time.

Lifting her arms, she looped them around his neck and drew him down for another kiss. Supine on the bed, offering herself to him, she had never felt so free or so right. *This was meant to be.*

He sprinkled kisses all over her face, gentle caresses that tried to be as reassuring as they were hungry. His hands began to wander over her curves, making them his, thrilling her to her very core. No one had ever touched her like this, stroking her as if he wanted to give as much pleasure as he took. Mel had been a grabber, and she had always told herself that sex was

318

something she didn't like, and had used waiting for marriage as an excuse not to go all the way with him.

She discovered differently now. There could be no future with Chase, and so she wanted whatever he could give her, wanted the emotional closeness that could come from lovemaking. Now she discovered she could be a creature of passion, and could want the sex as much as the closeness.

Soft little sounds formed in the back of her throat, and she lifted into his touches as unself-consciously as a cat. Her needs were taking over, driving all thought from her mind. Before he had even loosened a button, she was riding a wave that wouldn't let her off.

He cast his clothes aside. She knew a moment of distress when his hands and mouth stopped touching her, and she opened her eyes to beg him not to stop. What she saw made her breath lock in her throat. The male form held no shocks for her, but Chase's body was a thing of beauty. Lean, tanned, and hard-muscled from work and swimming, he suddenly seemed to her to have all the perfection of Michelangelo's *David*.

Propelled by wonder as much as need, she rose on her knees on the bed and reached for him, running her palms over him wherever she could reach, longing to learn him with all her senses, longing to engrave the feeling of him forever on her mind. She hardly noticed when he tugged her shirt over her head, felt annoyed when he interrupted her caresses long enough to pull away her shorts, her shoes, and her underthings.

And then she was as naked as he, and nothing, absolutely *nothing*, had ever felt so right and good. When he pulled her to him, and their bodies met full length for the first time with nothing between then, she discovered that there was no sensation more exquisite

319

than skin on skin.

The throbbing deep within her bloomed again, making her knees feel weak and her body feel languorous. As if he sensed it, he lifted her, the world spun, then they were lying on the bed, face-to-face.

"Perfect," he whispered as his hands ran over her, discovering every hill and hollow. She replied in kind, discovering his angles and planes. Each touch seemed to lift her higher on the crest of the wave, until she didn't know where he began and she ended. Each and every touch, whether hers or his, fueled the hard ache building deep within her.

He fondled her breasts with all the intensity of a man who had just discovered something of remarkable beauty and wonder, tracing their curves, testing their fullness, and finally, when she didn't think she could stand the anticipation another moment, kissing her there.

He drew her nipple into his mouth and sucked, and each time he drew on her, the tension in her center grew even stronger, spreading until it seemed to fill her entire being.

She was gasping and whimpering, taken so far out of herself that she hardly knew what she was doing. Eager to make him feel what he was making her feel, she reciprocated, twisting until she was able to find his small nipples with her tongue. He arched and groaned, pressing his hardness into her belly. Encouraged, she sucked on him as he had sucked on her, and felt ripples of pleasure run through him.

Power, she discovered, was a heady thing, and she had power then, the power to make him writhe and groan just as he did to her. Delight exploded within her, and she explored him further, discovering the hard planes of his belly with her mouth. But when she tried to move lower, he stopped her with a ragged laugh.

"You do that," he whispered roughly on short puffs of air, "and we'll be done before we start . . ."

Heady delight filled her, then gave way to a renewed rush of passion as he rolled her beneath him, pressing his manhood to her dewy center. The sensation was exquisite, so exquisite, and she adjusted herself to him, bringing him closer still, and arching her hips as she tried to get more of what she needed

Gently he rocked against her, sweeping her higher and higher as his mouth continued to forage her curves. Her body took over, taking her to places she'd never been, guiding her toward the place she wanted to go. The roar in her ears sounded like the pounding of surf, and she felt as if she teetered at the very top of a breaking wave, afraid of falling and afraid of not falling.

Then, with a long, slow thrust, Chase entered her. There was a moment of ripping pain that caused her to catch her breath in shock. He froze, cradling her head in his hands.

"Are you okay?" he whispered. "Calypso?"

The hot, burning pain was already subsiding, and she managed a nod even though the moment of shock had cast her down from her high pinnacle and thrown her back into harsh awareness of reality.

But her body hadn't forgotten its purpose, and when Chase began to sprinkle gentle kisses on her face and throat, and moved gently within her, it was as if the interruption had never occurred. She was once again dancing on the breakers, trying to keep her balance only to find that losing it was the answer she'd been seeking all along.

With a cry torn from deep within, she tumbled into

the calm pool of completion. Seconds later, she heard Chase's cry as he followed her.

Laughing like kids, they raided the refrigerator, and Chase made them both sandwiches from leftover chicken, waiting on Callie as if she were a princess. They ate at the table, sitting as close as they could get, touching often and frequently. It was the headiest, most perfect hour of Callie's life.

They talked about a lot of things, none of it important, both of them resolutely avoiding the shadows that lay ahead, seizing the moment because it might be all they ever had. A bittersweet feeling gradually filled the air.

"Let's go for a moonlight swim," Chase suggested.

Callie looked at him in amazement. He was proposing to face his fear of darkness and his fear of the water all at the same time. She was about to make an excuse, to spare him, but then she realized that in a way this would be a trial run for his dive. If he was going to panic in the dark water, it would be best to find out now.

She would have gone naked to the water, but then she remembered the red eyes in the woods. What if someone were out there? So she put on her maillot, though Chase didn't don anything at all. He teased her for her modesty, but his eyes said he understood her fear of watchers.

The moon was higher now, casting its silvery cascade over the world, driving the shadows farther under the trees. The water was warm, clinging to the day's heat, so comfortable that Callie thought this must be what it was like to float in the womb. Lying on her back, she let the waves rock her as she looked up at the thousands of stars overhead. Chase floated beside her, his hand

322

locked with hers.

After a while, Chase put his feet down and drew her close, kissing her gently as she floated. "Let's go in," he said. "I can feel you're getting cold."

But she stayed where she was, floating. "This is magical," she said softly. "It's like being in free fall. I feel as if I'm drifting among the stars."

"That's what it feels like diving," he said. "Floating free in the sunlight—at least until I go deeper. Flying like a bird . . ."

Fear settled like lead in her stomach, and suddenly she didn't find the night so enchanting. Dropping her feet to the bottom, she said, "Let's go in. I'm freezing."

"I'm sorry," he said, as they stood shivering in the bathroom, toweling dry. "I ruined the mood."

"It's okay," she said. "It's okay." No point in living in a fool's paradise any longer.

"No, it's not okay. I should have kept my yap shut."

"Why?" She looked at him, feeling the muscles of her face tightening with suppressed emotion. "Why shouldn't you be able to say what you're feeling? So diving is like flying. I can handle that."

"But you can't handle me diving."

"Sure I can," she said with more conviction than she felt. "You're going to do it, and I'm not going to stand in your way. Easy enough."

Dropping her towel on the edge of the tub, she headed for her bedroom. "I'm going to get dressed, then make something hot to drink."

She felt his eyes on her as she walked away, and wondered why she was feeling as if her heart had been flayed alive.

CHAPTER 18

MORNING ARRIVED ALL TOO QUICKLY, BRINGING harsh reality along with it. Callie slipped out of bed, taking care not to disturb Chase. The previous night she had wanted to sleep in her own bed, but somehow she had let herself be drawn into Chase's bed, where he had cuddled her close until she drifted off.

She had the feeling that he hadn't slept at all, at least not until the sun had risen. The lights had stayed on all night, and now she quietly turned them off. Pausing by the bed and looking at him, she thought he appeared exhausted. She stood over him a minute, and tried to quell the feelings of love, concern, and worry that came over her.

She was, it seemed, destined to lose everyone she loved. Chase would go on that dive and never return. Jeff would be convicted . . .

No! The word was like a thunderclap in her head. She couldn't allow any of that to happen. She might not be able to prevent Chase from taking his dive, but she could damn well do everything possible to ensure it was a *safe* dive.

And no matter what it took, she was going to discover what had happened on the *Island Dream* the day those two men had been murdered. If that meant letting Chase dive, she would do it. For him and for Jeff. Apparently that was the only hope she had of saving them both.

Stealing out of the bedroom, she went to the kitchen where she started a pot of coffee. She didn't feel like eating, but her stomach was rolling with nausea, so she made some instant grits to quell it. Standing at the sink while the microwave hummed and the coffeemaker hissed, she looked out on the sun-dappled morning and wondered how the world could look so beautiful when her whole life was going to hell.

"Good morning."

Chase's voice startled her, but she refused to turn and look at him. "Good morning," she said, her voice flat and heavy.

He came up behind her and slipped his arms around her. She shivered as he dropped a kiss on the shell of her ear, and wondered why her body wouldn't listen to her brain. It had betrayed her last night, and now it was about to do it again.

"Listen," he said. "I've been thinking about this dive. I understand why you're so worried about it. So . . . can we talk to Jeff's lawyer and see what she thinks? If she thinks it won't help at all to find out if Bill lied on his report, then I won't dive the wreck again."

Something inside her started to shatter, and she could feel grief beginning to ooze through the cracks, threatening to flood her. "You'd do that for me?"

"Yeah, I would."

She turned to face him then, tears beginning to blur her vision. "Caring about my feelings is a high-maintenance task, apparently. I ask too much of everyone."

"Callie . . ."

She shook her head. "No, don't tell me I'm not right. I know I am. I've been asking too much of Jeff for years, and now I'm asking too much of you. You go on that dive because you need to, Chase. Don't cripple yourself to spare my feelings."

He looked down at her, his expression grave. "Callie, you're entitled to your feelings."

"And so are you! That's my problem, you know. I

325

expect everyone I care about to do what I want so I don't have to be afraid or worry. If I had my way, I'd probably lock everybody I care about into a safe little box where nothing bad could happen to them. That's not fair to anyone! And I have no right to ask that of anyone."

He nodded slowly, but she wasn't sure he was agreeing with her. A tear escaped and rolled down her cheek.

"I'm selfish," she said. "I should be happy for Jeff that he's doing what he wants with his life. Instead I'm trying to turn him into something he would hate to be just so I don't have to be afraid every time he goes out in his boat. That's ridiculous! People go out to sea all the time and come back safely. God knows Jeff has been doing it since he was sixteen."

"Calypso . . ."

But she was in no mood to be silenced now that she was spilling her heart about her own flaws. "And you," she said. "How many dives have you made safely? Hundreds? And probably the only reason that anything went wrong on your last one was that someone sabotaged you. So why shouldn't you dive again? Because *I'm* afraid? Because I'm such a selfish scaredy cat, should you have to spend the rest of your life doubting yourself? Should you have to spend the rest of your life separated from something you obviously love?"

"Callie . . ."

But she kept right on going. "I'm trying to cripple both of you. *Both of you.* And for no better reason than that I can't learn to accept my father's death as one of those cosmic accidents of life. Because I can't learn to cope with a basic fact of human existence, a fact that all of us have to live with: that sooner or later we *all* lose the people we love."

"Callie . . . "

She shook her head. "You go on that dive. And when I get Jeff off this murder charge, I'm going to help him get a better boat. All he's ever wanted to do was go to sea, and I've been fighting him . . ." She trailed off into a sob and tried to turn away, but he caught her close and hugged her tight.

"It's okay, Calypso," he murmured, stroking her back and kissing her hair. "It's okay. You have every right to be afraid."

"Maybe," she said brokenly. "But that doesn't give me the right to cripple anyone else."

"Maybe not. But don't you *ever* think you don't have a right to be afraid. And don't you ever think that you don't have a right to express those fears and concerns. You're entitled to that, honey. Everyone is."

"But I'm not entitled to act the way I do when y'all don't agree with me. And I'm not entitled to ask people to change their entire lives because I'm afraid." Lifting a hand, she dashed away her tears. "You go on that dive, Chase. Because you need to. For yourself."

"I still want to talk to Jeff's attorney first."

"Then let me call her. Maybe we can drive in to Key West and see her for a few minutes. I need to sign those papers anyway."

"Okay. And I'll buy you breakfast."

"I can make breakfast," she protested.

He shook his head. "I don't want you waiting on me, or cooking for me, or any of that other stuff. I'm old enough to take care of myself, and I'm comfortable enough to buy us both breakfast."

She gave a choked laugh. "A liberated male?"

327

"Just an independent one."

Shirley gave them an eleven-thirty appointment. They stopped at a small place on Stock Island to eat, then drove to her office. As they were climbing out of the car, a man with an iguana on his shoulder came out of Shirley's and climbed onto a moped. He zipped away, the iguana looking content.

"God, I love this place," Callie said. "Where else would you see that?" And for the first time that morning, she genuinely felt like smiling.

The feeling went away, though, as soon as they were in Shirley's office. She had never been there except under the worst of circumstances. Shirley didn't even have to say a word before butterflies were churning in Callie's stomach.

As soon as she and Chase were introduced, Sylvia looked at Callie. "You understand I can't discuss the case with Mr. Mattingly present?"

"Why not?"

"Because it would violate attorney-client privilege. Also, anything I say in front of Mr. Mattingly would become a proper subject for questioning in a trial or deposition."

Callie nodded, understanding.

"I don't want to question you about the case," Chase said. "What I need to do is run a hypothetical by you and see if you think it might be useful."

Shirley steepled her hands and nodded. "Fair enough. I can listen."

"All right. Two months ago I was hired by Vantage Maritime insurance company to do a commercial salvage dive on a boat called *The Happy Maggie*. My area of expertise is vessel damage, and I was supposed to determine why she sank."

"She must have been an expensive boat."

"Actually, she was carrying ten million dollars in uncut diamonds."

Shirley's eyebrows lifted. "That's a good reason to check it out, all right."

As clearly as he could, he sketched his initial doubts when he learned the *Island Dream* had been found so close to where *The Maggie* had sunk, and how his suspicions had grown when he learned that two divers had gone out on the *Island Dream* on that last voyage, divers who hadn't been reported missing.

"There could be reasons for that," Shirley pointed out. "Some of them wouldn't be very helpful to Jeff. But you're right, the divers are missing, and someone by now should be looking for them if they didn't get home safely."

"You'd think so."

"And I'll grant you, the proximity to the sunken boat is intriguing. Especially with that much money involved."

"Exactly."

"But I need more than that, Mr. Mattingly."

"I know. Let me continue. I was injured on the dive I took and was unable to verify *The Maggie*'s damage. The other diver, Bill Evers, gave a report on the damage that doesn't at all match what the boat's owner claimed happened. He also said the diamonds weren't there."

"How do you know that?"

"I saw the insurance company report on the dive just a few days ago."

"But you didn't see the damage yourself?" She began to look doubtful, and Callie felt her stomach twist into a knot. Regardless of whether Chase made this dive, she had to make Shirley see the importance of this information.

"Shirley," she said, "don't you see? The prosecutor is going to claim that Jeff and Eric killed those men to get their boat. And everyone who knows Jeff knows how much he wanted a sportfisherman. It's been all he's talked about for years."

Shirley nodded. "I understand that Callie. Believe me. They've got motive and opportunity, and a circumstantial case that could be enough for a conviction. But I need something more than what Mr. Mattingly has given me so far if I'm going to pull their theory apart. Think about it. These waters are full of shipwrecks, some of them with millions of dollars in gold on them. People dive out there all the time looking for those wrecks. I can't simply get up before a jury and make a general argument that the missing divers were some kind of treasure hunters, and I can't link it to this boat Mr. Mattingly's talking about unless I have some specific proof that there was already hanky-panky surrounding the sunken boat. What's more, Mr. Mattingly just told me the diamonds weren't on the boat. Now how's that going to sound?"

Callie nodded reluctantly, her stomach sinking. "I still think ten million dollars in diamonds makes a better motivation than pirating a boat. And Chase thinks the diamonds were still there. Or that the divers believed they were still there."

"I need more than suspicions here."

Chase spoke. "Let me continue."

Shirley reached for a pencil and began tapping the eraser against the desk top. "Go on."

"Bill said the diamonds weren't on the boat. He also said the damage to the boat didn't match the owner's description of what happened. So Maritime is preparing to file a complaint of insurance fraud against the owner."

"I can see why. But I gather you don't think that's what happened?"

"I'm beginning to seriously doubt it. In the first place, I think those two divers who went out on the *Island Dream* were looking for the diamonds. The wife of one of the *Dream*'s owners said these guys wanted to do a deep dive. They went out beyond the reefs to deeper waters near the edge of the continental shelf."

Shirley nodded and rapped her pencil even more rapidly. "Interesting. Most people who dive around here want to do the reefs or nearby wrecks. Usually less than thirty feet, from what I hear."

"Exactly. Anyway, there's a private investigator looking for these divers right now."

"Good. He'll probably be more serious about it than local authorities. What else?"

"The diver who went down with me, the one who made the report to the insurance company, was found dead a few days ago. Shot in the back of the head."

Shirley's pencil was beating a rapid-fire tattoo. "Give me just a little more."

"The little more is that I'm proposing to dive to the wreck again. What if I find that the report was falsified?"

For an instant Shirley was perfectly still. Then she leaned forward, looking intently at Chase. "Prove that, and I think I'll have enough to make the state attorney reconsider these charges. If your friend lied about the damage, then there's a good chance he lied about the diamonds. What other reason could there be to falsify the report?"

Looking satisfied, Shirley sat back. "Bring me the

evidence, Mr. Mattingly, and I'll knock the pins out from under the state's theory of the case."

Callie was elated most of the way home. Chase listened to her bubble, a smile creasing his face. She was absolutely certain now that Jeff was going to get off. But by the time they reached the last stretch of road, past the salt marsh, doubts began to creep in.

"Knocking holes in the state's theory doesn't mean a jury would believe ours," she said in a voice gone tight. "What if Shirley can't get him to drop the charges?"

Chase turned a startled glance on her. "There's this thing called reasonable doubt, Calypso."

"I know all about that. I also know that if folks believe the state's theory, they're going to convict Jeff and Eric. Besides," she said, and her voice grew tighter still, "even if Jeff gets off, people are going to believe he's guilty. You know that. I know that. The only way to give Jeff back his life is to find out who really *did* kill those men. We've got to find those divers."

"I'll call Bruderson's lawyer and find out what's happening with the private detective. But, honey, the important thing right now is to get Jeff off. It's a lot easier to do it before a trial. Then we'll have all the time we need to find out where those divers are."

She nodded and managed to give him a wan smile. "I'm sorry. I'm just crashing from the euphoria, I guess. Things are certainly looking better than they did two days ago, and I've got to focus on that."

But it wasn't easy for her, Chase knew. She'd suffered some serious blows at the hands of life. Calypso Carlson wasn't a pessimist, but she knew that bad things, inconceivable things, could and did happen. She was a realist.

332

"One thing at a time," he said finally, the only consolation he could offer.

"You're right." She turned on the seat and looked at him. "Are you sure you couldn't have someone else do this dive? I mean, I know you have to make a deep dive. I know how much you need to. But—I don't know why, but I'm real nervous about you going back down to that wreck. What if—what if somebody has a reason to prevent you from doing it?"

"Tell you what. We won't let anybody else know I'm doing it, okay?"

After a moment she nodded. "Okay. That makes me feel better." She gave a little laugh. "I know it's stupid but . . . Chase, I keep feeling as if this black cloud is out there somewhere, and it's getting closer."

He could hardly argue with her about that. Black clouds had a habit of moving into her life.

They stopped first at his house so he could pick up some clothes and check his answering machine. There was one message, from Bruderson's lawyer, Peter Barton. "We've hired the private investigative agency, Mr. Mattingly. They're on the job. Mr. Bruderson wants to know when you plan to dive. Give me a call, please."

Chase looked at Callie. "It ought to be all right to let him know."

She hesitated. "But if they mention it to someone else . . ."

"Okay. I'll just pretend I didn't get the message." He wiped the tape and reset the machine, feeling uncomfortable about not answering the call. "But we did make a deal with them, Callie. I don't want to push it too far or they might yank the investigators."

"Finding those divers is as important to Bruderson as it is to us," she argued. "After all, he could be facing

333

criminal charges himself, on the insurance fraud thing."

"He could also start wondering if we've sent him on a wild-goose chase for reasons of our own if we don't cooperate.

"He'll call again first."

Chase let it go. This wasn't his usual mode of doing business, but then he'd never dealt with murder before.

When they reached the Carlson house, they found Jeff already there, painting the side of the house.

"What happened to Sara?" Callie asked him.

"She had to go to work." He wiped sweat from his brow with the back of his arm. "I feel like a slug not having a job. But I suppose you'll have a fit if I go fishing tomorrow."

Chase watched Callie, saw the hesitation and the tightening of her face. But then she said, "No, if that's what you want to do, fine. I wouldn't mind eating some fresh tarpon for dinner. Or even some mahimahi." She looked at Chase.

Jeff looked at her. "Hey, are you sure you'll be okay with me going fishing?"

Callie nodded. "Sure. It's what you do." Then she went into the house.

Jeff looked at Chase. "Is she okay?"

Chase shrugged a shoulder. "It varies according to what point on the curve you catch her. She's been way up and way down today."

"She must have a fever. She never lets me go fishing that easily."

"Maybe she's having a change of heart."

"Did you say something to her?"

"Actually, I think she's been saying things to herself." Uncomfortable discussing Callie with Jeff, and figuring that Callie would tell her brother what she wanted him to know, Chase changed the subject. "Listen, I want to make a deep dive. Can we use the *Lily*?"

"You're going down to the wreck, huh? Well, yeah, we can take the *Lily*, but wouldn't you be better off with a dive boat? Or something with a decompression chamber?"

"I can't afford a decompression chamber. And I don't want to rent a boat. I don't want anybody to know I'm doing this."

Jeff nodded slowly. "I can handle that. But if anything happens to you, Callie is going to have my hide."

"You've got it backwards, Jeff. If anything happens to you, Callie is going to have *my* hide."

The man and youth exchanged looks of complete understanding.

"When do you want to go?" Jeff asked.

"Tomorrow."

Jeff came into the house a little while later. Callie was in the kitchen making a useless stab at cleaning the refrigerator. "Where's Chase?" she asked.

"He went to get his air tanks filled. Said he'll be back this evening."

"Shit."

The word was so unexpected from Callie that Jeff's jaw dropped an inch. "What's wrong?"

She slammed the refrigerator door and threw the washrag into the sink. "What's wrong? Only that he's planning to make a dive down to nearly two hundred feet all by himself, and that he's probably planning on doing it soon. Like tomorrow."

"That's what he said. But, sis, it's not to two hundred

feet."

"No, only to a hundred and eighty-eight feet! Like that makes a big difference."

"Well, actually it does. See, if he goes down on heliox—which he should at that depth—and he really were going over two hundred feet, the likelihood of HPNS increases dramatically."

Callie gaped at him. "What are you talking about?"

"High pressure nervous syndrome. It was in the diving books Chase gave me. Yeah, going down below two hundred feet can sometimes be really dangerous on heliox. That's why they're testing hydrogen-air mixes . . ."

"Jeff." She interrupted him almost gently. "Jeff, I'm really thrilled you're learning all this, but I'd be very grateful if you wouldn't give me anything else to worry about."

"But that's what I'm trying to tell you. He's using the safest air mixture and going to a safe depth on it. Heliox doesn't cause nitrogen narcosis, and it's a whole lot less likely to cause the bends."

Callie's head lifted. "Really?"

"Oh, yeah. Because helium doesn't dissolve as easily in the blood."

"But then he shouldn't have gotten the bends on his last dive."

"Not exactly. In the first place, he probably had nitrogen in him when he went down. The only way to avoid that is by saturating with helium first, and I don't think he probably did that for such a short dive. Then, as fast as he came up, even oxygen could cause the bends."

"And if he wasn't on helium at all?"

"Then he was in a world of trouble, sis. He's lucky he didn't die. But that's not the point. The point is, *this* dive is going to be as safe as a dive can possibly be.

And if you want my opinion, from what I've been reading, I don't think Chase was on heliox on his last dive."

"That's what he suspects."

"I'm not surprised. From everything he told me went wrong, I'd bet somebody slipped him the wrong air mixture.

Callie's felt a fist grab her heart. She touched her brother's arm. "Jeff . . . Jeff, we can't let anybody at all know he's going to make this dive, okay? If somebody would do that to him once . . ."

Jeff nodded. "I know, Callie. Believe me, I know."

"Don't even tell Sara. Please. If word were to get into the wrong ear, I hate to think."

Jeff covered her hand with his own and squeezed. "Not a word anywhere, sis. I promise. I told Sara I was going fishing tomorrow, and I'm not going to tell her anything else. And what's more, when Chase gets back with those tanks, somebody is gonna watch them every minute."

That made Callie feel a little better, but when Chase still hadn't returned by seven that evening, she found herself on tenterhooks worrying that something serious had happened to him.

"God, I hate this," she finally said in a burst of utter frustration. Jeff looked up from the diving manual he was studying. They sat in the living room as the summer evening darkened with the threat of thunderstorms.

"What?" he asked.

"Worrying! I get so sick of worrying."

"You do a lot of that, sis." He put his book down on the battered coffee table. "You need to get a little more fatalistic."

"My problem is that I'm *too* fatalistic. I think

337

everything is going to turn out bad."

"No, your problem is worrying when there's nothing at all you can do."

"That's the definition of worry."

He almost laughed. She could see it in the way his blue eyes started gleaming, and she felt a brief surge of happiness that her brother was still able to smile and laugh despite the current mess. She'd nearly forgotten how herself.

"Look, he had to go all the way to Miami, I think. That takes time, and it's Friday besides. You know what the traffic gets like on weekends with so many people fleeing the city to the Keys."

"But how long could it take to fill a couple of air tanks?"

"I don't know. Maybe it's raining up that way. Maybe he got caught in rush hour. Just relax, Callie. He'll get here."

"I want him back before it gets dark. You know, I keep thinking about those people playing those pranks on him. There's something so . . . sinister about that. About the kind of mind that would do something like that."

"Actually, I think the kind of mind that would do something like that is pretty stupid. It starts to get too easy to get caught."

"Trying to convince someone they're crazy is sinister."

Jeff put up a hand. "Okay. It's sinister. But it's a far cry from actually trying to kill him. It's stupid, next to putting the wrong mix in his tanks before that dive."

"And what about his gun being stolen? That really puts me on edge."

"Maybe the guy who's flinging seaweed around just

338

wanted to make sure he wouldn't get shot while he was doing it."

"Maybe. But what if they did it so they could make it look like Chase committed a crime?"

"Kinda hard to do now that the gun's reported missing."

Callie shook her head. "No, it's not. Because Chase is the only one who said the gun is gone. No one else can *prove* that. So if somebody commits a crime with that gun, Chase could well be in serious trouble."

"Man, you have a devious mind. Maybe you should have gone to law school."

He was laughing at her again, and it irritated her. "Don't you see? Somebody might have taken that gun to set Chase up specifically so he can't do anything about *The Maggie* and the diamonds. If he gets charged with murder, who's going to believe him about the diamonds?"

"His fingerprints would have to be on the gun."

"They probably are, Jeff. They probably are."

"But they deteriorate with time, Callie. And somebody would have to hold the gun to fire it. Even if they used gloves so they didn't leave their own prints, that would probably smear Chase's prints beyond identification. I think you're making a mountain out of a molehill here."

"I don't think so." She smothered another sigh. "At least three people have already died. Somebody is willing to kill over this. Somebody is willing to wreck lives over this. I don't put anything past them."

"Maybe not, but I still think you're borrowing trouble. We need to just wait and see how this unfolds."

"Well, I'd do that a whole lot better if Chase would just get back here."

Jeff's expression softened. "You're crazy about him, aren't you."

Callie stiffened. "No, of course not. I just want to get this dive over with so you can get out from under the murder charges."

"Yeah. Right." He grinned. She threw a pillow at him. He laughed, and despite her frustration and fear, she had to laugh with him.

It had, she realized suddenly, been a long time since she had felt this comfortable with her brother. Maybe giving up her constant fight to change him would actually have some benefits.

He picked up his book again, and Callie sat across from him, watching him in the lamplight as the wind picked up outside. He was growing up, she thought. He really *was* growing up, and he was actually turning out pretty well—something she'd failed to see before because she hated his career choices.

Maybe she wasn't such a failure as a mom after all.

The night beyond the windows began to flicker with lightning. Jeff looked up from his book. "If this keeps up, Chase probably won't be able to dive tomorrow."

"How come?"

"Seas'll be rough, if this is a big storm system."

"Maybe I should check the weather."

"Won't make any difference. We'll have to decide in the morning anyway." He cocked his head. "I think I hear a car."

Callie jumped up but Jeff waved her back. "I'll go out there. We don't know who it is."

Callie, who never before in her life had worried about who might be pulling up to her house in a car, suddenly had a fractured feeling, as if the world had changed beyond recognition. This was crazy, she thought, to have to live with this kind of caution. "I'll go with you."

Jeff hesitated, then shrugged a shoulder. Apparently he, too, was learning that not everything was worth fighting over.

Callie followed him out the side door, and when she saw Chase climbing out of his Explorer she hit a full run, dashing down off the porch and practically throwing herself into his arms. "I was getting so worried!"

He laughed, his face lighting with pleasure, and swung her around in a circle before he set her on her feet.

"She sure was," Jeff said from the porch. "I think she wore a path in the living-room floor."

"Sorry I was gone so long. I had to rent some equipment because most of my stuff is up in Tampa. Then traffic was a bitch on the way back. Two accidents, right where you couldn't get around them. Nothing serious, but it felt like we crawled for miles."

Chase started walking toward the house, his arm around Callie's shoulders, but Jeff stopped him.

"Don't you think we ought to bring the equipment inside where we can watch it?"

"Good idea. I had the tanks sealed so I'll know if they've been tampered with, but why take a chance."

The tanks were considerably heavier than Callie expected, and bigger than the ones she frequently saw at the docks on the recreational dive boats.

"Five of them?" she asked. "Why so many?"

"I'm going to wear two of them. Then I'm going to hang one about ten feet down to use when I come back up. When I go this deep I always make it a practice to take a so-called emergency decompression stop at ten feet. Just an extra precaution. Anyway, the deeper you go, the faster you use your air, so I need quite a bit. The two extras are in case any of these leaks overnight."

It sounded as if he'd thought of everything, Callie reassured herself. There was also an underwater camera.

"I'm taking pictures of whatever I find down there," Chase said. "It's not going to turn into a swearing contest between me and a dead man."

Once they had his gear inside and stowed at one side of the living room, Jeff excused himself. He gave Callie a knowing look that made her blush and turn away quickly so that Chase wouldn't see it.

But as soon as they were alone, Chase turned her into his embrace and kissed her deeply.

"I missed you," he said simply.

"I missed you, too," she admitted shakily. It was a bad thing to miss him with the dive looming over them tomorrow. She didn't want to think about how she was going to feel if anything happened to him. All she could do right now was hope this was a big storm system so he wouldn't be able to go tomorrow.

It was appalling to realize how desperately she wanted just one more day before she had to face the terror. Suddenly scared by the depth of her own feelings, she pulled away.

"Hungry?" she asked, her smile brittle.

"I ate on the way back. Thanks." He looked at her, his expression thoughtful, as if he was trying to decide what her pulling away meant. Then he sat down and began to check his equipment and work calculations.

Outside the storm growled and rain fell. Inside all was quiet and filled with a sense of foreboding.

Finally, Callie could stand it no longer and went to bed alone.

A long time later Chase found her and slipped under

the sheet beside her. She went into his arms without protest and clung to him through a night that was far too short.

CHAPTER 19

"I'M GOING WITH YOU."

Callie stood on the dock and looked at her brother and Chase. They had just finished loading and securing all of Chase's gear. The day had betrayed her, turning out sunny and calm with no wind other than the usual westerlies. The water was almost as smooth as a mirror.

Chase looked over at her and put his hands on his hips.

Jeff spoke. "You hate the water, Callie. You won't even go fishing with me because it scares you to death to be out on a boat. You don't want to make this trip."

It was true her heart was pounding, and her mouth was dry, but she forced herself to ignore her instinctive terror. "You two are *not* going alone. If something happens, you might need help. There's no way I'm staying here."

Jeff hesitated. "Can you handle it?"

"Hell, yes, I can handle it better than waiting on the point again. I was out on boats with dad when you were still in diapers."

"That was before Dad died."

Callie set her chin. "I can handle it."

"Mainly I'm worried that if you get too frightened, you'll distract us," Jeff said.

Callie drew a sharp breath. She hadn't thought of that. "I'll be fine," she said firmly. "I'm far more worried about you two."

"Let her come," Chase said, speaking for the first time. "She'll be fine."

Ten minutes later, the *Lily* pulled away from the dock and headed out of the inlet. Callie felt a little queasy as she watched the shoreline fall away, but she forced herself to turn her attention to the sea.

The morning sun glinted off the gentle waves, and the water ranged in color from olive to light green to aquamarine. It was as beautiful as it had always been, but all that beauty held a threat she couldn't ignore.

She found herself remembering the times she had come out like this with her dad for the day, and remembered how happy those occasions had always been. Wes Carlson had been a serious commercial fisherman, but that didn't prevent him from fishing for fun when he had some time, or fishing just to bring home enough to fill the freezer. At an early age Callie had learned to mend the nets, to set them, and to haul them in full of catch.

And she had loved it.

But they had usually headed northeast, to Florida Bay, and they had rarely gone oceanside of the reefs. Even as she tried to recapture the joyous anticipation of her youth, she couldn't escape the awareness that they were going into deep water, water where the bottom wouldn't be visible from the surface, water so deep that the light didn't reach all the way down.

Chase came to stand beside her. "You okay?" he asked.

"I'm fine."

"You look awfully tense."

"I haven't been out on a boat in four years. I'll relax."

"I'm sure you will." Reaching out, he clasped her hand.

"How are *you* doing?" she asked him.

"I'm scared spitless."

She looked up at him and saw that he wasn't joking. She thought it took a very strong man to admit fear so readily. "Are you sure you want to do this?"

"Wanting isn't part of it. I *have* to do it. For Jeff. For me. For you."

"For *me*?"

His stormy gray eyes reflected some of the greens from the water. "I don't want you to be terrified every time I talk about going diving."

Every time? Would he be diving a lot after this? Was he thinking that their relationship would continue? But she didn't dare ask, and she didn't dare think about something so scary. She didn't know if she had the courage to risk loving someone.

But it was already too late, wasn't it? How far could she carry this game of denial she was playing with herself? Would it be any easier if she said good-bye to Chase at the end of the day, or if she waited for months or years until life took him away from her?

"This should be fun," he said. "Banish the clouds from your thoughts. We're going to have a great day full of sun and sea. Most people would consider this a holiday."

But she felt his hand tighten around hers, and knew that he wasn't much calmer about this than she was. He was just pretending better.

"You're sure you're up to this dive? It isn't too soon after your accident?"

"Honey, they decompressed me for days. Then they decompressed me a couple of extra times. If I've got any bubbles left in my body, it would be a major medical miracle."

"But you could have?" Her heart was suddenly in her throat.

"The possibility is so remote it's not even worth considering."

Which was not exactly the same as saying there wasn't any at all. She shifted her gaze back to the sea, trying to deal with the fear that was crawling up her spine.

"Look," Chase said, "even if I had some bubbles, they wouldn't cause any problem going down, and I'm allowing extra decompression time on the way back. I'm not only being conservative, I'm being ridiculously cautious, okay?"

She nodded but didn't trust herself to speak. The sea was looking more threatening by the minute, even though nothing out there had changed. The only thing worse than what she was doing now would have been staying home and wondering.

Finally, she summoned a smile, though, and looked at Chase. "Everything will be fine," she said firmly.

"Yes, it will."

The water began to darken as the depth increased, and the farther they got from shallow water, the stronger the waves grew. Nothing threatening, but swells were rolling them gently, and Callie felt herself balancing automatically against the rocking of the *Lily*.

Chase glanced at his watch. "Not much longer now."

It was going to be all right. She had to believe that.

"Why don't you go up on the bridge with Jeff?" Chase suggested. "He's probably wondering how you're doing."

So she climbed up there, ignoring an unexpected sense of vertigo as the ship's gentle roll was magnified. Jeff looked at her and grinned.

346

"This is the life," he said.

She forced herself to return the smile.

"You doing okay?"

"Just fine. I haven't completely lost my sea legs."

"Great." He beamed at her, as if he was just thrilled to have her sharing this with him. She felt a pang for all the times she had turned him down because she hated the sea. Standing beside him now, she realized it really wasn't so bad. Not bad at all.

Until she turned around and saw Chase pulling on his blue-and-black wet suit. Her heart fluttered wildly, and she gripped the rail until her knuckles turned white.

"We're almost there," Jeff said, reading the coordinates off the global positioning system. "I just hope those divers didn't detach the buoy when they went down for the diamonds."

"What if they did?" Callie asked.

"Then we'll never find the damn boat."

Which would mean Chase couldn't make the dive. Which would mean they wouldn't have the evidence to help Jeff. She couldn't remember ever having felt so torn between desires.

She found herself scanning the water, seeking the buoy, trying not to let all the hatred she felt for the sea rise up in her and drown her in bitterness. But she honestly could not escape the feeling the sea had made all this happen, that for some reason she and Chase and Jeff were all being manipulated to this point in space and time, forced to face their fears and desires head on.

"Callie?"

She looked at her brother.

Almost as if he had read her mind, he said, "You know what terrifies me more than anything else in the world?"

Her chest tightened. "What's that?"

"Losing this. Not being able to do this ever again. Spending the rest of my life in some stinking jail and never again putting out to sea. I think I could handle anything at all except that."

She stepped closer to him and slid her arm around his waist. His closed around her shoulders. The rocking of the boat on the swells was almost like being rocked in a mother's arms. "I'm sorry, Jeff."

"For what?"

"For trying to take this away from you."

He looked down at her, blue eyes meeting blue. "You couldn't take it away from me, Callie. I think you found that out. But it doesn't matter. I know you were trying to get me to do what you thought was best for me."

"No, actually, the sad thing is I was trying to get you to do what was best for *me*. I'm really ashamed of myself."

He squeezed her. "Don't be. You've been a good mother to me all along. Just consider it a difference of opinion, okay?"

Callie looked up at him and felt pride fill her. Her brother was turning into a remarkable young man.

"There's the buoy," he said suddenly.

Callie's mouth suddenly felt as if it were full of cotton. She didn't even want to look back at Chase, didn't want to know how close he was to being ready to go over the side.

The buoy was a small one with a strobe light on top of it. They pulled up nearby, close enough to read the painted warning that the sunken craft was being salvaged, but not close enough to foul them in the buoy line.

"Are they just going to leave that there forever?"

Callie wondered.

"I don't know," Jeff answered. "I'm surprised the divers didn't cut it loose after they recovered the diamonds."

"If that's what they were doing out here," Callie said. "We don't know for sure why they were out here."

Jeff looked at her. "Don't say that."

Callie, whose hopes about this were as high as Jeff's, understood what he was feeling. She was so full of hope and fear right now that it actually hurt.

Jeff cut the engines, then lowered the sea anchor to slow their wind drift. After a few minutes, he and Chase were satisfied they weren't caught in a strong current.

"What about that buoy," Jeff asked. "Why didn't those divers cut it loose?"

"Probably because it would have been too suspicious," Chase said. "See that warning on it? That prevents anybody except Maritime from legally salvaging the *Maggie*. Maritime's probably leaving it there in case they need to go down to the yacht for additional information during legal proceedings. As for the divers—cutting that buoy loose would be about as good as announcing somebody had been screwing around out here. The best way to leave no tracks was to leave the buoy."

Chase started to reach for his equipment, then paused and looked at Callie. "I'll be careful. I promise."

She managed a nod. "I know you will. I . . . just come back, Chase."

Jeff turned his back discreetly to give them privacy, and started fiddling with a boat hook. An instant later Callie was in Chase's arms, hugging him as if she would never let go.

"It's okay, Calypso," he murmured in her ear. "It's

okay, sweetie. I've done this hundreds of times. It's like walking across the street."

With her face pressed to his chest, she managed a nod. "I know," she said brokenly. "I know . . ."

He lifted her chin and looked deep into her eyes. "I'll be back." He said the words with a thick accent, reminding her of *The Terminator*. The unexpectedness of it surprised a broken laugh from her, and made it possible to keep her tears from spilling.

"You better," she said. "You better."

He gave her a quick kiss, then let her go.

The first thing he and Jeff did was lower a bar with an air tank and diving weights attached to it. The air supply for the last decompression stop, Callie surmised.

Then Chase pulled on his own tanks and fastened the harness securely. Instead of the diving mask she was accustomed to seeing, he wore a helmet-style mask that covered his head. He picked up the underwater camera, attached its strap to his belt, and gave her one last look.

She had a wild surge of panic and wanted to reach out to stop him, to tell him not to go, but he was over the side before a sound could escape her lips.

All she could do was watch him swim the few feet to the buoy. When he reached it, he paused and looked back, giving a little wave. Then he was swallowed by the depths of the Atlantic Ocean.

It was as if he had never been.

He went because of Callie. As he stood there looking over the side into the dark depths of the Atlantic, Chase had seriously wondered if he was going to be able to make himself do this. He could feel sweat breaking out under his wet suit, and fear tied his stomach into knots. No, he wasn't going to be able to make himself go.

350

Then he looked one last time at Callie, and knew he *had* to do this. For her. To help her brother. And to make himself whole for her. If he did any less, he would fail her.

Going over the side was the hardest thing he had ever done. Going under was even more difficult.

But the first thirty feet of the dive weren't bad. Enough light penetrated that Chase felt little except the unexpected joy of diving again. After that, though, it got steadily darker, and with the darkness came a resurgence of his fears. He had to remind himself to breathe, to keep the pressure in his lungs equalized, had to remind himself to clear his ears. One of his sinuses twinged, and he wondered if he had a blockage. A quick, sharp sniffle eased it though.

As the water grew darker around him, the pressure increased, and the feeling of being closed in began to trouble him. What had never bothered him before bothered him now, and he was painfully aware of his vulnerability.

He shouldn't be making this dive alone. He was violating a cardinal rule of safety, and he was grateful that it hadn't occurred to Callie to get stubborn about it. All that stuff he'd handed her about it being perfectly safe and his being excessively cautious went out the window the instant he came down here alone. But he didn't trust anyone else enough to ask him to make this wild-goose chase with him. So there he was, following a buoy line down to a depth that could kill him in a few seconds if anything went wrong.

That didn't make him brave, it made him dumb.

But he didn't want to think about that right now. Having a dive partner hadn't saved him last time. And this time he was relying on nothing and no one but himself and his own preparations—and the sea.

He felt her all around him, holding him in her watery arms, squeezing him as he went deeper, cutting him off from air and light. A spear of panic shot through him, and he paused in his descent, forcing himself to be calm, to breathe.

The light on his helmet cast a glow in the water around him, but beyond that glow there was only darkness, and the sense of shapes moving out there. Fish, of course, maybe some eels . . . Nothing to fear.

But he feared it anyway. At a hundred feet he seriously thought about heading back up. He was only halfway down, and his fear of the darkness was beginning to strangle him.

The camera banged against his leg, startling him, but he battered down the fright. Just the camera.

He'd done this hundreds of times, he told himself. Nothing had changed. There was nothing out there that hadn't been out there on all his previous dives. The sea didn't want to kill him. The sea was supremely indifferent to his invasion.

Except he felt as if he was being watched. And he probably was, he told himself. Fish were probably out there wondering what this light was. The image of perplexed fish drove his fear back, and he resumed his descent, checking his dive watch and his air gauge. Doing fine.

But foot by foot as he continued his descent, he became more and more aware of how alone he was. Fear crawled out of the increasingly cold water and latched on to his spine. He forced himself to ignore it, even when it soured his mouth and made his heart pound.

There was nothing to fear but fear itself. He'd had

that hammered into him back in SEALs training, and he chanted it silently to himself. Nothing to fear but fear.

Then a dark shape loomed out of the night of the sea. He had reached the bottom of the line.

Callie thought she was going to scream from the tension. Nightmare visions stalked her, filling her head with all the kinds of trouble Chase could get into. Her eyes searched the horizon, fearing that a buildup of storm clouds would suddenly appear. She imagined him getting fouled somehow in the buoy line, or caught in the wreckage below.

"How long is he going to be?" she finally asked Jeff.

"I don't know. He had several ascent plans worked out, depending on how long it takes him to examine the wreckage. The longer he's down, the slower he comes back up. He didn't think it was going to take more than an hour, though."

"What if it does?"

"Then it does." Jeff faced her. "Callie, he knows what he's doing. The real danger here is if he comes up too fast, and he's not going to do that. He showed me how he did his dive calculations—"

"When did he do that?"

"This morning while you were showering. My point is, he added extra time into the decompression stops. He's not even going to cut it close."

That should have relieved her, but other worries came to mind. "How's he going to get to those tanks we've got hanging over the side if he follows the buoy line? He'd surface first."

Jeff shook his head. "There's plenty of light down to nearly thirty feet, sis. He'll be able to stop following the buoy line long before he gets up to ten feet. He just has to swim over to the bar, and the boat's shadow in the water will be an obvious guide. Believe me, he can do it."

But when she looked over the side, the water appeared opaque to her, nothing visible except the surface. It would look different from below, she told herself. From below he wouldn't be blinded by the sunlight glinting off the water.

The water was getting choppier, wasn't it? But she couldn't be sure, and she tried to tell herself it was her imagination. There were no clouds anywhere, and the wind didn't seem to have stiffened at all. Of course, a large storm system somewhere out there could be making waves here even when it was too far away to see.

"How long was it supposed to take him to get all the way down?" she asked.

"I'm not sure. He said something about not being able to descend faster than seventy-five feet per minute, but I don't remember his calculations exactly. You've got to equalize the pressure in your ears and stuff as you go down . . ." Jeff shook his head. "I'm no expert, Callie. Hell, I wish I'd copied the times he calculated."

She wished he had, too. She would have liked to know where exactly Chase was as the minutes ticked by and her nerves stretched as taut as piano wire.

Her sense of foreboding was growing by the minute, and she tried to tell herself it was just her hatred of the sea. And maybe it was, but her mental arguments didn't help the feeling of doom that was settling over her. She scanned the horizon as if she half expected to see some movie monster appear while the sun pounded her.

The silence was eerie. The only sound in the world was the creak of the boat as she rocked on the waves, and the lap of water against her sides. And little by little even that was going away as the waters began to calm.

"We should have put a safety line on him," she said suddenly.

Jeff shook his head. "He said he didn't need one with the buoy line."

"Sure. As long as he can grab it." Her scalp was beginning to prickle. "How long?"

"Twenty-two minutes."

That was all? Time seemed to have turned to molasses, oozing by rather than passing. She gripped the rail tighter and told herself to calm down. Nothing was going to happen.

But almost as if the sea knew it was, they were suddenly becalmed. The wind stopped, the water smoothed out until the *Lily* was hardly rocking at all. Callie looked up at the sky and felt her heart thud as she saw a haze that hadn't been there moments ago.

"The weather's changing," she said tensely.

Jeff nodded. "It doesn't look bad, though. Just a haze . . ."

But she noticed he, too, looked around uneasily. The westerly winds almost never stopped blowing there.

"Maybe we're in the center of some high-pressure cell that's passing over," he said after a moment. "The breeze'll start again in a few minutes."

That was when Callie saw the boat approaching them. "Look." She pointed.

Jeff followed her finger. "What about it?"

"Is it coming this way?"

"I don't know. There are a lot of boats out here, sis. I'd be surprised if we didn't see one."

Callie nodded, but she kept her attention fixed on the boat, trying to tell if it was approaching them. They

355

might be out in the middle of the sea, but that didn't ease her apprehensions any. Not when someone had tried to kill Chase once before. Not when someone had been trying to convince Chase he was losing his mind. Not when someone had killed Bill Evers.

For all they had been secretive about this dive, it remained that someone could have seen them set out this morning. Or someone could have seen Chase getting his air tanks filled.

She glanced at her watch and started praying.

The hole in *The Happy Maggie* was in the bow, just as he would have expected from Bruderson's description. Just exactly as he had seen it in his dream. Chase photographed the damage, then took an up-close look himself.

The hull hadn't been damaged from within, he realized. Something had damaged it from the outside, and the more he looked at it, the more he felt that an explosive had been used, deforming the hull inward around the gaping hole.

The *Maggie* had been sunk deliberately.

He took a few more pictures, then had the worst urge to go inside and see if the diamonds were still there. But he was almost positive they weren't, and besides, going alone into a wreck would be an absolutely foolhardy thing to do. Too much could go wrong, and there'd be nobody there to help him.

He began his ascent feeling jubilant. Not only had he made the dive, but he figured he probably had enough evidence to help Jeff out. Of course, it wasn't enough to guarantee anything, but it was a giant step forward.

But he'd made the damn dive. The water whispered around him, and dark shapes threatened to coalesce, but he'd made it without blowing his cool. He could stand the fear as long as it didn't overwhelm him, and now it wasn't even strong enough to do that. With each minute he spent down there, he felt himself growing calmer. Instead of remembering his terror last time, he was remembering all the good feelings he'd always gotten from a dive.

He had a few more rocky moments on the way back up, but they weren't unexpected. Each time the darkness threatened to close in and crush him, he fought the urge to speed up his ascent and instead forced himself to stay right where he was. After a few seconds, the fear would subside again, seeping out of him and back into the cold, dark waters.

At sixty feet, he stopped, checking his dive watch, fearing that he was ascending too quickly. The stop wasn't necessary, but he took it anyway, facing a new fear: that he might get the bends again. It was enough to make him pause at that depth longer than was reasonable, and as soon as he realized it, he began his ascent again. Staying down here would only add to his required decompression time, not help.

It was when he was at last making his safety decompression stop at ten feet, hanging on to the bar that he and Jeff had lowered over the side, that he heard and saw a boat approach. Realizing it was coming too close, he checked his air, and saw that he had more than enough left. Letting go of the bar, he swam directly under the *Lily* and waited to see what was going on.

Callie and Jeff watched the other boat approach, coming directly toward them.

"This isn't right," she said to Jeff. "Something's wrong. We've got to warn Chase."

"He can't miss the other boat being here, sis. He'll know."

She looked over the side and saw the dark figure of Chase at the bar below. "He's almost up. Look."

"I don't want to look," he answered. "Stop staring, Callie. If these guys are up to no good, you don't want them to know where Chase is."

Her head snapped up, but she couldn't help stealing another look downward. Chase's figure had disappeared.

"He's gone," she said, her voice cracking.

"He probably went under the boat. Look, he's not stupid, Callie. He's probably as worried about this as we are."

She looked at her brother and saw that his face was drawn as tightly as hers felt. Instinctively, she reached out for him and he took her hand

"If . . ." She had to force herself to swallow and try again as her voice cracked. "If these are bad guys . . . let's lie about Chase. Let's say he's not due back up for a half hour."

"Why tell them anything at all?"

"We might not have a choice."

His frown deepened, then he nodded "Okay."

"Oh, I wish I had a gun." Turning around, she looked for anything she could use for protection, but saw only the boat hooks. She considered hefting one, then figured that if these guys were up to no good, they would have come armed. "Weapons. Come on, we've got to have some kind of weapon."

"It's not something I usually need when I'm fishing."

"The flare gun!"

He nodded and went to the equipment locker, digging it out and loading it. "Maybe we should cut away the air

358

tank," he said. "It's a dead giveaway that Chase is in the water. If we cut it away, we can always claim we're just out here fishing—"

"But he might need the air."

They looked at each other helplessly as the other boat drew nearer.

"He's not using them right now," Jeff said. "He must not need the air."

Callie took another quick look over the side. "Okay," she said. "Okay."

Putting his back to the approaching boat, Jeff untied the bar and air cylinder and let the rope go over the side. Callie watched it slip away, feeling her heart sink with it.

Chase watched the tank and bar fall away into the depths of the sea. There could have been no clearer message from Jeff and Callie. He checked his dive computer and realized he still needed another five minutes of decompression for safety's sake. Hell!

The hull of the approaching boat was visible now, and he watched it come up alongside the *Lily* and stop. The engine cut out, and the sea was suddenly the only sound he heard, the gentle whispers of the water as she rocked everything within her embrace.

He glanced at his watch again. Three minutes. The boats bumped, the sound loud in his ears. That was no friendly approach, he thought, sure now that the second boat meant danger. Friendly boats didn't pull up that close without permission, and he seriously doubted Jeff and Callie would have allowed it. Not when they were all so nervous about what might be happening. Not if they'd thought it necessary to dump his emergency tank.

He looked at his watch again. Two and a half

minutes.

You can do it, the sea whispered in his ear. Christ, was he losing his marbles? Hearing the sea talk to him? But he looked at the watch again and began to run a rapid mental calculation. He'd built in more than enough time, of that he was sure. He could probably shave these last couple of minutes off without any problem.

But the thought of the bends nearly paralyzed him. Fear reached up and grabbed him by the throat, trying to strangle him. Even if he was in a safe window on decompression, he shouldn't exert himself when he surfaced because exertion immediately after a dive could trigger the bends. But what choice did he have?

He forced himself to draw a couple of ragged breaths, then reached for the clasps on his harness. Callie was up there, and he needed to protect her. Nothing else mattered.

CHAPTER 20

CALLIE AND JEFF DIDN'T MOVE A MUSCLE AS THE boat pulled up alongside and bumped against the *Lily*. Callie could scarcely breathe. She knew what an Uzi looked like, even though she'd only seen them in the movies, and the man standing at the gunwale of the other boat was pointing one at her and Jeff. Jeff still held the flare gun at his side but from the look on his face she could tell he realized it would be suicidal to fire it.

Nobody said a word. It was so eerie, she thought, to have this boat pull up alongside, to have a machine gun pointed at her, to watch as two total strangers threw over a line and tied the two boats together. This couldn't be happening.

But it was happening, and it became suddenly, horrifyingly real as the man who was driving emerged from the covered bridge and faced them. Dave Hathaway. Chase's boss. What was going on here? Did he maybe think they were trying to steal the diamonds?

She decided to assume anything except what the horror creeping along her spine was trying to tell her: that Dave was behind this whole mess. "Hi," she called out, her voice wavering. "Is something wrong, Dave? What's with the gun?"

Dave smiled. He had a very nice smile, white teeth in a tanned face. "I'm looking for Chase."

She hesitated, trying to find a way to buy time. "Did he do something wrong?"

"He's getting in the way. Tell your brother to drop that flare gun, or I'll have my man shoot him."

Shock struck Callie, running through her like ice water. Jeff dropped the flare gun instantly. The sound of it hitting the deck was like a death knell. There was going to be no happy ending here, she realized. Not if this man was willing to threaten to shoot them. They were going to die because he couldn't afford to let them go now.

She had to find a way to buy time. If she could just win some time, something might occur to her.

"What the hell is going on?" she demanded, feeling shock give way to anger as adrenaline began to surge through her.

"You're getting in the way. All of you are getting in the way."

"In the way of what? For God's sake, if you're going to wave guns at us, can you at least tell us what's going

361

on?"

Dave mounted the gunwale of his boat and jumped up onto the *Lily*. With a flick of the wrist, he signed the other two men to come over with him. They came one at a time, each taking turns covering Jeff and Callie while they made the crossing. The man with the machine gun moved to the stern, keeping the barrel pointed at Callie and Jeff.

"It's like this," Dave said. "You should've kept your nose out of my business. Nobody at all had to get killed. They just keep poking their noses in where they didn't belong."

"Into what? Who's poking their noses in?"

"You are. Chase is. And those two guys who took my divers out. If they'd just minded their own business, they wouldn't have died."

"What did they do wrong? About what?"

Dave bent and picked up the flare gun, then tossed it over the side. "Keep an eye out over there," he said to the second man, who was now holding a pistol. Dave pointed to the side of the *Lily* away from his boat, the side near the buoy. "He's got to come up over there." The man followed directions, moving over to where the bar and tank had recently been suspended.

Callie touched Jeff's arm and began easing in the same direction. Jeff instinctively moved with her, a couple of inches at a time. She had to hope Chase would gauge this situation correctly, and not come up on that side of the boat. If he did, and if she could keep all these men looking in the wrong direction, he might have a chance to do something.

As if the sea were annoyed, the waves returned, beginning to rock the boats and make them bump together. It gave Callie an excuse to stumble and catch her balance even farther over. Jeff came to her aid, and now all the men had their backs to their own boat. She could only hope Chase wouldn't come up where he was expected.

But she didn't think he would. God knew he had enough reasons to be paranoid lately. There was no reason he should think the presence of a second boat was innocent.

"What did Rushman and Westerlake do to you?" she asked Dave Hathaway. "They couldn't have done anything to deserve being murdered."

"They couldn't mind their own business," Hathaway said. "Damn fools. They had to sneak a peek at what my divers brought up."

Callie took a quick look at Jeff, and saw that his eyes were darting around, as if he was seeking some means of acting.

She didn't know whether to hope he thought of anything, because the least move was likely to get them cut down by that Uzi.

"Just what did they see?" she asked, dragging her gaze back to Hathaway.

He laughed. "You know what they found."

"No, I don't. Look, I don't know what the hell is going on here, except that all of a sudden somebody I don't know is pointing a gun at me. I think I have a right to know."

"You don't have any rights at all." Hathaway's smile faded. "But what the hell. It doesn't matter if I tell you. Diamonds. The divers brought up diamonds. But you already know that, don't you? That's what Chase figured out, and you wouldn't be out here with him if you didn't know about it. So, which theory are you following? The theory that somebody already has the

363

diamonds, or the theory that they're still down there?"

"I don't know what you're talking about."

"Right." He shook his head and moved a little closer. "When is Chase due up?"

"Chase isn't here."

He shook his head. "Don't bother lying. My man saw him come out on the boat with you. He took diving gear aboard. When is he supposed to be back up?"

Callie thought frantically. What would be a reasonable time? She had no idea.

"Twenty minutes," Jeff said. "He's due up in twenty minutes, if nothing takes longer than he expected."

Dave Hathaway nodded. "Keep your eye out anyway, Marco."

"Sure," said the guy at gunwale who was watching the water.

Callie felt Jeff ease a little away from her. She had to fight an urge to reach out and stop him. "What about Bill Evers?" she said, desperate to distract Hathaway from Jeff. "Did you kill him, too?"

Hathaway shot her a glare. "Nosy little bitch, aren't you?"

"What difference does it make?" she said. "You're going to kill us anyway. You might as well tell us why."

"I already did."

"But what about Evers? He was on your side, wasn't he? Do you kill your associates, too?" Much to her pleasure, both of the other men were distracted by that question, and looked at Hathaway before returning their attention to their duties, one watching the water, the other watching Jeff and Callie.

"He became a nuisance," Hathaway said. "He got really pissed that I changed Chase's air supply. Hell, it wasn't my fault Chase reacted that way to the narks. He

364

was just supposed to get woozy and go back up above a hundred feet. How the hell was I supposed to know the guy was going to try to pull his mask off? If it had worked the way I planned, everybody would've been okay." He shook his head. "Christ, nobody had to get killed."

"So you killed Evers because he was pissed?"

I killed Evers because he let those two damn fishermen see the diamonds, after the second dive. He never should have given them the opportunity. But he was careless, and Marco had to rub them out. Evers went flaky on me. The deal didn't include murder, he said. So . . . I capped him."

Callie felt her internal chill deepen, and along with it came a frightful sense of resignation. "And now you're going to kill Chase, too?"

"He should never have started nosing around. He should have just stayed in his backwoods hole. Jesus. I was doing everything I could to keep him out of the way. Even paying a couple of guys to do things that would make him think he was losing it. All he had to fucking do was *stay out of the way* "

Hathaway's temper was rising, and Callie had the distinct sense that he was feeling out of control, that circumstances had snowballed in a way that he had never envisioned, and now he was trapped in a chain of events he couldn't escape.

Desperately she sought another option to offer him, but nothing occurred to her. He was already implicated in three murders. There was no escape from that, short of killing the three people who could link him to them.

The man with the Uzi spoke. "Let's just take care of 'em now, boss. It'll be less to deal with when the other guy comes up."

365

Callie caught her breath and felt panic lace itself tightly around her heart.

"No," said Hathaway. "I don't want to do anything that might tip him off."

"The boat's already tipped him off," argued the man.

"No, I don't think so. We might have been having trouble and pulled alongside. He'll have to surface to find out what's going on, and then we'll get him."

Desperate to buy time, Callie threw out the only thing she could think of. "You're not going to shoot us, are you? If our bodies wash up on shore, they'll know we were killed."

"They won't know who did it."

"You don't know that. We've talked to a lot of people about our suspicions. No, you should drown us."

Hathaway's jaw dropped. For an instant, everyone on the boat looked stunned.

"Except," Callie continued almost wildly, "I really don't like the idea of being eaten by fish. They take the eyes out first. Look, if you're going to kill me, don't I have some thing to say about how? It won't make any difference to you, but it'll make a whole lot of difference to me."

"Christ," Hathaway swore. "You're crazy."

"I can't help it. I get nuts at the idea of being eaten by fish. Look, maybe you could just tie us up in the cabin and leave us. We'd die of thirst in a couple of days. You know, tow us way out . . ."

"The Coast Guard," said the man with the pistol.

"They won't find us. They won't even be looking for us. Without a distress call, they would just ignore the boat if they *did* see it."

"You might get loose," Hathaway said. "Look, this is a stupid discussion. They'll never know who killed you.

I'm going to use Chase's pistol for the job."

Panic tightened its grip on Callie, clearing her mind in the strangest way. Grabbing Jeff's arm, she dragged him closer to the stern.

"Just don't tie me up and throw me overboard. At least let me swim. I'd never get to shore, but at least I could swim until I'm exhausted. Oh, God, don't tie me up and throw me over."

"I said I was going to shoot you."

"And there'd be blood everywhere . . . The thought makes me want to vomit." Bending over, she grabbed her stomach. "It's my death," she said, and gagged. "Don't I have anything to say about it?"

Chase had surfaced between the boats, the most dangerous place in the world, but the only one where he could be reasonably sure no one was looking for him. He listened until he was sure that everyone was aboard the *Lily*. Then he swam around the bow of the other boat, and pulled himself onto the foredeck. The cabin concealed him from the view of those aboard the *Lily*. And as if she understood his need, the sea grew restless, banging the boats together and filling the air with the lap of her waves. Covering any sounds he might make.

He made his way around the far side, peering through the bridge windows so he could see where everyone was on the other boat. They were at the stern, the bad guys facing the other way. He hoped that when Callie and Jeff saw him, they didn't telegraph his presence by their reactions.

He could hear Callie's arguments about her preferred method of death and he didn't know whether to be horrified or laugh, but as he listened he felt a surge of admiration for her. She was buying him time, buying them all time, and he promised himself that if they got out of this alive, he was going to give her a kiss she would never forget. And he was going to *kill* those men for doing this to Callie.

He peeked around the edge of the cabin and saw that everyone except Callie and Jeff was still facing the other way. He knew that Callie and Jeff saw him, but both of them quickly looked away, and Callie resumed her surreal discussion of modes of death.

Then he recognized Dave Hathaway, and his mouth turned sour with rage. That son of a bitch!

Stepping carefully down into the cockpit, he looked around for weapons. Two of the men on the *Lily* had guns, one of them an Uzi, and he didn't fool himself into thinking he could take both gunmen out in one blow. First he had to find a way to get to the guy with the machine gun, because he could do the most damage in the shortest time.

Moving silently, he made his way to the equipment locker and opened it. He could hear Callie talking frantically about how she wished they would kill her first so she didn't have to watch her baby brother die. Then Jeff chimed in, arguing he didn't want to watch her die either. Those guys must be feeling they had fallen in with lunatics.

In the equipment locker, he found a flare gun and, wonder of wonders, a speargun. He checked it out quickly, making sure it would still fire. It would. For backup, he loaded the flare gun.

When he straightened, he saw Jeff looking straight at him. Then the young man's eyes slid over to the guy who was at the side watching the water where Chase would presumably surface, his back to the group. Chase got the message and nodded. Jeff was going to push the guy overboard when Chase made his move.

Lifting the speargun, he aimed it at the guy with the Uzi. The spear did its job, flying across the intervening distance and hitting him in the buttock. The man screamed, and Chase gave a yank on the line attached to the spear. The man went overboard, and the Uzi clattered to the deck.

Jeff whirled around and with a single shove pushed the other gunman over the side. Chase leapt over to the *Lily* and launched himself at Dave Hathaway, catching him around the knees and throwing him to the deck. Dave swung at him and Chase hauled off and popped him a good one in the jaw. Dave looked stunned.

Callie spoke. "Chase, I've got the gun."

Chase looked up, keeping his hands on Hathaway's shoulders so the man couldn't rise.

Jeff was grinning. He leaned over the side. "What do you want me to do about these two guys?"

"Let 'em swim until I'm ready for them." He rose and took the gun from Callie, then looked down at his old friend. He had to fight an urge to nail Dave right between the eyes for threatening Callie and Jeff. "Jeff, you know how to use an Uzi?"

"Never had to."

"It's easy. Come here." He showed Jeff just how easy it was, then gave him the gun. "You keep watch. I'm going to tie them up, one by one."

Jeff took up his post on the flying bridge from where he could see everything. Callie retrieved rope from the locker and helped Chase tie up Hathaway.

"You'll never prove anything," Hathaway said. "This kid's wanted for murder. All I have to do is claim he was hijacking my boat."

Chase resisted the urge to punch him and satisfied

369

himself by yanking the rope tighter around Hathaway's wrists. "Shut up, Dave. If the law won't believe the three of us, then I'll just have to take care of you myself."

Hathaway blanched and fell silent.

"That's right," Chase said. "And I can make it a lot worse than life in prison."

When he was sure Hathaway couldn't get loose, he went and hauled in the man he'd harpooned. The gunman had yanked the spear out and had lost some blood, and that had taken most of the fight out of him. He submitted meekly to being tied up, and even thanked Chase for putting a bandage on his wound.

The third man was a bigger problem. He no sooner hit the deck than he attacked Chase. It took a couple of solid punches to subdue him, but then it was done.

Then, and only then, did Chase sweep Callie into his arms and hug her with all the desperation of a man who had come close to losing someone he cared about. God, it had been so close! She hugged him back, clinging to him with equal desperation.

But Chase was exhausted, not unexpected after a dive. Worse, he felt pain in his joints, joints that hadn't hurt before.

"Let's get back to shore as fast as we can," he said to Jeff.

Callie looked at him and felt her heart climb into her throat.

"What's wrong?"

"I think . . . I need to decompress."

"Can't you go back in the water and do it?"

He shook his head.

Callie turned to her brother. "I'll hold the gun, Jeff. Call the Coast Guard. Tell 'em we need medical help fast."

Chase sank down onto the stern and battled down a rising sense of panic. He'd exerted too much. But it wasn't that bad. It would wear off. It wouldn't be like last time. He started shivering, and hoped to God he didn't get an embolism in the brain.

Jeff came down from the flying bridge and gave Callie the gun. "You aren't supposed to exert right after you come up," he said. "I read that. You're not supposed to even help put your own gear away."

Chase managed a shrug and a tight grin. "Like I had any choice."

"Just call the Coast Guard," Callie said again. "They can airlift him out of here." She turned the barrel of the gun toward Hathaway. "I ought to shoot him," she said, her voice hard. "I ought to kill him. This is the second time he's done this to you, Chase."

"The second?"

"You were right. He messed with your air on your last dive."

"Hey," Hathaway said quickly. "It wasn't supposed to make that happen. All I wanted was to give him a case of narks so he'd come right back up. I never thought he'd pull off his mask. God, he's my *friend*."

"Some friend you are," Callie said bitterly. She saw Chase shiver again and handed him the gun. "Can you hold this while I get you a blanket?"

He nodded and she ran below, returning a minute later with an old olive drab army blanket. She wrapped it around his shoulders and took the gun back.

"Maybe," she said, "we ought to make these turkeys swim all the way back."

Chase managed a chuckle and pulled the blanket tighter around himself.

"Hey," Callie said, her voice softening and her heart aching. "Hey, you promised me you were going to be okay."

"I will be. I always keep my promises." But he was wondering if he was about to break this one.

Jeff reported that a cutter and a helicopter were on the way. Twenty minutes later a Coast Guard helicopter lifted Chase in a basket and swept him away.

The three men were taken into custody by the Monroe County authorities, and by five o'clock that afternoon all charges against Jeff and Eric were officially dropped. Callie drove to Stock Island with Jeff and picked up Eric, bringing both of them home with her. Eric was elated, but rather subdued, too, as if the experience had marked him in some way he didn't want to talk about. Callie thought it was better if he didn't stay alone, and Eric was glad to go home with her and Jeff.

Jeff, on the other hand, was ebullient. He recounted all the day's excitement to Eric, who wound up grinning almost like his old self.

Callie was feeling something altogether different. Chase had been taken to God knew where, and she had no idea if he was okay. The Coast Guard wouldn't tell her anything because she wasn't a relative. Frustration and fear made her want to wring someone's neck.

Finally, she walked out to the point, feeling that she had to make some attempt to find peace within herself. The sea, she thought, hadn't hurt Chase. Those men had hurt Chase. The sea had given up its secrets and given up Chase without harm. Except for those men, he'd be just fine. And if he died, it would be their fault, not the sea's.

Sitting down on the caprock, she wrapped her arms

around her knees and let tears of relief, release and fear roll down her cheeks. Her mind kept picking apart the events of the day, wondering if she could have done something different, something that would have prevented Chase from exerting himself. She couldn't think of a single thing.

Then, like a soft warmth growing in the depths of her mind, she remembered how calm the sea had been, and how rough it had suddenly become when the three men boarded the *Lily*. The sea had helped them, she realized. The sea had made it possible for Chase to board the other boat without being heard.

And that thought was no crazier than the ones she had had before about the sea being out to get everyone she loved.

This time the sea had helped save her loved ones.

Except Chase. She was scared to death about him, wondering if he was all right, if he would *be* all right. But she didn't blame the sea for what had happened to him. She blamed the men who had wanted to kill them.

The waves were rolling in gently, barely ripples in the smooth surface of the water, and she listened to the gentle lapping, feeling as if the sea were singing a soft lullaby. Mother Ocean. At least she'd made peace with that fear.

"I told you I'd be all right."

The sound of Chase's voice right behind her caused her to leap to her feet and turn around. He was silhouetted against the blazing sunset, and he opened his arms to her. She flew to him, felt him lift her right off her feet and into a world where everything was right.

He kissed her hungrily, holding on to her as if he wanted never to let her go.

"Oh, God, I was so worried," she gasped when he let

373

her breathe again. "I was so scared . . ."

"I'm fine. I'm fine." He set her on her feet, and his fingers traced the contour of her cheek. "I was almost over it by the time I got to the hospital. They decompressed me for only a short time. I'll have to take it easy for a few days . . ."

She wrapped her arms around his waist, hugging him close, burying her face in his shoulder and inhaling deeply of his scent. He was real. He was there. "Thank God. Thank God."

He stroked her hair and back, dropped a kiss on the crown of her head. "That was some song and dance you were giving those guys on the boat, arguing with them about how they should kill you."

A choked laugh escaped her. "It was the only way I could think to keep them off-balance. I had to buy time."

"You did a damn fine job of it."

She tipped her head back and looked up at him. "You're really okay?"

"Right as rain. What about you?"

"I'm perfect. Now that you're back."

The evening suddenly hushed. The waves grew still, the breeze stopped, and Callie had the feeling that the whole world was holding its breath.

Chase cupped her face in his hands and looked down into her eyes. In the failing light, his eyes were dark and mysterious . . . like the depths of the ocean. "I love you, Calypso."

She caught her breath, and felt her heart leap. "I . . . love you, too."

"Will you marry me?"

She could hardly believe her ears. "Marry you?" The words came out in a squeak.

"Marry me," he repeated. "I figure between us we can keep Jeff out of any serious trouble."

Her heart began to tumble. "You want to marry me to keep Jeff out of trouble?"

He started to laugh, throwing back his head and letting the sound rise to the blazing tropical sky. "Not hardly," he said finally. "Not hardly. I want you to marry me because my life would be empty without you. I figured that out today."

Then before she could question him further, or take umbrage, he lifted her off her feet and whirled her in a circle. "Marry me because I love you, Calypso. Because I love you."

It was the best reason in the world. They stood wrapped in each other's arms for a long time, watching the sun disappear into the sea, watching the burst of crimson and orange that came a few minutes later. Making plans for their future, Chase talked of starting a business, of making room in it for Jeff. He spoke of building a new life for them, and he spoke of the sea.

"Can you live with it, Calypso? I'll leave the sea if you really want me to, but . . ." He shook his head slowly, unable to express the loss that would mean to him.

But she didn't need him to express it because she understood what it meant to him. And she understood that taking him away from the sea would be cutting out some essential part of him. She loved him too much to do that.

"I can live with it," she told him, and looked out over the water, letting peace replace that last of her fear.

"It's over," Chase said finally. "The bad dream is over."

Callie nodded. She, too, felt as if she were waking

from a terrible dream.
  And stepping into a bright new one.

Dear Reader:

I hope you enjoyed reading this Large Print book. If you are interested in reading other Beeler Large Print titles, ask your librarian or write to me at

Thomas T. Beeler, *Publisher*
Post Office Box 659
Hampton Falls, New Hampshire 03844

You can also call me at 1-800-251-8726 and I will send you my latest catalogue.

Audrey Lesko and I choose the titles I publish in Large Print. Our aim is to provide good books by outstanding authors—books we both enjoyed reading and liked well enough to want to share. We warmly welcome any suggestions for new titles and authors.

Sincerely,

Tom Beeler

A00000106742935